BLIND *sided*

Nikki,

BLIND *sided*

BOOK ONE
IN THE
BY HIS GAME
Series

Game on!

EMMA HART

Cover Design by Louisa Maggio at LM Creations
Editing by Michelle Kampmeier at Mickey Reed Editing
Proof-reading by Kayla Jason Robichaux
Interior Design and Formatting by

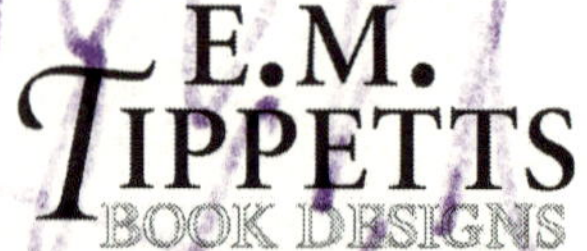

www.emtippettsbookdesigns.com

For my husband, who sat (and still sits) for hours, painstakingly teaching me all the rules of American Football, and never doubting that I could write a book on something I knew nothing about when I typed the first words.

Love you, honey.

Leah

"Run, dammit. Run!" I glance up from my drawing pad. "Go ahead, fumble it. Why wouldn't you?" I lean back against the sofa. "And this is supposed to be good preseason form. Good, my ass!"

"Leah? Why are you shouting? Are we being attacked?"

I look over at my elderly aunt as she enters the front room, her cane clicking against the floor with each step. "No. It's just the football. That's all."

"It's the what? The wall?"

"Football," I repeat, my eyes following the play on screen. "Are you wearing your hearing aid?"

"Oh!" She slides her hand into her pocket and removes the tiny device. "There," she says as she fits it.

"Is it turned on?"

She fiddles with it. "It is now."

I shoot her a fond smile. "Oh, go! Go!" I point my pencil at the screen. "Run, you useless—"

My mom interrupts me. "Shouldn't you be working?" My mom interrupts me.

"Um, I am. Kind of." I wave my pencil lamely in her direction and keep my eyes on the game.

She leans against the doorframe to remove her shoes. "I

still don't understand how you love football so much." She sets them in the hallway then enters the front room.

"Butts," Aunt Ada answers her. "It's the butts, am I right, Lele?"

"Yeah, that's it. I watch hours upon hours of football because of their butts. Hey!"

Mom waves the remote. "You have to get those designs submitted before Quinn sends you all your Fashion Week designs to finalize."

"I know." I swallow the bitterness that rises at the mention of New York Fashion Week. "It still sucks that I have to miss it."

"You could be honest."

"No." I fill in some detail on the shirt on my pad. "I told you before. I want to be successful for my work, not because my mom is Hollywood's sweetheart."

"And I respect that, honey, but you should be there for your show."

"Are they winning?" Aunt Ada butts in, perching on the sofa next to me. "What colors are they in?"

"Red and black, and"—I glance up—"yes, they're winning. Only just."

"Oooh, who's that?"

"Who's who?"

"That!"

"Corey Jackson," Mom answers. "He's the Vipers' quarterback."

"He's a handsome young man, isn't he?"

"Aunt Ada!" I snap my head up. "Are you seriously crushing on him? Don't you have bingo or something to go to?"

She cackles. "Not tonight, dear. Where can I find him?"

"Oh my God!" I smack the pencil down and look at her. "You are not going cougar on me!"

Mom laughs. "He'll be at the premiere tomorrow night. It's a shame your bingo will interfere with that, Aunt Ada."

"What? Since when?" I look at Mom.

"Since the invitations were sent out." She fixes her blue eyes on me. "Have you listened to anything I've told you about the premiere?"

No. "I, er… Not exactly."

"Leah!"

"What? I've been real busy. Plus, I am *not* interested in being asked when my big acting debut is going to be. If I have to tell everyone one more time that there isn't going to be one, someone's gonna get hurt." I raise my eyebrows and go back to my design.

Mom sighs, but it's obviously fake. "You know the drill. Turn up, humor them, watch the movie, hang around for an hour. Then you can escape out of the back door."

"Let's swap," Aunt Ada announces loudly. "I'll go in your place, Lele. You can stay here and work."

My eyes follow her line of sight to where Corey Jackson has a close-up on TV. "I hate to tell you this, but he puts out more than your friends on trash day."

"He's a young, handsome man. They all do."

"What do you know about young, handsome men?" Mom scoffs, walking into the kitchen. She opens the fridge and pours herself a glass of white wine.

"I was young once, Grace. And I knew a lot of young, handsome men."

"Whoa! Okay. TMI!" I shudder. "Let's move on. Crap. What's the time?"

Mom looks at her watch. "Six o'clock. Why?"

Dammit, I forgot to eat again. And dammit, I have to get dressed. I sigh. "Macey and Ryann are dragging me out for my birthday."

"Remind Ryann that she has an audition tomorrow," Mom says as I shut my sketchpad and get up.

"Sure." I tuck it under my arm and head for the stairs.

"Leah?"

"Yes, Mom?"

"Did you eat dinner?"

"Yes, Mom!"

"Are you lying to me, young lady?"

"Young lady? I'm twenty-two!" I holler down. "And no,

Mom!"

"Leah!"

I twist my bedroom door lock shut then dart into the bathroom. Reaching into the shower and turning the knob, I yell, "What was that? Sorry, the shower's on!"

"Leah!"

I'm so not getting away with that.

"My feet are killing me," I groan, leaning against the bar. "This is why I don't wear heels!"

"Nah, you're fine. You just need another drink." Ryann raps her knuckles against the top of the bar and flicks her hair. The bartender shoots down to us like a baby after candy. "Three tequila shots please."

"Aw, shit," Macey mutters. "Not tequila. Anything but the devil drink! That should only be drunk in the safety of my apartment."

I hold the tiny glass in front of my face. "It'll stop my feet hurting. I don't give a shit."

"I'll remind you that you said that when you call me tomorrow with a hangover."

"I promise I'll drink some water before I go to bed. My mom will kill me if I'm hungover tomorrow." I bring the glass to my lips and tip it back. "Holy shit." The tequila lights a fiery trail from my throat to my stomach. "Another."

Ryann smirks and throws my words back at me. "Your mom will kill you if you have a hangover tomorrow." Ryann smirks and throws my words back at me.

"Fuck off." I click my tongue. "It's my birthday, which, by the way, I've spent working and watching my half-assed football team almost throw a game. If I say another tequila, I want another tequila."

"Okay." Ryann shrugs, waving the bartender over again. "Three more, and three margaritas."

He nods and fixes the drinks. A few minutes later, they

appear in front of us, and I grab my purse.

"This is my round."

"Hell no!" Macey cries. "It's illegal to buy your own drinks on your birthday."

"But—"

"She's right," a smooth voice with a hint of a Texas accent says from behind me. "At least it is in Texas."

I spin on my seat and look into the devastatingly blue-green eyes of Corey Jackson. The very same man my seventy-five-year-old great-aunt was ogling on the TV earlier. And, okay. I get it. I *totally* get it. His dark hair curls over his ears, and his bright eyes are sparkling with the same smile that's twitching at his lips. And he has that jaw—you know, the kind of jaw that makes you want to rub your fingers over it repeatedly? Yeah, that jaw.

He's hot. The, er, tequila said so.

Smart, that tequila.

"Is that right?" I reply.

"Sure is." The twitch of his lips morphs into a slow, sexy smile.

"I hate to remind you, but this is California."

"Oh, I know exactly where we are. Where else am I going to be lucky enough to buy a drink for a girl like you?"

"Are you hitting on me?"

He rests his elbow on the bar in front of me and hands the bartender forty dollars between his fingers. "Does it sound like I am?"

"Is it supposed to? Because I'm sure Corey Jackson, L.A. Vipers golden boy, can find a thousand girls like me just by turning around." I nod my head over his shoulder. "Oh, look. I just found you a bunch of them."

Seriously, half the girls in this bar are in fan-girl mode. Or panty-dropping mode. I think they're synonymous where he's concerned.

He takes his change from the bartender, his smirk turning cocky. "Finally, a girl who recognizes me for more than what is under my shirt. Is this my lucky night?"

"If this is a lucky night, clearly California isn't doing much for you." I throw the tequila shot back.

"You could always tell me your name." He puts a hand on the back of my chair, leaning toward me.

"God, I just I *love* it when guys act like they have no idea who I am. It's so cute."

"All right." He holds his hands up briefly. "You got me, Leah Veronica. I'd recognize you a mile away."

"I'm flattered."

His eyes don't move from mine. "It's a beautiful name for a beautiful girl."

"Really? You're trying that one?" I raise my eyebrows. "It hasn't worked on me since I was fifteen. Nice try though, cowboy."

He laughs a deep, chesty rumble that makes my skin tingle. "You're hard work, you know that, Leah?"

I seal my lips around my straw and have a sip. "Have you ever met my mom? I'm afraid it's a Veronica thing."

His eyes rove over my face, taking in every detail from my blond hair to my glossy, pink lips. "I have, yes, and I fully believe you. Do you always make it this hard for guys to pick you up?"

"No." I meet his eyes once again and twist my lips in amusement. "I'm only this much of a pain when the guy is overly certain he can."

"Touché." He moves in a little closer. "How about we make a deal?"

"If you leave me alone, I promise not to yell at you next time you throw an interception?"

"There's definitely something to be said about you shouting my name," he murmurs in a husky voice, "but no. That's not it."

"Hit me. Hopefully you have better aim now than you did earlier tonight."

He smirks. "If you give me your number, I'll leave you alone. For now."

"Here's a better idea." I curl my fingers around his collar

and stand, bringing my face closer to his. "You realize I'm not interested and let me enjoy the rest of my birthday in peace."

"Are you askin' or tellin' me?"

That drawl tingles across my skin, but I hold my ground. "I'm telling you."

He covers my hand with his and pulls my fingers from his shirt. "You can enjoy your birthday all you like, Leah, but I don't believe you when you say you're not interested."

I snatch my hand from his grip. "What do girls see in you?"

"The money, the name, the body…"

"Figures. It sure isn't your charming personality."

He winks. *He fucking winks.* "Happy birthday, Leah," he says smoothly as he walks backward.

I shake my head and turn away. How does that guy get laid? Oh, yeah—that'll be the sexy smile and smooth lines that work only on desperate fan-girls.

"Was that…Corey Jackson? *The* Corey Jackson?" Macey puts her hand on her chest.

"The Corey Jackson?" I snort. "What is he, a football legend?"

"He plays football?" She blinks at me.

"How the hell are we even friends?"

Ryann laughs. "Damn. He's hot." She licks her lips.

"He's also the biggest serial dater in the league. In fact, I'm sure his dates are more like casual fucks. So yes, he's hot—"

"Very hot."

"Very hot," I correct myself, my eyes flicking to the back of his head across the bar. "But he's a total jackass."

Apparently my eyes linger on Corey too long, because he turns, his own blazing bright. I blink slowly. I've never felt anyone's gaze so intensely. His eyes are clouded with determination, a lusty heat flaring in their depths. His gaze tingles through my body the way his accent just did. I feel it right down to the tips of my toes.

How on Earth is he making me feel like I'm half naked in this bar full of people?

Macey continues. "You should have given him your

number. That would have been cool."

"This is Los Angeles," Ryann butts in. "It's not exactly a huge deal if some hot, rich guy has your number."

"Precisely," I mutter.

"But he's not just some rich guy!" Macey argues. "He's Corey Jackson. *The* Corey Jackson."

"You didn't even know he's a football player until two minutes ago!" Ryann cries in disbelief.

"Mace, why don't you go and get his number?" I ask snarkily. "I'm not interested in him. Got it?" I turn to the bar and wave my glass. "I'll have another."

I dig out a ten-dollar bill when bar guy brings it back, but he shakes his head.

"Mr. Jackson said all your drinks are on his tab tonight."

My eyes crawl along the bar to the corner table where he's sitting with two of his teammates. Corey raises his glass in my direction, and I purse my lips.

"Well, you tell Mr. Jackson thank you very much," I tell him. Bar guy makes to move, but I lean over the bar, grabbing his arm, my eyes still on Corey. "But I am perfectly capable of purchasing my own drinks, his supposed Texas laws be damned."

I slap my money in his hand, grab my drink, and turn without another word.

"*I am* not hungover."

Aunt Ada turns just as I slide onto the stool and bury my face in my arms. "You're not a bunger?" She frowns. "Whatever is a bunger?"

I open my eyes long enough to give her my best unimpressed look. "Never mind," I mumble into my sleeve. "Water?"

"Horter? You're making no sense, dear."

"Ughhhh," I groan. "Water. Wor-ter."

"You'd like some water?"

"Yes. Please!"

"Well, you should have said that!"

I flick my eyes open once more then give up. Oh, tequila, you bitch. You utter bitch. Why did I let myself have more than five shots? Why did I let myself have anything at all?

"Grace is going to kill you," Aunt Ada informs me, setting a glass of water and two pills in front of me.

"Sshhh. Don't say her name. You might summon her."

"Summon who?"

I sit up straight, wincing at the pounding in my head. *Ah, shit.* "Mary Poppins," I tell Mom, discreetly slipping the pills into my mouth and swallowing them with a drink.

"Smartass," she retorts, turning and studying me. "Did you have a good time last night?"

"I did."

"Did anything…interesting happen?"

"Macey went home alone."

Aunt Ada sniggers and places some French toast in front of me.

Mom's lips quirk into a smile despite her fight to remain stony-faced. "I'm certain that's more surprising than it is interesting. No, Leah. I meant with you."

I shake my head slowly, chewing. "No. I'm boring."

Her smile grows a little more, and she hands me the rolled-up magazine from under her arm. I frown and take it from her.

"You have it already?"

"Sasha dropped it by earlier." She waves her hand dismissively.

Right. I went out last night. Of course her assistant was up at the ass crack of dawn to get the tabloids.

"Oh! Is that Corey Jackson?"

"What?" I shriek in response to Aunt Ada's question and flip the magazine around.

Sure as hell, there we are—front page. The image shows him leaning down as I'm looking up. We look like we're about to kiss. *Oh holy mothercrapper.*

"Something to tell me, honey? Do you have a date for tonight?"

I look at Mom, my jaw dropping. "No, I don't! Oh my God. Is this for real?"

"Is he more handsome in real life?" Aunt Ada asks.

I ignore her. "Nothing happened. I swear. He is the last thing I need when I'm about to launch Lea V.!"

Mom's smile drops, sadness hinting her eyes. "I know, honey, but you're allowed to have a little fun."

I blink at her quickly. "Okay, so I'm taking fun as ha-ha-giggle fun and not the oh-oh-sexy fun, because I'm pretty sure you are *not* supposed to tell me to do that."

"I'd have fun with him if I were twen—forty years younger. Actually, twenty, too."

"Aunt Ada! God!" I gasp, looking at her. "You can't say things like that around me. You're gonna scar me for life."

"Char you for life? No, Lele. I'm not cooking you."

"Can you please get her that damn hearing aid? And maybe a gag?" I rip some French toast off with my fingers and shove it in my mouth. How is a girl supposed to keep any sanity around here? "Oh, I have a headache."

"Hmmm." Mom sweeps past me, hitting me with a suspicious glance, and stops in front of Aunt Ada. She bends, fits the aid in Ada's ear, then stands. "Is that better?"

"Lovely." Aunt Ada turns and hands her a plate of French toast, too. But she gets a kiss.

"Hey, why didn't I get a kiss on the cheek?"

"You refuse to tell me if Mr. Jackson is hotter in real life than he is on TV."

I'm a little alarmed at the level of her obsession with him. "Yes, he's hotter in real life, Aunt Ada. There. Are you happy?"

"Will you bring him for dinner? I'll make lasagna."

"We're, er, not exactly dinner buddies."

She looks at the front cover of the magazine pointedly. I snatch it from the table and dump it on the floor.

Mom rolls her eyes, grabs the magazine from the floor, and drops it back in front of me. "Leah? You need to go and shower. The stylists are here in an hour." She tugs on a lock of my hair before grabbing my shoulders and spinning me toward the door. "And Ada? I'll be sure to extend your dinner invitation to Corey this evening."

Fantastic. Let's encourage the crazy old bat. That's exactly what the world needs.

Chapter TWO

Corey

"I can do my own tie, Mom."

"I know." She straightens it anyway. "But it was crooked. You can't go to a movie premiere with a crooked tie."

I take a deep breath. "Of course I can't."

Mom leans back in the seat and smooths her dress out over her legs. "You know, it was lovely of Grace to invite you."

"It sure was," I reply, resisting the urge to loosen the tie. Fucking hell. I wear jerseys and sweatpants, not shirts and ties.

"Corey! Try and cheer up. You're acting awful."

"Laura, give the boy a break. Preseason games are tough after the break," Dad interrupts, handing her a glass of champagne to shut her up. "I'm sure no one will complain if the Vipers' star boy is a little on the quiet side. As long as he smiles for the cameras, who gives a shit?"

"Thank you," I mutter, adjusting my sleeves instead. This is the first and last time I do this shit. Next time, I'll have a headache or something.

The only reason I didn't back out at the last minute is because of the chance that Grace's daughter will be here. That blonde is one in a damn million. Every word I said rubbed her the wrong way and I loved every damn second of it. She's the first girl to challenge me, the first girl I've felt like I didn't have a chance with—if only because she's as stubborn as a fucking mule.

It was the spark in her eyes, the damn aggravating twitch of her lips every time she shot me down.

She was so confident with every word she said, and nothing about me swayed her. LA Vipers golden boy? Fuck off. Buy her drinks? Fuck off. Lean in close? Fuck *right* off.

Instead of being the top guy going after the girl, I felt like the fucking nerd going after the head cheerleader. Like I have no chance with this confident, gorgeous girl, like I'm destined to gaze at her longingly from the back of the room.

I'll be damned if that doesn't make me want her.

I'll be damned if it doesn't make me more fucking determined to have her.

Leah Veronica, daughter of Hollywood's darling, avoider of the media, elusive spotlight-hater.

Leah Veronica, a test to take, a challenge to be won, a mountain to be conquered.

I crick my neck to one side as my mother sets her half-empty glass down and picks up her purse. Dad nods as the car door is opened and steps out. He holds his hand out to help Mom down, and she exits with the grace of woman who's done it a thousand times. And she has.

I follow them from the vehicle, glad to finally stand up. Damn cars are cramped when you're as tall as I am. I've barely had a chance to blink when cameras flash and my name is shouted.

Yeah, definitely never fucking ever doing this again.

I follow my parents up the carpet like a good little puppy, stopping for photos, and damn...

"Corey! Can you tell us the Vipers' aim for the new season?" A reporter shoves a mic in my face.

"We plan to win the Super Bowl of course," I reply, smiling like I'm supposed to. "I've fully recovered from my minor injury and we're ready to start the regular season."

"Great news! Are you confident of your chances this year?

Didn't you almost lose yesterday?" the reporter pushes.

"We were in control of the game at all times. After all, if we won with ease, our fans would get bored. Now, if you don't mind, I'd like to head inside now." I step back and walk as quickly as I can to Grauman's Chinese Theatre. I'm not here to talk football. I'm here to do what's expected of me.

And find Leah.

"Corey? Are you ready to go in?" Mom asks.

"Yep." I loosen my tie the tiniest bit when she turns around and then follow her toward the door.

Grace is standing by the door, greeting everyone who's here to watch the movie. She takes a few moments to talk and laugh with each person before finally letting them go with a kiss to the cheek. Dressed in black, she's the epitome of class and elegance.

And next to her… My lips quirk. Wearing a figure-hugging, blue gown is Leah, smiling and laughing with each person, too. Her light hair is curled and smoothed to the side, exposing her neck, and the low neckline of her dress gives me a glimpse of her cleavage.

I hope she's sitting nowhere near me or this is going to be a very fucking uncomfortable movie.

"Laura, Justin!" Grace exclaims, happily hugging both of my parents. "How are you?"

"We're well, thank you." Mom smiles. "You know our son, Corey?"

"Of course I do. My aunt was *enjoying* the game yesterday." Grace winks and hugs me briefly. "And I believe you know my daughter, Leah."

"Yes, ma'am." I fight my grin but fail. Leah looks so fuckin' pissed. "Leah. It's lovely to see you again."

"It's a pleasure," she retorts.

Her eyes are spitting fire at me, and fuck, I can't resist. I take her hand, lean forward, and press a kiss to her cheek. She digs her nails into my palm.

"Enjoy the movie, won't you, Corey?"

I swallow my laugh. "Undoubtedly, I will." I step back, wink, and follow my parents into the theater, feeling her eyes burning a hole in my back the whole time.

"You're kidding me."

I look to the side and see Leah standing next to me. "Can't stay away, can you?"

She clicks her tongue. "I am going to kill my mother for this." She lifts her dress slightly and sits in the chair next to me. "I've never seen a more deliberate act in my life."

"Grace Veronica, the matchmaker. Who knew?"

"Grace Veronica, the joker," Leah replies, facing the front and demurely resting her hands in her lap.

"Oh, come on. Is it that bad to sit next to me for two hours?"

"Of course not. You can't talk to me when the movie is on—it's the reception after I'm not looking forward to."

"Can I get you a drink?" I motion toward the champagne bottle in front of me.

"You better. I'm sure as hell not getting through this sober."

I laugh and pour her a glass. "Here."

"Thank you." She takes the glass, her fingers brushing across mine.

I watch as her eyes flit around, making sure no one is watching. Then they go again as she brings the glass to her mouth. She tips it up and drinks it all in one go.

Three-hundred-dollar champagne, and it's gone in seconds.

"I'm gonna need another." She licks her lips and hands me the glass back.

I half grin. "You know alcohol lowers your inhibitions, don't you?"

"Yes, but thanks to tequila, I already know I can resist your lame attempts at hitting on me, so another, please."

I laugh again. She's something else. I pour her a second glass, and this time, I lean toward her, keeping a tight hold on the glass.

"You know," I murmur, my mouth hovering by her ear, "most girls would be half naked by now."

"You know," she replies equally as quietly, closing her fingers around mine on the glass, "I'm not most girls."

"I think I'm working that out."

She snaps her eyes to mine, amusement dancing in them. "Not nearly quickly enough, Corey." She says my name slowly, each syllable rolling off her tongue in an innocently seductive way.

I hold her gaze without taking my hand off the glass. The warmth of her hand seeps into my skin, and the steadiness of her stare adds another level to my want for her.

It would be so fucking easy right now to lean in and cover those shiny, pink lips with my own. It would be so fucking easy to close the small distance and make her realize that I can make her be like most girls.

It would be so, so fucking easy to make her melt beneath me, right here, in a room full of people.

Leah eases the glass from my fingers and straightens in her chair, turning her eyes to the front. I sit back, and my eyes linger on her for a moment longer.

By the end of tonight, I will make her breathe my name—one way or another.

The credits roll and the theater fills with booming applause. Naturally, the movie was incredible, as all of Grace's are. And as much as I said I'd never do this again, it was an honor to be amongst the first to watch it.

The lights switch on and Grace stands in front of everyone, a mic in hand. She bows dramatically, laughing, and brings the mic to her lips.

"Thank you, everyone, for coming here tonight for the premiere of Come Back to Me. It was such a fun and heartwarming movie to be in, and I'm thrilled you all enjoyed it." She pauses for the second round of applause. "Thank you. Now, if you'd like to walk through to the room to the right, there will be a selection of food and an open bar."

Another round of applause, this time filled with some happy shouts. Even Hollywood's elite love a free bar, it seems.

I move to stand, but Leah stays sitting. "Aren't you coming?"

"Yes." She sets her glass down. "But I'm waiting until the world and their mothers have gone through."

I look toward the large, open doors and see the people crowding through it. Makes sense. So I sit back down, and she quirks an eyebrow at me.

I sit back down and she quirks an eyebrow at me. "By all means, you carry on," she says.

"And let you walk through alone? Never."

"I've been doing this since I was eight. I think I can guide myself through to a reception."

"But I was raised a gentleman, and it would be rude of me to let you go alone."

She rolls her eyes. "Yes, Corey Jackson, serial dater and all-around one-night-stand guy is a gentleman."

"You seem to know an awful lot about my extracurricular activities, Leah."

She stands and brushes some creases from her dress. "You play for my team, and I live at the heart of L.A. I probably know more about your activities than you do. Including the fact that, every time you've been pictured with a woman, you've never once been a gentleman toward her."

I smile to her back when she walks away from me.

Or tries to.

In two long strides, I catch up with her and grab her arm. "Maybe because that's because they're not exactly ladies." I hook her hand in my elbow. "You act like a lady and I'll treat you like one." I softly pat her fingers.

She glances up at me, her lips pursed. "Fine. I'll allow you to escort me into the reception. Then you'll leave me alone. Agreed?"

"Sorry, darlin'. I can't agree to something I don't intend to do."

Something flits across her face. Then she sighs. "Are you always this pushy?"

"Are you always this prickly?"

"I'm not prickly. I'm simply a private person."

"How does that work? With your mom who she is?"

"Simple. I don't go looking for the cameras, and I don't give them any fun stories to run about me." She tucks some hair behind her ear. "Which means I definitely will not be seen anywhere near you in public."

"Ouch. I'm hurt."

"Oh, don't be. It's nothing against you. Actually, on second thought," she adds when I pass her a glass of wine, "it's everything against you."

"Fuck, Leah. Break it to me gently." I lean against the bar next to her. "I'm not that bad. Half of those girls never made it past a ride home."

"I'd imagine a ride is exactly what they got," she retorts smartly. "And last I knew, sex in a car is possible."

I laugh quietly. "I see the real reason you avoid the media. You'd tear them to pieces, and you obviously don't want to hurt their feelings."

"Oh, please. They don't have feelings. And after some of the bullshit they've run about my mom, I'd love to tear into them." She sips her drink, and her eyes find mine. "I just don't care to live my life in the spotlight. And if I do, it won't be because my mom is who she is. The media thinks the name on my birth certificate is simply 'Grace Veronica's daughter.'"

Leah saunters over to a free table, and my eyes drop to her ass. Damn. That dress really does hug it fucking incredibly. She coughs, drawing my eyes to her face, and half frowns, half smirks at me. I walk over to her, set my beer on the table, and hold my hands up.

"Babe, you wear a dress like that and you're gonna get looked at. Don't be blamin' me for it."

Her smirk swiftly changes to a full smile. "You're the most honest asshole I've ever met in my life."

"It's one of my better qualities."

"Of which there are few."

"You don't know a thing about me, Leah Veronica. For all

you know, I have a thousand amazing things about me."

She leans forward and rests her chin on her hand, her grin still in place. "Yet, equally, you could have even more bad things. Judging by what I know of you so far, letting me find out isn't a risk you should take."

"I love takin' risks," I murmur, tracing the shape of her lips with my eyes. "Especially when that risk is feisty and strong-willed."

"Are you calling me a risk, Corey Jackson?"

"What if I am?"

"Then you should be aware that you're never gonna get to take me—in any sense of the word."

"We'll see."

She sits up straight and her eyes flit away from me. A smile spreads across her face. "Cole!" She stands and embraces a guy with dark-blond hair. "You killed it! I bet your agent is drowning in calls already!"

Ah. Cole Dalton. Hollywood's new boy toy.

He smirks. "There might have been a couple."

Leah laughs. "Right. Tell me that in twenty-four hours."

"I promise I will, but you'll have to give me your number."

What the fuck? "I don't think we've met." I stand up and offer him my hand. "Corey Jackson."

Leah shoots me a hard look, but I ignore it and Cole doesn't even notice it.

"No way!" He puts his hand in mine. "Cole Dalton. Shit, I'm a huge fan. Leah, why didn't you tell me he was here?"

"I would have if you didn't change your number ten times a month." She smiles sweetly and sits down. "Do you want to join us?"

Now, she directs her smile toward me. My jaw ticks.

"I'd love to, but I'm afraid to sit down. Your mom is flaunting me like I'm her new boy toy."

"That's disgusting."

Cole laughs. "I'll e-mail you, all right? We'll do coffee or something."

"You still have my e-mail, right? You didn't lose that, too?"

He gives her the finger, much to her amusement, and disappears back into the crowd.

"You're friends with him?" I ask as soon as he's out of earshot.

"Jealous?" She shoots me a sassy grin and grabs a fresh glass of wine from a passing waiter. Then she turns, heading toward the door to the outdoor terrace.

I leave my drink where it is and go after her, the blue of her dress like a beckoning flag. She turns the corner at the top, and I follow her outside.

Leah sets her glass on one of the tables and walks over to the railings. You can see almost all of Los Angeles and the Hollywood Hills from this point, but all I can see is the girl leaning against the railings, looking like a fucking angel surrounded by bright lights.

I stop behind her and grip the railings on either side of her body. "Now why would I be jealous," I breathe, my mouth close to her neck, "when I'm the one up here with you and he's down there?"

"He's seen me almost naked." She turns her face into mine. "That seems like reason enough."

"Not exactly"—*Fucking lucky bastard*—"because I'll be seeing you completely naked soon enough."

"You are so certain it's comical."

She stops laughing the second my lips touch her neck. She smells like cotton candy and summer, and I brush my lips up her skin to her ear.

"Not so funny now, is it?" I whisper.

"If you have any sense, you'll let me go."

"Oh, I will. But not before I've done this." I pry her hands from the railing and flip her in my arms. The second her breasts brush my chest, I lower my mouth onto hers.

She tenses against me. I slip my hand up her back and cup the back of her head, my other hand holding steady at the base of her back. She has no choice but to give in and let me continue.

And she does.

Grabbing the lapels of my jacket, she tilts her face up to me.

I flick my tongue against her bottom lip, tasting the sweetness of the wine she's been drinking. She leans into me, and I kiss her harder, the softness of her lips consuming me completely.

"What are you—"

I silence her by kissing her again, this time more desperately, and she whimpers, opening her mouth. I slide my tongue against hers, teasing it, taunting it, until an all-out battle wages between us. Her hands twine in my hair and I kiss her until I can't fucking breathe anymore.

"Leah—I. Oh. Um."

She shoves me off her at the sound of Cole's voice. "Hi." She turns to me. "I'm leaving. And you"—she takes a deep breath—"are never going to do that again."

She lifts the bottom of her dress and runs across the terrace, leaving her wine left untouched on the table. Cole's eyes burn into me, a protective gleam there that tells me to fuck off.

Then he, too, turns and follows her downstairs.

I stare at the empty doorway, adrenaline pumping through my body, my dick as hard as a fucking rock. Her last words ring through my ears.

Yeah, right.

There isn't a fucking chance I'm leaving Leah Veronica alone.

I want her.

I want her a whole fucking lot.

And I get what I want.

Always.

Chapter THREE

Leah

One should make a note to remember that wine and or champagne will lower your inhibitions much quicker and much more drastically than tequila ever will. Surprisingly.

Shit. Shit. Shit, shit, shit! Why the hell did I let him kiss me last night? Why in the fucking hell didn't I demand to sit somewhere else and avoid him at all costs?

I should have known better. I *do* know better.

I've spent six years perfecting avoidance of anything that could destroy my career. I've stepped back from the media, except for my mom, and ignored the spotlight. I've turned down hundreds of acting jobs and opportunities so I could work on my dream—my own fashion label.

I've given up the easy road to success by keeping private and keeping Lea V. the world's most obvious secret.

I gave everything up when I was sixteen, threw everything into this dream. I watched every Fashion Week, never missing a show, studying every trend, predicting the next. Nailing it every time.

After four years of designing under the name Lea V., I finally got my break. My designs were finally noticed, and I was offered the contract of my dreams. My label. My line. To debut at NYFW. Everything I've ever wanted.

Now the only people who know who Lea V. really is are my boss Quinn, my mom, my aunt, and me.

Throwing myself into the spotlight will add millions of people to that list and give an acceptance I don't deserve. And Corey Jackson is most definitely the way to destroy every moment of hard work I've put into Lea V.

"I've never felt so awkward in my whole life."

I groan and bury my head in my hands. "I don't even know what I was doing. Cole, what was I doing?"

"I believe you were playing a round of very fucking enthusiastic tonsil tennis."

I groan again. "Thank you for stopping me. I mean… What the fuck is wrong with me? Corey Jackson?"

Cole smirks. "It could be worse. I'm sure hundreds of girls would love to kiss the quarterback."

"Ugh! This isn't high school. This is…wrong."

"Did it feel wrong at the time?"

I open my mouth then close it again. No. It didn't. How the hell could it have felt wrong when I could feel every inch of muscle beneath his suit? How the fucking hell could it have felt wrong when the sweep of his lips over mine, the probing of his tongue, and the sparks from his fingers against my skin hummed through my veins?

How could it have felt wrong when, for those few minutes his lips were touching mine, I felt so alive?

"I don't have to answer that."

Cole laughs. "There's my answer. Is that the first time you met?"

"No! What do you take me for?" I frown, pausing. "It was the second."

He buries his face in his hands, still laughing, and when he glances at me, I laugh, too.

"Oh God," I moan, covering my mouth with my hand. "He isn't going to leave me alone, is he?"

"Eh." He shrugs. "He definitely didn't like it when I came over to see you."

"And you didn't help! Mr. 'I'm A Huge Fan! Leah, why didn't you tell me?'" I mock, kicking him across the sofa.

"Hey!" He grabs my foot and knocks it away. "I am, all right?"

I roll my eyes. "He's coming for dinner tomorrow. Did you know that? Ada has the biggest, grossest, old lady cougar-crush on him, and Mom promised she'd invite him for dinner."

Cole stares at me. "No shit. A cougar-crush?"

"That's what you just took from all that? How about he's coming for dinner? To my house? With me?"

"Are you sixteen? Snap the fuck out of it!" He slaps my leg. "You are Leah Fucking Veronica, a take-no-shit, total badass. If you're gonna flail over a guy, it's gonna be me, movie star Cole Fucking Dalton, not some football-playing prick. You got that, sweetheart?"

I drop my head back and laugh. Hard. When all else fails, e-mail Cole Fucking Dalton for coffee and a good giggle.

"You're the best," I manage through my giggles. "Leah Fucking Veronica, indeed."

"You better fuckin' remember it!" He slaps my leg again.

I dig my toes into his thigh. "I'll put it on a Post-it and stick it to my mirror so I'll see it every morning."

"You do that."

"I will." I hold his light-brown gaze for a moment before giggling again. "Seriously, Cole. I don't need the drama or focus he'll bring to my life."

"It's always confused me how you can be so…quiet…when your mom is a megastar and two of your closest friends are Hollywood's new babies." He chews his thumbnail. "How are you not a movie star?"

"I don't know either," I lie, hating every second. Twenty years of solid friendship and he doesn't even know what I do. "I'm proud of all of you, and I love you all, but it just isn't for me. I guess I'm so immersed in this world that I see the less-than-glamorous stuff, too."

"Makes sense. It's pretty shitty sometimes," he agrees. "You're better off baking cookies or selling clothes or some shit."

"I'm not allowed to bake cookies. Ada steals them all and it rockets her blood pressure." I sigh.

"Come to my house and bake me and Dad cookies." He laughs and gets up. "I gotta go. Charlie will kick my ass if I'm late for another meeting. Apparently, her phone is ringing off the hook." He winks and backs out of the room.

"Bragger!" I yell after him.

He laughs. Then the front door shuts. His car rumbles outside as he drives to meet with his agent.

I swing my legs up onto the sofa and sigh heavily. It would be easier if I could just tell Cole about Lea V., because then my reasoning for staying away from Corey would make more sense. Right now, I just look like a flighty, indecisive little girl.

And let's be honest, I'm not going to talk to my mom or great-aunt about it.

With a heavy sigh, I grab my drawing pad from its hiding place in the coffee table drawer, open to my latest design, and get to work on next fall's collection.

"You know, Leah, I've always thought about going running."

My hand hovers over the coffee pot and I turn to Aunt Ada, her tiny frame swamped by a fluffy, pink robe. "Why on Earth would you go running?"

"For the same reason you do."

"I run to keep fit, Aunt Ada. Not because it's fun."

"A gun? Who said anything about a gun?"

I look at the ceiling and shake my head, but a smile creeps onto my face. "Don't worry. Coffee?"

"Toffee? No, dear. It'll stick to my dentures."

"Coh-ohff-ee," I repeat.

"Oh! Coffee. Six sugars please."

I choke back a laugh. One is more than enough for her. I don't even want to think about what'll happen if she has more than that. I pour two mugs and then join her at the island in the kitchen.

"You're missing five." She holds the mug out at me.

"Ada, you're not having six sugars." Mom's voice filters through the house. "Do you remember what happened last time? You ended up at the hospital because your diabetes thought it was Christmas for your pancreas."

I look down to hide my laughter.

"I'm older than you, Gracie."

"And you agreed to my rules when you moved in here." Mom walks past and opens the door. Nine thirty. Mail time.

"What was that? I can't hear you." Ada winks at me.

I smile and shake my head. Crazy old lady. "I'm going for a late run. See you later."

"Can I have your coffee?" Mom yells after me.

"Sure!" I tie my hair back as I step into the early morning Los Angeles sun.

From the entrance to Mom's sprawling house, I can see right across L.A., the skyline reaching into the sky and spanning the horizon. It's quiet and secluded up here, safe from the media, a total haven for those rich enough to own a house away from the craziness of the city.

I hit play on my phone, tuck it into my bra, and hook my headphones over my ears. Then I turn right and jog up the road, sweeping a loose lock of hair behind my ear. Running is freedom—the steady beat of my feet against the asphalt a constant rhythm I adore.

That's why, even with a folder full of designs to alter and finish and finals coming in for next month, I'm out here. It would be all too easy to hole myself up in my room and finish my work, sure. But I'd become a recluse, only emerging for a multipack of chips and cookies like a rabid kind of monster.

Something sharply connects with my ass, and I scream, turning around and swinging my fist at the body behind me. I make a connection with something solid, and I yank my headphones out in time to hear the resounding grunt.

"Corey! What the fuck?"

"Shit!" He rubs his arm. "Is your fist made of steel?"

"Did you seriously just run up behind me and slap me on my butt?" I shriek, my eyes widening. "You pig!"

He holds his arms up. "I thought you'd hear me coming!"

I hold my headphones up. "No. Oh my God." I rub my left ass cheek. Shit. That hurt.

"I'm sorry." He laughs.

"No, you aren't." I stuff the headphones down between my boobs and run away from him. "You just wanted an excuse to touch my ass."

"It's a fuckin' nice ass."

"Great. I always wanted your approval on it." I roll my eyes.

"You wouldn't be the first, babe."

"Good grief. You really do think a lot of yourself, don't you?" I glance at him and the way his dark hair curls over his forehead.

The muscles in his arms flex as he runs alongside me and he's barely breaking a sweat. And he looks good. Better than good.

Damn hot is what my eyes are feasting on right now.

"I only think what others say." He winks.

"Well, obviously." I pick up the pace.

"Tryna lose me, Leah?"

"Now what gives you that idea?"

"Your not-so-subtle speeding up."

"There're brains as well as brawn. I'm impressed."

He laughs, the deep vibrations of it crawling over me. "I love your attitude."

I raise my eyebrows and lean against a tree to catch my breath. Wiping my forehead with the heel of my hand, I reply, "I don't have an attitude."

"Oh you do." His eyes grab mine, an amused smile making the corners crease, and he runs his fingers through his hair. "And that's what makes you so damn attractive to me."

"My attitude?"

"Yep."

"Shit. If I had known that, I wouldn't have been nearly half as cocky as what I was when we met." I sigh and stretch upward. "Or on Sunday night."

He smirks, and his blue-green eyes flick to the strip of skin revealed by my shirt sliding up my stomach. He moves forward, closing the space between us. His body is so close to mine that I can feel the hotness of it radiating from him, teasing my exposed skin.

I drop my arms, looking up at him. Hell. If I took one tiny step forward, my front would be flush against his and he'd sure as hell be able to feel the little hop-skip-jump dance my heart is taking up.

Corey places his hand on the tree, barely a breath away from the top of my head, and I force myself to swallow the butterflies swirling in my stomach and rising up into my chest.

"No, you wouldn't," he says in a low, husky voice. "You didn't exactly push me away on Sunday, did you?"

"I should have."

"But you didn't."

My tongue flicks out and wets my bottom lip. His eyes flick down to the movement then back up. I flatten my hands against the tree, curling my fingers into the rough bark.

"You trapped me. I couldn't move."

His lips twitch—barely—and he steps forward. That space I was thinking about earlier? Yep. Gone.

His leg slides between mine, his free hand resting on my hip. His mouth—oh God. It's barely millimeters from me.

My head screams, *Get off!*

My body screams, *Get on!*

Traitorous little bitch.

"What about now?" he whispers, his breath ghosting over my lips. "Can you move now?"

I draw in a long, slow breath and slowly bring my right leg up. My thigh slips between his, and I hold it just below his dick. "I can and I will."

"No, you won't." He slides his hand up my side and cups the side of my face with a grin. His thumb traces the line of my jaw, and he tilts my face up. "Because you'll be needin' that pretty soon."

"So sure, cowboy," I whisper. "You caught me off guard once—"

"Twice."

"Twice," I correct, grasping his wrist and tugging his hand down. "Now, I'm telling you—move your ass or my thigh and your cock are going to get acquainted pretty *sharply*."

Corey shoots his hand out and pushes my thigh down. At the same time, he leans forward and presses his lips to mine. Then he kisses me hard, and when he pulls away, his teeth graze my bottom lip.

"You—" I start as he runs backward, winking.

"See you at dinner, darlin'."

chapter FOUR

Corey

That shower accomplished fuck all except for relieving a little of the sexual tension coiled inside my body.

Ever since she walked away from me at the theater, she's consumed my mind like a fucking addiction. One taste was all it took—one taste of those soft, sweet lips and I need more.

I crave more of her.

I should've run in the opposite direction when I saw her earlier. I was finishing, ready to head home, but then she was there. Her hair swinging in its ponytail, running pants hugging her hips and legs, her ass tight and round…

And fuck. I had to touch it. Had to know if it felt as good as it looked. And damn, the punch in the arm was worth it.

I pull some pants on and rub the towel through my hair. I wish to hell she'd just give in and let me fuck her. One night. That's all I want—one night to explore that tight little body, to explore its curves and contours, to make it tremble beneath my touch.

To make her scream my name.

To get her the hell out of my system.

I tug a shirt over my head, rub some wax into my hair, and then grab my phone and car keys. Dinner at her house. I should have said no, but no one in their right mind turns Grace Veronica down when she asks for something.

She asks, you do. Simple as fuck.

Plus, the opportunity to piss Leah off… It's like a game. Who can out-snark the other? Who'll win the battle of the bitch? And I love every second because the fire she gets in her eyes is sexy as hell.

I drive through the Hills until I reach her house. Then I put in the code Grace's assistant e-mailed me earlier and wait for the gates to open. When they do, I drive through and up the winding driveway that leads to the Veronica house.

Classy and modern with a hint of old Hollywood in the décor. Grace Veronica nails it once again.

I park my Range Rover in front of the large garage and pocket my keys. The house is huge, and as I walk to the front door, I realize the door is, too. Glass-paneled, double-door kind of huge. I am reaching out to press the bell when one of the doors swings open.

Leah stands in front of me with her lips pursed. Her eyes are spitting fire and anger at me, and I know instantly she's still pissed at me for earlier. Good.

"Corey," she says pleasantly. "I suppose I should let you in."

"Leah!" Grace snaps from somewhere in the house.

Leah takes a deep breath and her eyes focus on the ceiling for a second. "Corey. Come in." She plasters a smile on her face.

I step over the threshold and pause in front of her. "You could pretend you're happy to see me, you know."

"I am pretending," she hisses.

"You are?" I raise my eyebrows. "Now I see why you don't act. You're shit at it."

"I'm not afraid to hurt you, I swear to God, so you better start walking, cowboy."

I laugh and walk past her. She shuts the door and looks at me.

"Take your shoes off. Cream carpets."

I bend down wordlessly and tug my shoes off. Leah takes

them from me and puts them in the large coat room behind me then waves over her shoulder for me to follow her. She leads me through a large living area, not speaking a word, and just when she's about to guide me into another room, I grab her hand.

She freezes and looks up at me. "What are you doing?"

I don't know. "I'm...sorry," I say hesitantly. "I know I've pissed you off."

"Gee, say it like you mean it, why don't you?" She snatches her hand away.

"Do you want me to go?"

She stops and drops her head back. "No," she replies softly. "I don't. Just...cut the crap, okay?"

"Cut the crap?"

"Wow. You're dense." She shakes her head. "All the...well, all the kissing me. It makes me...uncomfortable." She swallows.

"You seemed comfortable enough to me."

"Corey!"

"Shit. I'm sorry." I hold my hands up. "Let me make it up to you."

"I can buy my own game ticket." She smirks.

Oh, she's hilarious.

I step toward her and push some hair behind her ear. "No, I wasn't going to suggest that." I match her smile. "I was going to suggest we do something. Together."

"Like a date?"

"Er..."

Her eyes widen at my hesitation.

"I guess."

"No." She spins and strolls out of the living area, leaving her sharp word echoing through the room and me wondering if she really fucking hates me that much.

Leah's great-aunt Ada has been staring at me all night. It's hovering somewhere between cute and creepy because she has the most adorable little grin she shoots my way whenever I catch her looking. Crow's-feet appear at the corners of her eyes, and her cheeks flush just a little.

I think she might have a crush on me.

Again, hovering between cute and creepy.

"Aunt Ada. Will you please stop looking at him like he's dessert?" Leah sighs, taking Ada's plate from in front of her.

"Stop hooking up with Bert? Whoever is Bert?" Ada replies, looking genuinely confused.

I quirk my eyebrow, and Grace leans across the table. "Hearing aid, Ada."

The old woman blinks then slips her hand into her pocket. She pulls out a small, nude-colored device and fits it to her ear. "Now, Lele, what was that you were saying about hooking up with Bert?"

Lele?

Leah catches my eye and gives me a death stare. "I didn't say anything about Bert. I asked you to stop looking at Corey like he's dessert."

"He isn't?"

I cough into my hand.

"Ada, it's late. I think you should, perhaps, go to bed now." Grace winks at me and stands.

"But we haven't danced."

"People don't dance at dinner now, Aunt Ada," Leah tells her. "They eat, they drink, they go home."

"Well, how boring. You young'uns don't know how to have a good time."

Grace swoops Ada out of the kitchen with her still muttering about "kids today."

"Oh, they do," Leah murmurs, loading the dishwasher. "They just don't invite old people along."

I grin. "Do you need any help?"

She shakes her head instead of answering me verbally. She hasn't said a fucking word to me since she rebuffed my offer of a date. Even through dinner, she managed to contribute to the conversation without directing a single sentence at me.

And it's slowly starting to really, really piss me off.

I watch as she scrapes the plates into the trash then bends over and puts them in the dishwasher. Her dress rides up her legs, the hem hovering at the very top of her thighs. If she bends over another half inch, her underwear will be fully exposed to me. So will her ass, and if she's that kind of girl, maybe her pussy, too.

My cock twitches at the thought. Fuck—I want to go over there and see. I want to flick that stupid fucking dress up and see what kind of underwear she wears, and if that doesn't make me hard imagining it...

"Are you staring at my ass?" she asks, her words slicing through the silence easily but sharply.

"On a scale of one to ten, how honestly do you want me to answer that?"

"Very honestly."

My eyes coast over her smooth skin. "About a fifty."

She slams the dishwasher shut and turns. "Seriously? Is me telling you to cut the crap an open invitation to ogle me?"

"No, but you wearing a dress that short and bendin' over is."

Her lips thin. "And you wonder why I won't go out with you."

"Maybe I'm not bothered."

"Yeah?" She rests her hands flat on the table opposite me and leans over. "So why've you been looking at me all evening like I'm a math puzzle you can't figure out?"

"Because you confuse the fuck out of me." I hold her gaze. "One night, you don't want me. The next, you're in my arms, fucking *whimpering* into my mouth. Then, not even twenty-four hours later, you're tellin' me where to go. That's why I keep looking at you." My eyes drop to her tits. "That and you're hot as hell."

She stares at me until I bring my eyes back up to hers. "Wow. And that right there is why I just told you no when you asked me out." She pushes off the table and stalks away from me.

She pushes off the table and stalks away from me.

"What the hell are you so mad for?" I get up and follow her out to the backyard. "You're the one sending me more mixed messages than I can keep up with!"

"Then this is the last one!" she yells, turning to face me. "No. That's the message, Corey, all right? I can't go out with you. I cannot be seen in public with you. I do *not* need the media craziness that will come with being associated with you."

"You're Grace Veronica's daughter. They photograph you getting a coffee for fuck's sake!"

"And that's why I don't need any more attention!" She runs her fingers through her blond hair. "I just don't, okay?"

"Why? It makes no sense."

"It does to me." Her eyes soften and she wraps her arms around her waist. "It's dangerous for me, okay? I can't explain why, so you have to accept that as it is. You have to take my no for a no and just leave it alone."

"See, that's where the problem is. I can't," I say, moving closer to her. She doesn't move. "I wanted you the moment I saw you in the bar. I wanted to fuck you, Leah. I still do. I'd love nothin' more than to have your body beneath mine right fuckin' now. But you turned me down with that sassy mouth of yours, and now, I'm intrigued by you."

"Intrigued by me? There's nothing to *be* intrigued by. I'm pretty boring."

"You're wrong," I mutter, dipping my face close to hers without touching her. "I want to get under your skin, darlin'. I want to consume you. Even if it's only for a night. I want to finish what I set out to start when I walked up to you in that bar."

"You can't." She swallows.

"I can and I will," I say, echoing her words from earlier. "I won't leave you alone, Leah. I will pursue you until I get what I want. Until I get you."

"You won't. Get me."

I cup her jaw and brush my nose along it. "I want you, Leah. And I always get what I want."

Chapter FIVE

Leah

"You look like you got attacked by a swamp rat."

I look up at my mom, my mouth full of Cheetos. I chew and swallow and shrug. "I'm working. All day. Which means I'm staying in my pajamas and eating a whole bunch of junk food."

"So I see." She casts her eyes over my bed, which happens to be littered with various full soda cans, bags of chips, and candy.

"Hey, I showered."

"Thankfully. Quinn said he'd e-mail the photos over at four this afternoon."

"Awesome." I add a capped sleeve to the dress I'm designing then erase it.

"Macey left a message on the phone. She might come by after work."

"Cool." I shove a Cheeto into my mouth.

"Ada is at the community center all day."

"Mmhmm." I crush my design into a ball and throw it in the general direction of my trash can. I miss.

Mom picks it up and drops it in. "Leah!"

"What?" I whine, turning around. "I'm trying to work!"

"I know, but I only want to talk for two seconds."

"Fine." I put the pencil down. "What is it?"

"Corey's on the phone."

I glare at her. "That better be on hold."

She nods.

"Good. I'm not here. Okay?"

"Leah."

"I said I'm not here. Okay?"

She sighs but nods. Then she brings the phone to her ear. "Sorry, Corey. She's not here. I must have missed her… All right. I'll tell her… Bye, hon." She throws the phone on my bed and looks at me pointedly. "He said he'll call again later."

I turn back to my pad, grab another Cheeto, and put my pencil to the page. "And I will still not be here." I shove the fluffy, orange chip in my mouth.

"Good grief," Mom mutters before shutting my door.

I don't even glance over my shoulder. I focus on the scratch of my pencil against the page, of the forming of the dress as it filters out of my mind and into reality. The shape of the skirt, the flare of the hem, the tuck of the waist, the dip of the neckline. I watch it take shape, become a real design, something I can change and manipulate until it resembles black-and-white perfection.

But it's not right.

I tear the page off, ball it up, and throw it toward my trash can. This time, I sketch a jumpsuit. Flaring the pant legs, I scratch up the page until I reach the neckline. Low, low, lower… I bring it back up, adding some structure to the neckline.

Not right.

Another—this time, a jacket.

Not right.

This time, a pant suit.

Not right.

Not right, not right, not fucking right!

I throw my pencil across the room and grab my cell. Then I dial Cole's number and drop back onto my bed, opening a package of Sour Patch Kids.

"What's up, buttercup?"

"I hate Corey Jackson."

"Intense," Cole replies. "What'd he do?"

"He kissed me again. Right after he told me he always gets what he wants."

"That's not the response one would usually expect from a girl he's kissed."

"Well, one isn't a girl he kisses. Until I am. Except I am. Except I don't know!"

Cole laughs. "He's obviously stopping you from doing something. You only get all bitchy when you're interrupted."

Shit. "I'm trying to find a job," I lie. "And I can't concentrate on writing my résumé."

"Really? Can't you just put 'Grace Veronica's daughter' down?"

And that right there is why I work in secret. "Yes, because that's my ticket to an easy life. Going off my mom's name."

"Wow. Do you have your regular visitor or something?"

"You're an asshole, Cole." I sniff. "No, I'm not on my period. Corey's just throwing me off, okay?"

"He must have done something big if you're this fucked up."

"Well, hey, I didn't know I was talking to Captain Obvious." I roll my eyes. "He said he isn't going to give up until I let him fuck me."

Cole laughs loudly.

"This isn't funny!"

"I'm sorry, Leah, but it kinda is. You're twenty-two and all flustered over him saying that. Just fuck him! Because, girl, he means it. You're not getting out of it until you let him stick it up in you."

"You're disgusting."

"Tell that to my date."

"You're on a date? A lunch date?"

"I get dates, you know."

"Uh, are you talking to me with her there?"

"No. She thinks I'm talking to my agent, so I'm gonna have to go or you're gonna earn yourself the title of 'Cockblocker.'"

"Fuck you, Cole." I hang up and drop the phone on the floor.

A lot of good that conversation did. He's such a fantastic friend—confirming what I already knew.

I slide to the floor and grab the phone. This time, though, I dial Macey's number.

"What?"

"Are you coming over?"

"About to. Why?"

"Bring alcohol with you."

"Who is that?"

"Who's who?" I roll my head to the side and look at Macey.

"That." She jabs at the screen on her tablet.

"Don't you mean 'him'?" I ask, squinting. "Jack Carr. He plays for the Vipers, too."

"Mmm. Do you think your new toy could hook me up?"

"Corey is not my toy," I protest with a sigh. "He's a very large, very hot, pain in my backside."

"Yes. Yes, he is." Ryann lies back on the bed next to me and puts her feet on the wall. "Hot, that is. And probably large. I don't want to know about the butt pain thing."

I slap her hip with the back of my fingers. "Ew."

"Right. Now back to Jack…" Macey shoves the iPad in my face. "Do we know where this guy lives?"

Ryann shrieks a laugh. "What, are you gonna go over there, knock on his door, and declare yourself available for a good fucking?"

Macey blinks. "I was considering it."

I briefly close my eyes and grab the wine glass sippy cup from my nightstand. Then I lie back down, drinking from the bright-pink spout. "You should," I say, resting the cup on my stomach. "God knows one of us three needs to get some."

"You have 'some' offered on a plate, sweetcheeks," Ryann offers helpfully.

"Some? No, Ry. She has fucking 'all' lying on a chaise lounge begging to be drawn like a French girl." Macey snorts, grabbing her own cup.

I laugh into my hand. "What? Oh my God. Now I have this horrific image of him lying on his side with his legs open and his head thrown back."

None of us speaks for a few seconds. Then we all laugh loudly. Seriously—I can't. I just... Oh my God.

The phone rings on the nightstand, and Macey rolls onto her side. "We should probably put the wine down now."

I grab the phone and tip my cup up to show her what I think of that idea.

"Agreed." Ryann tips hers up, too, giggling, then chokes.

I snort as I answer. "Hell—o?"

"Leah? That you?"

I slam the phone down the bed, my eyes widening. "Oh, fuck!" I whisper harshly.

"What?" Ryann hisses.

"Corey. Phone. Now."

"I want Jack's number!" Macey shrieks, diving over me to grab it.

"What? No, you crazy bitch!" I hold the phone over my head and scramble down the bed.

She grabs my leg. I respond by tugging myself away hard, and she lets go...leaving me to fall on my ass on the floor.

"Uh, hello?"

"Hello." I giggle into the phone. "I'm sorry. My friends are assholes."

"I didn't do anything!" Ryann shouts.

"Shut up!" I hiss across the room. "Hold on," I say to Corey.

"I thought you didn't want to talk to him?" Macey questions. Extra loud.

I shoot her a warning stare. Geez, what are we, sixteen? Can't I even get away with pretending I'm in my twenties?

I shut my bedroom door behind me and run into Mom's room. "Hello. Sorry. They're crazy."

"Hey," he replies, and I can almost hear the smile in his

voice. "Can you do me a favor?"

"Um, that depends."

"Can you let me in?"

Eyes. Widening. "I'm not home."

"Liar. Your car is outside."

"Macey gave me a ride to her place."

"Yeah?"

"Yeah." I nod. Because if I nod, I'll convince myself.

"You know we're not talking on your cell, don't you?"

I snap my head around to look at the phone. Sure as shit, I stare right at the silver house phone. "Oh. Um. Well, this is slightly awkward."

I pad down the stairs and through the house to the front door. His reflection is blurred by the glass of the doors, but he's definitely there. I swallow hard. Wow. He really did mean he wouldn't give up.

I pull the door open and look straight into his blue-green eyes. "Hi."

"Hi." His lips pull up to one side. "You can put the phone down now."

"Right." I step back and set the phone in its holder. "What are you, um, doing here?"

Corey shuts the front door behind him and runs his hand through his messy, wet hair. "Are you drunk?"

"No!" I purse my lips when he raises an eyebrow at me. "Maybe a little. A tiny bit."

He grins.

"Wine sippy cups," I explain unnecessarily. *C'mon, Leah. Does he care how you drink your wine?*

"Right." His grin doesn't falter. "I came to ask you something."

"Can I say at this point that I'd rather you didn't? Your questions generally don't lead anywhere good."

"Fine." He leans against the wall and folds his arms across his chest. *Mmm, biceps.*

Eyes up, girl. Fuck it.

"So you'll go? Fabulous." I grab for the door handle, but

he's quicker, his fingers closing around my arm.

"No," he says quieter. "If you won't let me ask you, I'll tell you."

"Really?" I stand up straight, snapping my eyes to his. "You're gonna tell me, huh? And how well do you think that's gonna work out for you, cowboy?"

"Probably as well as my attempts to fuck the hell out of you." He drops his voice and leans forward. "But I'm gonna give it a good fuckin' shot."

I stare at him stonily. Shit. Five minutes in his presence and I already wanna carve a satanic ritual into his balls or something. "I dare you."

"It's Reid's birthday tomorrow. His mom is putting on this fancy dinner at the Beverly Hills Hotel tomorrow night." He stops.

"Well, happy birthday to Reid."

"Funny girl," Corey murmurs, tugging me closer to him. "I want you to come."

"Translation: you need a date and you want me to be it."

"Nothing gets past you, does it, babe?"

"Not a damn thing." I smile sweetly. "And I'm sorry, but I'm busy tomorrow night."

"Doing what?!" Macey shrieks from the front room.

"Macey! Fucking hell!" Ryann cries. "What'd you do that for?"

"Uh, I wonder why!"

I close my eyes and take a deep breath. "Of course," I say under my breath. "Why wouldn't they be there?" I tug my arm from Corey's hold and step away from him. "You might as well come out, eavesdropping bitches."

They fight their way through the doorway then untangle themselves. Such a 'Cinderella's ugly stepsisters' moment. Sheesh.

"Hi." Macey grins. Widely.

"Hi." Ryann echoes, grinning, too.

"Hey." Corey smirks.

"Anyway," I interject, drawing the word out. "Sorry,

cowboy, but I'm busy. Maybe never, okay?"

"Maybe never? Ouch. You wound me, Leah."

"I'm sure there's some wannabe actress downtown who will kiss that better."

"Hold up." Macey steps forward. "This dinner. Is Jack going to be there?"

"We woke the beast," Ryann mutters.

"Yeah," Corey replies. "Why?"

Macey smiles widely. "'Scuse us." She snatches my arm and yanks me after her. Then she drags me into the front room, and Ryann shuts the door behind us.

"What the hell?" I look at Macey.

"Leah! Jack will be there!"

"I am not going to dinner with Corey just so you can get your panties wet." I fold my arms across my chest.

"Maybe you'll get yours wet." Ryann's eyebrows shoot up suggestively and she swigs from her wine cup.

I snatch the cup from her and finish it. "Nope. Still not feeling the urge."

"Please, Leah. We'll come with you and we'll keep you away from him," Macey begs. "I mean, Ryann will keep you away from him. Okay? It's kind of the same thing."

"You weren't even invited. I was. And I have no desire to do this." I feel like the sixteen-year-old I thought about earlier. God. Privately talking about hot guys like we're still virgins and wondering who'll get kissed first at this prom.

Except this time, it's who'll get fucked first.

And I don't mean in the sexual sense.

Dates with Corey Jackson—hell, one date with Corey Jackson—are a fucking in the literal sense. What if we went on a date, then I happened to like his arrogant ass, and one day, he discovers who I am? What I do?

That I'm that new chick in the fashion world with the most anticipated new line at New York Fashion Week?

That I'm the one every fashion designer wants? That I'm the one who is the future of the fashion world?

What if he finds out that I live every day in completely

secrecy, determined to unnecessarily take the hard path?

One word. One word is all it would take to tear apart six years of work.

"No," I say forcefully. "You can go, but I won't."

My best friends look at me like I've lost my mind, and maybe I have, but I'm sticking to it. I have to stick to it for my own sanity and safety.

I open the door, ignoring Macey's, "Unf—" and face Corey. "I have things to do. The girls will go, but I'm not. Sorry."

Then I turn away and head toward the stairs. Corey doesn't say another word. He just stares after me, and he lets me go.

And despite the fact that it's exactly what I want him to do, I don't like that he has.

Corey

"You threw without thinking!"

"Fuck off, man!" I point to the screen. "See that gap there? Where there are no Texans? That's where *you* needed to be! How do you expect me to get the ball to you when there's three of their defense right the hell there?"

"By waiting for two seconds!"

"And how's he gonna do that?" Reid raises his eyebrows. "He's the quarterback. Everyone moves for him the second he gets the ball. Corey's got a throw with the aim of a sniper."

My lips twitch smugly. That's one I haven't heard before, but I like it. Reviewing last season's tapes is always a nightmare, but we're fucked if we don't. There's no other way to make an impact in the preseason. And that's what preseason is—a chance to make an impact, to inject fear into the other teams.

In our case, it's to tell them that the Vipers are ready to intercept every throw, run every yard, and touchdown every ball.

It's to tell them that we're ready to take the fucking Vince Lombardi home next February.

Wes puts his hands in the air. "By running. He has feet, doesn't he?"

"Run friggin' where?" I jab at the screen again. Is this guy dumb or what? "They had me covered. They would have jumped on me if I'd sneezed in the wrong direction."

Wes sighs. "Fine. I'll remember to move my little peasant legs next time, Your Highness."

"All right, Wes, Corey. That's enough of your bitchin'." Lincoln Sparks, our coach, slams the door behind him. "Tactical meeting or not, whining at each other like a couple of girls ain't sorting it. Wes, you should have run into the space. Corey, you should have tried to shake off their defense. We're trying to get yards, not look good and get laid after the game."

I resist the urge to roll my eyes—this is my coach after all—because I can get laid either way. We all know it, so the only thing the yards count toward is winning the game.

"We just about killed it last weekend, but the preseason ain't over yet, and the regular season hasn't even begun. I want you go out there and live up to your damn team name! I want you to kick their asses and show them who the real champions of the National Football League are."

"We're on it, Coach," Jack pipes up. "What was it you said, Reid? Corey's got the aim of a sniper or something?"

Coach chuckles. "Never a truer word spoken. As long as he goes for the football equivalent of a headshot, we'll be just fine next game." He slaps my shoulder.

"I'll take 'em in one, Coach. Don't worry about that." I wink.

"Man, my head hurts," Jet groans, rubbing his temples.

"Get in Corey's way in practice, did you?" Reid laughs.

I smirk. "He'd be out cold if he did."

"Don't doubt that," Coach agrees. "I remember when you threw to Russell and he missed the catch—hit him right in the stomach and winded him."

I link my fingers and stretch them out in front of me, my knuckles cracking. "All in a day's practice, boys."

Laughter echoes through the room—because my words are true. They know it. I learned the game from the best fucking quarterback to ever play in the NFL. My father.

I learned the aim and the throw. I learned the run, how to outsmart the defense, how to whoop asses from their twenty-yard line to our touchdown zone. I learned how to run every fucking game with an iron fist and smash every opponent.

Relentless. Intense. Destroying.

They're the first words that come to mind when someone mentions the game. The three words that mean the goddamn world and more to me.

Except now there's another creeping into that collection of words. And it's more than a word. It's a name, a description, a verbal embodiment of a person.

Leah.

My dream and my motherfucking nightmare.

There's no other way to describe her. She's the thing I desire above everything else—maybe, right now, even above the Super Bowl—but she's also the thing I fear most. And I don't have a clue why. She's not scary, not with those baby-blue eyes, pouty, pink lips, and smooth, blond hair. She's the sweetest fucking thing I've ever known, but I'm terrified of her.

Terrified that maybe she really will stick to her 'no' and never give me the tiny slice of heaven she embodies.

I grab my bag from the locker room and sling it over my shoulder. The stadium is suffocating. I need to leave. I need to find a goddamn punching bag and work all of this shit out.

Leah Veronica is fucking with me in the worst kind of way.

I'm certain she knows. She has to. There's no way she can stand in front of me and not see what she's doing to me with her back-and-forth bullshit. There's no way she can curl into my arms, kiss my lips, whimper into my mouth, and not see or feel how much I want her.

One fuck. One goddamn fucking fuck. That's all I want. All I need. I just need to get this chick out of my system and move on.

She's the hardest fuck I've ever had to work for, so she better be the best.

"I ain't wearing a fuckin' tie," I say with my phone on speaker.

"You don't have to, man," Reid says. "Just a smart shirt or some shit. I don't know. My mom organized it. She thinks I'm twenty-one, not fucking twenty-six. I'd rather watch Avengers with Leo."

"Watching Avengers with Leo is an option?" I love Reid's son. The kid is awesome with a capital A.

"Man, if it was, don't you think I'd be doin' it?" he grumbles. "Mom hired a sitter so I have to go."

"Damn. Well, I got a white shirt. Will that do?" I throw the shirt on my bed. "Last time I went to this place, my mom made me wear a damn tux."

Reid laughs. "Bring your bow tie to pull the chicks!"

"Fuck off. Shirt and jeans it is. See ya." I hang up and throw my phone on the bed. That puts an end to the most damn teenage-girl-esque conversation I've ever had.

I dress quickly and grab my phone from the bed. Then I dial Leah's house number, but it goes to the messaging service. Fuck.

I'm gonna get this girl if it kills me.

After jumping into my Range Rover, I drive through the Hills to her house. The gates are shut and locked, but I lean out the window and press the buzzer anyway. There's no answer, like I expected, so I lean back in my seat and take the turn to downtown.

What if her 'busy' was seeing another guy? Fuck. No motherfucking way.

Her body belongs to me until I decide otherwise. Every fucking part of her, from her head to her toes, is mine. And only mine.

No other guy, no man, gets to see it. They don't get to touch it or kiss it or even think about it.

She doesn't know it, but I do. I know how she responds to me, how her heart thuds beneath my touch, how her pupils dilate when I get close. I see the way she inhales whenever her eyes meet mine. But her? No.

Leah Veronica has no idea how she feels about me.

She's oblivious to the obvious.

Luckily for her, I'm more than clear on the situation.

Leah Veronica belongs to me.

And she will until I tell her that she doesn't.

I park in front of the Beverly Hills Hotel and hand my keys to the valet without a word. Then I fiddle with my sleeve and walk into the hotel. The concierge guides me into the elevator then takes me two floors up. After stepping out, he makes me follow him down the hall and into a large dining room.

The room is filled with the team and their girlfriends. And Reid's mom, being the head of a modeling agency, has ensured that there are enough models and aspiring actresses here to keep any playboy happy. Several walk past me as I cross to the bar, and I give them a cursory look.

Shit, they're sexy, yeah. But that's all they are.

"You finally decided what to wear!" Jack laughs and slaps my shoulder. "Here. Have a beer. There are some fucking assholes walking around with champagne or some shit. I had to tell them to fuck off four times before they finally realized I'm not drinking that bubbly bullshit."

My lips tug to the side, and I grab the beer. "You know me well, man. When's dinner?"

"Half an hour," Reid says as he steps up next to me. "And your ass better be in that fuckin' seat or my mom is gonna kick it to Canada."

I laugh. "Ouch. She that excited?"

"Twenty-six, man. What the fuck is this?"

"She just wants to show off her itty-bitty baby," Jack coos, pouting his lips and reaching for Reid's cheek.

"Her itty-bitty baby stopped being a baby when he had one of his own six years ago." Reid punches his hand away. "So fuck off, asshole." He turns to me. "Hey, remember that blond chick you hit on in the bar?"

"Leah?" I frown.

"Yeah. She's here with two of her friends."

"And that brunette is fucking hot," Jack adds. "I would definitely give up celibacy for her."

"Yeah? And how's that celibacy workin' out for you, bro?

You made it past five nights yet?" I question.

"No. But I'm getting there. Once I've fucked her, that is." He nods in the direction of her.

I notice Macey first. Her bright-pink dress clings to her body, and if I preferred brunettes, she'd be at the top of my hit list. Standing next to her is Ryann, in an equally tight, if not longer, blue dress.

But it's Leah who stops me. She's here despite her protestations, and fucking hell, is she here. Her dark-red dress hugs her tits and waist and hips then flares at her legs. And shit. Fuck. She looks fucking gorgeous, her lips red to match the dress, her hair loose over her shoulders.

Just…fuck.

She looks up and her eyes find mine. There's a defiant spark in them that I can see from here, one that tells me to fuck off, that she doesn't want to be anywhere near me.

I smirk. Like that will happen. I can't stay away from that body. I couldn't stay away from her taste if I tried.

"She's sitting by us, right?" I ask Reid, never taking my eyes from my blue-eyed beauty's.

"Of course she is," he responds. "And if we don't sit down right now, my mom is gonna pull out her bitch streak."

He walks to the table closest to us and, coincidentally, the bar. I smirk as I take my seat because Macey is checking the seating chart right now.

"This is like a fuckin' wedding," Jack snaps, watching her. "Can't I just wave them over?"

"Don't fuck with the seating chart," Reid answers. "There. They're coming over."

Indeed, they are. Leah approaches with her eyes fixed on mine, and I follow her as she rounds the table and takes the spare seat next to mine.

"Should I be surprised, Corey?" she whispers, scooting her seat in.

"Not really, babe." I smirk. "Wine?"

"I'd prefer tequila, but sure."

I pour a glass and rest the bottle back in the ice bucket. Leah takes the glass from my hand and takes a long sip. She shivers as the chill overcomes her, and I slip my hand beneath the table to rest on her thigh.

She glares at me. "What are you doing?"

"Adjusting my balls," I reply, tickling just behind her knee.

Her leg jerks, and when she regains control, she jabs me in the ankle with her heel. *Fuck.*

"I told you," she whispers, leaning in. "Cut the crap."

"I planned to. Then you showed up in that dress and my cock got other ideas."

She turns to me, her expression wholly unamused…except for the twitch of her lips. "Behave yourself, cowboy."

"I don't know how to around you," I murmur truthfully, skimming my fingers beneath her dress.

She smacks my hand beneath the table, and I smirk, snatching her fingers. She jerks her hand from mine and grips her wine glass with it. I let my hand settle back on her thigh, my fingers dipping beneath the tight hem of her dress once more, teasing her skin.

She doesn't react—except every time I brush my fingers across her skin, she takes a sip. I lean toward her, smelling that sweet smell that is so very Leah.

"Watch it. You know what happened last time you were drinking wine around me."

Her nostrils flare as she takes a deep breath. Our food is set in front of us, and when the waiter puts hers on the table, she grabs him and requests a vodka and lemonade.

I can't help the smirk. It's like a fucking reflex around her.

"Vodka, huh?"

"It makes me a bitch," Leah replies without batting an eyelid. In fact, she's cutting into her potato all too calmly.

"Is your bitch side as hot as you normally are?"

"She sure as hell isn't afraid to call you out," she responds, examining the potato. "So I'd watch out for that if I were you."

"You didn't answer my question." I sip my drink. "But I sure as hell hope she is a bitch."

"Surprise, asshole," she snaps, finishing her drink as her

vodka is put in front of her.

My lips curve, because fuck. It's a kryptonite—annoying her. Like my own personal goal every time I set eyes on her. I figure she'll eventually be so angry that she won't remember why she is and she'll give in. One day.

One motherfucking day.

Chapter SEVEN

Leah

His eyes are crawling over me like he's never seen a woman before. I felt it the second he noticed me. The heat from his gaze was, and is, incomparable to all others.

Corey Jackson isn't the only man here tonight who's looking at me. But he's sure as hell the only man who means every inch of his stare. No other stare coasts over my body so thoroughly. No other gaze grabs every ounce of my body and makes it react to the intense pull.

No, it's only him. Maybe I want him.

Maybe, after all this time, I want to remember what it feels to have a guy's fingertips trail over my skin. And I do. I won't lie. I do—but not his. Sex is…something to me. It isn't something you give freely. It's something you own and control until the moment you're ready to hand all of you over.

I'm not ready for that.

I'm not ready to let go of all of my inhibitions and give myself freely to the one man who is sure to take it and run with it.

My eyes flit to Macey, who is flirting unashamedly with Jack Carr. He responds in kind, and I know that neither of them will be leaving alone tonight. Once Macey has her eyes set on someone, that's it. It's all systems go.

Sometimes, I envy her freedom.

Corey's hand finally leaves my thigh and I relax a little. Even if there is a chill snaking across my skin where his fingers just were. Jesus, this would be so much easier if I weren't attracted to him. If he were just…not there.

Yeah, that would be better. If he would disappear, that would be fabulous. Isn't there an away preseason game soon? A whole weekend without him here, in my face, making me feel unnecessary things.

Because he distracts me. The fight is exhausting, and it means I can't concentrate on work. I have a file full of photographs of models in my designs from Quinn to approve for the show and I can't. I'm here instead, struggling against the cockiest bastard I've ever met in my life.

His certainty isn't even endearing. It's annoying. Mostly because, every time he says something, he really does believe it, and for a second, my beliefs waver.

Eventually, he could wear me down and I'll give in to everything I don't want just for some semblance of peace back into my life.

I set my knife and fork down on the plate and take a sip of my drink. Then I studiously avoid Corey's gaze. I'm determined not to get drawn into his game tonight. That's what this is. To him, it's a giant game. Well, I'm not a pawn, and I don't want to play.

I always hated games.

My phone buzzes in my purse and I pull it out. The e-mail is from Quinn, and I open it below the table.

> *Leah, I need your approvals on the designs in twenty-four hours. We need to get the models into fittings. Overnight the file our usual way.*

I swallow my sigh. This is why I should be at home. Working. Right now.

> *Got it. Mom will call the courier.*

I hit send then bring up my messages and ask Mom to do exactly that. She responds with an, '*Okay*,' and I drop the phone back into my purse.

"Don't you know it's bad manners to use your phone at dinner?"

I look at Corey. "Don't you know it's bad manners to repeatedly not listen to someone?"

"Touché." He smirks. "Important?"

"Private." I drink.

He leans in. "Boyfriend?"

"Yes. I'm in the habit of kissing other guys when I have a boyfriend." I roll my eyes. "Please. If I were seeing someone, the media would make sure the world and its asshole knew about it."

"Just checkin'."

"Why? You wanna fill the empty slot?" I raise my eyebrows in disbelief.

He laughs and flips my hand over on the table. He grabs my arm, and his thumb traces little circles on the inside of my wrist. Shivers snake down my spine at the gentle yet erotic touch.

"Possibly," he murmurs. "Are you taking applications?"

"Absolutely, but there is a condition. Assholes need not apply, so looks like you're out of the running." I snatch my wrist away from him. "Excuse me."

I get up, grab my purse, and walk through the room. I say a few hellos to people I know, but I don't stop to talk. Hell no.

I shove the restroom door open and lock myself in a stall. Fuck it all—I'm leaving. Every time he speaks to me, he draws me into his game, playing me until I fall into his setup and he wins the round.

Someone get a bell to warn me of this shit.

The heels of my hands dig into my eyes, and I unlock the stall door. Then I head straight for the doors and hand my ticket to the valet. He nods and goes to collect my car.

"What are you doing?"

I look at Ryann. "I'm going home before I end up in an orange jumpsuit for the rest of my life. Thank you," I add to the valet, taking my keys.

"And when he asks me where you are?"

"Tell him I'm sick. Add 'of him' if you want to." I shrug and get in the car. "I'll call you tomorrow."

"All right. Hey...you're okay, right?"

"I will be when I get home." I smile and put my foot down.

I blow out a long breath as I drive away from the hotel. Jesus, I'm not this girl. I'm not the girl who fucking runs just because it's too much. I'm the girl who stays and battles through to the end because taking shit isn't something I was raised to do.

The problem is that it doesn't bother Corey. I can see it in his eyes. He thrives on getting me angry. It's funny to him, and he's slowly finding every one of my buttons.

He knows I'm not his type. He knows I'm not the girl who will roll over onto her back and beg for him. He knows—one hundred percent—I won't sit back and let him do whatever he wants without any consequences.

That's why he wants me. He said it himself. He wants the challenge. He wants to push me to my breaking point. Then he wants to bury himself inside me and tip me over the edge.

A part of me wishes I were his type, that I were the kind of girl who could stomach one-night stands. I'm not against them, but they're not who I am.

I enjoy sex as much as the next person. I enjoy slow, deep lovemaking, and I enjoy hard and fast fucks. But I respect it, too. I respect the connection that comes from being so intimate with someone, and I won't ever lose that. I won't let it go. Sex is for relationships, for trust and strong feelings, not hurried looks and drunken liaisons.

Which is why he won't get what he wants.

I lean out of the car and push the code in for the gates. They open, and I drive through, desperately wishing my mind could get the hell off him and onto the fifty possible outfits waiting for me on my desk.

I wish I could focus on scarves and neckties, on socks and gloves.

I park the car in front of the garage and shove my keys

inside my purse.

"Leah."

I turn at the sound of his voice. "What are you doing here?"

"What are *you* doing here?" Corey responds, slamming his car door.

"I live here." My jaw clenches.

He walks toward me, his steps strong, his gaze unwavering. I swallow as he gets closer because, although it's dark, I can see his expression. The light from the house gives me a full view of his tight jaw, his pursed lips, his strong cheekbones. The annoyance in his gaze glints bright green, and I wonder how he's the one who is annoyed when I'm the one he pisses off.

I stand steady, but he doesn't stop when he reaches me. Instead, he grabs me and pushes me against the wall, his fingers sliding into my hair and his mouth descending on mine.

I murmur a protest, but it's futile. He's stronger than I am, and he holds me in place as his lips attack me. I grip his shirt at his waist, curling my fingers into the soft material, and succumb to the sensation of his hard kiss.

He tugs on my hair and tilts my head back. His tongue slips into my mouth when my lips part, and the sweep of it against mine stokes a low fire in the pit of my belly.

My pussy clenches at the deepness of the kiss, at the way he controls it so deftly, so powerfully. My heart thuds at the way he hums low into my mouth, the vibrations seeming to flow through my veins.

I'm aching everywhere, just everywhere. I can't tell my heartbeat from my breath. I can't tell the adrenaline from the lust. It all mingles until I'm a tingling ball of sensation and my clit throbs painfully.

Corey pulls away and looks me in the eye, breathing heavily. "Don't ever fuckin' walk away from me like that again, Leah."

"Or what?" I reply, putting as much strength into my voice as I can muster.

He touches the tip of his nose to mine. "Or I'll be forced to fuck you on the spot."

He closes his mouth over mine once more then untangles

his fingers from my hair and stalks over to his car. I watch his powerful stride swallow up the driveway. He yanks open his car door and looks right at me.

"I'll pick you up at four o'clock tomorrow. Be ready. I hate waitin'."

"What for?" I shout as he sits in the car.

He doesn't reply. He simply revs the engine, turns the car around, and drives out.

I watch the white Evoque disappear through the gates and into the darkness, my heart still fighting to break free from my ribs, and let out a long, shaky breath.

I've never been kissed that way. Never has someone walked toward me with so much determination and kissed me until I couldn't breathe.

Never have I been so thrown by a single person in my whole life.

I open the door with a shaky hand and lock it. Mom's in the kitchen, and she watches as I kick off my shoes, leaving them scattered in the hallway.

"Leah, are you okay, honey? You're back early."

"Yeah." I walk through the room without stopping. "Just have a lot to do for Quinn."

"All right. Goodnight."

"Night, Mom." I run up the stairs and slam my door behind me.

I lean against it and close my eyes. Once again, he made me play his game, and he won. He left me in the dust with a simple demand and wet panties.

I take a deep breath and throw my purse on my bed. I rip my dress over my head and throw an oversized Vipers jersey on before heading to my desk. Then I open Quinn's file with a smile on my face. I don't want to play, but I don't have a choice. Not anymore.

Corey Jackson plays a good game. He knows all the rules, and he isn't afraid to bend them to his will.

I'm about to break every single rule he's ever written.

I'm ready to play him at his own game.

chapter EIGHT

Corey

She tastes like sugar and candy. She tastes like everything that's good but forbidden, like heaven and perfection. She tastes like fucking *addiction*.

She tastes like something that shouldn't have a taste, but she's it. She's addiction. Even when she isn't trying to be, she is.

I had to get the fuck out of there last night because the heated glaze over her eyes and the sharp breath she'd sucked in had nearly undone me. The worst thing is that she doesn't have any idea how sexy she is. She's oblivious to how tempting she is with her eyes wide and her lips swollen from *my* kisses.

My cock was throbbing for her. It was so hard that it was fucking painful, but I couldn't stop kissing her. I had to drink her in, touch every inch of her mouth with my lips and tongue, feel every fucking sensation she was handing me.

If she had any idea how badly I wanted to throw her into my back seat and drive her to my house, she would have run a mile to get away from me.

But shit. I want to know what makes her tick. What makes her laugh and where the hell she gets her smartass comments. I want to know what turns her on, whether it's a kiss to her neck or a stroke of my thumb on the inside of her thigh, and I want to try every fucking trick in the book until she's coming undone in my arms.

I need to know it.

I need to know how she likes to be kissed and how she likes to be teased. I need to know every damn thing about this girl until she's completely naked in front of me. For all the times she's tried pushing me away, all she's done is pull me closer. She's gone from an attraction, a one-night fling, to the obsessive addiction she tastes like.

And the problem with her being an addiction is that she's on my mind like one. I can't throw a ball for shit. I can't catch it, I can't pass it, I can't fucking run it—nothing.

"Pull yourself the fuck together, Jackson! Preseason isn't the time to turn into a mid-grade player!" Dante yells across the field.

"Yeah, man. What the hell is wrong with you?" Jack glances at me.

"Don't ask." I rub my hand down my face and grab the ball. "Can we finish this up?"

"Last run-through," Coach says into my ear. "Try not to mess this one up too, Corey."

"Got it," I reply.

I pass the ball and weave through our own defense team to catch it back. One throw to Jack and he flies into the end zone.

"If only it were that easy in a game," Jack sighs.

"It'll be impossible to win unless I figure my shit out," I mutter to him, heading toward the shower. I have a day and a half to get Leah Veronica out of my system before I turn the Vipers into the laughing stock of the league.

After showering and changing, I drop my bag in the back seat and tear out of the parking lot. I need a damn good run to get this frustration out of me. I turn toward the Hills, breaking the speed limit in my hurry.

Parking, I rest my forehead against my steering wheel and take a few deep breaths. No girl has affected me this way for as long as I can remember. Maybe they never have. Maybe it's just her.

When I look up, she's sitting on my doorstep, her eyes fixed on my car. I can see the tightness in her jaw from where I'm sitting, and I know the shit is about to hit the fan. Here comes my ass-kicking for last night.

An ass-kicking right now is dangerous. Real fucking dangerous.

"How did you know where I live?" I ask as I get out of the car.

"This is Hollywood." Leah stands, her hands on her hips. "You told me to be ready at four o'clock. It's almost four o'clock."

"Touché."

She's wearing running shorts and shoes, which tells me that she's here to prove some dumb point. We might as well have this conversation on the go.

"I'm going for a run. Are you coming?" I nod my head in the direction of the street and take off.

"I'm already done, but evidently, I don't have a choice." Her steps hit the asphalt hard as she comes up next to me. "What was that yesterday?"

"I don't know what you mean."

"Don't dick around, Corey. You know exactly what I mean."

"No, I don't."

"You're gonna make me spell it out? Really?"

"Yep."

"You're un-fucking-believable, you know that?"

"I have been told that."

She mutters something under her breath and I glance at her. Her blond hair is pulled up and back from her face, exposing her neck. My eyes graze over it and down her body to her slim figure and the curve of her ass. And her thighs. Those gorgeous, toned thighs I had my hand on last night.

"When you followed me home and kissed the living shit out of me. What was that about?"

"I kissed the shit out of you, huh?" My lips quirk on one side.

"Of course. Of course that would be the part of that you'd hear. Why wouldn't it be?"

"I wanted to kiss you. Is that a crime?"

"No."

"Shit. It probably should be though. Do you know I couldn't throw a ball in practice today?"

"So much for your epic skills."

"I have epic skills when I'm not thinking about kissing the shit out of a certain blonde."

"Maybe you should stop thinking, then."

"When I can still taste your lips on mine? How do you expect me to do that, babe?"

She chews on the inside of her cheek, and I know I've caught her off guard. Hell, I caught myself off guard. I hadn't meant to say that out loud.

"How am I supposed to answer that?" She glances at me.

"However you want."

We reach the top of the hill, and Leah leans against a tree the way she did the first time we ran together. She lets her hair down, and I look at her properly. She's wearing no makeup, and she's probably the only girl I know who can pull that off and still look red-carpet ready. Her long eyelashes, darker than her blond hair, curl over her eyelids, and her pink lips are naturally plump. The pink in her cheeks instantly sends me back to last night when the cause of the flush in them was me.

"You're infuriating, you know that?" Leah snaps her hairband around her wrist.

"You've said something like that before."

"Have I? I mean it more now. I'm still pissed you followed me home. How fucking dare you pull such an asshole move?" she yells.

"You walk away from me, darlin', and I'm gonna fuckin' follow you. Got it?"

She stands up straight and points at me. "I just… Argh!" She turns on me fully now, her eyes ablaze with anger and heat that sear right through me. They're shining, playing off her flushed cheeks, and her pouting lips are just begging to be covered by mine. "I can't even put it into words. That's how angry I am at you! And you know the worst thing? The absolute worst thing?" She pauses. "I'm not even mad that you kissed me. I'm mad you that followed me home. Okay, maybe I am a little mad that you did. I don't know. Shit! I'm not even making sense. I'm going home before I fling myself into this rock, because it turns out that I have no idea why I'm here."

She moves and I grab her arm, spinning her into me. I curve my hand around her back and hold her body against mine, trapping her in place. Her hands are flat on my chest, her fingers twitching as she breathes heavily. Her blue eyes are wide and angry and hard as they look into mine.

I run my fingers through her hair to push it back from her face and cup the back of her head, bringing my face close to hers.

"What do you want me to say, Leah? That I'm sorry? 'Cause I'm not. Not for one single fucking second."

"I don't want you to—"

"Do you want me to tell you how I fucked everythin' at practice today because all I could think about was the way your body felt against mine? How all I could taste was the sweet taste of your mouth? How I've touched your silky skin and wished there was nothing between us? How, now that I've had more than one taste, I don't know if I can give it up?" I move my face even closer to her. "Do you want me to tell you how badly I want to rip off your clothes and taste every single inch of your body? How I want to take you to the edge and push you over it until you can't breathe? Huh? Is that what you want, Leah?"

Her breathing is coming hard and fast through her parted lips, each breath heating my own, making me ache to kiss her again.

"'Cause if that's what you want, I'll tell you. I'll tell you how you've driven me fuckin' crazy for the last day. You've driven me fuckin' crazy since the day I met you. First because you said no and now because I want to fuck you so, so badly."

"No," she whispers. "I don't want to know that. I don't want to know it because knowing leads to believing, and if there's one thing a girl should never do, that's believe you." She knocks my hand from her head and steps back. My hand falls from her waist. "You've had your fun with me, Corey. That's all it's gonna be. Do you get that? I'm going crazy because I never know if what you're saying is true. How do I know that everything you just said is the truth? For all I know, you say that to every girl."

"Jesus Christ." I run my fingers through my hair and shake my head.

"What? It's the truth, isn't it? How many times have you said a variation of that speech to a girl? How many times have you meant it?"

"Hundreds!" I yell. "I've said it hundreds of damn times, but I've never meant it half as much as I do now." My eyes crash into hers. "And now you need to do me a favor and shut the hell up so I can kiss you."

"You think I'm gonna let you kiss me now?"

"Who said you had to let me? I'm gonna do it anyway."

I grab her back to me and crush my lips to hers. She tastes the same as yesterday, sweeter even, but this time, it's hot. Hotter than before because I can feel the anger radiating off her, yet she's not pushing me away. She's tightly gripping my shirt and sinking her body into mine.

My hand snakes into her hair, holding her face to mine, and I flick my tongue across her lips. She responds by nipping at my bottom lip. My cock hardens inside my shorts and presses into her stomach, and nothing is more tempting right now than pulling her shorts down and sinking inside her.

"I still hate you," she mutters, dipping her face away from me.

I smile. "Yeah, your dislike is obvious."

"I'm not afraid to kick your ass."

"I wouldn't. I'd probably like it."

She fails to hide her laugh and pushes away from me. Her hair is mussed where my hand has been, and her eyes are heavy, the way they were last night. She sighs and pulls her hair back from her face.

"That wasn't exactly how I envisioned this conversation going."

I follow her as she starts to run. "Babe, we haven't had a single conversation that's gone the way I've envisioned."

"That's because your conversations don't involve talking." She glances over her shoulder at me.

"They involve a type of conversation," I hedge.

"'Oh, Corey!' 'Oh yes!' and 'Right there!' do not make a conversation."

"There are plenty of other things said."

"I have no desire to learn what you say to the whores you pick up."

"I haven't picked any 'whores' up since I met you."

"Yeah? So you went home alone the night of my birthday?"

I don't say a word.

"Yeah. That's what I thought. So take that last sentence and shove it up your ass, Corey Jackson. And"—she stops and turns to me outside my house—"when you respect me enough not to lie to me two minutes after kissing me, you can come and find me. Until then, go fuck yourself."

I knock on her door and wait. There's no answer, so I push the bell. Shit. Two days of not talking to her and I'm done. I hate that she's so mad at me.

"Leah!" I yell, banging on the door again. "I know you're home!"

The door opens slowly and she peeks her face out. "What do you want?"

"To talk to you. No, I mean it. Actually talk." I put my foot in the door so she can't close it.

"I don't trust you."

"Please. Five minutes. That's all." I grab the door. "I won't even touch you."

Her blue eyes bore into mine for a few beats. "Fine." She pulls the door open and lets me in.

I follow her through to the kitchen. She pours a glass of orange juice and leans against the side.

"Five minutes. Talk," she demands.

"I want to apologize," I say quietly.

"I'm sorry. Did you just say *apologize*?"

"Yeah. I was an asshole, and you didn't deserve that. So… I'm sorry." I've never apologized to a girl in my life, yet she's had two. She's fucking ruining me.

"Well, apology accepted, I guess. Now you can leave."

The bell rings and she grabs the package on the table. I stand in the doorway as she signs something and hands it to the courier. Then she turns without shutting the door and looks at me.

"Well?"

I shove my hands in my pockets. "I'm not done talkin'."

"I am," she replies defiantly. "I'm not interested in talking to someone who repeatedly brings out the worst in me."

"You bring out the best in me, darlin', and I ain't goin' anywhere yet."

She slams the door shut and storms past me back into the kitchen. "That, cowboy, is probably because I'm the only girl who refuses to take your shit."

"And because you're the only girl who gives me a reason to be something other than what I've been."

"That's cute if you think I'm falling for that. Words don't mean a thing, Corey. Actions speak a million times louder than words ever could." She leans against the kitchen counter again. "You tell me so many things, but your actions don't back them up."

"You're right," I concede. "What are you doing now?"

"I'm about to eat all the Cheetos in the house and binge-watch Twilight."

I raise an eyebrow, but she's deadly serious. "I have a better idea."

"I'm not going anywhere with you. You're not going to romance your way into my pants, Corey. I wish you would understand that. You're not going to fuck me then walk away from me. That's the end of the story." She stares at me, the truth of her words evident in the harshness of her gaze. "Either we're friends or we're nothing at all, because I don't trust you as far as I could throw you."

I walk around the kitchen island to her and stop in front of her. I don't touch her—just like I promised—but I do grip the counter on either side of her body. "One chance," I whisper. "Give me one chance to prove to you that you're not like all the other girls."

"Of course I'm not like the other girls. I'm one in a fucking million."

My lips tug up on one side. "Right. So give me a chance to prove that you're one in a fucking million *to me*."

"And how long is your one chance, hmm? A night? A day?"

"A week. One week. If, in seven days, you're not convinced, I'll let you walk away from me."

"Really?" She looks at me. "You'll let me go?"

I nod slowly, even though I'm doubting the truth of my words. I'm not sure I can let her go until I've felt her pussy clenching my cock, but if that's what she wants to hear, then sure. I'll let her go in a week if she's still hating me.

Leah says nothing for a long moment, one that lingers heavily between us. I'm asking for a lot, especially when I can't guarantee anything she wants, but I'm fed up with the back-and-forth.

"Okay, fine." She swallows and meets my eyes fully. "One week, but you have to let me go anyway. Even if you convince me that I'm not just any other girl, you let me go."

I clamp my jaw shut. "That's not what I said."

"That's what I'm offering. Take it or leave it."

Leah

Rule one: broken.

I never expected him to agree to what I said. I never expected that he'd agree to let me leave. I thought he'd fight me, argue until I gave in, but all he did was look at me for an agonizingly long moment before he agreed.

I'm not sure what it says. Does it say that he doesn't actually care if he's willing to let me go so easily? Or does it say that he respects me enough to let me have it the way I want it?

Playing him at his own game would be much easier if *I* knew the rules.

I throw my purse onto the floor of his Evoque and climb into the passenger's seat. He smiles at me across the car. Just a smile. No words. Maybe he's afraid that, if he talks, he'll piss me off.

It's a good call, to be honest.

His hair is wet, and the big bag on the back seat tells me that he's come straight from practice.

"Hi."

"Hi," I reply. "Good day?"

"Yep. You?"

"It was okay." I hug my knees.

"Nice jersey."

"It's all right, I suppose." I shrug. "I'm hungry."

He glances at me, his lips twitching. "You wanna get food?"

"No. I regularly get hungry and don't eat." If only that weren't true. I skip dinner way too much when I work.

"Takeout?"

"Only if you guess what my favorite is."

Corey laughs. "Chinese."

"Shit." I punch the seat. "That was too easy."

He laughs again. "Lucky guess," he says, turning onto his driveway. "Just don't make me order for you, all right? I will fuck that up."

"I'm not that mean." I sniff, grabbing my purse. "Although it would be funny to watch."

Corey's lips thin as he grabs his bag. "Don't make me smack your ass, girl."

I grin. "You wouldn't," I say, turning and walking backward toward his front door. "Because that would be counterproductive."

"Not exactly. I'm not really an ass-slapper. Unless it's your ass."

"Thanks. I think." I frown and follow him inside.

"You're welcome." He lightly taps my butt with a cocky smirk.

I shoot him a look and he lightly shoves me in the back.

"Come on. Let's go order food. You want a drink?" he asks.

"Please."

"I have wine."

"Me plus wine plus you never equals a good combination."

"I like bad combinations." He sends a smirk my way and pours a glass anyway. "Here." He puts the glass in front of me. "Sorry. I don't have sippy cups."

"Fuck you." I narrow my eyes, fighting my smile. *Asshole.* "Are you ordering my food or not?"

"Fuckin' hell," he laughs. "Give me a minute, all right? We just walked through the door."

"But I'm hungry."

"Let me find my phone at least."

"I'll take a chicken chow mein, egg fried rice, and crispy beef strips. Thanks."

"Shut up before I kiss you."

"Try it."

He steps next to me and dips his head. I put my phone against my mouth and he pauses, his lips hovering above it.

"I found my phone." I grin.

He sighs, closes his eyes, and then takes it from me.

"There's a takeout on speed dial five."

He stops. "Are you serious?"

"About food? Always." As long as I'm not working, that is.

His eyes don't leave me as he dials and reels off our order. He hands me my phone back when he's hung up, making sure his fingers brush mine. "Done."

"Thank you." I smile sweetly. "Did I tell you I'm paying for mine?"

"No, and you're not."

"I am."

"You're not. Stop being fuckin' difficult."

"I'm not. But if you pay for it, that makes this a date." I grab my glass and follow him into his front room. A sixty-inch TV sits in the corner, and a PS4 and Xbox one sit on a shelf in the media center. "Really? You need both?"

"Yep. And I don't give a shit if me paying for dinner makes this a date. I'm payin' for it and that's the damn end of it."

"So your idea of a first date is Chinese in front of the TV?"

He snaps his head around and looks at me. "You're the one who won't be seen in public with me for whatever reason. Take it or leave it."

"Usually, I'd leave it, but I'm so hungry that it isn't an option." I sigh and sit on the sofa next to him.

Corey gets up and grabs two Playstation controllers. Then he drops one in my lap. "Here."

"What is this?"

"It's a controller," he replies with a smirk. "If you win, you can buy your own dinner. If I win, I pay."

I blink at it and put my wine glass on the coffee table. "I'm at a serious disadvantage here, you understand? I don't own a PS4."

He says nothing. Just lets his lips tug up and starts the game.

"Look, I wasn't lying. I said that *I* don't own a PS4. It's my mom's."

Corey stares at me in disbelief over the table. "Your mom owns a PS4?"

I hold my hands up. "Hey, I asked her, and she said she needs it to shoot people because people piss her off, and if she shot them in real life, she'd be in jail. It's hard to argue with that kind of logic, you know?"

"Shit, man. I can't believe I just got my ass kicked at Call of Duty by a girl."

"A one-in-a-million girl," I correct him, shoving noodles in my mouth.

"Yeah, I think you just went up to one in ten million. Fuck."

I smile and chew. The look on his face was priceless. I wish I'd had a camera because I'm pretty sure he's never had his ass handed to him that way before.

"Look, it isn't hard to play. You just aim and shoot."

He stares at me blankly. "What about the guys aiming and shooting at you?"

"Well, that's simple." I put my fork down. "You shoot them before they get you."

"And if you don't know they're coming?"

"Then you die."

"Oh, simple." He shakes his head slightly. "Just when I think I'm starting to understand you a little bit."

I grin and get up. "Don't kid yourself, cowboy." I drop onto the sofa. "You'll never understand me. I'm way more complex than the fuck-and-go girls you're accustomed to."

"Now *that* I know. I knew that the night I met you." He sits next to me.

"I really can't believe you haven't given up yet."

"I told you I don't give up. Besides, I have a whole week, remember?" His eyes flick over my face. "There isn't a chance I'm giving up when you can shoot better than me and make a hobby of screaming my name every game day."

I raise my eyebrows. "Is that opposed to hearing a different person scream it every night of the week?"

"Believe me, Leah. No one says my name the way you do." He leans back against the sofa and rests one arm along the back of it. His fingers tickle my bare shoulder, just ghosting across my skin. "I wouldn't want anyone to say it the way you do."

"I would hope not."

"Besides, no one else could get away with calling me cowboy."

My lips twitch and I grab my glass from the coffee table. I finish the wine, put the glass back down, and then stretch upward. My jersey rides up with the movement, and Corey's eyes drop to my exposed stomach, lingering there before climbing up my body.

"What?"

"Nothing," he replies, meeting my eyes, a fire burning in his.

I poke his thigh. "Don't look at me like I'm a chocolate chip cookie then say, 'Nothing.'"

"If I'm only looking at you like that, then I'm worried, because in my head, you're way sexier than a fucking cookie."

"God, you say all the right things, don't you?" I shake my head.

"You compared yourself to a cookie."

"Yeah, and that's where you were supposed to say, 'You're not a cookie. You're more like a chocolate fucking sundae, sprinkles and all.'"

"And that's opposed to saying you're sexy?"

"There are other ways to compliment a girl on her looks, you know."

"I know." He leans over me, his eyes fixed on mine. "But when you're wearing my team jersey with *my* name on the back, you bet your tight little ass you're fucking sexy."

"How do you know it has your name on it?" I murmur.

He lowers his face to mine. "I notice everything about you, Leah. Like how your cheeks flush when I call you sexy and how your lips part when mine are close. I also notice that I'm very, very close to starting to wear you down."

"And how have you worked that out?"

"You're here."

Smartass.

His lips brush down my cheek to my jaw. "I can see it in your eyes, babe." He presses his lips to my neck.

I draw in a sharp breath. Shit.

"I can hear it when your breath hitches like that." His fingers trail down my arm, drawing an easy path on the underside, until they finally meet mine. Then he links our fingers and whispers, "And I can feel it in the clenching of your fist."

"That's so I can punch you later."

"Mhmm..." He dusts kisses up my neck, making me swallow because he's right. He does affect me—crazily. "But until that happens, I'm definitely wearing you down."

"You're a dick, Corey."

He smiles against my skin. "I know, but that doesn't change the fact that I'm going to fuck you by the end of the week."

"You're still so sure, aren't you?"

"If I don't have my certainty, I don't have much of anythin', babe. Don't shatter my dreams." He hovers his lips in front of mine.

"Fine—you stay in your delusional little bubble, and I'll stay in the real world."

His lips curl. "What happens when they collide?"

I rest my hand on his cheek. "Then you're going to be very, very disappointed."

He laughs and sits back down but doesn't let go of my hand. "What are you doing tomorrow?"

"Nothing."

"Good. I'm taking you on a date."

"Not outside, you're not."

"Hey." He runs his thumb across my bottom lip. "Trust me.

Okay?"

"That's what I'm afraid of doing."

What the hell was I thinking? Agreeing to go in public with him? *Sure, let's keep a low profile, Leah. Let's do that by going on a date with the hottest fucking guy in the city. Let's do that!*

Ugh. He's a master manipulator, kissing my neck and making my heart pound then touching my mouth so softly. He made me go gooey. Fucking gooey.

Leg-tremblingly, heart-stutteringly, stomach-flutteringly gooey.

What the hell did I do that for?

He's dangerous, I know that, but he needs a sign or a tattoo or something to remind me. Unfortunately, my mind wasn't in control yesterday. My hormones were. And hormones control my body, and they're impulsive little bastards.

Impulsive little bastards who need to keep themselves under control today. The only reason I agreed to this week is because he agreed to leave me alone. Jesus. How dumb was that? He won't leave me alone.

The brown wig on my head is evidence of this.

"This is dumb."

Corey grins. "But you don't look like you, so it's okay."

"Great. I'll get to see myself in the papers tomorrow referred to as a mystery woman. I love that."

"Better than your name being associated with mine, huh?"

There's a little bitterness in his tone, and I wince a little. "It's not like that, and you know it."

"No, I don't know that."

I grab his hand and stop him before we get the tickets. "Well, it isn't. I just… I can't tell you, okay? It's complicated."

Complicated because I'm the only person in this city who won't take the easy way into one of the toughest industries in the world.

Corey nods. "All right. Come on." He gets our tickets and

we step in. "Disneyland. I can't fucking believe I'm taking you to Disneyland."

"It's my favorite!" I nudge his elbow. "*I* can't believe you asked my mom where to take me!"

His mouth spreads into a beaming grin. "Smooth, huh?"

"Yeah, if you like your smooth crunchy."

"Excuse me, are you Corey Jackson?" A little boy looks up at him.

"Sure am," Corey replies.

"Can I get an autograph?" The little boy shoves a pad at Corey.

"Sure, buddy." He leans down and scribbles on the autograph book. The little boy's mom asks for a picture, and Corey agrees, putting his arm around the boy's shoulders.

I smile, putting my hands in the pockets of my shorts. He's a jackass almost all of the time, but he has another side. That's clear to see, because he now has a small crowd of kids around him clamoring for an autograph and a picture.

But he doesn't complain. He doesn't ask for peace or to be left alone. He signs every book, smiles for every picture, and hugs every kid.

And it's the hottest thing I've ever seen.

When the kids disperse, he grabs my hand and tugs me into the park. I laugh as it hits me: he's trying to escape the madness.

Disneyland: the happiest place on Earth. Unless you are Corey Jackson. Then it's apparently your own personal slice of hell.

"Smile. You're scaring all the kids away." I knock our hands into his hip. "It's the happiest place on Earth!"

He looks at me flatly. "I've signed ten autographs and we haven't even been here for fifteen minutes. I'm not a Disney character."

"But isn't that what makes you so appealing? Your fame?" I throw a sassy glance over my shoulder as I skip off toward a candy store.

"All right, all right. You win."

"Smart guy." I wink. "Is it really that bad here?"

"Yes. No. I don't know. I feel like I don't belong here."

The temptation to grab a pair of Mickey Mouse ears and put them on his head is almost too much. Damn that almost. I giggle to myself. He does look a little out of place—the famous quarterback in a kids' resort. I feel a little bad. I mean, he clearly hates it here, but this is my favorite place ever, so he's just gonna have to deal with it.

Besides, he's the one who asked my mom where to bring me.

"Look, we're in Frontierland. Let's do the shooting." I pause, glancing at him. "You can shoot, right?"

"Leah, I grew up in Texas. My granddaddy owned a ranch. Of course I can shoot. The question is whether you can."

"Only on COD." I grin, pretending to look at the rifle in a bit of confusion.

He hands over two tickets for twenty-five shots each. Then he rolls his eyes.

He rolls his eyes. "Watch me."

"Ooo-kay."

He leans forward, concentration etched on his face, and fires off a round of bullets, hitting some targets and missing some. I stand by, idly watching him, my hands clasped together. After another few shots, he turns to me.

"I'll help you."

"Okay." I shrug and get behind the gun.

He stands next to me and wraps an arm around my shoulders. His hands cover mine and his fingers ease mine into position as he breathes right near my ear.

It's always been obvious how fit he is, how much muscle is packed into his body, but it's not until now, with that muscle against me, that I can feel how solid it is. How toned every part of him is. Even with his stomach pressed against my side, I can feel all the dents and dips of the six-pack that's clearly there, and I force myself to let out the sharp breath I just took.

Those pesky hormones.

"Like this, aim, and pull the trigger. Got it?"

"Got it."

I line the barrel of the gun up with the first target and flick my eyes to the others. I pull the trigger and hit the first one, and the second, and the third, and every one until the first ten are down.

"Like that?" I turn my face toward Corey's. His mouth is open and he's staring at me in disbelief.

His mouth is open and he's staring at me in disbelief. "What the fuck did I just see?" he mumbles.

"Surprise!" I laugh. "Favorite place on Earth. *My* grandpa taught me how to do this game when I was six."

He stands, releasing me, and rubs one of his hands down his face as he goes back to his rifle. "I'm not sure if that was the scariest thing I've ever seen or the sexiest."

"Probably both."

"Now who's got a big ego?"

"Yours is rubbing off on me, clearly." I look over to bright, blue-green eyes.

"So many things I could say to that. So many." He shakes his head slowly.

"None of which are fit for Disneyland." I fire off the last of my bullets, hitting more targets than he did, and grin.

"I thought that was supposed to make me feel better," he grumbles as we walk away.

"It was. I didn't realize you were so crappy."

"I'm not crappy. You're just scarily and sexily good at that." He shakes his head. "I'm picking next."

"As long as you pick food."

"Okay. Pizza?"

"What kind?"

"Pepperoni, of course."

chapter TEN

Corey

Leah runs her tongue around her mouth and licks off the sauce at the corner of her mouth.

I'm fucking mesmerized by the movement. Slowly, she traces her bottom lip then wiggles the tip of her tongue to catch the lingering sauce. She misses, and I reach across the table to her. I swipe the sauce with my thumb, smirking, and meet her eyes.

"Move your thumb before I bite it," she mutters, looking down at my hand.

"You're a biter?" The words escape before I can stop them, and I know she's going to look at me as if I'm completely hopeless before the expression flits across her face.

"Is there a sentence you won't turn sexual?"

"'I'm pregnant.'" I chew some pizza. "I'd run a fucking mile. And then some."

"Can you picture the headlines? 'Corey Jackson, dad-to-be, finally runs more than five yards!'"

I stare at her across the table. "You're real cocky. You know that, darlin'?"

She grins and runs her finger along the piece of pizza she's been picking at. Her finger is covered in sauce as she lifts it toward her mouth, and my eyes gravitate there. She closes her lips around her fingertips and sucks. Hard. Her cheeks hollow a little—and fuck.

I shift in my seat. I've truly never wanted something I couldn't have. As a kid, I had everything I could dream of thanks to my father's success, from game consoles to bikes to the latest sneakers. As a teen, I was the quarterback on my high school team. Then again at college, which made me the guy to be seen with. If I wanted the cheer captain, she was mine—and her sister was once, too.

When I came to L.A. four years ago and broke out as the rookie to watch, I became the guy to bag. I was at the top of every girl's fuck list—because here, sometimes the only way to get to the top is to fuck your way up. None of them considered that, if they'd give it up that easily for me, they'd give it up for another guy, too, so the only up they were going was up my dick.

I've sure enjoyed them trying though. The seductive glances and sex on tap has been good. It's an easy life outside of football, but no one's even come close to getting me for more than a quick fuck.

Except the girl opposite me. Because she really is one in a fucking million.

"Corey? Hello?" Leah throws a piece of pepperoni at me.

"What?" I meet the soft, blue eyes regarding me curiously.

"You were looking like you wanted to eat me, so I thought it would be polite to remind you that you've just finished your lunch."

"I'm always hungry."

"I wouldn't taste very nice, I'd imagine." She stands and we leave the restaurant.

"You taste fuckin' incredible, babe. Don't doubt that."

She blushes.

She actually blushes.

"Are you blushing?"

"No!" she insists, hitting my arm lamely. "You just caught me off guard, Corey."

I love the way she says my name. It rolls off her tongue in

a crazy mixture of exasperation and seduction that shoots right through me. Every single time she says it, I want to grab her and kiss her until all she can think of is the feel of my mouth on her. I want to take her home and hold her under me until the only thing she can say is my name.

I want to do so many things to this girl, and fuck me if it isn't killing me not to.

"Isn't it my turn to pick what we do now?"

"No." She flicks her fake, brown hair over her shoulder. "You picked lunch."

"Actually, *you* picked lunch, and we decided what to eat together, so it's my turn."

"Damn, you're right." She sighs. "What are we doing?"

Nothing suitable for this park.

"How about the Haunted Mansion?"

"Er..."

I walk backward in front of her, my eyes trained on hers. "C'mon, babe. Don't tell me you're scared of a haunted house designed for kids who can only just write their own names."

"Obviously not." She folds her arms across her full chest, pressing her tits up. "Let's go to the haunted house, then."

We get on the monorail to the New Orleans Square section of the park. She ignores me the whole time, and I can tell she's not a haunted house kind of girl. She's too put together, too girly, too... Not a shooting kind of girl either, but she royally kicked my ass at that.

I have to stop making assumptions about her and just take it as it comes, even if that freaks me the fuck out. She's marching to the beat of her own drum, and I love it and hate it.

"I can't believe I'm doing this," she mumbles, looking up at the ragged building in front of us.

"You've never been in here, have you?" I smirk.

"No, and I never intended to be."

I push the door open, and she edges in behind me, as close as she can be without touching me, as we walk into the foyer. The Ghost Host begins to taunt us, and the portrait room ahead of us starts to stretch as we slowly walk through. The portraits reveal fates of previous 'guests,' from a lady over crocodile jaws to a widow above a gravestone.

And then the lights go out with a booming clap of thunder.

Leah screams and grabs my arm. A ghostly apparition appears above us, illuminated by flashes of lightning, before it goes dark again. A blood-curdling scream rings out, making Leah scream again and scoot into my side. I wrap my arm around her shoulders, and she tucks her face into my neck.

We climb into a Doom Buggy, Leah never letting me go, and begin to move. Bangs and screeches come from the doors on either side of us as we head toward the séance room. The 'ghost' recites the séance, and we pass through into the ballroom, where there seems to be a party or something. I don't know—but I do know that, if Leah grips my shirt any tighter, she'll tear it off me.

Not an altogether bad thought, but this isn't the place I envisioned her doing that.

In the attic, there are endless pictures of a bride with different grooms. Their heads disappear one by one to the sound of a hatchet coming down, and each time it does, the girl tucked into my side flinches.

I feel like a bit of an asshole for dragging her through this.

"I think that's the worst for this bit," I whisper in her ear.

"You think?" she whispers back, turning her face forward.

But I'm wrong. So, so wrong. Just before we leave, the bride floats in front of us, moaning wedding vows while holding a hatchet. She appears quicker than I can blink, and Leah shrieks and moves closer to me.

I tilt my body into her and put my other arm around her. She's actually shaking, and this is a whole different side to the girl I'm coming to know. The hard-ass, quick-witted Leah has a softer side.

And as long as that soft side is near me, I think I like it.

I rest my head on top of hers as we go through the rest of the mansion, closing my eyes so I don't make the mistake I did a minute ago. She doesn't need another reason to kick my ass when we get off here. Hell, she has plenty already, and I have no doubt she's gonna take every advantage of them.

Screams ring out from the others in the buggies. She moves even closer to me, gripping me more harshly. I tighten my arms around her for the last few seconds before we get out of the buggies, and when we do get out, she runs out of the mansion.

She. *Runs.*

"You're an asshole!" she cries, her hands clasped to her chest. "I can't believe you made me do that."

Her eyes are wide and shocked, and I want to laugh at the way she's shaking her head. But I don't. Instead, I apologize. Again.

"I'm sorry." I hold my arms out. "I didn't think it would be that bad."

She takes a deep breath. "Bad? Bad? I nearly peed myself in there!"

My lips twitch.

"Don't you dare smile at me, Corey Jackson! Just when I was thinking you weren't the world's biggest jackass, you put me in there!" She points angrily at the house.

"I'm sorry. Really, I am!"

"No, you're not. You're loving this."

"Is it wrong if I say I am a little?"

"God! Are you twenty-four or fourteen?"

"Twenty-four with a mental age of fourteen." I wink at her and she clicks her tongue.

"There is only one thing that could possibly even this out."

I watch as she heads back toward the monorail and gets on. "Leah!" I jump on after her.

I'm feeling a little anxious at the determination shining in her eyes. She definitely strikes me as the kind of girl who gets her revenge in the most evil way possible.

"Leah. Leah!" I scramble after her at downtown Disney. "What are you doing?"

"You'll see."

I have a horrible feeling that I don't want to see.

I wait outside as she heads into a store. I don't know want to know what she's buying in there. Probably the single most embarrassing thing…

Aw, fuck.

"You're wearing these."

"Hell no!" I back up a couple of steps.

"Hell yes." She walks toward me.

"I'm not wearing fuckin' Mickey Mouse ears."

"Why not?" She pouts. And shit. She looks so damn adorable doing it that I almost want to give in to her.

"Because I don't want to."

"I didn't want to go in that stupid mansion, but you made me."

"Okay. That's fair. But I'm not wearing them!"

"You are."

Leah runs toward me, and I reach out and grab her waist. She moves onto her tiptoes and places the headband on my head. Then her face breaks into a huge smile, and as her eyes drift from the ears atop my head to mine, she slowly lowers back down to her heels and looks at me for a long moment.

She looks at me like I'm something other than the jackass who pisses her off every time he opens his mouth. Like I'm more than the devil-may-care playboy the media makes me out to be—that I act like. She looks at me like I'm a real fucking human being, and when she drags her teeth across her bottom lip while still looking at me, my heart thuds loudly.

My fingers flex against her slim waist. Every part of me is screaming for me to step forward and cover her sweet mouth with mine. I want to take this moment of her not hating me and spin it into something more.

She steps back from my hold and whips out her cell phone. Before I can say a thing, she snaps a photo of me with the ears on and laughs. The look on her face is pure delight, and that combined with her musical laugh means I have to smile at her. I move closer to her and pull out my own phone.

"What are you doing?" She raises her eyebrows.

I put my arm around her and tug her into me. "Smile," I whisper into her ear before taking my own picture.

I look at the screen. We're both smiling, and it looks totally natural. No pained, faked smiles.

"What did you do that for?" Blue eyes look up at me.

I push some of the horrid, dark hair from her eyes, letting my fingers linger on her soft cheek. "So I can remember the thirty seconds where you weren't actually mad at me for something."

I pull into the driveway outside her house and kill the engine. We get out silently, and I follow her to the door. Night is beginning to fall, and I know that, if I look out at the city below, I'd see thousands upon thousands of bright lights making their mark in the darkness.

But looking anywhere other than at Leah doesn't seem plausible right now.

She puts a hand on the door handle and drops it again. "Thank you," she says softly, turning to me. "For today. I actually had a really nice time."

"Nice? Ouch. That's an insult pretending to be a compliment."

Her pink lips twist on one side and those gorgeous eyes find my gaze. "Fine. Aside from you dragging me through one of the nine circles of Hell, I had an amazing time."

"Now you're just trying too hard," I sigh.

She laughs and slaps my arm. "Shut up. I mean it. I wasn't expecting to, but I had a lot of fun."

"Me, too. Even if it was at Disneyland."

Her eyes glitter, and she reaches up and tugs the wig off her head. "Yeah." Then she throws it at me. "Good thinking on the wig, cowboy."

"Do you think it worked?" I lean against the wall.

"You'll know tomorrow morning. I'll be either happy to talk to you or leaning over your bed with a heavy object."

"She's a comedian as well." I dip my head. "Now, are you gonna let me end this date with a kiss or do I have to steal one again?"

Her eyebrows shoot up. "Why, are you asking me if you can kiss me?"

"Right now? Yes. In five seconds, it might be a whole other story."

Leah laughs, and I'm starting to think that I really fucking like that sound. She rests her hand on my waist and leans up onto her tiptoes, tilting her face up. Her lips press against mine, soft and sweet, the sugary taste of the cotton candy she was eating an hour ago still lingering on her mouth.

"Night, cowboy," she whispers, stepping away and opening the front door.

"Night, babe." I walk backward toward my car, not taking my eyes off her, because how the fuck am I supposed to? How am I supposed to look anywhere other than at the girl who's edging her way under my skin?

"Hey, Corey?" she calls from the doorway.

"What?" I spin, my hand on my car door.

A small smile appears on her face, one that lights up her eyes. "Check your call log."

I look down and scroll to the log, and sure enough, the last call is from Leah. My eyes go to the door, but its shut and she's inside. I bring up my messages and text her instead.

Looks like I finally got your cell number.

Wrong. I got your number. SUCKER.

A laugh bursts from me as I get in my car. *When did you do that?* I reply before driving. It takes me two minutes to get to my house, and when I do, she's already replied.

When you went to the bathroom at lunch. Can I give you some advice?

You can.

Don't leave your phone around a girl you're trying to pull, especially if she shoots better than you. If she can do that, she can probably pull better too.

You're not letting me live that down, are you?

Never. In fact, I'm probably better than you at most things. All you have on me is throwing a football, and I'm probably pretty close there, too.

I smirk and lock my door behind me. We'll see, Leah. We'll see.

chapter ELEVEN

Leah

I went on a date in public. With a very public, very hot guy. *And it isn't all over the papers.*

Well, it is. The front page of the L.A. Reporter is a large picture of us at lunch. The photo was taken from behind me, but you can see Corey's face well enough. And the accompanying headline?

> DISNEY DATE FOR THE VIPER KING! IS HIS BITE LOSING ITS STING?

I laugh at it. I have to. He has a soft side. I saw it. The way he held me close to him in that damn haunted house when I was terrified for my life—quite literally, I might add—melted my heart just a little. It warmed a part of me toward him because it proved that he's not all asshole and dickhead. Although that part is warmed, it's still wary.

Because I have no idea what's his game and what isn't.

And that little part of me, the part that likes him, is vulnerable. I'm aware of it, that slither of a 'maybe he's not playing you.'

It breaks through into the rest of my body, and it's a fight inside to keep that maybe away from the almost certainty that he is.

I don't want to fall for him. I don't even want to trip. Hell, I don't want to freakin' *stumble.*

It's too risky. And not even for my job. That doesn't matter—not when my heart is involved. My job is my world, the one thing I live for, and the secrecy that shrouds it controls every part of my life. It isn't my heart though. It isn't even close. My heart is the gentle, regular beat of every day, waiting, just waiting, for the person worth pounding for. It's waiting for the person worth thumping against my ribs for.

He could be it, but I doubt it. To be a heart-pounder, you have to be trustworthy, and I wasn't kidding when I told him that I wouldn't trust him as far as I could throw him.

I pull the pin from between my teeth and secure the waist of the dress on the mannequin in front of me. "Yes. That's right," I tell Quinn. "I always saw it with the mocha scarf, not the mahogany one."

"Right," he replies down the phone. "And the leaf-patterned dress? What are you putting with that, darling?"

"Nothing much. Do you have the thick-knit, tan cardigan? And the chunky boots with the flip-over tops."

"Just that? No jewelry?"

"No. Just that." I pin the other side of the dress then grab my scissors. "And the maroon pants—pair them with a cream blouse, the one with the brown collar."

"Why didn't you put this in your notes?"

I slice through the collar. "You didn't ask me. I'm working on next fall's collection. It's hard to concentrate on this season's collection when I'm consumed by this."

"You mean it's hard when you're not here."

"Yes." I sigh, dropping the scissors and leaning against the wall. "Dammit, Q. I wish I were there. I'd give anything to see my designs walk down the runway and all the crazy backstage fun. I'm gonna miss it all. And that sucks big time."

"I know, Leah darling, I know," he says softly. "But you picked this path—and I commend you. You could do it easily, make your mark in this world because of who you are, but you won't. That's honorable."

"Really? Is it? When I'm going to miss out on everything

I've ever wanted? When my dream is going to happen without me there?" I squeeze my eyes shut. "I know I have to do this. I want to be accepted for me, dammit. Not because of Mom. It just hurts a little. That's all."

"Just remember who refused your designs. Remember all those designers who broke your sixteen-year-old heart because they thought you couldn't deal with the pressures."

"But you were there," I say quietly. "You believed in me before you knew I was a Veronica."

"Precisely," he replies triumphantly. "Because you have talent, Leah. You have real fucking talent, girl. So, in two weeks, I'm going to stand at the end of the runway watching your designs kill it and I'm gonna be proud as hell of you. I already am. You got that?"

"Got it." I stand up. "My designs are gonna create waves, I'm gonna kick ass, and you're going to video every second and send it to me after, right?"

He laughs. "Exactly that!"

"Awesome. Now I have to go and work before my boss kicks my butt."

"I agree. He's a tough guy."

I laugh as I hang up. Quinn wouldn't hurt a fly—much less kick my ass. Slap it, pinch it, yes. Kick it? No way. He appreciates a good butt too much.

I grab some pins from my box and hold them between my teeth. I have no idea what I'm creating. All I know is that the neckline dips severely, the skirt clings, and the sleeves… Well, they're flappy pieces of pinned-on material right now.

Sometimes, when the designs don't come out on the page, they come out on the mannequin. The secret design room just down the hall from my room is my favorite place in the house. The walls are covered in designs I've sketched since I was six, because this was my eighteenth birthday present from my mom. A place that was wholly mine, where I could go and let it all go. There's even a giant desk in the corner where I'm supposed to sit and design, but I prefer my room for that.

This is where I get to create a giant mess.

It's fitting, really, given my emotional state. I fight it. I swallow it back and pretend I'm okay, but only because I have to. If I could let it all flow and have the mother of all cries, I'd be really okay.

The thought that my dream is within touching distance but my fingers will never even skim it is heartbreaking.

But, like Quinn said, I have to remember who believed in me. Who imagined I could be someone when they thought I was no one. He's the person. He took a risk on the little sixteen-year-old, and when, year after year, my designs got noticed, he's the one who took a risk on the kid with a dream.

He's the one who got me a line, a show, a place in the spotlight. He's the one who encouraged me to draw until my fingers bled and think until my brain hurt. He's the one who taught me to add details until my eyes sting with the concentration and my body shuts down with the pressure.

He's the one who taught me to believe.

He taught me to believe in the little things. And maybe in my life, I'm so busy looking at the bigger picture that I've overlooked the tiny details.

But the tiny details—they're all Corey. And, to be honest, I don't want to think of all the little things. I don't want to focus on the way his eyes sparkle whenever they meet mine. I don't want think about the curvature of his lips when he smirks or the smoothness of his fingertips ghosting over my skin. I don't want to think about the dip in his cheek—the one I can't decide whether it's a real dimple or just a wannabe. I don't want to think about anything past playing him at his own game because it's too easy to get lost in a game.

It's so easy to forget the rules. It's so easy for the rules of the game to bend, to distort, to become another reality altogether. It's so easy to twist and contort your expectations with those rules.

It's so, so easy to lose, even when you think you're winning.

I could give him my body. I could let him peel my clothes from my body and take me to a crazy level of this Earth I might not have experienced yet. I want to. I'll freely admit that. I want to fuck Corey. I do.

But, as my dream proves, you can want something and not get it. And that's okay. Because being denied something you want will only make you work harder, make you more determined.

I drop the pins on the floor. Fuck. Fuck fuck fuck, of course.

Denying him is why he's so fucking hung up on getting me into his bed. It's why he's so goddamn determined to slip inside me and keep up with everything he's ever promised me.

Because I say no.

He wants me, and I refuse him.

I thought—naïvely—that the way to get him to leave me alone was by denying him. That, eventually, he'd listen to my protestations and give up.

I was wrong. Fuck, was I wrong.

The way to get him to leave me alone is to give him the very thing he wants, even if it defies my beliefs.

I'm going to have to sleep with Corey Jackson.

And soon.

Great-Aunt Ada walks into the room wearing a giant fruit hat.

No, that isn't the opening line to a joke. It's the absolute truth.

I blink at her. "What on Earth is that on your head?"

"On my bed? There's nothing on my bed, dear." She stops in front of the mirror on the wall and adjusts the monstrosity.

"Head!" I shout. "What is that on your head?"

"No need to shout." She meets my eyes through the mirror. "It's my new birthday hat. What do you think?"

I think her age has caught up with her and she's gone batshit crazy. "I, er… It isn't your birthday for another month."

"I had to try it on."

"Naturally." I ignore the knock on the front door. "Do you have to keep it?"

Ada turns to me. "What's wrong with it?"

I blink at her again. Jesus. Does she really not see the problem with wearing a *giant fucking fruit hat?* "Can you, er, ask me what's right with it instead?"

"Are you sassing me, Lele?"

"No. Just asking."

She narrows her eyes as there's another knock.

"I'll get it, shall I?" Mom yells.

"Yeah. Thanks, Mom," I call back, still staring at the old woman in front of me. "I just don't see how it'll go with your wardrobe."

"Oh, Grace took me shopping today. I have the most fabulous yellow dress to wear with it."

"I'm sure you— Oh my God, my eyes!" I snap my eyes shut and cover them with my hands. Fuck. No. That dress should not exist. The frills, the drop hem… Good God. "Please put it away and never show me it again."

"You have no taste," she scoffs. "Corey! Do you like my new dress?"

Pause. "It's wonderful, Ada. The hat, too."

I drop my hands and stare at him. "Are you serious? You're encouraging this?"

Ada faces me, still clasping the dress.

I cover my eyes again. "Please. Put it away."

"Grace knows better than you."

"I've dressed her for the last three years!" I stare at Mom in disbelief. "How could you let her buy that?"

"Since when have you ever denied your aunt anything and been successful?" Mom retorts, raising her eyebrows. "Precisely."

"Aunt Ada, please!" I implore, waving my hands at her. I've honestly never seen such a hideous item in my life. I hope they don't expect me to go out in public with her wearing it. Mustard yellow and frills are not a stunning combination.

She huffs and folds the dress, putting it back into the bag. "A fashion major with no taste. Well, I never."

"You're a fashion major?" Corey asks, looking at me.

Thank you, Ada. The old woman looks at me with wide eyes.

Something that is, thankfully, missed by Corey.

"Yep." I stand up and avoid my aunt's gaze, lest I send her six feet under. "Why do you sound so surprised?"

"I just never pictured you drawing dresses and shit."

Drawing dresses and shit. Oh. My heart hurts.

"Good thing I don't, then, huh?" I raise my eyebrows. "Why are you here?"

"Uh…" He looks around at my mom and aunt.

Mom smiles. Wide. Then pours a glass of wine and settles in at the kitchen island.

Corey's eyes flit between her and Aunt Ada, who is staring at us like she's never seen a couple of twenty-somethings talking before. I can feel the intensity of my family's gaze, and Corey doesn't look comfortable at all.

"Oh, for goodness' sake, you two!" I grab Corey's arm and tug him after me. Then I lead him through the kitchen and into the backyard, and no, I am totally not focusing on the firmness of his biceps against my fingers.

Not. At. All.

Okay, maybe a little…

"What are you doing here? Wait." I clap my hand over my mouth. "That's rude. I'm sorry. Let's try again. Hi. What's up?"

Corey's lips twitch up to the side, and the smile adds a little glimmer to his eyes. "Hi." He pushes some hair from my face and tucks it behind my ear.

Stepping forward, he leans in, his lips a breath away from mine. My eyes flutter shut, and then…

"Why is your aunt pressed against the kitchen window?"

I push his hand away from my face and spin on the balls of my feet. Ada jerks out of the way of the window, but not quick enough.

"Fuck my life!" Once again, I grab Corey, this time by the front of his shirt, and pull him around the side of the house where there are no windows.

He laughs. "Number-one reason I live alone."

"No, you live alone so your mom doesn't question the endless stream of girls coming in and out of your room."

"Or so she doesn't question the amount of time I spend in there."

"Oh, how romantic of you."

"I try. Now, third time's a charm." The words are a murmur falling from his lips, and he steps forward, cupping my chin. His thumb is rough as he traces it along my jawline. Dipping his head, he softly touches his lips to mine, just the barest brush. "Hi."

I smile. "Hi."

"Good day?"

"Mhmm. You?"

"Hard. It's better now that I've seen you."

"Of course it is. I'm wonderful."

I grin, and he laughs and rests his forehead against mine. "There's no shortage of self-confidence here, is there?"

"Says Mr. Certain."

"Darlin', when you look like I do, there's no need to be uncertain about anything."

"I like it when you call me darlin'. It's very cowboy of you."

"Watch out. One day, I might turn up with a cowboy hat and boots and charm my way inside your pants."

"It would be around ninety percent more successful than your current arrogance," I admit. "I love a good cowboy novel."

"What do books have to do with me wearing cowboy boots?"

"Nothing. I'm just saying, I like cowboys, okay?" I put my hands on my hips.

"So you like me."

"I never said that."

"You call me cowboy."

"It was originally supposed to be derogatory."

"Then what happened?"

"It kind of…stuck." I shrug. "So now you're cowboy to me. Is that all right?"

He pulls my hands from my hips and tugs my body flush against his. "All right by me."

"Great. Now, remind me what you're doing here."

"I never said." His lips brush along my jaw.

"Now would be a good time. Corey!" I wriggle in his hold when he kisses my neck. I hate it when he does that, because last time, I really, *really* liked it. "What do you want?"

"You. In my bed. Naked. Under me."

"Stop it." I wriggle again when he swirls his tongue in the dip of my collarbone and digs his fingers into my hips. Then, oh, he kisses my up to my pulse point and sucks lightly, his tongue caressing my skin. My clit aches. "Fucking hell! Corey!"

He drops his head against my shoulder and chuckles quietly. "I'm not even sorry."

"You will be if you don't tell me why you're here."

"Okay, okay." He pulls back. Not without one last kiss to my neck though. Obviously. "Our preseason game is at home tomorrow."

"Yes. At one o'clock. Against the Giants. Where are you going with this?"

"It's really hot when you go all football fan on me."

I roll my eyes. "Corey. Focus. My eyes are up here." I snap my fingers in front of my nose and he jerks his eyes up from my tits.

"Sorry. Kind of," he adds, glancing back down again.

I reach between us and tug my shirt up so it covers my cleavage completely.

"Good call," he mutters, meeting my eyes. "And I got you tickets."

"Tickets? There's only one of me. My ass isn't big enough that it needs two seats."

He laughs. "No. I thought maybe you'd want to take… someone."

I lick my lips and grin. "Go on. Say his name. It won't hurt you."

"Cole," he grinds out. "I thought you might want to come watch the game with Cole."

Is it bad that I'm hovering in delight right now? Oh, God, it is. So bad. So, so bad.

"It's kind of short notice. I'll have to call him," I say

dismissively. "I don't know if we can."

"Fuck 'we,'" Corey half growls, forcing me to look at him. "You're gonna be there whether he is or not. I couldn't give a shit about the pretty boy. I only got him a ticket to be fuckin' considerate."

"God, it's hilarious when you get jealous," I tease him.

"I'm not fuckin' jealous!"

"You're cussing. You so are."

"Leah, I swear to fuck, keep it up and I'm gonna kiss that sass right out of you."

"Tempting." I purse my lips. "But okay. I'll stop. I'll call Cole and see if he's free for a football date."

"What?" Corey's eyes blaze.

"Wait—I think that came out wrong..."

I smile as he pushes his mouth onto mine. It soon drops, though, because damn. His mouth is on fire, every ounce of the jealousy I just teased him about pouring into my body and consuming me. Corey's lips are hot and unrelenting, and the grip his fingers have on my hips is almost possessive, as if they're telling me who I belong to.

As if his fingertips, which are digging into my skin almost painfully, are telling me that I belong to him. That my body does, that I'm his, that it's his—no fucking arguments.

I ignore it though. I won't let him make me believe that I'm his, because I'm not. I'm my own. I belong to me and no one else. But if he wants to believe it...

"That definitely came out wrong," I whisper. "I didn't mean a *date* date."

"Fuckin' better not have," he whispers back, his voice harsher than mine.

I won't tell him that Cole's dad has been quietly dating my mom for the last few years. Or that he's always been closer to my brother than a dating prospect. Cole knows my feelings on the Hollywood lifestyle, and I know his on the jet-setting fashion world. We decided way back when we were seven that we could never date because it would just be impossible.

Besides, his fashion style is awful.

"A friend date," I clarify, sliding my hands up his chest.

"Damn right it is. Seven days, Leah. You said you were mine for one week."

"And I didn't lie. Just like you didn't about letting me go at the end of it, right?"

"Right." His jaw clenches through his lie.

Because that's what this is; it's a tangled web of lies that weave into and around each other. The longer we pretend, the more intricate the web becomes and the more the untruths combine with reality to make something that's neither truth nor a lie.

And we're hovering, balanced preciously in the middle. Our words are neither truthful nor untruthful. There are obvious words that are so full of shit it's hilarious. He'll let me go. I don't want him. Then there are the truths. But I'm starting to believe there's only one truth in this whole weaved perception.

And that's that I'll walk away in five days.

I have the strength. I have the desire to. I won't stay. I don't trust him, and I have more respect than that.

"I'll call Cole and let you know," I say softly, breaking through the tense silence that accompanied my thoughts.

"Yeah," Corey responds, his voice tight. He leans in once more and touches his lips to mine. "And, Leah?"

"What?"

"You better be wearin' my motherfuckin' jersey."

I smile against him. "Sure thing, cowboy."

chapter TWELVE

Corey

Seeing a jersey hanging in a locker with my name on it is something that still doesn't feel real to me. Since being drafted four years ago, I've played more games than the average newbie, but looking at that jersey makes me feel exactly the same as it did the first time I saw it.

It's a reminder that this is real, that I play for one of the biggest teams in the NFL. It's a rush of adrenaline, a boost, and I hope to fuck that this feeling never gets old. I want to feel this way every single fucking time I open my locker door. I want to feel the rush every time I see my name lettered on the back of the jersey, every time I hear my name called on the team roster.

I take the game day program and sit down, scanning it. It might be preseason, but it's the same as always. The schedule never changes—what happens might, the outcome will, the team does, but the timing never changes. That routine keeps us disciplined, strong, determined.

Unlike the other guys, I can't sit still. I won't sit still until later when I head for a massage, because game day makes me antsy. Preseason or fucking not. The nerves inside are always too strong for me to stay in one spot for too long. They won't head to the bathroom to meditate until later, but it's the first thing I do.

It's how I keep calm and focused when I'm on the field. If I don't meditate as soon as I get my ass through the locker room door, I'll go batshit crazy. I have my father to thank for that. He taught me to go first, to let go of the stress before everyone else does. He taught me that even the seemingly insignificant games matter as much as the big ones do.

And that's where I stand now—in the locker room with the program clutched tight in my hands. I breathe deeply. I clear my mind of everything except the game. The ball. The field. Right now, that's all that matters. The game. Winning.

Nothing else is more important than winning today.

This is my third season, and after losing the Super Bowl last year because of that stupid bullshit injury I got, I'm determined to win it this year. I don't care if we have to take out the biggest teams or injure the league's best players. We're gonna fucking get there. We're gonna show America who's boss in this beloved sport.

Nothing about the fight to win this year will be easy.

That's all this is. It's a fight to be the best and prove you're the best. I know I'm the best young quarterback out there. Now I just have to prove it to the rest of them because they still doubt me. They said that my injury in the Super Bowl was inevitable. I said, "Fuck off." It was bad luck, pure and simple. I got caught wrong—or right if you were the defensive team—and had to step back. And now, months later, I still say, "Fuck off."

I say, "Fuck off and watch your motherfucking back."

As everyone heads into the bathroom for their meditation, I make for the shower. Energy runs through my body and invigorates it as the water beats down, and I shake my arms out as I head for my locker. I can feel it now, the excitement and adrenaline that always floods me after a shower. It's as if the simple act of standing under the intensive hot water flow wakes me up and prepares me for everything.

Phil Collins's "In The Air Tonight" blasts through the training room as we get taped up. Reid is sitting next to me, getting acupuncture in his shoulder. I wince when the needles go in, and he smirks.

"It doesn't hurt."

"Fuck that." I eye the needles sticking out of his skin. "That's like the seventh level of Hell."

"Hey, if it means I can catch whatever is thrown at me tonight, I'll go it through Hell ten thousand times. This is our hardest preseason game."

Fingers dig into my shoulders, and I hiss as the masseuse hits a big knot by my shoulder blade.

"Jesus Christ, Corey. You got a sailor in there tying your muscles up?" Flora pushes a little harder and works it out.

"Sure I do, Flora." I grit my teeth. "He's in there just so I can see you every week of the season, sweetcheeks."

She barks out a laugh. "I'm nearly fifty, boy. Your charm ain't working on me."

"Would you believe me if I said that it was sarcasm? Ow!"

"Well now." She works down my spine, having freed another knot. "Aren't I good enough for the famous Jackson charm?"

"Only when you're not breakin' my back."

"You want a massage, you're gonna get one. It's not my fault you got knots tighter than my pops was."

I bite my tongue as she works her magic across my back, loosening up the last part of me that was holding any tension. A massage works pretty much the same way as sex, and I know which I'd rather have.

As I wander onto the field I know like the back of my hand, I scan the seats where the crowd will be very soon and wonder if Leah will be here. She never said that she would be. She never texted me like she'd promised, and that pisses me off. It knots the muscles Fiona just untangled, because fuck. I don't care if she's here with Cole. I don't care if the guy wants her until he's blue in the face.

I'm also a fucking liar, because the idea of someone going to a game with my girl drives me fucking crazy, even if I paid for it. For her. Because I'd do just about fucking anything at this point to get her to realize hat I want something more than she's expecting.

Shit. I don't even know what I want from her. It's somewhere between sex and a casual fuck. Something that makes no logical sense, but the thought of her screaming my name sends all sorts of shit through my mind. Things that should be thought with my dick and not my head.

Because I can't afford this shit right now. Preseason or not, I need to stand on this field and instill fear into the defense opposite me. I need to send a warning to every other team in the league. And if my head keeps thinking about the way she'd look beneath me, her hair wrapped around my fingers and her eyes glossed over as I move inside her, we'll be in dangerous territory.

Very fucking dangerous territory.

I push my wet hair from my forehead and sling my bag over my shoulder. We won by a mile. We slammed the defense, and ours fucking destroyed their offense.

"You didn't fuck up."

I look up at my car. Leah's sitting on the hood, her knees bent, her arms spread behind her. I could slip right between her legs, climb up, and fuck her so easily. Instead, I drop my bag, place my hands flat on the hood, and lean forward.

"I had you screaming my name. How could I fuck that up?"

Her smile turns to a sexy grin. "I knew that would do it. I was disappointed though."

"There's always a catch, isn't there?"

"You didn't celebrate."

"What?"

"I wanted to see your robot. You didn't celebrate."

I slide my arm around her back and pull her to me. Her body hits mine and I cup the back of her head, leaning her back on the hood of the car. My lips find hers, and I kiss her hard, savoring the taste of candy on her tongue as she flicks it against mine. She curls her hands around my neck and pushes her body to mine. I don't know who's controlling this kiss anymore. I don't know if I'm holding her against the car or if she's clasping me against her.

I just know that it feels good. Too fucking good. Addictive. She feels incredible below me, her legs bent at the knees and her fingertips digging into the back of my neck. When she pulls back and takes a deep breath, I look into soft, blue eyes on fire.

I put that fucking fire there.

The swell in her lips is from mine and the red on her chin is from the stubble on my chin she loves.

She's mine. I know this much is true. It's more than a fucking game, more than a try. It's something so simple. Something so much more than seven days of seduction.

Four days to go and she's fucking mine. Her smile, the glint in her eye, the grip of her fingers—it's all mine. More than she'll ever know, she's mine. Off-season, preseason, regular season, playoffs, Super Bowl. Leah Veronica fucking belongs to me because I said so, because her body said so.

Because when our bodies come together, shit gets crazy.

Convincing her of it will be a whole other ball game, but when she's on my car, wearing my team's jersey, her body alight for mine, she belongs to me.

And I'm not giving her up for anything.

"What was that?" Leah breathes when I pull back.

"That was how I celebrate a win."

"I'm afraid to see how that ends up after the preseason."

I thread my fingers through hers and curl our arms around her back, holding her against me. "Don't be afraid of pleasure, darlin'." I smile against her, and as my teammates exit the stadium, she shoves at me.

"Don't be a dick," she says, fear lacing her voice.

"Whoa. Hey." I step back and let her slide off the hood. "What's wrong?

"Can we go? Please?" She snatches her hands from mine and grabs the passenger's side door handle. Her eyes are downcast, no part of her body willing to acknowledge mine.

"If you want." I answer her because I don't know what else I have to do.

She'll go to Reid's birthday and sit next to me. She'll sit on the hood of my fucking car waiting for me. But she won't be recognized by my teammates?

What kind of bullshit game is she playing with me?

I slam my car door behind me and rev the engine more forcefully than necessary. What the fuck is her aversion to being seen with me? What the fuck did I ever do to her?

I don't reply as I tear out of the parking lot and onto the main road. Leah keeps her head down and her knees up, her phone tucked into her lap. She plays on it, doing whatever it is she does when she shuts herself off from me. I drive. I just fucking drive.

Past her house.

To mine.

She looks up but doesn't say anything. Her eyes remain fixed on the road, on our destination, on the trees that line the road that leads to my house.

And hell. I just need to touch her the right way, kiss her in the right places, and tease her until she's on the edge and begging for more. I need to take her so close that she's saying my name in whispered pleas, because the only thing I can think of that would be better than her screaming my name is her whispering it as she comes undone in my arms.

I park in the driveway and get out. She follows me, holding her stomach.

"Hungry?" I ask over my shoulder as I unlock the door.

She nods, her mouth forming a silent yes. Whatever the hell that was back in the parking lot has really gotten to her. I wish I knew what it was so I could soothe it, even a little.

"I'll make dinner," I offer.

She nods then crosses the room to my sofa. She drops back on the plush leather and swings her legs up to the back of it so casually, like she's done it a thousand times. And fuck. She looks like she has. She looks like she should do it a thousand fucking more times.

She hums to herself across the room, her eyes fixated on the television. I know she's trying to cancel out noise in her head.

I want to silence that shit for her. Whatever it is, it's serious if she's gone from gripping me tight to pushing me away in seconds. Fuck.

But it's hard to focus when she's lying back on my sofa, her legs in the air and kicking in time to whatever tune she has in her head. She looks relaxed, and finally, a small smile is playing on her lips.

She looks like she fucking belongs there. That's it. She looks like she's supposed to be lying on my fucking sofa, wearing my fucking jersey, in my fucking house.

She looks like she's supposed to be fucking mine. Like she was meant for me and me alone.

I chuck my shirt off and try to focus on the pasta I'm cooking. I try to focus on the boiling of the water and the softening of the hard pasta, but I can't. I keep glancing over my shoulder at the blond beauty who's lying on my sofa, distracting me.

I don't do distraction. I don't do anything that pulls me from the game. I don't do anything that has the chance to become my number-one priority over throwing a pass that will make a touchdown.

Until her.

Fuck, until her. She's more than a fucking distraction. She's a thrill, something consuming, something all-encompassing. Every second seems to be about her. It doesn't matter that it's only been ten days since I spoke to her for the first time.

What matters is that it's been ten days since she royally handed me my fucking ass and went from utterly hating me to wanting me—even just a little.

And now I look at her. She's still relaxed across black leather, the bright red of her jersey a stark contrast to the lightness of her hair, and I walk across the room to her and lean over the sofa.

Her eyes are closed and her lashes are fanning over her cheeks. She lied before. Maybe every time she's said it, because she does trust me. Maybe only a little, but if she didn't, she wouldn't be so comfortable around me. If she didn't trust me, she wouldn't be lying on my sofa in this position with her skirt around her hips. And she sure as shit wouldn't be showing me a glimpse of the tiny, white lace panties she's wearing.

I lower myself over her and softly cover her mouth with mine. "Dinner's ready."

She opens her eyes to mine. "Help me up."

"Isn't it supposed to be me saying that to you?" I ask as I take her hands and stand her up.

She tucks her hair behind her ear and smirks. "In my limited experience, you need absolutely no help getting up."

I swear to God she adds a little extra sway in her hips as she goes to the kitchen island. That skirt sure wasn't swishing like that earlier.

I sit opposite her and keep my eyes on her as we eat. Her gaze flickers to mine a few times, her cheeks flushing every now and then. I love knowing that I affect her. Even if it's just a flush of her cheeks, a glow in her eyes, I know something I'm doing is getting to her.

She chews slowly as she regards me. After several long minutes of silence, she says, "You aren't wearing a shirt."

"I don't usually wear one at home."

"It's not a complaint."

"How can you complain about this?"

"Corey. You're being an asshole."

"I can't help it, babe. It's in my DNA."

Leah hands me her empty plate and I put our dishes in the dishwasher. She swallows and walks over to the sofa, perching on the edge of the seat like she can feel the tension, too.

"What do you want to do?" I ask, sitting back next to her.

"Do you have any decent movies?"

"I do. Not that I have any time to watch them. They're in the cabinet by the TV."

She crawls across the floor and opens the doors to the unit. Fuck. Beneath the hem of her skirt, I can see her thong, which is barely covering her pussy. The soft, pink flesh peeks out, or through, the material. I don't even know.

I lean my head back and close my eyes. She knows exactly what she's fucking doing to me. She knows and she does it anyway. There's no way she doesn't want me when she's doing this.

Or maybe she doesn't. Maybe she's torturing me just because she can. There's no way she can crawl across the floor like that and be ignorant to the fact I can see what's under her skirt.

My cock is rock hard and straining against my jeans when she joins me on the sofa. She glances at my crotch with a small smile on her lips but doesn't say a thing. Fuck yes, she knows. She knows how fucking tortured I am right now.

Keeping my eyes on the movie is impossible when I can see her in my peripheral, her skirt exposing her long legs. It's impossible when I know exactly where those legs lead to. Because fuck. What even is this shit on TV? What the hell has she put on?

She leans into my side. Her hand rests on my stomach, her fingers teasing across my abs, but all I can think about is the skin waiting for me beneath that skirt. That jersey. That fucking bra. Those fucking panties.

I want to see her come apart so fucking badly. I want her to have some idea of what I can do to her. I want to make her come so hard with my fingers that she's actually afraid of what I could do with my mouth and my cock.

I trace my fingers up her thigh, making her shift against me, and smile into her hair. "What's up, babe?"

"You're pushing it, Corey."

I flip her on top of me. She squeals, but I overpower her easily, and then I sit up.

"I'm pushing it? You think you can wear those panties then bend over right in fucking front of me and I'm not gonna be turned on by that? I've been thinking about what you're wearing under that skirt since you walked out of that stadium. Since you were sitting on my fuckin' car."

I hook my thumbs under her skirt and push it up. My hands cup her ass perfectly. It's tight and firm, fitting in my palms like perfection. Like it was made for me.

"What are you—ohh."

I touch my lips to her neck and kiss my way down it. My

tongue swirls around the dip in her collarbone, and I drag my mouth up to hers. Her fingers curl into my neck as mine probe her butt, bringing her closer to me.

Our tongues swipe against each other's, and she grazes my bottom lip with her teeth. I kiss her deeply, tasting every inch of her sweet mouth, and she grinds against me. I slip one of my hands up to her back. She pushes her hips toward me, gripping me tighter. My finger slides beneath the string connecting the back of her thong to the front and travels to the front.

Her hips push even further to me, and she makes a whimpering noise into my mouth. She's wet. Shit. She's so fucking wet. My thumb easily grazes over her clit, pressing against the tight bud of nerves. She takes a deep breath in mid-kiss, and I smile against her mouth, knowing this is what she's wanted. She hasn't said it, she hasn't forced it, but I know this is what she wants me to do.

I run my fingers along her pussy and slip one inside her. She breaks the kiss and tilts her head back, giving me perfect access to her neck as I work my fingers against her wetness. She grips my hair, tugging hard, and she moves her hips in time with the movements of my finger and thumb. At her moan, I put another finger inside her and she clenches her muscles around me.

"Thought you didn't want me?" I whisper in her ear. "Hasn't that been your motto for days?"

"I…don't…" she replies breathily.

I curl my fingers inside her and push down on her clit. "Don't give me that shit, Leah. My fingers are inside your gorgeously tight pussy right now. Don't tell me you don't fuckin' want me."

She drops her head forward onto my shoulder as I continue to work her, to rub her, to bring her closer to the edge. Before she goes, I pull my fingers from her and hold her face in front of mine.

"Corey," she whispers. It's deep and low, seductive and begging, and it's music to my fucking ears.

"Tell me you want me." I graze my teeth across her bottom lip. "Tell me you want me and I'll give you what you need."

"I want you." Her breath fans over my mouth.

"Say my name."

"Demanding bastard." She manages a laugh, but it's breathy and desperate. "I want you, Corey. Okay? I want you."

My whole body goes taut, tight. Yes. Those are the words I've fucking wanted. I don't care if I've had to tease her with my fingers and hold an orgasm for ransom to get them. What matters is that she said them, and she can't take them back—not when she's gyrating her hips against my hand.

"Corey," she moans softly. "Now finish me off, for the love of fucking God."

I move my fingers quickly inside her and rub her clit. And I look at her. I watch her lips part and her eyes close and her cheeks flush. I feel her breath quicken and her muscles tighten around me and her juices over my fingers. And finally, I hear her cry out as she comes. I hear her cry my motherfucking name into my shoulder as she comes.

My. Fucking. Name.

Her body collapses against mine, and I press kisses along her jaw to her lips. I cup the back of her head and hold her to me. Her falling apart in my arms is the most goddamn beautiful thing I've ever seen. The glaze over her eyes, the quickening of her breathing, the moans from between those lips.

"You. Bastard," she whispers into my neck.

"I'm going to bed."

"I don't—"

"And I'm carrying you in there," I murmur into her hair. "I'm carrying you into my bed. I'm going to peel your clothing from your body and I'm going to hold you against me as I sleep, and I'm not going to let you go. Do you understand that?"

She doesn't reply despite the heavy breath she exhales, and I grip her tighter.

"Do you understand?"

"Yes," she whispers. "I understand. Completely."

chapter THIRTEEN

Leah

Our legs are tangled under his sheets, the rough hair on his lower legs scratchy against my smooth skin, but not uncomfortably so. His arms are wrapped around my body, holding my back flush against his chest. I can feel every dip and rise of his muscular body, and I can feel his breath against the back of my neck, hot and oddly comforting.

I never thought I'd find myself waking up in Corey's bed. His determination to have any and all of me is admirable—I have to admit it. Not to mention his surprising resistance to not take it any further last night. It would have been easy for him to carry me into his room, slip my underwear to the side, and fuck me.

And maybe, in my delirious, post-orgasm state, I wouldn't have refused him.

After all, he's already had a part of me. That intimacy between us wasn't asked for, but it was freely taken. I'm not ashamed of the fact that, the second he touched me, I didn't want to move. Hell, I *couldn't* move. I took what he was giving me and I reveled in every damn glorious second of it. I rode every wave of pleasure he sent my way. And there was a *lot* of pleasure. Maybe he has magic fingers.

I glance down to where his hand is resting on my stomach.

His fingers, long and perfectly sized, are splayed across my skin. He twitches in his sleep, and the tiny movement sends a bolt of delight across my body.

Yep. He definitely has magic fingers.

He is…surprising. I'm not sure how else I'm supposed to describe him. I can't get over the fact that he didn't take any more than I was willing to give last night. That he didn't even try to. It seems so contradictory to his everyday behavior.

If I'm totally honest with myself, I wish he would have followed through. I wish he would have taken everything I probably would have given him, because then it would mean that this whole damn charade could be over.

I would be the mountain conquered, the war won, the question answered. I would no longer be a thrilling prospect for him to overcome. The challenge would be fulfilled.

Lying in his arm this morning, warm and snug, I wish I were all of those things. Because every second we spend together blurs the lies a little. It's natural to spend so much time with someone and want to know more about them.

And I do, I think, want to know more. I'm curious about the man behind the mask, because that's what I think he is. He's hiding behind a mask. For whatever reason, I don't know, but I kind of want to.

I think I want to know about his life before the Vipers, what he does when he's not training or playing, what he likes, what he doesn't. I think I want to know who Corey Jackson is, because I'm almost certain that the person he portrays to the media is not him.

It's dangerous. It's a dangerous line to cross in this dangerous game. Too much information, too much of an insight into who he is, could shatter everything. My conviction could—and probably will—be destroyed. Too much information and I could hand over a lot more than just my body.

As it is right now, I know wholeheartedly that I will have sex with Corey Jackson and it won't mean a damn thing.

One of the most important things my mom has ever taught me is that a woman's body isn't a toy. It's not to be played with and discarded like a broken train set. A woman's body is a work of art to be admired and revered, and you shouldn't settle for less than anyone who'll treat it like it's worth a thousand priceless paintings.

I have no doubt that Corey would worship my body, but the real question is whose pleasure he would be worshipping it for.

And to that, I already know the answer. Yet my conviction is already staring at me, broken on the floor at my feet.

I shift my gaze from Corey's hand to the clock on the nightstand. "Oh, fuck!" I yank the sheet off my body and shove his arm away.

"What the…"

"Crap, crap, crap!" I grab my clothes from the floor. Quinn will be calling me in T-minus fifteen minutes and there's no way I can be around Corey for that.

"What's wrong?"

I turn to look at him. He's sitting upright, the covers pooled at his waist and exposing every glorious pack of muscle on his stomach. My eyes shamelessly trace the indentations of his body then drop down farther. The sheet is tenting, and…

"Leah? It can't be that serious if you're staring at me."

His words jolt me from my trance. I blink harshly and snap my eyes up to his. *Think, Leah. Think.*

"I have a job interview in, like, forty-five minutes. I need to shower and change before I leave!" I lie easily.

"Okay. You need me to give you a ride home?"

"Uh, yeah!" My eyes widen. "I look like I just got dragged through a bush by a bobcat or something."

He laughs. "Do me a favor?"

Ten minutes. "I don't have time for your fooling around, Corey."

"No. Just put your clothes on, for fuck's sake, or I'll be driving nowhere except into you."

I look at the fabric in my hand. Crap. I'm panicking so much that I almost forgot to get dressed. "Fine." I throw the jersey over my head then slide the skirt up my legs. "Happy?"

"Not really," he grumbles, swinging his legs out of bed.

My eyes flick to him as he stands. Since he's wearing just his boxer briefs, I can see the outline of his erection clearly, and I swallow. Hell, I knew he wasn't exactly small—I've had it pressed against me enough times—but I didn't realize he was quite that…big…either.

"You're not fuckin' helpin'."

"Sorry. Going. Now." I turn and run out of his room before my hormones make crazy decisions for me.

"You don't have to!" Corey yells after me.

"Oh, I do," I mumble to myself then I shout to him, "Just put some damn clothes on and take me home!"

Macey and Ryann stare at me across the living room.

"Let me get this straight," Macey starts, leaning forward. "You slept together, practically naked, and you *didn't* hit a home run?"

"I'm with her," Ryann agrees with a grimace. "For once. Girl, what is wrong with you?"

According to my friends, a hell of a lot. "It's not my job to start that. It's his."

Macey rolls her eyes. "Right. Because it totally wasn't my job to lean over the table and whisper a very dirty thought in Jack's ear the other night."

"But that's you. I don't…whisper dirty thoughts. Unless I'm asking my mom to do my laundry because I can't be bothered."

"Look, you're crazy. Totally crazy. Get in that man's pants and get out before you're in so far that his waistband is holding you there."

Ryann shakes her head. "Mace, not everyone is as anti-love as you are. What if they're falling for each other?"

I choke on my drink.

Macey looks triumphant. "See? You don't choke if you're falling in love, Ry."

"Okay. I'm not falling in love with him," I clarify. "I don't even like the guy half the time."

"You like him enough to let him play ping-pong with your clit."

Ryann coughs loudly.

My mouth drops open. "Where do you get these things?"

"Well, it's true," Macey implores, nudging Ryann. "Ry, tell her. She can't dislike him that much."

"Hey, you sleep with people you don't like all the time."

"But I might like them. I just don't get to know them well enough to know if I do. You and Corey, however, do know each other well enough to know that."

I rub my temple and finish my drink. "Okay. No, we don't. I just…"

They both stare at me for a long minute.

"What?" Ryann prods me.

"I'm fucking with him, okay?" I slam my glass down. "I just want him to leave me alone, so I'm fucking with him like he is with me. It's about him getting laid and getting the heck away from me."

Macey laughs loudly. "Yes! I knew you had it in you." She gets up and walks to her fridge for another bottle of wine.

"Okay, as much as I think you're insane for not hitting that, you do know what you're doing, don't you?" Ryann asks me quietly. "Because you can't listen to Macey. She's just afraid of commitment and thinks everyone else should boycott it, too."

"Yes, I'm sure. And do you blame her? Mitch was Lord of the jackasses," I remind her. "He's driven her to putting out whenever it tickles her pickle."

"I don't think there's any pickle-ticklin' happening."

I giggle. "There's plenty of tickling. Believe me. I heard the Jack story this afternoon, and the way she told it, *I* needed a hot shower afterward."

Ryann whistles. "So, what? Jack Carr is an animal in bed?"

"Hotter than midday on the equator, apparently."

"There's no apparently about it." Macey strolls across the room, unscrewing a wine bottle. "I had a fire that needed stoking, and that baby lit me up good."

I share an amused glance with Ryann.

"I think she was a teenage boy in a previous life," I whisper.

"Heard that." Macey fills her glass. "Just because I'm getting some."

"Technically, I could have it whenever I want it."

"Again, I ask, so why don't you?"

"Because…I guess I don't want to. Not for the want of pleasure, at any rate."

"Okay, saying you don't want pleasure sex is insanity." Ryann shakes her head. "We're in the middle of casting the lead opposite me in Chasing Tucker—"

"Oooh! Cole's in the running for that!" I gasp.

"Precisely!" she sighs. "I swear to God, I need me a vibrator, because every time he walks in the room, I burn up like *whoa.*"

"I'd recommend the Rabbit Pearl." Macey sits opposite us.

"I'm starting to wonder if you're addicted to sex, y'know," I tell her.

She shrugs. "There's no complaints from me."

"A commitment-phobe addicted to sex. There's something you don't hear every day."

"It's actually perfect if you think about it," Ryann muses. "She can get her kicks and not worry about getting her heart broken because she doesn't get attached."

Macey sits forward. "Unless it's Mr. Rabbit. I'm very attached to him."

"Wait. You *named* your vibrator?" I raise my eyebrows.

"Well, yeah. What else am I supposed to shout out when I O?"

chapter FOURTEEN

Corey

Two weeks into the start of the preseason and I've never been happier to have a day off.

All day, from beginning to end, belongs to Leah. Every second is dedicated to this girl. To kissing her, to teasing her, to bringing her so close to the edge she fucking begs me.

I can feel it—she's so close yet so far. One moment, she's in my arms, soft as fuck. Then the next, she's jumping from my bed in God evil underwear, leaving me with a raging hard-on and a shower to eliminate it.

The next time she's in my bed, she'll be writhing beneath me with my name on her lips. Fuck yes, she will be.

Ada blinks at me in the doorway. "Ria? Who's Ria, dear?"

"Lee-ah," I say slowly but loudly. "Is she here?"

"Oh! Leah. Why didn't you say so?" She shakes her head and steps back, opening the door. "She's upstairs. Do you want me to call her down?"

"Is Grace in?"

"No."

"Do you mind if I go up?" I wink at her, giving her my most charming smile.

She stares at me for a long moment. Then a grin breaks out on her face. "Oh, go on. Just don't tell Leah I said so, okay?"

"You got it, Ada." I kiss her wrinkled, powered cheek, and she laughs.

With another wink, I dart past her and to the stairs. I take them two at a time, needing to see Leah more than I can comprehend, and stop at the top of the stairs. Fuck. I don't know which room is hers.

"Leah?" I call hesitantly.

"Corey?" she shrieks, opening a door at the end of the hall. "What are you doing here?"

"I came to see you." I shrug.

"Okay. Hang on." She shuts the door behind her.

I frown when she reemerges a second later with her cell in her hand and locks the door.

"What's that?" I nod toward the room.

"My space," she answers evasively.

"Your space?"

"Yeah. I go there to chill. It's no big deal." She pushes her bangs from her forehead and opens her bedroom door.

"Isn't that what your bedroom is for?" I ask, taking in the white-and-dark-pink décor.

"Well, yeah, but it's just…my space." Her voice finishes quietly. "Just…leave it, okay?"

I raise an eyebrow. "Is it like a secret sex chamber full of whips and shit?"

She gasps and turns, her mouth wide open. "Corey!" she laughs. "What the hell?"

"I'm just askin'!" I grab her and pull her to me. "Well, is it?"

"No!" She manages through her giggles. "God. What kind of pervert am I seeing?"

"You're seeing me, huh?"

"I… Um." Leah's blue eyes widen, hesitance and fear in them. "I think I said that, but I didn't mean to."

I slide my hand around to her back and beneath her tank top. "Is that the same as dating?" I lower my face to hers.

"N-no…" she breathes. "That comes before…before the D-word. Will you stop tickling my back?"

I swallow my chuckle. "I'm sorry. So, we're not quite single but not quite dating. Is that what you mean?"

"I… Um… I…" She swallows. "I'm going to go shower." She wrenches herself from my grip. "Make yourself comfortable," she shoots over her shoulder, opening her bathroom door.

Nice evasion. I groan. "How the fuck am I supposed to get comfortable knowing you're naked in the next room?"

She smiles. "You're not." She disappears into the room, and the lock clicks.

Shit. Fuck. That was plan B.

I stare at the door, especially when the water runs. She's in there, naked. Fucking naked. All lightly tan skin and smooth, toned curves. She's in there, no makeup, wet hair, water droplets coasting down her skin.

Water droplets begging to be licked up by my tongue, wiped away by my fingers, completely eliminated by me.

I lie back on her bed and switch on the TV. This is ridiculous. My cock is straining against my pants. Nothing is going to calm that bastard now, least of all thinking of my girl naked.

My girl.

My girl.

Fuck. Now, even in general thought, she's mine. Three days ago, she was 'that girl.' Now she's fucking 'my girl.' Like I'm attached to her. Like I want her for more than a quick fuck.

The water stops, and I stare at the door despite the TV being on. Nothing on TV will beat the view about to walk out the door—I can guarantee that.

"What are you doing?" she asks, looking at me and opening the door.

"I was attempting to make myself comfortable." My cock throbs. "Not so much now."

Her eyes drop to the bulge in my pants. "Well, this is kind of awkward." Then she bends over to retrieve her hairdryer.

Fuck, I need to remove that image from my mine.

I need to erase the image of her bending over and exposing her bare, perfectly pink pussy to me.

"What's awkward is the fact that I can see your ass under that towel, never mind the fact that your pussy was just on full fuckin' show for me, and I can't do a damn thing about it."

"I can see how that would bother you." Her eyes flick to my pants again, and this time, they linger for a moment.

"Leah," I warn, my eyes trained on her.

Studiously, she avoids my eyes in the mirror and turns on her hair dryer. She blasts the hot air through her hair, running a brush through it at the same time. Still, she fucking avoids my gaze. Like she can't feel it. Shit, I can feel it reflecting back onto me.

She puts the hair dryer down and walks to the dresser. After opening the drawer, she grabs a pair of white panties and bends over once again, this time hooking them over her ankles.

"Fuck. Fu-uh-uh-uck!" I curse and slap my hand over my eyes. I'm trying real hard to be good here. I'm trying real hard to not flip this girl onto her fucking back.

"You can look," she says, amusement tinting her words. "I'm decent."

I drop my hand and stare at her, my eyes landing on hers, and she shivers. "Darlin', the only decent thing about you right now is your underwear and how fuckin' good they'd look on my floor."

She raises her eyebrows. "For the price I paid for them, they're pretty damn decent on, thank you very much, cowboy."

I watch as she pads across the room and shifts some papers to find her makeup bag. She files the papers into a pile and shoves them into a drawer. Then she grabs a brown leather bag.

I watch as she carries the bag over to the mirror and sets it down. As she bends forward, searching for makeup, her dress rides up her thighs. Fuck. This girl—she has no idea how sexy she is. She has no fucking idea how incredibly hot she is. If she knew for a second what she could do to me, she'd know how incredible she is.

If she knew just how turned on she could make me with a glimpse of her underwear, she'd realize how fucking irresistible she is to me.

I scoot down the bed to where she's standing and grab her thighs. She gasps, dropping her mascara into her bag, and steps backward. My fingers trace up and down her thighs, the skin beneath my fingertips silky soft.

The hem of her dress rides up as my thumbs do, and when she draws in a sharp breath, I touch my mouth to the curve of her ass. *Shit.* Her muscles clench beneath me, and I curve my hands around to the front, letting them brush her panty line at the apex of her thighs.

My nose, brushing her ass cheek, twitches. She's wet. Fuck. I can smell her, sweet and strong, wet and ready for me. I tug her back so she's sitting between my legs, her ass barely perched on the bed, and flatten my hand against her stomach. She isn't fucking moving. I want to feel her give herself over to me again.

My cock pushes into her back, and I'm ready for her. Shit, I'm ready for more than her giving herself over. I'm more than ready to give myself. To feel that tight, sexy pussy clenching around my rock-hard dick.

"What are you doing?" she whispers breathlessly, my fingers trailing up her inner thigh.

"I'm tryin' not to rip this sexy-as-fuck bit of lace off of you so I can fuck you," I whisper in her ear. "And you're makin' it hard, Leah. You're makin' it real hard."

"You can handle it," she exhales sharply.

"This is me handling it." I graze my lips down her neck in a blazing trail, and she shivers. "The only reason I'm not fucking you right now is because we're not alone here." I slide my fingers beneath her lame excuse for underwear, her juices instantly coating my fingers. "But trust me, babe. If you pull this shit again, I'm gonna be balls-deep inside you in a fuckin' millisecond."

My fingers push inside her at my words, and she gasps sharply. Her muscles clench with that sharp inhale, and fuck, fuck. Her clit is swollen beneath the pad of my thumb, and she drops her head back onto my shoulder. She moans—not quietly. Despite the thrill it sends through me, *because I fucking caused that,* I slide my hand from her and trail from her stomach to her mouth.

"Shhh," I hiss into her ear, kissing the spot below it. "No

sound, babe."

"Dickhead," she breathes on a jolt of pleasure. "Total dick… ah…head."

My hand cups her jaw, holding her head back on my shoulder as my fingers work her pussy. I harshly pump them in and out, my thumb rubbing her clit. She trembles and quivers in my arms, and my cock gets harder and harder, painfully so.

"Corey, fuck!"

Her whisper is music, a sweet fucking melody I'll never hear again, and I push deeper, rub harder.

"Say it again," I groan.

"Cor—shit!" She pushes against my hold on her jaw, but I'm stronger, and instead she bites onto my finger. Her cry is long and high-pitched. Her shudder is everlasting, finished by a heavy moan, and her pussy is clenched tight, clamped onto me.

She stills, her chest rising and falling with each breath, and I bring my hand to my mouth. I turn her face toward me and insert my fingers into my mouth. I lick every last drop of her off myself, and it's sweet and harsh and as fucking addictive as I imagined it to be.

"Corey, I—"

I close my mouth over hers, making her taste her lingering juices on my tongue. "You nothing. You fucking nothin', babe. Now go and clean yourself up before I finish what I just started."

She breathes in sharply, stands, and turns to me. "You're a pain in my fucking ass."

I cup her neck and pull her down to me. "Leah, darlin', I appreciate your sass. I fuckin' love your sass. But if you stand here much longer, talking to me this way, I really will finish this shit." I press her mouth to mine. "And the next time I make you come, it'll be with my dick. It'll be buried so fuckin' far inside you that you won't be able to think. You won't be able to breathe or function. It'll be buried so far inside your pussy, there'll be no fuckin' doubt that you're mine."

Her knees buckle, but she stays standing. "I got it, cowboy. I got it."

I slap her ass lightly. "Good. Now get in that bathroom, tidy up, and let's go."

Reid and Jack eye Leah with curiosity. Their eyes flit across her body, Jack's lingering on her chest a little too long. I cough, and he diverts his eyes. Leah glances at me, her lips twitching, and then she regards my friends with mild amusement.

"Are you done looking at me like you've never seen a woman before?" she asks, looking up at them with a smirk.

"Yeah. Y'all already met her, or did you forget that?" I grunt.

"I've never stood in front of a girl this hot that didn't want me," Jack says in wonder.

"From the sounds of it," Leah replies, "you guys don't do much standing in front of girls. More lying with them."

"She's incredible." Reid turns to me. "Really. Please don't piss this one off."

"Too late. I do it on a daily basis." I shrug. "She's used to it now."

Leah rolls her eyes. "Yeah, I work three hours into each day purely for you to annoy the crap out of me."

"I'm honored."

"You should be. One of those hours used to be for kicking your ass. Now, I allow thirty extra minutes for that."

"I think I just fell in love," Reid mutters.

"Well, thanks, darlin'," I say, ignoring Reid and keeping my eyes on Leah. "But I can think of something better to use that half an hour for."

"Keep trying, cowboy. Keep trying." She smirks again, tapping my chest.

"Wait, wait, wait." Jack pauses, looking between us. "You're telling me you haven't fucked her yet?"

"*Her* is right here." Leah waves.

"Not for a lack of tryin', man. Her pussy is clamped shut tighter than a bank vault."

"You know, Corey, I'm about to use that half an hour of ass-kicking time." Leah smiles sweetly at me.

"I can't believe you're still around," Reid tells her, sitting on the sofa opposite us. "It sure isn't for his fucking charm. Does he have some redeeming quality we haven't discovered yet?"

I grimace. Assholes.

"I'm still looking," Leah answers, her eyes trained on the TV. "It's quite the dig."

"My redeeming quality is my cock, babe. You don't have to dig for that. He'll pop right up if you ask him nicely." I brush my thumb across her neck.

"Will he stay down if I ask him nicely?"

Jack guffaws into his hand. "She's got your number, man."

"Nah. She wasn't asking it to stay down an hour ago."

Leah leans forward and grabs the bowl of Doritos I set out. Seeming completely unaffected, she pulls the bowl onto her lap and shoves one in her mouth.

"She looks like she'd like to tear it off right now." Reid smirks.

"True story," Jack agrees. "Hey, Leah, do you want his cock up or down?"

"He can shove his dick up his butt if he really wants to." She chews.

Jack raises his eyebrows. "Feisty."

"Non-fuck-giving," she corrects him. "Quite literally."

I tug on a lock of her hair and bend my head forward. "How can you be so stressed out when you had the best orgasm of your life not so long ago?"

"And what the hell would you know about the quality of my orgasms, Corey Jackson?" She sits up and stares at me. "Maybe my own fingers have given me better orgasms than yours have."

The guys choke on their laughter.

I stare into her eyes. "Wanna prove it?"

"Maybe I should. Your ego could do with a good sanding off." She doesn't flinch. She holds her ground perfectly, her gaze unwavering, the tightness of her clenched jaw showing me just how angry she is right now.

"Again, man, she's got your number," Reid says.

"She's several tickets behind having my number," I reply, my eyes staying on hers. "She's just got this awful sassy side that makes her mouth contradict everything her body says. She whispers my name while her body screams it."

She takes a deep breath, her chest heaving. In a split second, she drops the bowl on the coffee table and gets up. "Excuse me," she says tightly, slipping past me.

Shit. "Leah." I grab for her hand, but she moves out of my way.

She stops at the doorway. "Follow me, Corey Jackson, and I'll do more than sass you. I'll rip your fucking arrogant balls from your body." She turns, her blond hair swinging with the sharp movement, and slams my front door behind her.

I stare at the empty doorway, and fuck, my heart drops. It's a jolting drop, a guilty one, a fucking 'what the fucking hell did you just do, you asshole?' kind of drop.

I swallow. Shit. Why do I hafta turn into such an immature prick when these guys are around?

"Wow," Reid says flatly, his eyes traveling from the doorway to me. "I think she just friend-zoned you, bro."

"I think she just fucking *enemy*-zoned you," Jack adds.

"She something-zoned me, and it ain't fucking good." I run my fingers through my hair and drop my head. "Shit."

Silence lingers in the room. It's heavy and so saturated in my regret that I could reach out and grasp a handful of it. Fuck, fuck, *fuck.* Why do I always hafta be such a fucking shit? She deserves better than that.

Leah deserves the whole fucking universe handed to her on a silver platter with a red rose and a heart-stopping declaration of love.

Saddest thing is that maybe I could fucking give her that. If I weren't such an immature, impulsive asshole, maybe I could give her everything she deserves and everything she doesn't know she wants.

But no—I couldn't. I can't. She deserves someone better than me, someone who won't get to know her just because she's hot and would probably be a good fuck. She deserves someone who'll adore her for her, because she's fucking incredible, amazing, and the closest thing to fucking perfection you'll find in this city.

She's adorable and she's honest and she's totally gorgeous. She's sassy, yeah, but she's strong. She's hard but she's soft, she's secretive but open, and…shit.

I just fucked up royally.

"You're going after her, aren't you?"

I look up and meet Reid's gaze. He's concerned but amused. Yet he's confused because this shit makes no sense. I'm not supposed to feel anything for this girl unless it's arousal. I'm not supposed to give a crap if I piss her off or make her hate me. I'm supposed to move on and find someone else to warm my bed.

But Leah…

"Pussy-whipped," Jack says, breaking the silence.

I stand and dig my keys from my pocket. I unhook my spare house key and throw it at them. "Lock the door on your way out."

Then I follow her.

chapter FIFTEEN

Leah

I slam the front door behind me and throw my keys into the glass bowl on the side so harshly that the clanging sound rings out downstairs. I kick my shoes off and they bounce off the wall. But they're messy, all over the place, and that makes me mad, too. Why can't they fall right? Why can't they just line up perfectly against the wall?

I grab the pumps, yank open the closet door, and throw them in. I slam that door, too, because I need to get rid of this anger. It doesn't matter that I ran home. It doesn't matter that my feet hurt because my pumps aren't made for running or that there's probably a blister or two on my baby toe.

It just matters that I'm angry. So fucking angry.

"Leah?"

I storm into the front room and stop in the middle of it. I don't know what I'm supposed to do. I feel…disoriented. Like I'm here but I'm not, like something is missing.

"Honey, are you okay?" Mom stands up and steps toward me.

"I don't know," I answer, throwing my arms up. "I don't know."

"What's wrong?" She moves again, but I hold my hands in front of me, because no, I don't want to be touched.

I want to be alone—completely alone.

"Why are guys such fucking assholes, Mom? Why do they feel like they need the need to treat women like their playthings, huh? God!" I run my fingers through my hair and tug on the ends. "Why was I so dumb?"

"Leah, what happened?"

"Corey Jackson happened—that's what. That childish jackass happened." I release my hair and stroll into the kitchen for a glass of water. I'd prefer vodka, but whatever. "Seriously, I don't know what I did to deserve to be treated like I'm a piece of meat, but he's got it figured out."

The doorbell rings, which is followed by a series of loud knocks. "Leah!"

I turn to Mom. "I swear to God, Mom, don't you dare let him in!"

She looks at me, completely torn. "It's no good yelling at me, honey. Tell him this. Not me."

"Mom! Oh my God!" I slam the glass down when she disappears and the front door opens.

"Is Leah—"

"Yes."

Fuck this. There isn't a bone in my body that wants to see that asshole. Not a single fucking *cell.* I run through the kitchen and up the stairs. Footsteps thunder after me, louder and harsher than mine, desperation reeking in every step.

"Leah."

"Fuck you." I reach for my bedroom door, but Corey's quicker, and he grabs my arm.

He spins me to him. "I'm sorry, all right? That was fucking dumb of me. I shouldn't have treated you that way."

"No." I meet his eyes and shake my head. "Fuck you, Corey. Seriously. Fuck you. Absolutely. I'm not interested in your apologies because they're for one reason and one reason only."

"No. Leah, you don't—"

"Don't what? Understand it? Get it? *Fuck you!*" I shout, fighting to get him to release me. When he doesn't, I shove his chest. "I'm not your toy. Do *you* get it? Do you *understand* that?

I'm not gonna roll on my back and let you do whatever you want just because you're Corey Jackson. I'm Leah fucking Veronica, damn it, but I'm also a woman, and I will *not* be treated like some whore off a street corner just because some asshole can't dedicate his cock to someone for more than an hour!"

"Leah, shit!" He cups my face with his free hand, pulling me toward him. "It's not like that, all right? Not anymore. You're more than that!"

"I call bullshit. I call fucking bullshit on every word you say. You're a charmer, Corey. I'll give you that. You're a charmer and you're a sweet-talker, but you're also a complete and utter manipulator, and you can kiss my fucking ass."

"Feel this." He presses his lips to mine. They're hot and they're heavy; they're bruising and they're breaking; they're desperate and they're pleading. They're kissing me the way every woman wants to be kissed. Intensely, endlessly, like every second is inching closer to your final breath.

"Feel this, asshole." My palm connects with his cheek. "Get out," I say steadily, but I'm shaking. "Get the hell out of my house right now."

"Leah—"

"Get out!" I shout, my eyes stinging. "I'm worth more than your opinion of me. I'm worth more than the way you treated me ten minutes ago, so get out. Whatever game you're playing, I quit. I'm done. It's over. Go play with someone who doesn't care, because I do. Too much." I let out a shuddery breath at my admission. "Get out, Corey, and don't come back. Ever."

He stares at me. The moment is everlasting. Like a thousand angels are hovering between us, their hearts breaking one by one.

"Go," I whisper, finally snatching my arm from his grip. "Just go."

"That's what you really want?"

I nod. I want him away from him. I want him so far that I won't be tempted to grab him or fold my arms into him or kiss him. I want him so far that I can forget that he exists—even if it's only for a second.

"Fine." His voice is low, quiet. Defeat threads through every syllable.

My heart wants him. Oh, Lord, my heart wants to wrap itself around him and secure him against me. But my body and my mind? They want him to go. They want him away because then…then, it won't hurt.

Corey swallows hard. Then he releases me and chills filter across my skin. "Fine," he says. "Fine. All-fuckin'-right." He steps back, his foot dropping onto the second stair, his eyes on mine. Always his eyes on mine. "All right. If that's really what you think of me, babe, then all right."

"It is," I whisper. Except the words are so quiet that I don't think anyone but I can hear them. They're so quiet that I'm not sure they're true at all, because if I had meant them, surely I'd have yelled them. Surely I'd have shouted them from the rooftops, ready to announce to L.A. my opinion of him.

Surely I wouldn't be standing here, tears stinging my eyes, watching him walk away from me.

He does. Walk away from me. One step at a time, he descends the staircase, each inch another farther from me.

I get angrier. I want him to fight, dammit. I want him to run up those stairs and claim me, make me his. I want him to stay in this house until I'm one hundred percent sure I'm his.

But he doesn't. In typical Corey fashion, in typical playboy fashion, he hits the bottom step and walks. He doesn't even turn around.

The ache—it grows. And my eyes—they burn. The sting is a little stronger. Everything, I feel it everywhere, because maybe I've been kidding myself.

Mom appears where Corey just was. "You want me to call the girls?"

I shake my head. "Cole," I manage. "Please, Mom. Cole."

She nods, turning away.

I stare at the stairs. How could he have walked away so easily? How could he have left me so simply? That isn't how it was supposed to go. He was supposed to fight. He was supposed to ignore my demands and make me believe he's more than the guy he appears to be.

He was supposed to prove that he cares.

But he doesn't.

And I do.

I lost my own game.

I slump down against the wall, wanting the only guy who's ever made sense to me. I want Cole to make sense of Corey.

I curl up into a ball. As curled as I can get while sitting upright, that is. I hug my knees tight because they're all I have to hold on to. They're the only anchor in my life right now.

I don't know how much time passes when I finally hear him say my name.

"Lee?" Cole says softly.

"What did I do for him to treat me so fucking badly?" I look up at him, swallowing hard.

"Baby girl," Cole whispers back, walking across the hall to me. Then he sits next to me and loops his arm around my shoulder. "Nothing. Absolutely fucking nothing."

"I don't even want to care. Do you know that? I'm mad. I'm so damn mad." I can barely feel anything else other than that anger. "So why do I care?"

Cole doesn't answer—he doesn't need to. I already know why, and so does he.

Movie debut week for Mom is always crazy. It's a mixture of calls from her agent, e-mails from random publications who can't be bothered to contact her publicity team, and scheduled appearances.

I try to be there. I do. Every year, I've been backstage at every interview, ready to hug her and tell her that she's perfect. But this time, I'm shut in my design room, surrounded by material and pins.

Frills and lace and polyester consume me without distracting me at all. They don't calm me either. My escape isn't working.

I step back to look at the mess of red and white fabric on

the mannequin. Jesus. Is that a coat or a dress? I don't… I don't even know what the hell that looks like.

I rip the fabric from the fake body and pins scatter across the linoleum floor like a thousand tinkling raindrops. I grab a stubborn red scrap and tug hard, and the mannequin goes, too. I jump back as it crashes to the floor. Then I kick it.

"Stupid piece of crap." I throw the fabric on top of it and drop onto my plush, leather chair.

"Leah? What's wrong?" Aunt Ada pokes her head around the door.

"I'm broken," I mutter, staring at the mess on the floor.

"Broken my backside," she retorts, walking into the room. "I thought I taught you better than this."

Oh hell. Of all the times for her to have her hearing aid in. "I'm fine, Aunt Ada. I just need…something."

She claps her wrinkled hands together. The sharp sound rings out around the small room, and I jump. My eyes snap to hers.

"A man pissed you off. So what? It's in their job description to be irritating bastards, dear. And what we do when a man pisses us off?"

I shrug. "We drink lots of wine and eat cake?"

"Leah Veronica! Most certainly not! Women do not feel sorry for themselves." Ada frowns at me. "Why are you angry, really? Is it because he pissed you off or because he left when you told him to?"

I open my mouth. Then I close it again because I don't want to say it out loud.

My old aunt smiles. "Ah-ha. Now, it makes sense." She hobbles across the room and puts her hand on my cheek. "Dear Lele, listen to Great-Aunt Ada. The best way to get a man to come back is to make him think you don't want him to."

"I don't want him to."

"Sure you don't. Call Macey and go and meet another guy, then."

"I don't want to do that either."

"Sounds like you don't know what you want, dear."

Something like that. "Can we get to the point of this seemingly pointless conversation?"

Ada laughs and drops her hand. She straightens and looks down at me, her eyes sparkling fondly. "When a man pisses you off, one does not sit back and wallow in one's self-guilt. One gets up, gets beautiful, and pisses him off straight back."

With those words, she turns and leaves the room. I stare at her as she walks down the hall to her bedroom and disappears through the door. What was that?

If only it were that simple. If only I really could get up, get dressed, and piss him off.

He's probably already moved on.

I ignore the sting that that thought brings. Because hell, if he's moved on, and I'd bet my ass he has, then I can, too.

I grab my phone from my desk and call Macey.

"Hello?"

"Mace."

"If you're gonna go 'Heartbreak Hotel' on me, then I'm sorry. I'm closed for business."

My lips twitch. "No. I want some advice."

"On the quickest way to remove balls from a guy's body? Or how far up their ass they can go?"

Tempting… "I want to know how to piss off a guy without making it seem like I want him to come back."

Silence. Then a loud, gleeful giggle. "Why, you get dressed and you come out with me, of course!" The sound of a door shutting comes down the line. "I'll be over in thirty minutes. Order pizza. I'll bring the wine."

chapter SIXTEEN

Corey

I flick the beer cap up. It spins in the air then drops down onto the table with a clunk.

My house is too quiet, which means the thoughts in my head are extra fucking loud. Each one is a painful scream begging me to listen to it. One after the other, they circle until my temples throb and there's a steady pounding at the base of my skull.

I drop back onto the sofa and run my fingers through my hair. I've fucked up many times in my life, but this is the biggest one. And the worst thing is that I don't have a clue what I have to do to fix it.

I don't know if there is anything I can do.

I've already given her something I've never given anyone—a chance at more. Even if she doesn't know it. I'm afraid that, with every word she's ever spoken, every smile she's ever given me, every kiss she's placed on my lips, she's wriggled her way under my skin. She's clawed her way through the asshole act and hit my fucking heart.

"What?" I open my front door.

"Did I interrupt a jack-off?" Jack laughs.

"Fuck you."

He follows me inside. "You see the news?"

"Do I look like I've watched the bullshit?" I motion toward my TV and grab a beer from the fridge. I offer the bottle to Jack and he nods in response.

"You should."

"Or you could just tell me what the hell you're talkin' about."

He takes the beer from me. "Apparently, the media vultures had a new plaything downtown last night."

I raise an eyebrow.

"Leah went out with Macey. Pictures show her leaving Vibe with some guy."

I freeze. "You fuckin' what?"

Jack pulls his phone from his pocket and swipes his thumb across the screen. Then he drops it on the kitchen table and slides it to me. "See for yourself."

I ignore the words, my muscles tightening. I want to see the pictures—I want to see that it isn't fucking true and they don't fucking exist.

They do. And it's sure as shit her. Long legs, curves hugged by black fabric, blond hair swept to the side. Then some asshole standing next to her with his arm around her waist.

His arm. *My* girl.

Fuck no.

I throw Jack his phone and drop my bottle in the sink. It falls over, the undrunk beer spilling out of the top, filling the sink. After tucking my phone into the pocket of my jeans, I grab my shoes and shove my feet into them.

"Whoa—where are you goin'?"

"Leah's house." I grab my keys.

"How many beers have you had?"

"Four. Maybe."

Jack snatches my keys. "You aren't fucking driving, you idiot."

"You won't stop me going 'round there."

"I'm not trying to. Despite the fact that you're probably safer sending roses or some shit, I'm telling you to get in my car. I'll give you a ride." He puts his bottle down and opens my front door. "I'm not offering this shit again, so get in or walk."

I sigh heavily and follow him to the car. I'm… I don't know how the fuck I feel. I'm mad and I'm confused. I'm torn and I'm fucking fuming.

Two days ago, she was standing in front of me, trying to not to cry as she demanded I get out of her house. One day ago, she was leaving a club with some prick.

My girl, my Leah, was leaving with someone else.

Someone else was touching her, kissing her. Someone was taking everything she had denied me.

I slam my fist into the dashboard. "Fucking asshole!"

"Agreed." Jack slams on the breaks outside her house. "I don't understand this feelings shit you seem to have going on, so I'm just gonna say don't fuck up again. Maybe try giving her an orgasm. Chicks are way happier after an orgasm."

I blink at him across the car. "You're a dick."

He laughs and I get out. He salutes me before driving away, and I walk up to the gates. Then I punch in the code and slip through the gap as soon as they open.

Was this driveway always so long?

Grace is leaving just as I reach the front door. I open my mouth, but she beats me to it.

"Yes, she's in. No, she probably doesn't want to see you. And, honey?" she whispers, stepping forward. "Don't believe everything you read."

She kisses my cheek and leaves the front door open. A small smile twitches her lips as a black car rumbles up the drive. I stare at her.

"It's open. Your choice." She smiles wider and gets into the car, turning to face the front.

My choice. Like there's a choice other than walking through that front door and staying until Leah sees sense. Until she sees that she's…something…to me.

I close the front door behind me and check every room downstairs. It's empty, so I take the stairs two at a time. Then I knock on her bedroom door twice, and when there's no answer, I shove it open.

"Leah?"

"Corey?"

I turn around. She's standing in the doorway of her room at the end of the hall, her space, and as soon as my eyes meet hers, she steps forward. The door slams behind her, and she fumbles with a key to lock it.

"What are you doing here?" She doesn't move from the end of the hall. Even wearing sweatpants and a tank top, her hair shoved messily on top of her head, she's fucking beautiful.

"Who was that? Last night?"

"It isn't your business." She puts the key in her pocket, the shake of her hand betraying her calm words.

"It is. It's every bit my fuckin' business."

"You decided it had nothing to do with you when you walked away from me, so no, it isn't, thank you."

I cross the hall in three long strides and stop in front of her. "You're mine, Leah, so you'll find that it is my business. Now, who the fuck was it?"

"Not. Your. Business," she repeats, her eyes steady on mine.

My lips crush to hers, my hand cupping her jaw. Her body jolts, and I step forward, pinning her to the door. She raises her hands to push me away, but I grip her wrists and flatten her hands against the door. The whole time, our mouths move together, desperately, fervently.

"Tell me again that it isn't," I growl quietly. "Go on."

"It isn't!" She fights my hold and I let her go. She steps around me and walks to her room. "None of me is your business. Not my mind, not my body, not my actions. You walked away, Corey. You made that decision."

"You told me to go!"

"Well, you weren't supposed to!" she yells, turning back to me. "You weren't supposed to fucking leave. You were supposed to tell me to shut up, that you were sorry, that you didn't mean it. Damn it!" She slaps her hand against the door and turns to it. Then she rests her forehead against the wood. "You were supposed to tell me that you care."

I stare at her, leaning hopelessly against the door. I'm fucked if that's what 'Go. Get out. Leave now,' actually means. 'Cause, shit…

"You think I don't care?"

"How can you? The way you treated me…" She shakes her head. "I can't, Corey. Every word you said proved to me that I really am just a toy to you. You don't disrespect someone you care about."

"So you went to find someone else. Is that how it works?"

"Yes!" She looks at me. "Yes. It is. Because when one guy is an asshole, there's another nice one out there who will treat me right."

The thought that she was with someone makes me sick. Physically fucking sick. I walk to her and pull her against me, burying my nose in the sweet softness of her hair.

"How are you so sure?" I ask quietly, lowering my mouth to her ear. "Did he make you feel like I do? Tell me, darlin'. Did his kiss set on your body on fire? Did he make you tremble with one touch? Did he run his hands all over your skin and skim his fingers up the insides of your thighs to your tight pussy? Did he make you breathless with pleasure? Did he make you feel even half as good as I do? Because if not, then he definitely isn't fuckin' treatin' you right."

"You couldn't treat a sunflower right," she breathes, keeping her eyes trained on the floor.

"You can't give a flower an orgasm, darlin'." I touch my mouth to her jaw. "You haven't answered my question."

"He can give me respect."

"Still not answering my question."

"I don't know!" she snaps, finally looking up at me.

"Interesting. Why's that?"

"Because he didn't touch me!"

"Really? What a fuckin' gentleman."

"I stopped him, you asshole!" She shoves at my chest, but it fails. Instead, she wraps her fingers around my shirt. "I couldn't do a damn thing because you pissed me off so badly."

"You couldn't do it because you're mine." I drop my face to hers. Our lips are a breath apart, so close that I can feel them brush when I speak. "You couldn't do it because your body belongs to me. Every part of you belongs to me, Leah. You can't do a goddamn fuckin' thing unless it's with me."

"I hate you," she whispers, turning her head away.

"But you're still mine."

"Then why did you go?"

"You told me to," I answer. "You think I wanted to? You think I wanted to fuckin' turn around and leave you, babe? You think it didn't gut me to see you with tears in your eyes?"

"I think you didn't care. You still don't. That you're here on some jacked-up level of your game."

"I care about you, Leah. I care about you more than I've ever cared about anyone."

She lets go of my shirt and puts some distance between us. "Prove it," she says softly. "If you really do care, you'll do whatever it takes to make me believe you. If you want me that badly, it won't matter."

Shit—if only she knew how much I want her. If only she could fathom for just one single fucking second how badly I want her.

"You owe me three days." I brush my thumb down her cheek. "My original offer still stands. Except this time, I'm not promising to walk away. This time, you have to promise to leave. But only if you still don't trust me. I won't leave again."

Leah swallows, and a long moment passes. "You have one week," she whispers to the floor. "That was the deal. I'm not gonna make it easy for you, but you have your week. Then I can go."

"You can go. But you won't."

Her eyes travel up my body to mine. "You're so certain."

"I believe in my epic powers of seduction and flawless charm."

A smile tugs at her lips. "Not everything we believe is real."

I grin and close the distance between us. "You're right. But some things are, and this is one of them."

"We'll see."

"We always do," I murmur, covering her mouth with mine.

chapter SEVENTEEN

Leah

I stare at my mom, furious at her. Just because Corey and I are talking again doesn't mean she's off the hook. I also don't care that she's scrambling for Tylenol because she had one too many glasses of champagne last night.

"Please stop looking at me like you're my mother and I broke curfew," she grumbles, shaking two pills from the bottle.

"I'm not, but you did," I tease her, sipping my coffee. "You came in at seven a.m.!"

"Alex had some extra champagne and we decided it would be easier if I stopped over last night."

"Riiiiiight. Easier. Is that what you call sex when you get old?"

Mom chokes on her water. "Leah!"

"Oh, whatever. I'm twenty-two. You stayed at your boyfriend's house and got drunk. Mom, please. Don't insult me."

"You're not supposed to say these things to me. I'm your mother."

"I'm sorry." I set my mug down and look at her innocently. "I hope you had a wonderful time with Alex last night. Cole tells me the spare bed is very comfortable."

Mom's lips twitch. "Don't sass me, young lady."

"I'm mad at you. I'll sass you if I want to."

"Mad at me? What for?" Her eyes twinkle.

"You know exactly what, you witch!" I grab a grape from my bowl and throw it at her. "Letting Corey in last night?"

"Right. But you're friends now, aren't you?"

"We're not friends."

"So you're sleeping with him."

"I thought we weren't supposed to talk about sex."

"Did he stay over?"

"Mom. Seriously."

"Are you using condoms?"

"Mom!"

"Do you want me to stop by the drugstore for you?"

"They're cheaper on Amazon, but whatever. Oh my God." I cover my eyes. "Macey said so. Double whatever. This is so wrong!"

Mom laughs and sits opposite me. "See? It's not nice."

I look at her dead-on. "We're not sleeping together, he went home around midnight, and there are condoms not being used in my nightstand. Okay?"

"Thank you. And for the record, I did not spend the night in Alex's spare room."

"Thanks, Mom. Now I have all kinds of sick images in my mind."

"Well, at least we cleared everything up." She nods. "But I won't apologize for letting him in. He thought you came home with…"

"Liam."

"Liam last night. You thought he didn't care. He was there, and you got all of your drama out of the way. Now, maybe you'll both stop playing around and just start dating."

My laptop rings with a Skype call from Quinn. "We both know that dating Corey Jackson isn't a good thing."

"Who's dating Corey Jackson?"

I look at the screen. "No one is. It's just…hypothetical."

"Awesome. So you had fun at Disneyland?"

"What the— Mom, did you tell him?"

"She didn't tell me anything, darling. I worked it out all by myself. I love a good gossip rag, you know. They make wonderful toilet reading." Quinn beams.

"It's the morning for bad images, isn't it?" I rub my hand down my face. "I assume that, since you're calling, you finalized my designs."

"I did." He claps his hands. "I'm on my cell so I can show you them. Let me know what you think."

The camera angle changes. I wave to Mom and she comes around the island to look over my shoulder.

Quinn focuses on the first outfit: a white, knee-length dress teamed with a dark jacket and brown scarf. Then the next: a pantsuit accented with elaborate stitching in the shape of a tree on the inner leg. Next, another dress, this time an evening gown, glittering with gems. A skirt teamed with a dark-brown leather jacket, a yellow necktie, and long boots.

I swallow. This… This is it. This is the product of my hard work over the last six years. This is what I stayed up late designing, what I dreamed about when I finally got to sleep. My own collection rolling out in front of me.

This is everything I won't see in two weeks.

My stomach sinks. They're so close to being perfect. Quinn has done them fabulously, but they're not mine. I'd tie the necktie a little tighter, lift the hem another half inch on the skirt, do up another button on the jacket.

This is it, and it hurts.

"They're amazing," I say softly when the camera clicks back. My phone rings and I ignore it. "Thank you. For bringing them to life."

"You brought them to life, Leah darling. I just gave them breath."

"Thank you," I whisper. My phone shrills again and Mom passes it to me. Corey's name appears on screen. "Can I have a minute?" I ask Quinn. He nods and I get up. "Hello?"

"Hey. Are you busy?"

"Er, kind of."

"Will you be in around ten minutes?"

"Not really."

"Good." There's shuffling. "I called Coach—do you wanna come watch practice today?"

"Are you serious?" I shriek a little.

"Hot football fan girl," Corey sighs. "Yes. I told him you were my good-luck charm. I fucked everything up yesterday."

"That's why they call it practice." I laugh. "I'm in my pajamas."

"So get dressed. I'm leaving in a few minutes and I'm already running late. All right?"

"I guess. Do you still have the stupid wig?"

"Fuck the wig," he hisses. "The guys won't say a thing. Just put sunglasses or something on."

I swallow. "Okay. See you in a few minutes." Then I hang up and go back to the island. "Hey," I say to Quinn. "Is that all you needed me for?"

"Who was that?" he asks. "And where are you running off to?"

"No one, and nowhere."

"Why are you blushing?"

"I'm not. Oh my God!"

He grins. "That's all I needed you for, darling. Go have fun on your date with Corey Jackson."

I walk backward, pointing my finger at the screen. "Not. A. Date."

~

"So, how's this for a date?" Corey asks as I climb into his Range Rover.

"This isn't a date."

"Shit. I was hoping for brownie points."

My lips twitch. "You get brownie points, cowboy, but it's not a date."

"Is it a date if I do this?" He leans forward, grabbing my neck and kissing me firmly.

"No," I mumble against his mouth.

"Is it a date if there's a guaranteed orgasm at the end of it?"

"No." I sit back and look at him. "That's extra brownie points. And I thought you were late."

He laughs and puts his foot down. "I am. Some chick kept me up late last night."

"Oh? Who is the poor girl?"

His eyes flit to me. "You're hilarious, babe. Really."

"There's a spot of dirt on your car, by the way. Right under the hood." I stroke the leather seat.

"How the fuck did you see it there?"

"It's bird shit." I smile widely.

He turns to me, his lips twisted in annoyance. "If you're fucking with me, I'm gonna slap your ass, 'cause I know you hate that."

"I don't hate it. And I'm just saying that she's dirty."

"Darlin', you're here so I can concentrate, not to piss me off."

"Then we probably shouldn't mention my underwear."

His fingers flex against the steering wheel. "You're right. Or I'll have ideas of your pretty little ass hugged by those lace panties you like to wear."

"I'm wearing pink today," I say casually.

"What kind?"

"Of panties? Lace ones."

"Shit. But no. What kind of pink."

"That would be telling, and since you're going to do your best to find out later, I don't want to spoil your fun."

"Shame. I like you in white." He shoots me a heated look.

I grin. I'm not wearing pink at all. I'm wearing white, but he doesn't need to know that. And hey. I did warn him that I wouldn't make it easy for him.

"Wait. What if I don't like pink?" he asks, parking in the Vipers' stadium parking lot.

"Then your practice is about to get a whole lot more productive, isn't it?" I grin, pushing my door open. "I have to admit, my ass looks way better in white than pink."

"You're wearing white, aren't you?"

"No."

He grabs his bag and slings it over his shoulder. "I can see your bra strap, and I bet you're the kind of girl who always wears matching underwear."

"What gives you that idea?"

He slips his arm around my waist and leans in. "Because you've got class, Leah Veronica, and classy girls wear matching sets."

"Come across many of them, have you?"

"None. Until you."

"Sweet-talker."

"I warned you about my charm." He winks and kisses the side of my head. "You know how to get to the field, right? I've gotta go get ready to practice."

"Practice what? Throwing an interception?"

His hand connects with my ass. Sharply.

I squeak.

"Watch your mouth. I can think of several ways to silence it."

"Hey. I've seen you throw enough interceptions."

"You wanna get on the field and do a better job?"

"Nah. I don't wanna show you up. That would be embarrassing."

He catches me in his arms. "You'd show me up everywhere if only you'd go out in public with me. I guarantee that, when you do, everyone will look at you before they look at me."

I mock gasp. "Oh no. How will your ego cope?"

"It knows I'm the one who'll get to fuck you," he murmurs, closing the distance between our lips. "Again and again. That's all it needs to know."

I smile against his mouth. "Are you practicing? You know making out with me won't win you the Super Bowl, don't you?"

"Couldn't have said it better myself." Reid opens the door behind us. "Corey, Coach said to get your ass on that field if you want to play any games this season."

Corey laughs. "Because he's gonna play Anderson over me."

"He's thrown less interceptions than you." I whistle as I link arms with Reid.

He laughs and tugs me toward the field.

Corey shoots me a look. "Get your hands off my girl, North!" he yells at Reid, disappearing into the locker rooms.

"His girl, huh?" Reid looks down at me.

"It's easier to let him think what he wants." I shrug.

"True that. Ever been here before?"

"In the stadium? Sure. I've held a season ticket since I was seven. Cole's dad used to bring us." I look around the majestic building, at the large, green field, and the endless seats.

"Cole? Dalton?"

"Yep."

"You know"—Corey steps between me and Reid—"Anderson spent less time on the field than I did last season."

I roll my eyes. "I know, but look at your ratios. He has the better track record, s'all I'm saying. You need to figure your shit out, cowboy."

"Oh, man." Reid laughs loudly. "Coach, can we get this chick on our sideline on game days this season? She's brilliant." Reid cocks his thumb back to me.

"What is it with you and my interceptions?" Corey stares me down.

I shrug a shoulder. "You gotta work on it, okay? I'm bored of seeing you throw points away. Keep doing it and you'll probably find you'll be getting yourself off a lot over the next few months."

"She's hired," a graying man I recognize as Lincoln Sparks, the L.A. Vipers' coach, laughs. "Lincoln Sparks. And you must be Leah, the girl who drove my quarterback halfway to insanity yesterday."

I shake his hand. "I assure you, sir, he makes me far crazier."

"I can believe it." He turns to Corey. "Well? Get your ass on the field, Jackson."

I smile at Corey and he wraps an arm around my neck, pulling me into him. His lips brush my temple.

"It's a good fuckin' thing you're my favorite girl in the

world, Leah Veronica." The words are whispered in my ear seconds before he runs onto the field to practice.

I can't help the smile that curls my lips as I watch him go.

He knows what to say and when to say it. Maybe he does have some kind of charm after all. It sure as hell isn't flawless, but it's there. And those words are tingling through me right now.

I put my purse on the bottom row of seats and sit down. I can't believe I'm actually watching them practice. It's kind of surreal, something I've wanted to do for years. How many people can say that they've done this?

I watch them run through several basic plays without contact. If any of them got injured this season… It doesn't bear thinking about. Last year, we were close—so damn close—to lifting the trophy, to being the champions. Then we watched our chance shatter right before our very eyes.

Of course, there are the backup players, but if they were that good, they wouldn't be backup.

Lincoln moves backward and leans against the wall separating me and the field. "What are they doing wrong?"

"Excuse me?" I look at him.

"What are they doing wrong?" he repeats. "Every time Corey throws to Trent, they fuck up. You look like a girl who knows her stuff."

I raise an eyebrow. "You know exactly what they're doing wrong."

"I know. I just want to see the look on Corey's face when he gets his play instructions from a female."

My lips curve. "I wasn't paying that much attention, to be honest."

"Again," he says into his mic then turns to me. "Watch now."

I turn my attention to the field and watch as Corey throws to Trent. Sure enough, the ball goes sailing past him and he kicks the field. Corey's arms go in the air, and I hear a faint "What the fuck, man?" sail across to us.

"Trent isn't turning soon enough, and he isn't getting into

enough space. It doesn't matter how the defense lines up—he has a crap-ton of space on either side." I shrug my shoulders. "And it wouldn't kill Corey to keep the ball in his hand for longer than two seconds. He has legs to move."

Lincoln smiles widely and relays that into Corey's earpiece. He nods. "Oh, and your girlfriend said you can move your ass before you throw." Lincoln winks at me.

"I'm not his girlfriend," I mutter.

Corey turns, and I grin.

"Right." His coach laughs next to me. "He said he'll try to remember that from the girl with a fashion degree."

I need you. Now.

I look up from Cole's text to Corey. "Take me home. I have to go to Cole's."

"What?"

"Just…hang on and take me home." I hit reply. *What's up?*

Check Google alerts. Your mom will have pinged.

Wait, what? I bring up my browser, sign into Google, and bring up the alerts. Sure as hell, there's a whole list of them—all within the last half an hour.

"What's she done now?" I mutter, clicking on the top link.

HACKER TARGETS HOLLYWOOD.

"What the…" I scroll down and read the article. Pictures, documents, e-mails—all exposed. All spread across the Internet, hacked from the backup cloud of people's phones. My mom is threatened, my best friend is exposed… "Shit. Shit!"

"What is it?"

"Fuck my house. Drive to Bel Air. Turn off now!" I smack the dashboard.

"Whoa—is everything okay?"

"No. No, no, no." Guilt eats at me.

Cole doesn't do pictures—at least not naked ones—but we dared him once. He crashed girls' night and we dared him to take a full-frontal pic and send it. He did on the condition that Macey showed him her tits. She never did, but she got the picture. It was deleted, but…

"Fucking asshole!"

Corey reaches over and slides his hand around my thigh. "Where's his house?"

"Third turn, the one with the giant apple trees," I mumble, looking out of the window.

Corey pulls up, and I wrench my way out of the car. Then I run up the driveway and bang on the front door. Cole answers with a weak smile, and it hits me straight in the gut.

I wrap my arms around his neck and hug him tight. "I'm sorry. Shit, this is my fault."

"Why? Did you hack Hollywood's stars?"

I shake my head and let him go. "But I made you take the picture." I walk past him.

"Hey, you didn't push the button. I did. It was a laugh—even if Macey still owes me a tit pic. I had no idea it was saved to the cloud."

"I can't believe you were hacked! What kind of bullshit is this?" I run my fingers through my hair. "Who else did they get?"

Cole goes to the laptop and brings up the article. He reels off the names of several of the biggest movie stars and singers. "My agent called me. She has alerts on all of us—the second my picture went up, she knew."

I swallow. "What are you gonna do?"

He shrugs. "Get laid more often?"

"Cole!" I stare at him. "I'm here feeling guilty because we made you take the pic and you're thinking about your dick?"

He holds his hands up. "Hey, it was a good picture. It's a legitimate thought."

I blink. My best friend: the only hacked person in Los Angeles thinking about how much more sex he's going to get.

"Seriously though," he continues, quieter. "I don't know. We're negotiating for Chasing Tucker. It'll be my first big lead and this could ruin that. My dad's out now seeing if he can do any damage control, but short of finding the hacker and wringing his neck, I'm not sure he can do much."

"You can sue," Corey says.

I had no idea he was here. I thought he was still in the car.

"There's no one to sue," I reply.

He nods. "You can sue whoever operates your cloud. They're supposed to be safe. It's an invasion of privacy."

"Right." Cole brightens. "I'll call my dad and get him to call his lawyer."

"I have a better idea." Corey pulls his phone out. "You got somewhere I can make a call?"

"Sure. Go through to the kitchen." Cole waves over his shoulder, looking at me.

I shrug, perching on the sofa. Corey winks at me then walks past, his hair still wet from his post-training shower.

"What happened here?" Cole motions between us.

"We…made friends," I answer vaguely.

"So, you're dating."

"Not defined." I crane my neck around to the kitchen to see him. "Is it bad if I go spy on him? I wanna know what he's doing."

"He's making a call," Cole replies dryly.

"Now I get why you're up for the lead in a romantic comedy. You're fucking hilarious."

He laughs, and I'm glad. I'd rather have the laughter over the sad look that was in his eyes a few minutes ago.

"Sorry," I whisper again, looking down. "You want me to get my mom to make sure you keep the contract?"

Cole nudges my arm with his elbow. "Fuck off, Leah. I don't need your charity. I'll go in tomorrow and charm the hell out of the producers. I swear, Shannon Hunt has a crush on me."

"Ew! Shannon's, like, fifty."

"I'm not against the older woman."

"Ew, Cole!" I slap his thigh.

He laughs just as Corey walks back into the front room, pocketing his phone. He stops in the middle of the room and grins.

"What did you just do?" I ask suspiciously. I'm not sure I

like how his eyes are glinting.

His smile widens, and he walks toward Cole. "You got your phone?"

Cole nods and hands it to him. I frown as Corey inputs something before handing it back.

"That's the number for my dad's lawyer, Neil Harmon," he says. "He said to call him and arrange a meeting. He'll waive fifty percent of his fee since you're a friend of mine."

I blink at Corey. Quickly. Because—what?

"For real?" Cole stands up. "I'm not fussed about the waiver, but seriously—thanks, man."

They shake hands then do that guy hug thing where they smack each other's backs, and the whole time, I'm sitting here, staring at them.

Is this the fucking Twilight Zone? Did I get sucked into a parallel universe?

"I gotta go meet my mom for dinner, but I'll call you when I've seen Neil, all right?"

I jolt my eyes from Corey to Cole. "Of course." I hug him. "Say hi to your mom for me."

"Nah. If I do that, she'll make you do dinner again. I won't make you suffer through that shit, too."

I wrinkle my nose. "New boyfriend?"

"Boy toy," he replies with disgust, letting us out of the front door. "Hey, Corey. Really, thanks."

"No worries." Corey smiles, wrapping his arm around me and guiding me to his car. Then he opens the door and I get in without saying a word.

I'm confused. I don't know—I don't understand—why he'd do that. For whatever reason, he hates Cole. At least, I always thought he did. But now…

I stay silent as we drive out of Bel Air and toward the Hills. Corey surprises me at every turn. There's always something. It's not always good, I admit, but it's something. I'm starting to wonder if, one day, he'll surprise me so much that my heart will just give up the game and go kaput.

And I don't mean the romantic kind of kaput. I mean the

'what the hell? I'm done' kind of kaput.

I get out of the car at his house and grab my purse from by my feet. Chewing the inside of my cheek, I follow him inside and text my mom to make sure she's seen the threat the hacker made when he posted the pictures. But I can't linger on it. My brain is so fuzzy.

Is Corey using Cole's misfortune to prove to me that he cares? Is it all a manipulation game, or does he genuinely want to help him?

I drop my purse at the side of the sofa and kick my shoes off. Corey walks into the kitchen and grabs the phone.

"Pizza?" he asks.

I nod, not looking at him.

"Pepperoni?"

I nod again.

"Cheese? Stuffed crust?"

I nod for a third time, and I can't even find it in me to smile. He just got my favorite pizza in one shot, like a fucking pro, but I'm so hung up on this Cole thing that I can't even like that. Or—hey. Maybe it's Corey's favorite pizza and he's taken advantage of my silence to order it.

I don't really know him at all.

"You all right?" He walks over to me and puts a can of Diet Coke in front of me.

I nod. I feel like a fucking motorized toy. Nod, nod, nod. Over and over. I'll nod my head off my neck soon.

"Sure?"

Again with the nodding. Jesus. I just don't trust myself to speak. It would be easy. So easy to speak. So easy to ramble a bunch of words that mean a lot but make no sense at all.

Corey sits next to me and hooks his arm over the back of the sofa. His fingers play with my hair, and as he grabs the remote and turns the TV on, a shiver cascades down my spine. I fail to mask it, because his hand stills for a second.

Even the hair-playing is messing with me. Sending tingles from my scalp and across my skin. It's a surreal feeling, especially when I was so angry with him forty-eight hours ago.

And now… Now, I have to admit to myself that I don't want to be anywhere else but here.

Even if he does have me mind-fucked.

"Seriously. What's up?" He shifts so he's facing me.

I raise one shoulder, playing with my fingers in my lap.

"Babe," he says in a low voice. "I'm pretty sure I didn't fuck up again already, so what is it?"

"Why'd you do it?" I look up at him, letting my hand relax. "Call your dad's lawyer?"

"That's what's buggin' you? That I did something *right*?"

"I… Yeah."

"You confuse the fuck out of me, darlin'."

"I'm a woman. Confusing guys is what I do."

Corey shifts a little more and cups my cheek with his hand. "Look at me."

I shake my head, but he fights it and I find myself looking at him anyway.

"You panicked. Do you know that? When Cole texted you, I've never seen you so afraid. You yelled at me, Leah. When you realized what had happened, you screamed at me to drive to Bel Air because you needed to fix it. Then we got there, you talked, and I realized what was happening. And, babe"—he strokes his thumb across my cheek—"the second you knew you couldn't help, it hurt me. You looked so fuckin' helpless. Your best friend was hurting and there was nothin' you could. But I could."

"But why?" I whisper, my eyes finding his. Blue, bright, gorgeous. "Why did you do it? You didn't have to."

"If Cole's happy, I know you are. I knew that, if he could smile, you could, too. And, Leah, if there's anything I'm afraid of, it's that I won't get to see you smile again." Corey leans forward, his nose brushing mine. "So I did what I could."

"Neil isn't waiving the fee, is he?"

"What?"

"You're paying it, aren't you?" I pull his hand from my face. "For me."

"No. For Cole. Because he doesn't deserve this shit. It's a

violation."

"But you're doing it for him, for me."

"Yes," Corey admits. "Because I'm selfish, too. Because I want to look at you and see you smile. I've seen you sad all too much the last few days, and I don't want that again."

I swallow and edge away from him. Not because I don't want him to touch me. I do. God, I want him to fold me into his arms and hold me until every ounce of confusion is swept out of my body.

"I want him to be okay," he says softly, letting me have my distance. "Because as helpless as you felt, shit, babe. I felt helpless, too, because you stood there staring into space, hopin' for some kind of fucking miracle. The least I could do was be the miracle."

I exhale slowly through my nose, emotion building, swirling, going totally crazy inside me. Then, without another thought, I lean forward, my lips sealing over his.

His arms go around me firmly, and he pulls me on top of his lap. I straddle him and wind my fingers into his hair. His lips are hot against mine, searing into me. Sparks flow through my veins with every sweep of his mouth, and I push myself toward him, further and further.

Because, oh my God. I know Neil Harmon. I know his fees. Mom has used him in the past. For Corey to pay half his fees... Six figures for approximately a month's work is standard.

Instead of the doubt I felt earlier, there's a renewed vigor inside me. As my fingers tug Corey's hair and my lips caress his and his hands tease beneath the hem of my shorts, something else ignites inside me.

The need to know him. The real him. It's stronger than before. Now it's all-encompassing. I need to know Corey Jackson. What makes him tick. Why he has to be the arrogant asshole the media adores portraying him as when I know he isn't.

"Leah..." My name falls from his lips in a thick whisper, and he flips me onto my back. He easily slides between my legs, his hard cock straining against the tightness of the denim separating us. I feel it rubbing against me, teasing my clit, hinting at more.

I hook my legs around his back. In this moment, the game can fuck itself. The rules can fold and anything from outside can go find something else better to do. In this moment, it is me and Corey, desire and lust, desperation and insanity, all coiled into a throbbing ball of impending pleasure, begging for release.

All there is is us. Leah and Corey. Passionate touches and feverish kisses and maybe some hope, too. It's an intoxicating mix, a dangerous one, but one I want to play with.

For the first time, I want to play with danger. I want to tease the edges of our connection and see if it's really as real as it feels.

His hands… They slide beneath my shirt. His fingertips are soft yet rough against my skin, and they're probing, digging into my skin in a deliciously painful way. My brain says that it's because he needs to hold on, too, because he can't do anything else but hold on.

And for now, I will believe.

Because.

"Fuckin' pizza," he breathes against my mouth.

Every inch of my body is aching against him, for him, with him, but I sigh as the doorbell rings again.

Corey parts my legs and gets up. But before he goes, he grips the sofa, and still leaning over, he whispers, "We aren't fuckin' done here, babe."

I touch his face before he disappears. His eyes burn into mine, blazing bright blue.

And I whisper back, "I'm counting on it."

chapter EIGHTEEN

Corey

I can feel her skin, silky and smooth, like perfect satin, beneath my fingertips. My hand ghosts across a soft curve until it hits lace. The rough material is enough to jolt my from my hazy half-sleep into full consciousness.

Leah shifts, curling her arm around her body until her fingers wrap around my forearm. I shuffle closer to her, relishing the silence. Relishing the feel of her in my arms, still, relaxed.

There's a sense of calmness in me. I've always been the crazy one, the wild one. I've never stopped to smell the roses or think about something other than right the hell now. I've never stopped to think about anything seriously.

Except football. The game was always the number-one thing in my life. Nothing else meant a thing. It was all fleeting.

Until this girl.

Until she handed me my ass, sassing me royally, and told me where the fuck to get off on the dickhead train.

Leah Veronica has crawled beneath my skin. With every word she speaks, she inches a little deeper. Every time she laughs, she gets a firmer hold on me. Every day, she grips a little tighter, cementing herself in my life as the most important thing.

She cares. I care.

That's the problem with playing a game. That's the problem when you set out to play without knowing the rules. No one can win. At least they can't win the original prize. Because over time, that prize changes. It becomes more than a carnal need, than a fleeting hour of slick flesh meeting and pleasure reigning.

No. It becomes something stronger. Something so fucking real, so solid, that you can barely grip it. Something so real that it can collapse as easily as it was built.

The prize isn't her body. It isn't her pussy, her pleasure, or her nails in my back.

The prize is her heart. It's the sparkle in her eye, the tremble of her hand, and the security of her in my arms.

The game is convincing her that I'm everything she could ever need.

"What did the student say to the teacher?" she mutters, half asleep.

"What?"

"Stop asking me to find your 'x.' I don't know 'y' she left."

My lips curve. "That was fuckin' awful."

"I know." Leah opens her eyes fully. "But you were looking at me like I was a math problem, so I thought it was appropriate."

"Math is never appropriate at seven a.m."

"It's seven in the morning? Ugh. Go back to sleep, you weirdo." She attempts to roll away from me, but I leap on top of her and straddle her. "What are you doing?" she moans, covering her eyes with her arm.

"Some of us have a job to go to." I touch a light kiss to her lips.

"Yeah, well, some of us have sleeping to do. You're seriously disrupting that." She bats at my head. "And you don't have a job. You have a ball to throw around."

"And team tapes to study, and tactics to discuss, and weights to lift…"

"All right, so you're the all-American football star." She drops her arm. "I, however, am not. I'm a twenty-something girl with a love of sleeping in."

"Yet you run almost every day."

"I run when I wake up at, like, ten. Macey used to run at five. That was the first time I seriously questioned our friendship," she says, her blue eyes wide. "The last time was when she went to Reid's party with the sole objection of sleeping with Jack."

"I admire a girl who knows what she wants," I murmur against her.

"So, you don't admire me?"

"No, babe. You want me. That's more than admirable. That's heroic."

She laughs, pushing her head back into the pillow. "Oh my God. You're something else, Corey Jackson. For real."

I grin slowly. "Well, duh. I'm sexy, charming, and funny. You don't get guys like me that often."

"Thank fuck!" Her laugh tinkles now, wrapping around me, making my slide my fingers into her hair. "If there were any more than one of you, I'd go crazy!"

"Hey." I descend my lips onto hers. "You know there'll never be another me. I'm too fucking fantastic."

"Yes," she whispers. "That's it. You're so fucking fantastic no one can live up to you."

"You sassin' me, darlin'?"

"I'm always sassing you, cowboy. I'm just waiting until you realize it."

I smile, and the curve of my lips matches hers. "I love your sass. It makes you sexy."

"So, I'm only sexy when I sass you?"

"Why do you hafta twist everything I say, huh?"

"I'm a woman. I'd twist a steel rod given half a chance."

"Shit. Please don't. My cock likes being straight."

She laughs again. "You're awful, you know that? Just because you have two heads doesn't mean you should think with them both."

"Babe, if I thought with them both, I'd fuck you before I let you sleep in my bed."

She wriggles her hips. "Feels like he's ready to sass *me* for sleeping in it without fucking you in it."

"When you put it that way..."

"Don't you have to practice not throwing interceptions?"

"Bitch." I tickle her sides and she writhes beneath me. It does nothing for my growing erection, because fuck, her pussy rubs against my dick, her legs clench, and she grips my biceps.

"Corey! Cut that shit out!" She lightly slaps my shoulder then sighs. "Well, now you've woken me up. I hope you plan to cook me breakfast."

I sit up and pull her with me. "Shit. Someone's demanding in the morning."

"Take a note, cowboy. Don't wake me up."

"You mean you'll let me sleep with you again?"

She darts her eyes to mine, and she smiles almost shyly. "Depends how nice you are to me."

"Is that an anagram for 'every night'?"

"Oooh, someone's getting cocky."

"Someone has a cock to be cocky with." I slide my hands to her hips and yank her forward. "He'd like it if you stayed every night."

"Would you?" she asks quietly. Her nails trail light scratches up my arms, and her eyes follow the movements.

I wrap my arms around her so tight that her body is flush against mine. "Every night," I whisper honestly. "You up for the challenge?"

"For five more nights?"

"And whatever happens after."

"Corey Jackson, are you asking me to be your girlfriend in some jacked-up way?"

"Are you telling me you'd be comfortable in public with me?" I cup the back of her neck and brush my nose against hers.

"No," she answers honestly, letting out a long breath. Her hands still at the base of my back. "I wouldn't be comfortable. But if you wanted me to try, then maybe I could."

"Leah Veronica," I murmur, my mouth running across her jaw to her neck. "Are you telling me you'd like to be my girlfriend?"

Her throat bobs as she swallows, and her fingers grip me a little tighter. "You gotta stop asking me questions I can't answer."

"Can't answer, or won't?"

"Maybe both."

I kiss the spot beneath her ear. I want to push her. Fuck, I want to tear the answer from her. I want to wine and dine her. I want to wrap my arms around her and kiss the ever-loving motherfucking life out of her right in front of a photographer.

I want the whole damn world to know that this sassy, gorgeous, confident woman belongs to me. And me alone.

I get up and throw some sweatpants on. We've known each other for all of a couple of weeks, and they've been the most harrowing two weeks of my life.

"What do you want for dinner tonight?" I ask her when she pads into the kitchen behind me.

"How very domestic of you," she replies, amused.

I turn around to look at her. She's wearing one of my Vipers T-shirts, and it swamps her, the hem skimming her thighs. My eyes hover on the material moving against her skin as she walks.

"Corey. Hello?"

"What was the question?" I look up. "You're distracting me."

Leah rolls her eyes and sits at the table. "I said 'surprise me.'"

"I don't have any candles and I've never bought a bunch of flowers in my life, so I think you're gonna be pretty disappointed, babe."

"Candles are overrated and flowers just die." She shrugs. "Just...decide on something for dinner and I'll figure out the rest, okay?"

"Got it." I pass her some toast. "What are you going to do today?"

"Work."

I pause and glance over my shoulder, the butter knife resting on my own toast. "I thought you didn't have a job."

Her eyes snap up. "I don't. My mom joked once that my work is looking for a job. It kind of stuck."

"Right." I look away but glance back. She doesn't notice my

eyes back on her, but I notice everything.

The long, quiet breath she lets out. The visible relaxation of her shoulders. The slight shake of her head.

And instantly, I know—Leah Veronica has a job.

One she's keeping secret.

Not for long.

Talk. She wants to fucking talk.

That's her plan for the evening. I cook dinner and then we talk. 'Get to know you' kinda talk.

My dick planned on a different kind of conversation.

"You're whipped, man. Completely pussy-whipped." Jack shakes his head.

"What does she even want to talk about?" I drop the controller next to me on the sofa. "I'm fuckin' awesome, I play football like a boss, and I'm hot as hell. What else could she want to know about me?"

"Don't ask me. Ask your girlfriend."

"Leah isn't my girlfriend." Kind of.

"Who the fuck are you kidding, Corey? You haven't so much as looked at another girl since you met her. She has dinner at your place all the time, you have sleepovers, and now, she wants to talk."

"That doesn't make her my girlfriend."

"So, you're gonna finally get in her pants then dump her?" Jack questions me, raising an eyebrow.

I run my tongue across my teeth. No. I'm probably gonna get in her pants then roll her over for another round.

"She's not my fucking girlfriend." I get up and grab a beer from the fridge. "Ask her yourself when she gets here."

"Ask me what?" Leah strolls into the front room and puts her hands on her hips.

"Dickhead over here"—I cock my thumb in Jack's direction—"reckons you're my girlfriend."

Her lips twitch and she turns to Jack. "That's real cute. Did you think of that all by yourself?"

He smirks. "Right after I left Macey's place again yesterday."

"You mean you managed to give a girl an orgasm and actually think after? I'm impressed." Leah perches on the arm of my sofa and stretches her legs out, just inviting me to stare at them. They go on forever, all long and tan and toned. I love looking at her legs and touching them, and I'd bet fucking anything that I'll love the feel of them around me. My waist. My neck.

"Right. I'm not sitting here and watching you undress her with your eyes." Jack stands.

"Suit yourself."

"Shall I pass a message on to Macey for you?" Leah smirks at him.

"Better not. Twice with the same girl is a fluke. But if I had time for the relationship shit, she'd be the one I'd tie down. She's a fucking animal in bed." He winks and goes, leaving Leah shaking her head.

"Do obnoxious bastards gravitate toward each other naturally, or is it just you two?" she asks, her eyes finding mine.

I grab her hands and tug her toward me. "Just us, babe. If there were any more of us, the city would explode."

I run my hands down her body and over her gorgeous curves. My fingers curve around her thighs and tickle the insides of them, slowly edging higher, and I brush a kiss to her neck.

"Stop it." She wriggles. "We haven't eaten yet. Or talked."

My fingertips ghost over the crotch of her jeans, making her shiver.

"Corey."

"Saying my name isn't the way to make me stop." My mouth covers hers.

"Corey!"

"Leah, every time you say my name, you're inviting me to fuck you. Do you realize that?" I kiss her harder.

"We're not"—kiss—"doing this." Kiss. "We're"—kiss—"supposed to be"—kiss—"eating and talking." Kiss.

"What about?"

"You."

"I'm boring."

Kiss.

"Corey! For God's sake!" She pushes up off me. "I want a real conversation. About you. About me. You know, with words?"

"Words are overrated."

"Oh? And sex isn't?"

"Hey, it's called body language for a reason."

She gives me a hard look. "I'm being serious."

"So am I." I sigh. "So am I."

"Drama queen." She rolls her eyes. "Well, while you and your dick are sitting here feeling sorry for yourselves, I'm going outside. Come and join me when you've A, cooked me food, and B, remembered how to word-speak, not sex-speak."

Fuck. I'm a guy. I don't do word-talking. I don't do heart-to-hearts and I sure as shit don't do life stories.

Yet my newest problem is that I'll do just about fucking anything for this girl.

I follow her to my yard and find her in my pool. She's floating on her back in a tiny string bikini that barely covers her breasts. My cock gets hard at the sight of her, and a groan escapes my mouth.

"What?" Leah swims to the side of the pool and gazes up at me.

I adjust my pants. "You want to talk to me and you're wearing that? Are you trying to fuckin' kill me?"

A smile pulls at the corners of her mouth. "It's kinda hot today. I wanted to cool off."

"And you couldn't wear a swimsuit or something? You had to pick this?"

"Should I take it off?" Her eyes are full of innocence, but the smirk on her lips is anything but.

"Take that off and I can promise you that the only talking you'll be doing is my screaming fucking name."

"I'll leave it on then. For now." Her smirk changes to a sassy smile, and the innocence in her eyes gives way to a playful spark that doesn't help the hard-on trapped by my jeans. She dips under the water, her blond hair fanning out behind her, and I turn back into the house.

There isn't a chance I'm getting in that pool in jeans. Besides, jeans and erections don't go together.

I change into swim shorts and head back outside. I feel her eyes on me as I walk toward the pool and sit on the edge. I feel them as they trace over my body, from my shoulders to the lightly defined 'v' muscle dipping below the waistband of my shorts. I feel the heat in them, the approving gaze.

"See something you like?"

Blue eyes crawl up my body slowly and meet mine. "I'm still deciding."

Of course she is. "Well, then. Now is a perfect time to have your talk."

"So it is."

"What do you want to talk about?" World's worst question right there. And not one I thought I'd ever ask.

Leah swims across the pool to me and slips between my legs. I hook my feet behind her back. She slides her arms around me and links her fingers, keeping herself afloat.

"You," she says softly.

"You know everything about me."

"No, I don't."

"Yeah, you do. You know I'm a shit-hot football player, that I'm an arrogant, self-confident dickhead, and that my seduction skills are sexy as fuck. What else do you need to know?"

"That's not everything, cowboy. I don't know anything about you before you became a Viper. I don't know what your favorite food is, your favorite movie, your favorite video game… I don't know what you do in your spare time, why you're a football player, how you grew up, why you grew up in Texas although your dad played here, why, of all the tattoos in the world, you got a tiger on your back…"

Jesus Christ. She wants a verbal autobiography. Shoulda written her an e-mail.

"No one knows any of that stuff. Believe it or not, I'm kind of a private guy."

And that's the truth. I might not be physically private, but when it comes to me, not many people really know me. Not even the guys. We're not like girls, where life stories are a requirement for fucking friendship. All we care about is if you like sports, you like girls, and you like beer. If you do, good job.

"But I want to know it," she replies, tracing her finger across my thigh.

"Why?"

"Because it's important to me."

She blinks up at me, her eyes wide and earnest, and I can see that it is. For some reason, she wants to know everything about me.

"Really? It's that important to you?"

She nods. "I've been thinking about what you said. And while I don't necessarily trust your motives in you asking me to be your girlfriend—"

"I never confirmed I was askin'."

"Precisely. But on the rare chance that you do, knowing you will make a difference, Corey. I want to know you. And I do mean the real you. You show me glimpses of him sometimes, and truth be told, I kinda really like him."

I run my fingers through her wet hair and let my arms come to rest on her shoulders. Jesus. Manipulator. Gorgeous fucking manipulator.

"Okay. But only because it's you."

A smile pulls at the edges of her lips. "You grew up in Dallas, right?"

"Yep."

"And?"

She's not gonna make this easy for me.

"And I had an easy childhood. My dad got drafted to the Vipers after winning the Heisman then married my mom. She lived out here until I was two. Then she decided she didn't want me to grow up influenced by Hollywood. So she moved us back to Texas, where my grandparents lived."

"But football was in your blood, right?"

I laugh. "My dad was the best quarterback in fifty years, and I lived in Dallas. I was throwing a ball before I was walking. A love of the game, natural skill, and money meant I went to the best college. We spent every summer in L.A. to be there with Dad during the preseason. When I was fourteen, I started spending my summers at their practices. I wanted to be my dad."

"What about your mom?"

I shrug. "Most of the time, she was with my baby sister, who whined at any chance about being in my shadow. She could have broken out if she'd wanted to. She had the same opportunities I did—private school, top college, private tutors—but by age sixteen, she realized she got just as much attention for being 'poor little Lottie' as she would for actually doing something, so she didn't bother. We're not close at all. She practically threw a party when I moved here permanently, never mind that she's at college in New York."

Leah rests her head on my thigh. "That's sad. That you're not close."

"Yeah, I guess, but it's always been that way. Even when I knocked out her ex-boyfriend for cheating on her, she still hated me."

"Nice. So I guess you haven't seen her since you moved here?"

"A few times. She goes to Dallas every break except for Christmas. Even then, she only stays a few days before flying out to stay with our grandparents."

"Wow." She looks up. "But to summarize: you were a privileged, little rich boy who grew up to be a privileged, self-entitled bastard, am I right?"

I run my fingers through her hair again and smirk. "Your words, babe."

"So now I know about you growing up."

"Yep. Are we done yet?"

"No. The tattoo."

I roll my eyes in a move that's so very her. "You gonna tell me about yours?"

"You noticed that?" A smirk curves her lips, and she shrugs a shoulder. "It says 'always believe.' Just…'cause, you know. Sometimes you forget to."

"Philosophical," I remark. "I got a tiger because it was my favorite animal as a kid. It was my twenty-first-birthday present to myself after the Vipers drafted me."

"Shouldn't you have gotten a Viper?"

"Probably, but it wouldn't look half as good on my back as the tiger."

"Okay. I get that." She smiles. "What's your favorite food?"

"Fucking hell, babe," I groan. "There are better uses for your mouth, you know?"

She smacks my thigh. "I'll answer if you do."

Hello, Leah's pinkie finger. Nice to meet you—it looks like I'm wrapped around you for the foreseeable fucking future.

"Twinkies," I reply.

"Twinkies?" Leah laughs. "Seriously?"

"What's wrong with Twinkies? When they announced they were taking them off the shelves, I went crazy and bought about fifty boxes. They're in the pantry, hidden on the top shelf."

"Okay, Twinkie King."

"What's yours?"

"Frozen yogurt. When I was eighteen, Mom asked me what I wanted for my birthday, and I said frozen yogurt. I was joking, but she's a regular comedian and bought a freezer full of fro-yo in all the flavors. It took me, like, a year to get through it all."

"Really? I never pegged you for a frozen yogurt girl."

"Everything you've pegged me for has been completely wrong, so I don't know why you're surprised."

"True."

She straightens up and hooks her fingers in my waistband. "Favorite movie?"

"Rocky. All of them. I met Sylvester Stallone when I was ten and it's the closest I've ever come to fainting. Yours?"

"Aw, fan boy cowboy." She grins. "I would pay to see that. And my favorite movie is Magic Mike."

"Oh, original. Real original." I run my hands down her back.

"You asked."

"I know, I know. Are we done now?"

"My next question was your boxer size."

I quirk an eyebrow. "Do I get your bra size?"

She smiles suggestively. "You get to guess it."

"Boxers are large," I say quickly and drop my eyes to her chest. "You realize I can't tell from looking though, right?"

"Sure you can. You're a guy. You have a scale or something in your head for bra sizes. You look at a pair of tits and you just know like it's a freaky psychic power." She wriggles out of my hold and floats across the pool.

"I need to make sure it's accurate by touching." I drop into the water and swim after her.

I come up behind her, and she tilts her head to one side, exposing her neck. Then I press a kiss to her bare, wet skin, my lips wiping away any lingering water droplets.

My hands slide up her stomach to her breasts. They fit in my hands perfectly, round and firm, and her nipples pebble as my fingertips graze over them. She lets out a long, heavy breath when my fingers slip beneath her bikini top, and she rests her head back on my shoulder.

"We're done talking, aren't we?" she whispers.

"Mhmm." I spin her in my arms.

Our lips lock together, and I untie the strings holding her bikini top to her. I tug on it and it comes away, leaving her bare breasts to press up against my chest.

She gasps into my mouth when her nipples rub my skin. My hair is wrapped around her fingers, and she moves her mouth against mine, every kiss increasing in intensity. As I hold her to me, the only parts of us I want bare so fucking badly are covered. My cock is hard against her thigh, throbbing almost painfully, ready and waiting to slip inside her tight pussy.

But she's still holding a part of herself from me. This is the last time I'm playing this game. This is the last time I plan to have her pressed against me and not fuck her after.

I lift her onto the side of the pool, get out, and pull her over to one of the lounge chairs. I push her down, and she looks up at me, her body soft beneath me, her bare breasts heaving with her frantic breaths, her eyes heavy and lidded.

She looks up at me, temptation embodied, sin and innocence…pleasure and torture in one fucking painfully beautiful package.

"You're beautiful, you know?" I whisper, leaning down over her. I cup her breast and flick my thumb across her nipple. "I'm not sure I've ever told you that."

"No, you…" she trails off when I close my lips around her other nipple and suck gently. "Haven't."

"Well, you are." I pepper kisses up her neck. "You're beautiful, and you're sexy, and you're gorgeous."

"Had to get 'sexy' in there, didn't you?"

I smile against her mouth and trail my fingers down her flat stomach. "Yep."

My fingers disappear inside her bottoms and rub along her wet pussy. She half gasps, half whimpers, and I slide two fingers inside her. She instantly tightens her muscles around me and lifts her hips toward me, a silent plea for more.

She clutches at the back of my neck as I move my fingers inside her. Her breath is hot on my skin as I kiss down her neck, and the tiny whimpers she's making are driving me fucking insane. I'd give anything to tear off those bottoms and replace my fingers with my cock, ready to tip her over the edge and back again. I want to fuck her so badly that it hurts, and the want only grows with each whimper that gets louder.

"And you're so close to perfection that it scares me," I murmur in her ear, flicking her clit with my thumb. "And I want to taste you. All of you. Every last inch of this gorgeous body needs my lips on it, Leah. Can you imagine that, babe? Can you imagine my lips and my tongue where my hand is right now? 'Cause I can, and I bet you taste fucking incredible."

She squeezes my fingers hard, her breath harsh and heavy, and a moan leaves her mouth when I push my fingers inside her deeper. She's so close to the edge. So fucking close…

I give her clit one last caress and take my hand from her.

"And when you're ready to feel that, just say the word."

Her eyes snap open and follow me as I casually stroll back into the house. I'm a bastard. A real bastard. But she shouldn't give if she can't take it. Right now, I imagine she feels a lot like how I've felt since my lips first touched hers.

"You fucking asshole, Corey Jackson!"

I smirk. And that right there is how you even the playing field.

chapter NINETEEN

Leah

Oh hell fucking no.

Hell. Fucking. No.

This jackass is not leaving me lying by his pool, naked, on the brink of an orgasm he has no intention of finishing. I want him so badly that I'm aching. My lips are aching to kiss him, my fingers are aching to touch him, and my body is aching to be wrapped up with his. *I hate him for it.* I've never felt this way. I know what he can he do to me and I want it.

Every part of my body wants to feel that release. I want the tingles across my skin where he touches me and the shiver down my spine when he kisses the back of my neck. I want my muscles to tighten when he runs his fingers across the tops of my thighs.

More. I want more, because I want more of him. I want to see the look in his eyes when *I* kiss *his* neck, when I run my hands across his stomach to the waistband of his pants and slip my fingers inside it. I want to know how his eyes look when I curl my fingers around his hardened cock, and I want to hear the breath escape his mouth when I wrap my lips around it.

Because I have never, ever wanted someone the way I do Corey. Equally, I've never had someone want me as much as he does. I've never had someone push me and push me until I've felt like I want to break, but he does that. He makes me want to break every single one of my own rules, and I will.

I never thought it would come to this. I never imagined my body would take over my mind where he's concerned, but it has—and rather spectacularly. Emotions haven't even really factored into the crazy and scary relationship we have.

It's all based on pure, carnal need.

I need to feel his body in a way so intense and raw that it scares me. And now?

We talked my way—and he's about to find out that I'm more than skilled at talking *his* way.

I run after him into the house. Hearing his footsteps on the stairs, I dart through the house and up them. I don't care that I've never been upstairs. The running shower water directs me to exactly where I need to be—his bedroom.

I burst through into the en suite in time to see him standing in front of the shower. Naked. All packed, tight, carved, and sculpted muscle, remaining drops of water from the pool running down his body to where his cock is standing to attention. It's long and large and perfect, veins drawing wiggled patterns down his shaft.

My clit throbs as if to remind me why I'm up here.

"You!" I storm forward and wrench his hand from the shower door. Then I slam it shut and turn. "Are a fucking asshole."

Corey smirks. "Welcome to how I've felt since I first looked at you."

"Good. Because you're about to carry me to your room and finish what you just started!"

His smirk drops. His eyes darken, and when he steps forward, his cock so close to brushing my lower stomach, a thrill runs through my body. "Leah Veronica, are you asking me to fuck you?"

"I don't ask, beg, or plead," I breathe. "I'm telling you to fuck me. And mark my words, Corey Jackson. I won't fucking do it again."

He opens his mouth, but it isn't to answer. He closes it over mine—harshly, almost—and grips my hips. Our bodies slam together, his cock pressing up against my stomach, his hands running all over my back and my ass.

And fuck. All I can focus on is the demanding movements of his lips against my own, the forceful way they caress mine, taking everything I have. I don't even know how this feels, how I'm supposed to explain it. I'm supposed to hate this, to not want it, but all I can think about is keeping him right here against me so I can keep feeling the jelly in my knees and the begging clenching of my pussy. I want to keep on feeling the tingles down my spine, the thump of my heart, the heat swamping my body, and the desperation clinging to him in my fingertips.

Corey pulls me back through to the bedroom, his grip never easing, his kiss just as forceful. Then we fall, together, onto the bed, a mass of tangled limbs, wet hair, and pure, unbridled wanting.

Our skin is slick against each other's with water, but that barely matters with the heat rushing down in my body.

I'm hyperaware everywhere he's touching me. His lips are on fire against mine and his fingers splayed on my back send sparks to places of me I didn't know could feel a kiss.

And he kisses me this way, long and hard, probing and heated. And he cups my breasts, teases my nipples. And his cock rubs against my pussy lips, teasing my cli, until there isn't any air left in my body and all that's in my head is his name.

Until all that's on my lips is his name, because I don't beg, but… "Corey, condom."

He leaves me with a bite to my bottom lip and reaches over to the drawer in the nightstand. After fumbling for a few seconds, he pulls out a foil square and tears it open. I look down as he pulls the condom out and rolls it over his cock in a swift motion.

"Last chance," he murmurs, opening my legs and taking my hands in his.

"Shut up and fuck me," I reply, pushing my hips up. I'm done fucking around.

His answer is his cock easily and quickly pushing into my

wetness. I gasp, the filling and stretching sensation stronger than I expected, but oh, God, good, too. So fucking good.

He rocks his hips against me, each thrust pushing deeper and deeper, getting quicker and quicker. Corey's lips take mine and he releases my hands, his fingers winding into my hair. I steal a breath between each kiss, my whole body burning.

Heat and desire—they swamp me, swamp us. His strokes are deep and easy, and each one is as intense. All there is is this—us, heavy breathing, low moans, and sweaty skin. All there is are my fingers gripping his back, his tangled in my hair. Our mouths battling, our breath mingling, our bodies fusing together.

"Fuck," Corey groans against me.

I open my legs for him to fuck me deeper, and he does, but harder, too. He fucks me harder and faster and deeper until there's nothing I can do but take it, live it, breathe it. I'm defenseless as his rough movements take me closer to the edge of the pleasure cliff coiling in my lower stomach.

I'm defenseless as, with one powerful thrust, he pushes me.

I spiral up, down, and around as he ignites the fire inside me and it explodes, rushing through my veins, forcing its way through my spasming muscles until I don't know left from right, reality from a dream, hot from cold.

Only one thing breaks through, and that's the sound of him saying my name in a long, tortured groan as he finds his release with mine.

"You probably shouldn't be sitting with your legs against the back of my sofa when you're not wearing panties."

I tug Corey's T-shirt down and catch the material between my thighs, covering myself. "Better?" I chew on a piece of crispy chili beef.

"No." He leans his head back and covers his eyes with his forearm.

"Oh, come on. It's not that bad."

"Babe, it's worse than bad." He drops his arm and turns his face toward me. "I know how fuckin' incredible you feel."

I roll my eyes. "Well, I don't have panties. And my bikini bottoms are wet."

"I can put them in the dryer." He moves.

I laugh. "And I still have no clothes for tomorrow."

"Wear the ones you wore today and I'll take you home in the morning to change and stuff."

"Or..." I swing my legs around and sit up. "You could go to my house now and get me some clothes."

Corey blinks at me like I just asked him to recite Shakespeare in Mandarin Chinese. "No."

"Oh, come on!"

"I'm not going to your house, where your mom and aunt will ask me suggestive questions and watch me with a knowing grin."

"Fine." I grab my phone from the table.

"What are you doing?"

"Hey, Mom," I say, looking at Corey. "Can you do me a favor and pack me a bag for tonight? Corey will come pick it up."

"Oooooh!" she coos down the phone excitedly. "Do I need to pack condoms?"

"Um, no. Just clothes and stuff, okay? Okay. Thanks. Bye." I hang up before she can ask me all sorts of other inappropriate questions.

Corey's still looking at me in shock. "I cannot believe you just did that."

I shrug. "I need clothes."

"Fine," he says after a moment. Then he leans over me, his face close to mine. "But we're going on another date. In public."

"'Where people can see us' public?"

"'Where people can see us' public," he confirms in a murmur, cupping my cheek. "I fucked you, Leah. And now, you're really, really mine. So I'm gonna get your clothes. Then, tomorrow night, we're going for dinner, and every-fucking-one is gonna know it."

I swallow and fight the shiver that wants to snake down my spine. I know I shouldn't; I know I should quit now.

But I can't.

Because a part of me is accepting the fact that I am absolutely becoming his.

"Okay," I whisper. "One date."

"For now." He kisses me softly, his lips searing into me despite the gentleness of the touch. Then he pulls back and grabs a T-shirt. "By the way, how did your job search go earlier?"

Guilt bites at me. Just a little. "Not great." I shrug. There's a suspicious spark in his eye that flares to life when I answer. And maybe... "You know, maybe I'll come back with you."

"You do that."

"How am I supposed to fold these?" He holds up a pair of panties.

"I don't know." I shrug. "I usually just throw them into my drawer. As you can see." I motion to the drawer he's standing in front of.

"Right." His eyes flick down to the scrap of material and back to mine. Then he drops it onto the floor.

"Uh, what are you doing?" I look down at my panties crumpled on the rug.

A smirk tugs at his lips. "That's where they'll end up anyway. I'm savin' you the hassle of putting them on."

"And you say you aren't a gentleman." I snort and bend down to pick them up.

Corey steps up behind me and places his hands on my hips, his lips tenderly brushing the base of my neck. "I'm the best kind of gentleman, darlin'. I'm polite in public and filthy in private."

I wriggle out of his hold. "That must be the famous Jackson charm you've been telling me about."

"Is it working?"

I drop my pants into the bag and glance at him. "Yeah,

kinda. That was a good one."

He grins smugly and leans against the dresser. I fumble for my phone charger on the nightstand then tear my eyes away from Corey to find it. Shit. Where's the cord?

I look at the plug socket, but it isn't there either. Crap…

"I gotta go get my phone charger. I'll be back in a second."

"You want me to go get it so you can finish here?"

I shake my head quickly. "No. It's okay." I dart out of the room before he asks any more questions and pull my keys from my pocket. After locating the key for my design room, I put it in the slot, turn, and yank it out.

I give the door a nudge so it closes behind me and go to my desk. Sure as hell, it's there, lying across the top of my laptop. Note to self: stop moving the phone charger.

I bend down and pull the plug from the wall, giving it a tug so the cable falls down the back of the desk. One, two…crash. Oops.

"Are you—what's this?"

I freeze at Corey's voice. "Nothing."

"Right. It looks like nothing. Do you always hide under tables when you lie?"

I harshly pull the charger and get up. Pencils are scattered across the floor where I knocked the holder over, and I focus on them instead of Corey.

"Leah."

"I said nothing!" I snap. I wind the cable around my hand and storm out of the room.

Shit. Shit. I should have locked the door behind me. Fucking shit!

"Why do you have a room for designing clothes? I thought you only majored in it."

"I did," I say honestly. "I still do some design now. For fun." That time, I lied.

"Right…" Corey stops on the other side of the bed. "Now you wanna explain why you have letters and shit in that room from a big designer?"

"For my mom." I zip my bag to disguise the shake of my

hands.

"You're a fuckin' terrible liar," he says quietly. "Tell me the truth, Leah."

"What if I can't?" I whisper, lifting my eyes to his. "What if I actually, physically can't tell you?"

Corey swallows. "I've always been honest with you, babe, but it seems like you ain't givin' me the same courtesy. If you can't tell me, then we're done. I'm an asshole, sure, but I don't fuck around with lies."

A sharp breath fills my lungs. This is it—my way out. It's my escape from his life, from this rouse, from everything he expects of me.

But I don't want to take it.

The rouse is real.

"I don't… I don't know," I reply, looking away again as apprehension coils in my belly. "I don't know if I can."

The floor creaks when he steps back. "I'll be downstairs. If you ain't down there in twenty minutes, I'll know what choice you made."

I close my eyes as he backs out of the room. My door slams, and I drop onto my bed. Crap. Why can't he just accept that I can't tell him right now? Why can't he accept that I have to have a secret? That something has to remain shrouded in mystery?

I run my fingers through my hair. Of course he was going to find out. It was inevitable. The moment I followed him upstairs earlier and we had sex, I knew he'd find out.

I knew then that I was done. That this seven-days thing is bullshit.

And now the one thing I can't tell him could ruin everything before it has even started.

Would it hurt to tell him?

The whisper is there, growing steadily louder, in the back of my mind. Would it? I don't know. Maybe. Maybe not. Maybe he wouldn't say a word. Maybe he would spill the beans to every media outlet in the country.

Maybe you can fall for someone before you trust them.

Maybe falling should be enough.

But it isn't. This is my dream, my life, my career. If I tell him, it'll discount everything I've worked toward and the last few years of lying to my best friends about half of my life.

If I don't tell him, he'll leave.

Our relationship has been built on lies. Lies to each other, lies to ourselves, but this may be the biggest one of all.

The biggest lie is that I wish he'd leave with the same breath that I wish he'd stay.

chapter TWENTY

Corey

Looking for a job my fucking ass. Designing for fun my motherfucking ass.

This chick works as a designer and for one of the biggest fucking fashion houses. I know because it's my mom's favorite. Because she previews QD's collection before the shows. I know because she's raving about the fall collection for whatever fucking season it is.

And for some reason, Leah can't talk about it.

I should be glad for the chance to leave. I should want her to stay up there and not explain herself to me, but fuck, I want her to. I need her to. I want her to bring her hot little ass down here and tell me every fucking thing she's been hiding.

"Corey? Are you okay, honey?"

I look up at the sound of Grace's voice. "Yep," I reply tightly.

"Oh, dear. Let's make you a cup of tea," Ada rambles, sweeping past her niece and into the kitchen.

"I'm good, Ada. Really. Thanks."

"It's good for the soul, you know," she insists, reaching for a mug in a high cupboard. "Grace…"

Grace laughs and gets the mug for her. "There." Then she turns back to me. "Where's Leah?"

"Upstairs."

"Have you two had a fight?"

I glance at my watch. "I'll let you know in five minutes."

"No," Leah says softly, appearing in the kitchen doorway.

"I'm confused," Grace sighs, leaning against the island.

"You and me both," I mutter, causing her to raise an eyebrow.

Leah walks across the kitchen and sits on the stool next to me.

"You're pregnant, aren't you?" Ada asks, putting tea in front of me. "Oooh, a baby! How lovely."

"No!" Leah shouts. "Jesus. If I am, it happened very fucking quick," she adds under her breath.

My lips twitch. Fuck—no. Don't talk about sex. If I start thinking about her nails in my back and her pussy hugging my cock, then my threat to leave will be a waste of breath.

"Well, what happened?" Grace asks, her own lips curving.

Leah glances at me, her big, blue eyes hesitant. "I'm staying with Corey for a couple of nights, and I grabbed my phone charger from my design room. He followed me in…" Her voice trails off and she swallows. "And he saw everything."

"Ah." Grace grabs a stool opposite us.

"Ah, fuck," Ada adds, sitting, too.

Stop ahhing. Stop ah-fucking. Just tell me.

"He saw the letters and stuff from Quinn that I have pinned to my board, and, somehow, it appears this big football-playing goof knows who Quinn is." Leah looks at Grace. "And now, I'm trying to figure out if I can be honest. Any ideas, Mom?"

"You made your choices for your own reasons. You have to here, too."

"Can someone just explain somethin' to me?" I ask, looking at them all. "'Cause all y'all seem to know what the fuck is going on and I don't have a clue."

"I have a job," Leah responds, turning her face toward mine. "I have since I was seventeen. When I was sixteen, I started sending designs to various designers in the hope that they'd let me intern during the summer. Quinn did more than that—he gave me a chance. I worked for QD while I worked toward my bachelor's degree. Then, a year ago, he asked me to design a whole collection and get a name for it."

"He gave you your own line?"

Leah nods slowly. "I did it. I'm pretty sure my fingers were bleeding for, like, a month after, but I did, and in ten days, it'll debut in New York."

I stare at her, amazed. What the fucking hell? "And this is a secret…why?"

"Because no one knows," she whispers. "You're the first person outside of my family and Quinn to know what I do."

"We'll leave you to it," Grace says softly, and she and Ada get up.

"But wouldn't all the designers? The ones you sent stuff to?" I frown.

"No. I sent everything under a different name," she explains. "I know what you're going to say," she says hurriedly when I open my mouth, "and that's exactly why. I wanted a career in fashion for my work, not because I'm a Veronica."

"Wow." I stare at her. I just stare at her, because she really is amazing. Everyone else would have taken the easy way out. Hell, I kind of did. "No one knows? Really?"

She shakes her head and turns her body to me. "Macey, Ry, and Cole always tease me because I'm 'too fussy to work,' but I have to pretend so they don't find out. They think I'm still sending stuff to designers."

"Wow," I say again. How the hell has she kept this up for so long? "Did you ever plan on coming clean?"

"Yes. When I was established and people respected my work for my work, then I was going to be honest." She meets my gaze. "I don't do it to be deceitful, just selfish."

"No, babe. No." I push some hair from her face. "You do it because you're fucking incredible. That's why."

Pink colors her cheeks. "Maybe to you, but it's hard. Like my mom is gonna go and see my show and I'll be sitting here at home, watching it on my laptop." She casts her eyes downward. "That hurts because I've worked so hard for it."

"My mom will be there, too." I keep my voice low. "I wish

I could come watch it with you, but we have a game that day."

"I think your mom is going to the show with mine."

"Yeah…" I say slowly, realization dawning. "Mom's a huge fan of QD, and she said that Grace mentioned this new collection he's bringing out. And it makes sense," I finish on a mutter.

"Lea V." Leah's voice is a whisper. "That's what I called myself when I was sending my designs out, so now it's my collection name."

My lips curve upward. Widely. "You're hiding in plain sight. Clever girl." I stand up and close the distance between us. "I'm sorry I made you tell me," I apologize softly, cupping the back of her neck.

She swallows again then lets her eyes crawl up my body until they find mine. Her fingers curl around my forearm. "I'm not. I trust you, Corey."

I drop my forehead to hers and close my eyes. *Fuck.* I didn't know how much I needed to hear her say those words until now. I didn't know how much it fucking mattered until relief floods my veins right now.

"You shouldn't," I whisper against her mouth. "I don't deserve it."

"I know. You gotta start earning it," she replies just as softly then tilts her face so our lips mesh completely.

"Let's go." I break the kiss. "Talking is better after fucking."

Leah shakes her head but gets up and goes upstairs anyway. I stare at the doorway as she goes, as she disappears, and as she walks back through it. With her bag slung over her shoulder, she walks up to me and pauses.

"Let's go be roomies," she teases, pushing up onto her tiptoes to kiss me.

"We're more than fucking roomies," I say after her, following her outside to my car. "Get in."

"That was my plan."

"She's sassy now that she's come clean."

She grins and leans over the center console. "She's sassy because she bagged the unbaggable."

"Sassy *and* sure. Sexy." I grab her hand and bring it to my lips.

"You're rubbing off on me, you know? One day, I'll walk past a mirror and be like, 'Damn, I'm hot.' Then I'll need to punch myself in the face with a brick because I'll be a female Corey Jackson."

I laugh. "Babe, I don't need a mirror to tell me I'm hot."

"Of course you don't."

I park in my driveway, unclip my belt right before hers, and pull her over to straddle my lap. She squeaks as she tries to keep her head from hitting the roof of my car, but I grip her ass and lower her down. Her fingers curl into my shoulders, and the escaped tendrils from her messy 'do tickle my face.

"It's in your eyes, Leah. Whenever you look at me."

"Is that right?"

"Hmmm." I hum the words into her mouth then pull back. "I bet that look is in your eyes right now."

She reaches down and opens my door. Her other hand pulls my keys from the ignition. "If you can catch me, I'll let you look." With a laugh, she extracts herself from me and jumps out before I can tighten my grip on her.

"Bitch!" I laugh, jumping out after her.

She disappears inside the house, and the crash of my keys hitting the side table breaks through her laughter. I slam the door behind me and look into the front room. She pops up from behind the sofa and blows a raspberry.

"Leah…" I warn.

She darts into the kitchen, and when I go after her, she's on the other side of the table, grinning. "I hope you're a better catcher than you are thrower, King Interception-Thrower."

"Shit, that's some fightin' talk there, beautiful girl." I grab my side of the table. "Sure you wanna go down that route?"

"Too late."

"Damn right." I jolt to the left.

She shrieks a giggle and runs around the table. She's barefoot, her feet slapping against the tile floor, and as soon as she gets close to the door, she runs through it, full speed, into the front room.

Fuck this. Time for game over.

I jump over the back of my sofa, loop my arm around her waist, and slam her down onto the cushions. She screams, still laughing, and lands in a heap beneath me.

"Bam," I murmur when she opens her legs and wraps them around my waist. "Blindsided."

"Smartass," she murmurs back, tangling her fingers in my hair and pulling my mouth down to hers.

I sit up and bring her with me, keeping the connection of our mouths. My fingers slip beneath her shirt and splay across the silky skin stretching over her back. She pushes into me, and my cock hardens quickly, throbbing with the knowledge that her pussy is three thin layers away from it.

I pull her shirt over her head and kiss my way down her neck. She gasps when I unclasp her bra and seal my mouth over her nipple. I cup her gorgeous, full tits with my hands, and she tugs at the neck of my T-shirt.

I pull the material over my head, and when it's gone, I grab her body closer to mine. As I run hands over her curves, every quick breath she takes is music to my ears.

She reaches between us and unbuttons my pants. "You have a—"

"Pocket. Just in case."

She smiles then lifts herself and shoves her hand into my pocket for the condom. Her fingers graze along my cock, making it twitch. Fuck. It's a tiny touch, delicious but torturous, and I groan.

Leah gets up, the foil packet between her teeth, and rolls her panties down her legs. Her bare pussy is right in front of my face—right in fucking front of me—and the urge to taste it, the temptation…

I lift my hips and push my pants and boxers down to my ankles. Then I reach forward, grab her hips, and make her step forward. I kiss the smooth mound of skin just above the place my cock is begging for. Leah inhales heavily, and the condom packet scratches my neck as she grabs me.

I kiss down, farther and farther, her legs parting just a tiny bit. Just enough… I flick my tongue out against her warm, wet pussy, and a small moan of delight leaves her. I do it once more, really tasting her, then sit back and pull her with me.

Snatching the condom, I rip it open and roll the rubber onto my dick. With one hand on Leah's back, the other around the back of her neck, I pull her against me.

"Get on my cock. Now."

She drops her hips and takes me in one motion. Fuck. I groan. She's so fucking wet and ready, and she hugs me tight, rocking slowly as she adjusts to my invasion.

Because that's what this is. I want to invade her body the way she's invaded my life and my heart.

Her fingers grip my hair, her mouth breathes hot air into mine, and her hips… Shit, them hips. They rock and gyrate, and she bounces, too, taking me from the tip to the base. Her gorgeous pussy is literally swallowing my cock.

I flip her beneath me without withdrawing from her and kiss her harshly. It's not enough. I need to hear her scream my fucking name the way she did earlier. I need her to get lost in me, because I'm sure as hell lost in her.

And I pound into her again and again, and like the addiction she is, she consumes me until all I know is her.

The sound of Leah's hair dryer blasting fills my dressing room, and I glance through the door at her. She's sitting on the chair in front of the mirror and built-in vanity, a bright-blue towel wrapped around her body. Her hair is flying everywhere as she fires the hot air at it and desperately tries to run a brush through it.

I dump my shirt on the bed and walk into the dressing room. Her eyes meet mine in the mirror, her lips curving. I smile back and take the brush from her. Then I run it through her long hair, controlling it better than she just was. Her smile continues to grow as I brush right to the ends halfway down her back.

"What are you doing?" she asks over the hair dryer.

I shrug. "I used to do it for my mom. My dad told me once that I'm the biggest pussy of a quarterback he's ever known."

Leah laughs. "He's right. Look at you. Big, hard man brushing a girl's hair."

"Not just any girl," I correct her.

"Oh, I'm sorry. Look at you. Big, hard man brushing your girl's hair."

"Better." I nod and quickly kiss the top of her head. "See? I can be a gentleman."

She laughs again and turns the hair dryer off. After setting it on the vanity, she takes the brush from me. "A gentleman. Right. Is that what you were being at four a.m.?"

"Look, babe. If I wake up with your tit in my hand, you can bet your hot little butt that my cock is gonna wake the fuck up, too."

"I'll sleep in a spare room tonight, then."

"I dare you to try." I lightly tug her hair. "I have practice until two. What are you doin'?"

"I'm going shopping with Macey. Then I need to call a bakery. It's Aunt Ada's birthday on Sunday and Mom wants me to get her a cake. Not that she can eat it because of her diabetes," she adds. "But still."

"You wanna make her one?" I call over my shoulder.

"For real? You can bake a cake?"

I shrug and throw my T-shirt over my head. "How hard can it be?"

Leah grins. "Famous last words, cowboy. Famous last words."

I wink. "If I can handle you, I can handle making a cake. We'll do it Sunday morning."

"Because you're playing the Bengals at home on Saturday at one thirty, right?"

Seriously. She is so fucking hot when she talks football to me. "Right."

"Then you'll go out with the guys to celebrate the inevitable win." She gets up and walks toward me, still wrapped in the towel.

"Maybe. Or maybe I'll come home and party with you." I wrap my arms around her and kiss her.

"Or you won't, because I'll be with the girls for Ryann's birthday." Leah beams.

"Of course you are. Just make sure every guy in the club stays away from you, all right?"

"I have no doubt that, at some point in the evening, you'll find us and glue yourself to my side without causing a huge scene."

"Babe, I will cause a scene so big it'll be the next fucking blockbuster." I kiss her again. "I have to go. Oh, and do me a favor."

"What?"

"When you go shopping, buy something for our date tonight."

"Oh. Yeah. The date."

I raise my eyebrows. Yeah, the date. The public date where we'll be seen together. The public date that will put us on the front cover of some tabloid and as the main entertainment story online.

And I couldn't give a fuck.

chapter TWENTY-ONE

Leah

"So, he's your boyfriend."

"No. We're dating, I guess, but he isn't my boyfriend."

"There isn't a difference," Macey sighs.

"Sure there is." I pull a red dress from the rack then put it back. "Dating is, like, going out on dates and stuff. Boyfriend-girlfriend is when you do everything together."

She looks at me. "Like eat-together, sleep-together, go-watch-him-practice kind of together?"

I open my mouth then close it again. Crap. "We're just doing it backward. That's all."

"Well, duh." She hangs a pair of jeans over her arm. "I thought you hated him."

"I never hated him. Just severely disliked." And now, my heart hurts at the thought of him leaving. Go figure.

"So you're in love."

"No. I'm in lust. Very severe lust," I add.

Macey's face transforms from a frown into a big grin. "You finally fucked him!"

"Please say it a little louder. I'm not sure the whole store heard you."

"Oh my God. I'm dying. I'm so proud of you. My baby

finally decided to hump it without a love declaration?"

I shift uncomfortably. "Well. I mean. He's hot," I finish lamely, shrugging.

Macey laughs. "Hell yeah, he is! I can't believe it took you so long. Was it good?"

"Do we have to talk about this here?" I give her a stern look and glance at the sales assistant, who is listening with a little too much interest. "I'm used to seeing my yoga-pants-clad butt all over the media, but I don't want anything else there."

Macey rolls her eyes. "Okay, okay. Did you find a dress?"

I shake my head.

"Okay. Lemme get these jeans and then we'll go find your dumb expensive stores."

I smile. She can say what she wants, but she loves swooning around the designer stores. Maybe one day, she'll find someone who'll buy the shop for her.

"So what about you and Jack, hmm? You tapped it more than once," I say when we step onto the sidewalk.

"Eh. Don't get me wrong. The guy is a fucking magician between the sheets. But Mitch has really put me off dating for a while." She adjusts her sunglasses. "Would you believe my aunt sent me an ultrasound picture on Facebook?"

I wince. As if her ex-boyfriend's knocking up her cousin while they were on a break weren't enough, her aunt sends ultrasound pics? Ick.

"Pssh," she carries on. "He's welcome to her, to be honest. I hope he enjoys her mommy-body and remembers my non-mommy-body."

Sometimes, I forget that she's a bitch.

I lead her into Chanel and one, two, three… Macey happy sighs. I knew it. Every time.

I scan the rows of clothing one by one, trying not to focus on the fact that this date tonight will change everything. Not between me and Corey, not whatever we have, but everything else will be different. Every time we step foot outside, we'll be stalked and snapped. We won't be able to do so much as buy a coffee without being big news.

And, yes, it scares me, but I know Corey's right. I know something has to give, and while I'm a private person, he's very much in the public eye. He likes it that way, but I just...don't.

"I like that," Macey says when I pull out a black, knee-length dress.

I turn it to see the back—or, rather, lack thereof.

"I don't know. It's kind of...fleshy..." I hedge, looking at it.

"Try it on. Now." She turns me and frog-marches me into the dressing room.

I sigh but hang the dress up. I know I can't leave here until I have tried it on because I can see her feet beneath the door. Yep. She's on guard duty.

I strip and grab the dress from the hanger. It's tight, and I really have to wriggle to get inside it and get it to sit right. I do after a few agonizingly long minutes and then look in the mirror.

Oh, now it makes sense.

The high neck gives security for the girls. I'll need a little tape for the sides and an invisible bra to stop any nipple mishaps, but they're firmly encased in the fabric. The plain material hugs my body perfectly, stopping at my knees, so I turn. The back dips down, ruffling at my lower back. Another inch lower and my butt would be on show. It's risky, but I really, really like it.

"Holy motherfucker!" Macey pokes her head in the door. "If I were a guy, I'd be ripping that off and fucking you before you could say hello."

"Thanks." I laugh, turning slowly. "Okay. I'm gonna get it."

"Want me to take it and have them put it on your mom's account?"

"Please." I pull the dress over my head, put it on the hanger, and hand it to her.

She shuts the door, and I dress quickly, fluffing my hair afterward. It's all static from the friction of pulling the dress over my head.

"Oh. I don't know," Macey says, looking around.

"What's up?" I ask, coming up next to her at the register.

"Um. Was there anything you needed to get?" Her eyes

widen and she shakes her head just barely.

"No…" I answer as confidently as I can. "Not today."

The sales assistant smiles at me, and I recognize her.

"Ms. Veronica," she greets me.

"Hi," I say brightly. "What's going on?"

"Ms. Kelly was just requesting her dress be put onto the Veronica account, but we had a call this morning from Mr. Jackson requesting that any purchases she makes go onto his account."

"Mr. Jackson?" I cough and knock my chest. "Did he give a reason?"

"No. Just that any and all purchases made by Ms. Macey Kelly are to be charged to him."

I look at Macey slowly. *What the hell is he playing at?* "Charge it to him, then."

"Very well."

"What the fuck?" Macey mouths at me.

I shrug and watch as the sales assistant folds the dress and puts it into a box.

"Might as well get some shoes," my friend mutters, raising a questioning eyebrow at me.

I shrug again. "I…I guess."

Macey walks over to the shoe section. A few minutes later, she reappears with a bright-blue stiletto. "Do you have these in a seven?"

I fight my smile.

My size.

I tug the dress down over my butt and look in the mirror. My hair is curled and falling free over my shoulders, stray locks tickling my bare back. My hands are shaking, and I wish I knew why.

It's not like I don't know him. It's technically not even a first date. I'm trying to blame it on the fact that my ass is about to be hounded for a quote or a picture or something.

Really, I'm just afraid that everyone will be finding out, and that pressure might be too much. It was for my parents. My dad couldn't take it. He couldn't deal with the media scrutiny every time he and Mom stepped outside the door. He left when she was pregnant, and I've only ever met him a handful of times. Figures he couldn't handle being there for me either.

I'm not entertaining the thought that Corey and I will grow old and have babies and stuff, and it's different because he's famous, but still.

The scrutiny will, and has, destroyed a lot of relationships. Sometimes, the pretense is just too much for people, the needing to put on a smile just to run to a grocery store after a fight lest their whole relationship be torn apart on front pages.

If I'm pissed off, I kind of like going to the grocery store looking like a raging bitch and not worrying that my whole life will be dissected in an article.

"I bought that, right?"

I bring my eyes up in the mirror to Corey's blue ones. His darkening, blue eyes, which are crawling across my body like he's never seen a woman before.

"I wouldn't know. Only purchases for a Ms. Macey Kelly were charged to your account."

"Mhmm." He clasps my waist and kisses my shoulder. "And I'm guessing you two figured it out."

"Yes, we did. Thanks for the warning, by the way."

"You're welcome." His lips travel across the top of my back. "I didn't want to spoil the surprise."

"Surprise? I was so shocked I nearly had a heart attack. Corey Jackson doing something romantic!"

He looks up and grins. "Smooth, huh?"

"Very," I acquiesce. "But how did you know I would go to Chanel?"

"I didn't," he whispers by my ear. "I actually left an hour early for practice, and I called every store I could think of just in case."

I pause. "Seriously? You did that?"

He nods. "I told you. I'm a gentleman."

"Okay. I'll give you this one. This time." I spin in his arms. "Thank you. It was very sweet of you."

"Sweet?" he grunts into my kiss. "It was fucking amazing of me. I deserve boyfriend of the year for that stunt."

"Boyfriend, huh?"

"Yeah. I figured, since we're about to be the media's new plaything, we should probably get the status of our relationship straightened out. I decided you're my girlfriend." He trails his fingers across my bare back. "So I'm your boyfriend."

"How very high school of you." I grin and step back so I can see him.

He's wearing a white shirt, the top button undone, and it's tucked into black dress pants. The black shoes on his feet are shiny, totally clean, and the pants are pressed to perfection.

"You clean up well," I tease, running my finger up the buttons.

He snatches my wrist. "I believe this is where you tell me I'm the most handsome man ever created."

"You're pushing it, cowboy."

He pulls me close to him. "Say it," he breathes, "and I promise not to smack your ass all night. Which, it should be noted, is incredibly tempting in that dress."

"You are the most handsome man ever created."

"Babe, you could at least pretend to mean it."

I laugh and skip into the bedroom, where my shoes are sitting at the end of the bed in their box. I lift it onto the bed, sit down, and unwrap them.

"Shoes, too?"

"Ms. Macey Kelly really took advantage of your account." I slide the blue heels on and stand up. "Good thing she did. These are hot shoes."

"They're fuck-me shoes," Corey laughs, taking my hand. "Get your purse and get downstairs or we'll be late, and I know how stressed you get when I don't feed you."

"I do not get stressed!" I huff, grabbing my black purse and making my way downstairs.

He follows me to the front door and opens it for me. Then,

by his car, he opens the door there, too.

"Well, damn," I mutter. "Who swapped Hugh Hefner with Romeo?"

Corey's laugh rings out through the car, loud and low and rough, and I shiver. "I'm a Texan, darlin'. I'm a dickhead, but I have more Southern charm and manners than you can shake a stick at."

"Do those manners extend to the bedroom?"

His eyes flick to mine. "First rule of being a gentleman: never, ever be a gentleman in bed."

"Seems legit to me. I mean, who wants a gentleman in bed?" I roll my eyes.

He grins. "Precisely. Don't worry, babe. I'll treat you like a gentleman. Then, at the end of the day, I'll fuck you like a porn star."

"Oh, baby. Romance me!" I giggle. "Your powers of seduction are second to none, Corey Jackson. Really, they are."

He winks, his grin growing, and turns the car onto Sunset Boulevard. Los Angeles is thriving as night falls, the bright city lights illuminating the road and sidewalks. There are people everywhere as stores close and everyone heads out for dinner.

I gaze out the window at the darkening skyline as Corey turns and pulls up in front of Alati restaurant. "Wait," I say, looking across at him. "How the hell did you get us in here? They're booked six months in advance!"

"Not for me."

Without any more of an explanation, Corey gets out and walks around the car to me. Flashes start, and I take a deep breath. Corey opens my door then takes my hand to help me out. I hesitate just before I do, but he tugs on my hand.

"Trust me," he whispers.

I nod despite the sliver of doubt. My heels touch the ground, and Corey hands his keys to a valet. Corey slides his fingers through mine and pulls me toward the front of the restaurant. As soon as I step onto the bottom stair, the light gives me away, and my name is shouted.

It takes them seconds to crowd us.

Corey snatches his hand from mine and wraps his arms around me. I cover my face with my purse as a security guard pushes his way through the photographers and gives us space to get into the restaurant.

My heart is pounding, and my hands really are shaking now.

"Are you okay?" Corey asks, resting his hand on my cheek.

"Um, we're never going out in public ever again," I answer, glancing toward the door. There are a few security guards there now, but the paparazzi are still scrambling and fighting for pictures.

"No kiddin'." He laughs quietly and turns to the hostess. "Jackson. Table for two."

"Of course, sir." She runs a finger down the book in front of her. "If you'd like to follow me."

Corey takes my hand again, and we follow the woman through the star-packed restaurant. She seats us at our table, thankfully away from a window, and sends a waiter over. Corey orders a bottle of white wine and reaches across the table for my hand.

"I'm sorry," he says softly, brushing his lips over my knuckles. "I didn't think they'd be quite that insane."

"It's okay," I reply just as gently. "I mean, it would have happened sooner or later. After all, you've got the It Boy of football and the daughter of Hollywood's It Girl on a date."

"You're an It Girl in your own right."

"Being yours doesn't count."

His lips tug up. "Oh, it does, but I meant you're an It Girl for the you-know-what." He pinches his shirt and flaps the material.

I look down and laugh silently. "Yeah. I'm the secret It Girl, right?"

"You are. My mom called me this afternoon to see where we're staying when we play the Jets, and she brought the show up again. She's going with my sister." His jaw ticks. "Then we're expected to do dinner. How fun."

"Oh come on." I stroke my fingertips across his palm as the

wine is poured for us. "It won't be that bad, will it? Just eat, have a drink, then leave."

"You haven't met my sister," he says dryly. "She's like rain in the Bahamas when you're on vacation—a giant pain in the ass."

"See? You have something in common!"

"Beautiful and funny. Such a catch." The teasing lilt in his voice makes me smile. His gaze catches mine, and he holds it. Then his smile drops a little. "You know somethin'?"

"What?"

Corey lifts my hand again and kisses the inside of my wrist. "I'm real glad you handed me my ass on a silver platter when we met."

"Know something?" I smile. "Me, too."

chapter TWENTY-TWO

Corey

And I am.

I've never been gladder of anything in my life.

She pissed me the hell off when she did it, mind you. But now, I see why she did it, and it makes sense. Leah Veronica isn't the girl you fuck and run from. She's the girl who'll tilt your whole damn world upside down and make you look at it through different eyes.

She's done that for me. So I'm still the same arrogant asshole I always have been, but she touches the softer side of me. She makes me want to care for her. Hell, I don't think it would matter even if I didn't want to. I'd do it anyway because she's that girl.

She's infectious and endearing. She's soft and hard, her edges rough in some places. She's strong and confident, and she's beautiful and she knows it. She has so much damn respect for herself and everyone else around her that it's a wonder any guy has ever let her go before me.

Fucking sucks to be them, though, and everyone else, because I don't plan to.

Somewhere along the way, she became more than a prize. She became a gift—to me, from me. And this is one gift I'm not going to let collect dust at the back of the closet.

Somewhere along the way, she made me fall for her. I can't help but miss her, even if we're only apart for ten minutes, and fuck, the way my heart thumps whenever I see her is, to be honest, terrifying.

She's the scariest thing I've ever known.

"You're staring at me."

"You're not exactly hard on the eyes, babe."

"It's a curse," she sighs, setting her knife and fork down. "Where's the wine?"

I grab the bottle and pour the last of it. She's now on her fourth to my one, but I think she needs it after the media assault we experienced on the way in. I'm sure as hell not putting her through that on the way back out. If I knew they'd be that bad, I would have gone and got McDonald's drive-through or something.

"Thank you." Leah picks up the glass and sips. "When do you go to New York next week?"

"Thursday. We'll be back Monday morning. Then a few days off before regular season starts. Which means"—I lean across the table—"you get me all to yourself for a few days. Aren't you lucky?"

"Oh, yes. I get four days completely free of you!"

"Your sass is terrible." I run my thumb across her bottom lip. "Someone's gonna have to shut that mouth of yours up."

"Try it," she replies, looking at me flatly. "I dare you."

"I could fill it."

She takes a big mouthful of wine and puffs her cheeks before she swallows. "I just did."

I laugh. She's right, and it's one of my favorite things about her. Not that she's right—that pisses me off because I'm supposed to be right—but that she'll take my dumb sexual comments and completely flip them upside down.

Leah looks over my shoulder at the doors. "Do we have to go back out there?"

I shake my head. "No, babe. We'll go out the back way."

"I can kick some cameraman ass if I have to," she responds, relaxing back into her chair again. "Wouldn't be the first time," she adds under her breath.

"There's a story there, isn't there?"

She looks away. "There might have been this one time where some guy got too touchy with my mom trying to get her to answer one of his questions. I might have swung my very heavy purse at his balls." Her blue eyes flit back to mine, dancing in amusement and faux innocence. "He might have ended up on his butt."

"Tough chick," I tease. "Is that a warning?"

"To you? Maybe. Don't annoy me when I have anything in my hands."

"I'll keep that in mind." I smile. "Are you ready to go?"

Leah nods and drinks the last mouthful of wine in her glass. I motion for the bill, and when the waiter brings it over, I ask about leaving through the back. He goes to arrange it, and I pay, adding a tip on top of the total.

"The valet will have your car right outside the back door, sir," the waiter says. "This way."

I clasp Leah's hand with mine, and we follow him through a long corridor to the back door. He opens the door to the valet.

"Mr. Jackson, if you and Ms. Veronica would like to return for another evening, please ask to enter the back way when you book. We'll make the necessary arrangements for your discreet evening." He bows his head.

"Thank you." I shake his hand then take my keys from the valet.

Leah shivers as we step outside, and I open the passenger's side door so she can get in. She throws her purse on the floor, and I grab her waist, hoisting her in.

"Come on, slow poke."

She laughs, and I get in on my side.

"Got plans for tonight, have you?" She turns in the seat and looks at me.

She looks tired, and, honestly, I am, too.

"No, babe. Not tonight." I take her hand in mine. I fucking love the feel of her fingers sliding between mine. "Tonight, when we get back, we get undressed then cuddle."

"Okay," she says with a soft smile. "But no more four-a.m. boob grabs. You got it?"

"I'm not promising anything."

Leah looks at the magazine with her mouth twisted to the side. Her mom reads the article over her shoulder, but all I can see of it is the front page. Which, unsurprisingly, is a picture of us entering the restaurant before shit got crazy.

"Well, they weren't assholes," Grace reasons. "But I'd appreciate it if they'd stop calling us now."

"Why do you think we left Corey's place?" Leah sighs, dropping the magazine on the cushion next to her. "We left our cells there, too. Like, three phones, all ringing repeatedly. Then there are the tweets and the texts and the e-mails."

"My favorite text was Cole's." I sip my coffee. "He wanted to know why I hadn't asked him to dinner instead."

"Legitimate question," Grace says, fighting a laugh. "Why didn't you?"

"He's a little clingy, and since I already got him tickets for the game on Saturday, I didn't want to give him too much of the wrong impression, y'know?"

Leah rolls her eyes at me. "Nice to know you're getting along, but where's my ticket?"

"Next to Cole's on my dresser."

"I didn't see any there."

"You weren't looking for them." I shrug, leaving the empty mug on the island and joining her and Grace. I pick up the magazine, give the cover a cursory glance, then drop it on the coffee table.

"You aren't reading it?" Leah turns to me.

"No." I sit next to her and rest my arm over her shoulders. "Their bullshit reporting and speculation aren't going to change my life any. It'll piss me off a little, and since I have training this afternoon, I can't be fuckin' bothered with it."

Grace's lips twitch. "Couldn't have put it better myself.

Leah, hon, you know better than anyone what they're like. Just ignore the articles and comments and focus on you two. It's only going to get worse."

"I know. I guess we should probably answer the question they're all asking though, right? It's too close to the show for them to be all up my ass, discovering what I ate for dinner last night."

"I agree." Grace stands and reaches for her phone. "Do you want me to get Charlie to put something out? And what do you want put out?" Her eyes glitter as she asks that last question.

Leah sighs again, and I stroke the side of her neck with my thumb.

"Tell Charlie to call my agent," I say. "It's Michael Wilson. He's already waiting for me to call him."

"Sure. But what are you telling them?" Grace asks again, the glee in her tone all too amusing. To me, at least.

"That they can fuck off," Leah mumbles, leaning into my side.

My lips twitch, and I press them to the side of her head, my eyes on Grace. "Tell them that we're confirming that we're in a relationship."

"We are?" Leah asks.

"We are."

Grace smiles widely, and she jumps up happily. "I'll go call Charlie now."

Leah rests her head on my shoulder and curls her body into mine. Ever since we woke up at six a.m. to our cell phones going crazy, she's been quiet. Every word has been softly spoken, no matter how angry they were, but she's been like a shadow of the girl I know.

I feel guilty for having made this happen. I wish beyond belief that I hadn't pushed her into taking this public. That, at the very least, I'd waited until after her show. Really, ten days wouldn't have fucking killed me. But no.

I needed to stake some bullshit claim to the world because sometimes I look at her and wonder if she is going to leave in a few days.

"You're going to hurt yourself." She runs her thumb along my jaw. "You're thinking."

I capture her hand and kiss her fingers. "I do that sometimes, you know?"

"Sometimes," she agrees. "Not often though."

"Hey." I tickle her side and she wriggles.

"Just don't apologize to me, okay? It's not just me that's affected by it. Hell, I can float aimlessly between my house and yours until they give up. You actually have to go out in public and get hounded by them."

"Yeah. The gates sure do protect us from their stupid cameras." I shift so I'm facing her better. "You really sure you're okay?"

She nods and offers a small smile, but as she leans in to kiss me, she doesn't look okay at all.

My stomach tenses when I feel Leah's lips brush across it. Slowly, she kisses downward, and her soft mouth ghosts along the patch of skin above my dick. Her fingertips follow her mouth, and each touch is like velvet, soft and tantalizing at the same time.

I open my eyes and look down in time to see her slowly drag her tongue from the base of my cock to the tip. Her eyes meet mine for a brief second, and they twinkle with heat and sensuality.

"What are you—"

She wraps her mouth around me before I can finish speaking, and I drop my head back. Holy fuck.

She doesn't respond to me in words. She responds with her body. She curls her fingers around the bottom of my cock and swirls her tongue, wetting my skin and taking a little more into her mouth. Her wrist twists, her fingers tightening slightly around me, and that beautiful mouth takes me again.

Her hand and her mouth work with each other but against each other, her hand coming up when her mouth comes down.

Her pressure and speed vary, fast and deep to slow and sensual. She knows exactly what she's doing—from the gentle graze of her teeth as she comes up to the stroke of her tongue on her way back down.

My hands find the back of her head and I tangle my fingers in her hair. I jerk into her mouth and she holds me tight in her hand, taking me farther back in her throat. She swirls her tongue again, lavishing attention on my swollen head, and gently sucks it.

"Fuck."

I bend my neck up. I want to watch her wrap those beautiful lips around my hard cock and suck it. And she's naked, *completely fucking naked,* on her hands and knees. Her ass is in the air, and her head bobs as she takes me deeper and deeper into her mouth with each suck.

Fuck, fuck, fuck.

She picks up speed, working her hand quickly beneath her mouth. I don't want to push her head down but—shit—I can't help it. I hiss out a breath when I hit the back of her throat and she doesn't gag. She does that again and again, and my dick swells.

I groan, and she sucks hard and slow on her way back up. She's switching speeds faster than I can cope with it and it's driving me insane. I can feel my release building inside me. My muscles are clenching, spasming with each suck. My balls tighten like they're in an iron vise, and my hips jerk up. I let go, my come spilling into her mouth with a fervent groan, but she doesn't move. Instead, she sucks softly until I'm done.

Adrenaline and pleasure are rushing through my body, and when Leah moves up the bed, I pull her on top me.

"Fucking hell, Leah," I mutter against her lips, my hands splaying across her body. "You know how to wake up a guy."

She runs her hand through my hair and smiles down at me. "Happy game day."

"Happy game day in-fuckin'-deed. If we win, can we make this a regular thing?"

She laughs, and the smile on her face is so much brighter

than it was yesterday. "We'll see. I have to get ready so I can meet Cole."

"Ah, yes. I get to hear you scream my name for a couple hours."

"I'm not saying it'll be in a good way," she warns, sliding from my hold and skipping into my bathroom. I laugh, but stop when I hear the spray of the shower.

I laugh, but stop when I hear the spray of the shower. "Are you offering shower sex?" I sit up.

"Ha!" She pokes her head around the bathroom door. "No. You got a blow job, so now I get breakfast. Off you go." Her eyes shine with laughter.

"Orgasms… Breakfast… There's a difference?"

"Corey."

"You have me whipped, Leah," I sigh, getting up and throwing some sweats on. "Completely fuckin' whipped."

chapter TWENTY-THREE

Leah

I love game day. Preseason or regular season—it's an exciting escape from the pressures of every day. In the crowd, I'm not somebody. I'm just another person cheering on her team.

And today, I really, really need that.

"Two guys in three days. What a fucking scandal." Cole laughs and passes me a coffee.

"Hmm." I glance over my shoulder at the photographers outside Starbucks. "I'm just gonna pretend they're not here for me and that they're trying to get inside the head of Hollywood's hottest property."

"Well, you know, I'm sure a couple are," he answers noncommittally. "After all, I did just get the lead in Chasing Tucker."

I roll my eyes. "Yes, yes, I know. Los Angeles knows. Hell, the country knows." I knock his foot with mine under the table. "I'm glad they didn't hold the photo thing against you."

"They were charmed by it. I told you—after that picture got out, I'm the hottest fucking thing this world has seen."

"And apparently, you just stole Corey's crown as the most arrogant."

Cole half grins. "Someone has to be the most eligible bachelor now that he's tied down."

"Right. You fill those boots oh so well, huh?"

"Fill boots, pants, pussies—whatever you wanna call it."

I cover my face with my hand. Am I surrounded by people who are obsessed with sex?

"And if you didn't like Ryann so much, I'd be happy to—"

"Say it." I snap my eyes up. "Go on. Dare you."

He mimes zipping his lips shut.

"Good boy." I sip my drink and glance at the screen of my cell. There's a message from Corey, and I swipe to open it.

Photographers just got so close that I think one gave me her uterus and another got me pregnant.

What? I laugh loudly and cover my mouth. *You're crazy. I'm being stalked at Starbucks,* I send back.

Kinda sounds like a low-budget porn movie.

You're sick.

Pregnancy hormones are messing with me.

Shut up. Is it that bad there? Do I need to creep into the stadium Mission Impossible style?

You probably shouldn't come as yourself.

I sigh and put my phone down. Great. Now I can't even escape into a football game.

I look up at Cole. "I'm real glad you're driving because you're gonna have to put them muscles to good use and be my bodyguard."

He lifts his arm and flexes his muscle. "On it."

"You're such an idiot," I mutter fondly. "Did you hear back from Neil Harmon after your meeting?"

"Yeah. I'm not the only person who's approached him about it—seems like three-quarters of the hacked people did. He told me that some of the others got warnings about more stuff being leaked."

I wince. "Shit. You don't have any more sordid pictures tucked away, do you?"

"Yeah, I mean, there's a whole bunch of porn movies I never told you about. I'll be bummed if that shit breaks."

I stare at him flatly, and he looks back at me seriously. I raise an eyebrow, and he cracks, his lips curving to one side.

"All right. You got me," he admits. "No. I have no more sordid pictures. Just one. God, I'm boring, aren't I?"

"I have none, so you're more exciting than me." I push my empty cup to the side with a giggle. "Come on, Mr. Muscles. Get me to your car without being assaulted by the media and I'll buy you a hot dog."

"Flashing the cash, as always."

"I'm a big spender. What can I say?" I link my arm through his and pull open the door.

Questions and pictures are fired at me from all directions, and Cole makes easy work of getting these fuckers out of our way. We reach his car in a minute or so and bundle in, slamming the doors behind us. We buckle up, and he flips it around, driving straight at the photographers.

"They move," he informs me gleefully when I grip my seat.

"I get the feeling that you enjoy this," I mutter in response.

His answer is a laugh. "Come on. Let's go watch your boyfriend throw some balls around."

Of course Corey just threw an interception. I mean, he is Corey Jackson, after all. Interception is his middle name.

"If they'd run it instead of passing, they'd be back on first down!" I thump my hand against the wall separating us and the sideline. We're sitting behind the Vipers, unsurprisingly, and we have a perfect view of the action.

"Run, run, run!" Cole yells along with thousands of other people.

I look to the sky as Reid makes the first down. "Fucking hell. It's a clusterfuck."

"They got the down," he shrugs. "Look—it's first and goal. Not even Corey can fuck this up."

I watch as the ball is fumbled. "You were saying?"

There are only a few more plays until the end of the game. I think it as Cole says it, and I nod in agreement. I know. I also know that this game doesn't actually mean anything, but I really, really hate losing.

Especially because I can look at Corey and I know that his head isn't in the game. It's probably somewhere with those fucktard photographers outside.

"He looks like shit!" Cole shouts into my ear as we finally score the touchdown.

"I know." My eyes follow Corey's number-eight jersey as he walks back toward the team. "He was bugged by the media before the game."

Cole shakes his head. "Shit, Lee. He has that all the time, even if it is kind of fucking crazy right now for you two."

So, that wasn't what I wanted to hear. Yes, it's crazy. Yes, it's always on my mind, And yes, it is taking its toll on me. I thought that, today, they'd lay off a little since they'd gotten the information they'd wanted. But they haven't. It's just as bad—if not worse.

Mom's agent is even managing the situation for me because, well, I haven't needed a manager until now. She's fielding all the calls and telling them to fuck the hell off in a far more polite way than I ever could.

I grab Cole's arm. "Do me a favor, okay?"

"What?" he looks at me.

"On the count of three, yell, 'Get your shit together, Jackson.' Okay?"

"Is this some kind of freaky foreplay you do?"

"Cole! I'm serious."

"He won't hear you."

I watch as Corey stands. "We have to try. Please?"

"All right, all right. Now?"

"One, two..."

We yell it in unison, and he's right—it's completely drowned out by the crowd. But Corey's step falters, just barely, and his head turns toward us.

"He heard, he heard!" I excitedly tug on Cole's sleeve.

"Sorry. What was that? You deafened me." He rubs his ear.

I laugh and let go, bouncing on the balls on my feet. This time, when the ball is snapped and Corey throws, Reid runs it twenty-five yards before he's tackled.

The rest of the game goes like this. Over and over, they throw, they get first down, they score. Our defense shuts down the offense, and our offense destroys their defense.

And in minutes, it's all over, and with one preseason game left, the Vipers are undefeated.

"Uh. Shit." Cole scrolls on his phone.

"What?" I lean over and see that the screen is full of text from an article.

He puts the device in front of me and taps the screen. I blink to adjust my eyes to the text, read, and freeze.

"Shit." My eyes rise to meet Cole's. Then they move toward Corey as he's leaving the field. "We need to go. Now."

I hug my knees to my chest on the hood of his car. It all makes so much sense now. The hacker released a second batch of photos, and there are two or three of Corey. I have no idea what they look like or what kind of context they were taken in, but it doesn't matter.

I just need to know that he's okay because, dammit, that's what matters. My heart physically dropped when I read those words, because despite everything, I've come to care about this guy more than I really ever thought possible.

A door slams and male voices drift across the parking lot. I look up and see Corey and a few of his teammates walking toward the cars.

"There's a chick on your car," someone says, and Corey lifts his head.

His eyes meet mine in the afternoon light, but that's the only light there is. His eyes, normally so full of life, are dull and shadowed. His brows are furrowed, the expression only adding to the darkness of his gaze, and the downturn of his lips makes me want to tease them with my fingers until they curl up again.

I want to see the cocky glint in his eyes and the smug smirk he loves so much. That I love so much. That's him. This isn't my

Corey at all.

He stops in front of the car and takes a deep breath. "Leah, I don't… I…"

I slide down and slam into his body before he can carry on. My arms wrap around his waist tightly and I bury my face in the side of his neck. *I feel his pain.* He doesn't even need to drop his bag and curl his arms around me the way he is. I feel it so acutely.

"It doesn't matter," I whisper. "I don't care."

"I didn't even know they existed," he starts.

I shake my head and look up at him. Then I slide my hand up to his face and cup his cheek. "Not here, okay?"

Corey looks around as if he's forgotten where we are. "All right. I have to go to my parents' place." He releases me and throws his bag in the trunk. He stops and looks at me. Slowly, he raises his hand and runs it through his hair. "I didn't think you'd be here."

"Dumbass," I say softly, stepping toward him again. I reach up and press my lips against his firmly. More firmly than I ever have—answering the unasked question that's on his lips.

I'm not leaving now. I'm not leaving in a few days when I have the option.

I want to stay.

"Got it," he replies quietly, leaning in for one more kiss. "I can take you home if you want."

I stare at him for a second, blinking. He's so cute. Grabbing the car door, I open it and then climb in. It slams behind me as I reach for my seatbelt.

"Got it," he repeats, getting in next to me and jamming his key into the ignition. The Range Rover roars to life and he tears out of the parking lot without a word to his teammates.

I want to know how he knows about the pictures, because if he knew when he texted me, he'd have told me, surely. I want to know what pictures they are and why he took them and why he never mentioned it when the first images were leaked only days ago.

But he doesn't want to talk at all. Not if the harsh set of

his jaw and whiteness of his knuckles as he grips the steering wheel are anything to go by.

Instead of asking, I sit back, set my hands in my lap, and stare out of the windshield as we drive toward his parents' house in Calabasas.

After what seems like ages, we arrive at the majestic house and I follow him out of the car. Corey walks ahead of me, his shoulders visibly tense, and pushes the front door open.

"Hello?"

"Corey?" his mom calls. Her voice is followed by footsteps, and in seconds, she appears in the large hallway. "Oh!" She runs forward and wraps her arms around him. She's only five foot something, and against his six-foot-plus, muscular frame, she looks positively tiny. But she still embraces him with the force of a mother's love.

"All right, Mom. I'm okay," he lies, trying to extract himself from her. "Did Dad speak to Neil?"

"Don't you lie to me, Corey Jackson. I can see that you're not okay," she admonishes him. "And yes. You don't have to do a thing. Your father is figuring it all out." She turns to me, and I smile weakly. "Leah, honey. I wish we were meeting again under different circumstances." She hugs me as tight as she just did Corey.

"Me, too," I reply, meeting Corey's eyes over her shoulder.

His mom straightens and sighs. "It's a shame the first girl he brings home has to be under a shitstorm."

I raise an eyebrow at Corey. He shrugs, indifferent, and somehow, I don't think it would be a much difference response if this visit weren't shrouded in darkness.

"Come and sit down," his mom says, guiding us both away. "Your dad's in his man-cave, as he calls it."

"Man-cave?" I question.

"Games consoles, dartboard, pool table, bar—that sort of thing." She waves her hand dismissively. "I ignore it, mostly."

I step closer to Corey and brush my fingers along the back of his. He snatches my hand and squeezes my fingers, the tightness telling me everything I need to know about his mood.

He releases me and greets his dad, who hands him a beer and tells him to sit on a large leather couch. After kissing my cheek, Justin sits me next to Corey with a light shoulder shove.

"Laura, hon, can you get you and Leah a glass of wine?"

"Oh, I'm okay," I insist.

Laura smiles but hands me one anyway. "My son would have me believe that about him."

I smile slightly. Maybe she can see on my face the worry I'm trying to keep inside. Because I am worried. For Corey. I'm mad, too. Hell, I'm real fucking mad, because whoever this hacker prick is, they've targeted two of the most important people in my life.

But Corey seems far more affected than Cole ever did.

"Well? Where'd they come from?" Corey asks. "Because I've sure as fuck never stood in front of a mirror and snapped a picture naked."

"That's what I'm trying to find out," Jason says, sitting forward and twirling his beer bottle between his fingers. "My friend who called me did some digging during the game, and according to him, there are three of you lying in bed. The angle suggests that you weren't the person to take the photos…"

"So you believe me?" Corey asks, looking between his mom and dad.

"The fact that you're sleeping in them with your hands empty is another indicator." Jason cracks a small smile, but it drops quickly. "The question is who did it. Any ideas?"

I slide my hand beneath Corey's and my fingers between his.

He shakes his head. "No fuckin' idea. Probably someone I met and took home…"

His mom coughs, and Corey looks at her.

"If you don't wanna hear it…"

When she doesn't say anything else, he goes on.

"Shit, Dad, I never had a chick there the next morning. It could have been anyone leaving in the night."

"But weren't only celebrities hacked?" I look between them all. "How many of those did you take home?"

He shrugs. "This is L.A. I don't know who the hell is a celebrity or who isn't, much less names. They could have been on my phone, uploaded, then deleted for all I know."

Jason rubs his fingertips over his forehead. "I see. Well, I have Neil pulling a case together now with many of his other clients, so all I can say to you two is to be careful." He meets our eyes, one after the other. "Because of who you are, son, you're going to be their new plaything. And, Leah? If the media can dish up dirt on you, they will."

I swallow, unable to meet Corey's eyes. "I know. They love a scandal," I say softly, ignoring the light squeeze of my hand.

chapter TWENTY-FOUR

Corey

If it isn't an ass-battering from Coach about all the media attention swarming me since Leah and I went public about our relationship, it's the pictures I didn't even fucking know about until yesterday being leaked.

And if it isn't that, it's the frostiness that's lingered between us since we left my parents' place last night. It's the slow withdrawal of her from me. And the worst thing is that it's my past. The one thing I didn't think would make a difference to us when I proved to her that this is it.

The fake way I lived could destroy the realest thing I've ever known.

Yet she's still here. So she lay pretty much fucking still last night, both of us barely sleeping but neither of us talking, and she's said all of two words to me this morning, but she's here.

She's. Still. Fucking. Here.

I rub my temples and glance at her. She's crouched on the floor in front of the coffee table, paper spread out all over the wooden surface. Her pencil flits across the page with ferocity, the scratch somewhat audible over the sound of the TV. I'm too far away to see what she's drawing, but it doesn't take a fucking genius to work it out.

It's a cruel reminder of everything she works to hide. A

cruel reminder of everything that could be taken from her in an instant if someone digs too far.

She's still fucking perfect though. It feels like there are a thousand years spanning the few feet between our bodies, but I can't help but stare at her. She's the only thing that makes this whole situation better. She's the only fucking thing that makes all the bad shit melt away.

That's the thing though. Be enough of an asshole, and when shit finally goes right, it'll get taken away from you.

I've never been as scared of anything as I am that this girl will get up and walk away from me.

Right now, I want to handcuff her to me, lock her body against mine with a thousand solid padlocks. I want to keep her right here with me, because that's where she belongs.

Hell, never mind that. I belong with her. One hundred fucking percent, I belong with this girl.

I belong with my girl and she belongs with me. The end. Happily fucking ever after.

I get up and walk around and crouch behind her. She doesn't move as I do, her focus entirely on the page in front of her. I can see now what she's drawing. It's an evening gown, long and flowing, and I've never seen anything like what she's creating right in front of my eyes.

I sit with her and wrap my arm around her waist. I rest my chin on her shoulder and watch her work. She's completely at peace, her hand moving nimbly across the page, her eyelashes fanning her cheeks when she blinks. She nibbles at her lip as she works, denting the pink flesh with white with every bite.

"We have to bake Ada a birthday cake," she says out of the blue, her pencil stilling. "Did you find out how to make one?"

"Uh…"

"Corey." She puts her pencil down and shifts so she can look at me. "I thought you were going to learn."

"I was. Then I got…distracted." Not a lie.

She sighs. "It's a good thing I can make a killer chocolate cheesecake, isn't it?"

"Wait," I say, stopping her from getting up. "You can make

a chocolate fucking cheesecake and you wanted me to learn how to make a sponge?"

"Um, yes. Pretty much."

I pull her to me and brush my nose against his. "Fuckin' hell, babe. Good thing I didn't learn, huh?"

She nods. "I'll teach you how to make chocolate cheesecake. I already bought everything."

"I don't want to learn."

"I like chocolate cheesecake." She taps my nose. "So if you ever happen to piss me off, which is a regular occurrence, as we both know, then you can make me a cheesecake and I'll be your friend again."

"Friend? You've never been my damn friend. You skipped straight from enemy to lover."

"So I did." She grins. "Come on. We have to cook it now before we have to go for dinner."

"In a minute." I bring her face back toward mine and seal my mouth over hers.

She doesn't fight or back away like I expected her to. Instead, she cups my face with her hands and holds her lips against mine.

"Now?" she asks.

"Fine." I sigh and stand up with her. "I can't bake to save my life, for the record. Not even fuckin' cookies."

"I guessed that when I discovered that I had to buy a cake pan." She throws a sassy smile over her shoulder and pulls said pan out from a cabinet I don't think I've ever used. "Just do what I tell you to, okay?"

"Okay."

"Now take off your shirt."

"What the hell does that have to do with baking?"

"Nothing," she admits, still smiling. "I just like the view."

I smirk and toss my shirt on the table. "Better?" I step up behind her and cup her hips.

"Hmhmm," she responds, tilting her head to the side and grabbing a package of cookie. "Now be a doll and crumble these into this bowl."

I sigh and let her go. "Yes, ma'am."

She purses her lips, but the happy twitch gives them away. "Just do as you're told, cowboy, and this will go smoothly."

"I prefer things rough."

She flattens her hands on the counter and drops her head back. "If there's anyone up there," she directs to my ceiling, "I could do with an extra bucket-load of strength to deal with this guy. Thanks."

I laugh at her exasperation and, in my distraction, crumble cookie all over the floor. "Shit!" I laugh even harder.

"Corey! Oh my God! How can you fuck up crumbling cookies?" Leah looks at the floor then at me. Then she shakes her head. "I… I don't… Just don't make any more mess, okay?" She looks away, her shoulders shaking lightly.

"I know you're laughin'," I utter under my breath.

She glances over her shoulder and pokes her tongue out, the dancing of her eyes warming me inside. *There's my girl.*

She drops another pan on the stove and throws some butter into it to melt it. I keep crumbling cookies into the bowl until she tells me to stop and throws the melted butter in with some sugar.

"I'm trying to decide if I want to let you mix this." She stares at the bowl. "I'm going to regret this," she says, handing me a spoon. "Try not to flick it everywhere, okay?"

"Yes, ma'am."

"Stop saying that!" She narrows her eyes and lightly jabs my arm. "Now be quiet because I need to concentrate."

I focus on mixing as she does whatever else she needs to do. Then, so I don't look totally stupid, I slide my phone onto the counter and Google a chocolate cheesecake recipe. It's pretty dumb since she's already guessed that I'm like a virgin in a strip club when it comes to baking, but hey.

"Uh, babe?" I look up from my phone. "Isn't this supposed to go into the fridge before you do the chocolatey stuff?"

Leah's eyes snap to mine. "Yes. But we don't have time because I forgot to do that this morning. How did you know that?"

"Lucky guess." I discreetly put my phone back in my pocket.

"Corey Jackson, did you just Google a recipe?"

My eyes widen. "No. I'd never do that."

"You're such a liar!" She gasps, turning the stove off. "I can't believe you."

I grab the bowl and stir in front of my body because she looks like she's about to put this spoon somewhere uncomfortable.

After a long moment, she turns away and pours some melted chocolate into some cream and sugar. She grabs a cream-covered whisk and glances at me every few seconds, her eyes narrowed. Shit. I'm in trouble.

Maybe I should stick to being a baking reject next time.

Next time? No. Fuck this. I'm not baking shit ever again.

Leah puts the chocolate mixture down and goes to the fridge. I set my bowl next to hers and dip my fingers into the chocolate, my lips twitching. She turns, and I swipe my finger down her nose.

"You did not just put chocolate on my face."

I grin and step back into the counter. "Me?"

Her lips twist into a half smile, half purse, and she advances on me, her own fingers dipping into the mixture.

"Now, darlin', think about what you're doin' here…"

I hold my hands up, but quick as lightning, she launches herself at me and smears three fingers across my cheek. I laugh and scoop some back off, going after her. I get her cheek, some of it spreading onto her mouth.

She pauses to lick up that mixture. Then, with a tiny, "Mmmm," she shoves her hand in the bowl and presses it flat against my cheek.

It covers one-half of my face, still warm from when the chocolate melted. I stare at her in disbelief. She giggles, backing up against the counter, her face and hair brown from my attack.

I pin her to the counter then rub my mixture-clad cheek against her clean one.

"Corey! Coreeeey!" she shrieks, trying to get me away, but it's entirely in vain. I'm stronger than she is, and besides, she's too busy fucking laughing at me.

"What?" I ask, pulling back. "Hey, it's a good look for you."

"Dick!" She reaches behind her and grabs the sponge.

Instead of wiping her own face, she throws it at mine. Soaking wet. It smacks me in the cheek and hits the floor with a loud, wet *thwack.* I bend down, grab it, and wipe my face clean.

It smacks me in the cheek and hits the floor with a loud, wet, *thwack.* I bend down, grab it, and wipe my face clean. "Thanks, babe."

"What about me?" She looks at me, her last laugh still playing with her lips, her eyes wide and sparkling.

"You threw it at me. I didn't know you wanted it." I rinse it under the tap. "Did you?"

She pouts.

"Okay, fine. Here." I push it onto her nose and water drips everywhere. It runs down her chin and neck and soaks her shirt.

She gasps, grabbing the sponge and blinking at me. "Oh my God."

"I'm sorry!" I swallow my laughter and take it from her. "Here. Let me help you."

"I don't trust you at all!" She darts under my arm. "I'm going to shower and you can clean this up. Okay? Good."

I watch her go then spin to see the kitchen. Yeah. There are crumbs all over the floor, and they're now accompanied by water puddles and chocolate drops and smears.

I'm going to join the shower thing.

I run upstairs after her and shrug my jeans off in my room. My boxers go down with them. Then I walk into my bathroom and yank the shower door open. The large space inside gives enough room for us both, and Leah turns, unsurprised.

"I knew you'd do that," she sighs, running her fingers through wet hair.

Her tits bob as she roughly rubs her scalp, and my eyes fall down to them. Her nipples pebble beneath my gaze, and I grasp her waist.

She moves toward me without my urging, her wet body pressing flush against mine. I ease one of my hands up her body, my palm rubbing over her nipple, and cup the back of her neck. Her lips part as I tug her head back, and she shuts her eyes. I look at her for a moment, ignoring the begging of my cock, before I finally take her mouth.

She whimpers beneath me and slides her hands up my back to my shoulders. She curves her hands around them and moves so close that I know there isn't an inch of space between us. I want nothing more right now than to push her against this wall, slip my cock between her legs, and fuck her. I want to let go of the stress of the last twenty-four hours with her.

But it isn't right. I need more. She needs more. So instead of flipping her back onto the wall, my hands fall to her ass and curve around her thighs. I lift her, and she wraps her legs around me. My cock bobs against her pussy, the temptation coiling all my muscles.

I carry her into my room so I can drop her on my bed and lean over her. Her eyes crawl over my body and she draws in a sharp breath, ghosting her fingertips over my stomach. She sits up halfway, her hands on my sides, and brings her mouth to my chest.

"No." I grab her hands and pin them to the bed. Then I lower my face to hers so she feels my words instead of just hearing them. "This is the part where I get to kiss every inch of your body, not the other way around. There are so many spots I haven't touched yet. So many spaces I need to taste, to touch, to feel."

She gives a small gasp when my mouth lowers to her breasts. I wasn't fucking lying to her when I said that I want to kiss every inch of her body. I should have done that way before now, but I needed her too badly. I needed to be inside her more than anything else.

Now, it's all about her. It's about me and her, more than a fuck. It's about us getting something from nothing. Right now, I intend to show her the time of her goddamn life.

Her chest rising and falling as her breathing picks up, and I feel her stomach clench beneath my lips as they travel along the skin above her bare pussy. Breast to belly button, I brush my lips over her body. Belly button to hip, my tongue swirls.

Hip to hip, I dot hot, openmouthed kisses along the invisible line there.

I lift her leg and brush my nose down it, pausing just before the apex of her thighs. Then I do the same the other side. Being so close to her pussy and not touching or tasting it is driving me insane because I can smell her. Shit, I can see her wetness glistening on her gorgeous, pink flesh.

She shudders when I kiss her thigh and pushes her hips up. I flatten my hand on her stomach to keep her hips against the bed and kiss her. Just barely. A sharp gasp meets my ears, and I smile. I love knowing I can do this to her when I've barely touched her. I haven't truly started yet and she's already wet enough to take me without blinking.

My mouth hovers above her and I blow on her tender skin. Then I drop my mouth, and I run my tongue all along her pussy in one smooth, long stroke. *Fuck. Fu-u-uck.* Her taste fills my mouth, driving me to taste her more, to tease her and please her and make her come.

Leah fights my holding her down, and when the tip of my tongue finds her swollen clit, I push down as I tease it. Her back arches as I work her, gaining speed then stopping to explore the rest of her.

The taste of her is all over my tongue and I love every second of it. She really does taste like perfection—sweet and addictive and fresh. I'd do this all day, every fucking day, if it meant I'd hear the breathy cries leaving her mouth right now, if I meant I got to taste her.

I glance up when the sheet moves. Her fingers are gripping it tightly, her head thrown back, sweat glistening on her damp skin. I'm done fucking around. I want to see the look on her face when she really comes apart from just my mouth.

Her legs tense and a shudder wracks her body as I push hard on her clit, rubbing and teasing. I keep my eyes on her face until she throws her head back, crying out, and gives herself over to her orgasm. I run my tongue along her pussy again as she comes, taking every last bit of her before kissing my way back up her body again.

I grab a condom from the nightstand and roll it on. Leah reaches between us and rubs her thumb over the head of it, and fuck, I wish there weren't a layer of rubber between us.

"You need to fuck me now," she whispers roughly, her voice shaky.

I laugh huskily, bringing her mouth up to mine. "No, I'm not going to fuck you, Leah." I lower my body to hers, my cock touching her pussy. "I'm going to make love to you. I'm going to sink myself inside your swollen, wet pussy and make love to you so slowly and deeply that you'll be begging me to fuck you and make you come. But I won't." I push into her, her muscles clenching around me, and roll us onto our sides with her leg hooked over mine. "I'll keep making love to you just like this until you come, and I don't care how it long it takes. I don't care if I'm inside you until tomorrow morning."

She digs her fingers into my back as I start my slow assault of her. "Why?"

"Because." I wrap my arms around her so every part of our bodies is touching. "You're a beautiful woman who deserves to be loved in the purest and rawest way. No frills, no sugarcoating, no bullshit. This is my way of doing that."

She slams her mouth against mine and cups my neck. Her hand comes between us and stops me going back inside her.

"You're clean, right?" she whispers.

"Always."

"Take it off." She positions her hand at the base of my cock as if she's asking permission.

"Take it."

She rolls her hand down my cock, removing what I just put on, and guides me back to her opening. I ease into her, her wetness so much realer than before. Her pussy really is hot and tight, and it clings to me mercilessly as I rock my hips against her slowly.

She feels more amazing than I ever thought. Being inside her with nothing separating us is exactly the way this should be. Fuck knows I've fought long enough to be this close to her, to have her here, so there's no space for a condom to be between us.

chapter TWENTY-FIVE

Leah

"I have something to tell you," Mom says, strolling into the room.

I blink at her from my laptop. "You're renting my room out?"

"No." She laughs. "Although, are you planning on spending any time there anytime soon?"

"Couple of days. I only agreed to stay at Corey's for a week." I go back to Facebook.

She puts her purse on the table and looks at me. "Don't you want to know what my surprise is?"

"No offense, Mom, but your surprises don't have a track record of being good."

"My last surprise got you a boyfriend."

"With a whole bunch of bullshit attached to it," I say pointedly.

It's been two days since Corey's surprise pictures were leaked online and his dad reminded me of how ruthless the media can be. And are. Of how they'll dig until they have something good on me, too.

"You'll get past it," Mom reassures me.

"I've had periods longer than our relationship. You're awfully confident."

"Sounds like I believe more in you and Corey than you do."

"Probably." I sigh at her raised eyebrows. Shutting the laptop, I say, "It's not that I don't believe in him, okay? It's just that the whole reason I stayed away from him was because of this very thing happening, and the only reason I stopped staying away from him is because I thought that was how I could get him to stay away from me."

Mom blinks. "That's a lot of staying away, honey. But it sounds like you don't know what you want."

"I want Corey, okay? I didn't, but now, I do, but I don't know if I can have him. Which isn't fair at all." I swallow and look at the table. "Why does nothing ever work out like it's supposed to?"

"Because that's life, Lele." Mom comes around the table and strokes her hand over my hair. "But I know one thing that's worked out right."

"Which is?"

She slides an envelope in front of me wordlessly.

"What is this?" I pick it up and flip it over. The QD logo is embossed onto the flap, and I tear it open. "Are you serious?" I shriek, pulling two tickets out of it. One has her name. The other has mine.

The show?

Mine.

"I spoke to Quinn," she explains excitedly. "You can't be backstage, sure, but why can't you be in the front row with me? You've been there before. It won't be suspicious at all!"

"Are you serious?" I repeat. My hand is shaking, and fuck, my heart is pounding, but I don't want to believe it because this can't be real.

"Deadly serious, honey. I'm not going to let you miss your own show!"

I drop the tickets and hug her tight. My eyes are stinging with tears, ones that are full of hope and happiness, because I can see my dream after all. And it doesn't matter that I can't be backstage fiddling with clothing and other things.

It just matters that I'll see my designs. On a runway. On real people.

In five days.

You know your relationship is about as serious as it gets when you're bundled into a car at nine in the morning with two suitcases and no idea where the hell you're going.

I eye Corey as he drives out of Los Angeles. A smile has been teasing his lips all morning, and I knew the second I woke up that he was up to something. It was obvious when he didn't get ready for practice like he should have.

Hell, it was more than obvious the second his morning glory wasn't followed up by an attempt to get inside my underwear. I actually thought he was sick until I saw a playful, secretive spark in his eyes.

"Where are we going?"

"If I tell you, it won't be a surprise."

"I hate surprises."

"Of course you do."

I smack his arm. "Tell me. Please."

He shakes his head. "You'll just have to trust me."

I narrow my eyes. "I did. Then you threw me in here."

"I don't throw you anywhere, babe. Except maybe into bed, but that's totally acceptable."

So he has a point there... "Fine. You coaxed me into it."

"Actually, there was no coaxing involved. You really want to know where we're driving to?"

"Yes."

"Long Beach."

Two suitcases for Long Beach?

"Why are we at Long Beach?" I get out of the car and look at the building in front of us. "At a fucking helipad?"

Corey just smirks at me and pulls the suitcases from the trunk. "I said to trust me."

Trust you my ass. "Are we flying? 'Cause you should really warn a girl if you're gonna send her into the air."

"Relax, Leah. It's not like I'm flying you to London. It's only fifteen minutes."

I eye him and follow him toward a waiting helicopter. I've only ever been in a helicopter once, and I can absolutely say that I prefer a plane. Helicopters are kinda…rocky.

"Can you just focus on the whole 'taking you away for the night' instead of where we're going?" Corey murmurs in amusement when we're inside.

"Yeah, I'm still trying to connect Asshole Corey with Night Away Corey," I tease him. "You've been really nice lately—if you ignore the chocolate thing—so we'll have to come back to this when I've got you figured out."

He laughs as we put on the headsets and strap ourselves in. Actually, I can't do up my belt, so he does it for me.

"Good luck with that." He takes my hand in his.

The helicopter lifts off the ground and I chew my thumbnail, looking hesitantly out the window. "Now can you tell me where we're going?"

He shakes his head, a smile teasing his lips, and looks out of the window.

Bastard.

I've heard of Catalina Island, but surprisingly, I've never been. Great-Aunt Ada swears by it as the perfect mini retreat to escape the hustle and bustle of Los Angeles, but I've never needed to escape it. Until now.

This tiny island is a small slice of beauty just off the coast of insanity. From the golden beach to the pier stretching out and the brightly colored houses, it's incredible. There are no reporters, no photographers, no people trying to figure out how we feel about the change in both of our lives.

I look around the quaint street we're standing on. How have I never been here before? Why have I never bothered to jump on a boat and escape here?

Corey leads me into a two-story, turquoise house that would

look out of place anywhere but here. Until you walk inside. Here, it looks like something out of a magazine with two cream leather sofas, a wide-screen TV, and walnut coffee table. A few pictures hang idly on the walls, and my curiosity gets the better of me. I walk to the biggest wall, to a photo of a guy in his teens. There's a football tucked under his arm and unruly, brown hair flops down into smiling, bright-blue eyes.

"Is this you?" I point to the picture and raise an eyebrow at Corey.

"I should have guessed you'd get it in seconds. Yep, that's me." He comes up next to me and his thumb brushes the frame. "I was fifteen, and that was taken right after we won the state championship."

"So I'm gonna ask a really dumb question now, but how does your picture just happen to be in this house?"

He smiles. "My parents own this place. They came here for their honeymoon and Mom loved it so much that Dad bought her this house. Once a year, right after the season ended, Lottie and I would be shipped off to our grandparents and they'd come here for some time together. Then, before training started, we'd all go as a family."

"That's so cool." I walk along the fireplace, looking at the pictures. "And this is your sister?"

"Yep, that's Lottie. Nose in a book as it always was."

"You look alike."

"I might have to spank you for that."

I grin at him and step back. "You're not touching me until you tell me why we're here, cowboy."

Corey's eyes wrinkle with his smile. "All right. But I am touching you." He steps forward and wraps his arms around my shoulders. I circle mine around his waist and look up at him. "I brought you here because it's somewhere we don't have to worry about being watched," he says in a low voice. "Somewhere we can hide from the media and just be us before we both go to New York for the weekend."

I squeeze him tight. "You're the sweetest asshole I've ever met."

He laughs. "Hey, I have my moments." His fingers brush my forehead as he pushes some hair from my face. "The last few days haven't been the same. I wanted to bring you somewhere where you can remember that, in the end, all that matters is us. That you, me, us—we're real to me, Leah. It didn't start that way, but that's how it's finished."

I swallow. His eyes are intensely focused on mine. I'm trapped by both his gaze and his arms, and I realize how important those words were. How much I needed to hear them. I didn't even know I needed to—a part of me wanted to, sure, but needing is something else.

And needing something from someone past just their body, whether they care about you or not, is a dangerous thing for anyone else to do.

Needing means you open yourself up to them. Needing makes you vulnerable. Easy to hurt. Easy to break. I don't do needing, I don't do vulnerable, and I sure as hell don't do easy.

Until Corey came along and slowly smashed all of that. Because I care. I care, and he matters. Somewhere between all of our fights and teasing, I started falling for him. It's been hidden beneath my determination to keep him away and my judgment of him. It's been hidden beneath what I thought was right but was actually very, very wrong. Slowly, it's become real, and falling for him has become real, too.

I was vulnerable to him the moment his smooth, soft, Texas accent floated to my ear on my birthday in the bar. I needed him the second his lips touched mine, and the moment the words he just said left him, I became like glass—one touch just a little too heavy and I'll shatter.

Corey Jackson is my exception in everything.

"And I've looked at you and realized that maybe this is too much for you. That I am," he says just as softly, his fingers curved around the back of my head and holding our faces close. "And that, when we come back from New York, you might walk away."

"I don't want to," I whisper.

"I know, babe." He kisses me softly. "But just in case. This is for us."

I bury my face into his chest. I don't want to talk about leaving him although I know it's a very real possibility. I was so afraid of him being the weak one when it came to the pressures of having a relationship fully in the public eye, but maybe I'm the one who's weak.

chapter TWENTY-SIX

Corey

"Fish and chips. Ladies and gentlemen, welcome to the world's most unromantic meal on the most romantic island," Leah mumbles, walking off the boat. "It bugs the hell out of me. It should be fries."

I smirk as I study her. She's been talking about the 'chips versus fries' thing since we walked into the restaurant two hours ago. Never mind that the owners are British or that fish and chips aren't out of place in America. She's adamant that it should be fish and fries.

"Leah, it's just a name."

"I know, but chips are crunchy and come in packets. Not next to a piece of fish on my plate." She sighs.

I shake my head and jump in front of her. I take her hands in mine and link our fingers together, pulling her toward me. "Does it matter that much?"

"Well, no."

"Shut the fuck up about it, then." I bring my lips to hers. "I can think of plenty of better things you can do with your mouth instead of complaining."

"Hey."

"I'm just sayin'," I say against her smiling mouth. "Don't tell me you can't think of anything better to do with mine."

"I can, actually." She takes her hands from mine and flattens one of them over my mouth with a loud giggle.

"God, you're a real comedian." My words are mumbled into her hand. "I bite, you know."

"Do you?" She quirks an eyebrow, pulling one side of her mouth up in a suggestive smirk.

"Sometimes." I nip her hand and she removes it, stepping onto the beach. I wrap my arms around her shoulders from behind and bury my face in her hair, slowly walking with her. Even her hair smells like candy, fresh and sweet.

"Are you sniffing my hair?" Amusement laces her tone.

"It smells the way you taste," I murmur. "I'm liable to bite now."

She laughs and wraps her fingers around my arm. "Is that a promise?" She turns her face into mine.

"Do you want it to be?"

"Depends where you bite."

I love hearing her laugh. It's soft and warm, the kind of laugh you can't help but respond to, whether it's a smile or a laugh of your own. I love that it's so easy to make her laugh, to put that wide, beaming smile on her face.

"I'll keep that in mind." I release her and drop onto the sand. Then I pat the spot between my legs for her to sit.

"Why haven't you done it before now?" She slowly lowers herself down between my legs and rests her back against my chest, her fingers linking between mine as they rest on her stomach.

"Bitten you?"

"Yes."

"You want me to?"

"I already told you, cowboy. It depends where you do it." She taps my hand with her fingers and leans back fully onto me.

"Relaxed?" I ask, kissing her jaw.

"Very. I should have come here before." She rubs her thumb across the back of my hand. "But I'm glad I'm here now."

"I go into shock every time you say you're happy to be somewhere with me."

"Well, hey now. I didn't say a thing about you."

I flip her around onto her back and lean over her. Sparkling, blue eyes gaze up at me, and the smile playing on her lips is a teasing one. She looks like our conversation never happened, that the idea of us being apart was never brought up.

I wish it were true. I wish I could look at her and know I could promise us both always. But it isn't in my hands. It's her choice. I can only fight for her to make what I think is the right one.

"That's what you get when you get all presumptuous," she teases, tapping my nose.

"It's hard not to be sometimes. You know you're here with Corey Jackson, right?" I lower my face, murmuring, "People want me, babe."

"God." She shakes her head with a laugh and traces my jaw with her thumb. "Your ability to be an It Boy never ceases to amaze me. You know that?"

"Yep. And every It Boy needs his It Girl." I close the small distance between our mouths and savor the taste of her. She arches her back so her lips are firmer on mine, so there isn't an inch of space between us.

She arches her back so her lips are firmer on mine, so there isn't an inch of space between us. "Secret It Girl," she reminds me, sinking her hands into my hair.

"Secret It Girl," I reply, correcting myself, and sit up.

She stays lying down, but she looks up at me, her eyes big and blue and her hair spread on the sand. I reach over and run my fingers along her jaw. They trail down her neck to the curve of her chest, and she shivers when I tease the skin along her bra line.

She sits up and curls into me, hooking her legs over mine. Then she slips her arms around my waist. I feel her take a deep breath and turn her face out to the water, where the sun is setting in the sky.

I breathe her in. All of her. As the sun lowers and her grip on me never loosens, I realize something that should have been clearer than simply believing that I want and need her to be close to me.

I'm falling for this girl.

Fuck anyone who says that you can't fall for someone in just a few weeks. Love doesn't have to be a slow simmer. It can be a fast burn that only intensifies over time.

And while I know I'm falling a little more each day, I know I could hit the bottom soon. I know I will. One day, I'll fall so fucking far that she'll consume me.

She's so under my skin that she couldn't even be cut out with a fucking knife.

chapter TWENTY-SEVEN

Leah

I drop back onto the hotel room bed with a happy sigh. New York City—my favorite place in the world. I've been here plenty of times, yet it never seems to be enough. There's something about the magical charm of the city that sets it worlds apart from L.A.

There's also the fact that my designs are in this city right now. So close that I could touch them, fiddle with them, and alter them… But still, I can only dream of it.

I slap my cheeks. I'm not going to think of the fact that I'll only get to experience New York Fashion Week as a spectator. Maybe one day, my work will be respected enough that I can step from the shadows and experience all the Fashion Weeks around the world as a designer.

My phone buzzes in my pocket and I pull it out. "Shit!" It drops onto my face and I rub my nose, bringing Corey's message up at the same time.

Are you here yet?

My lips form a smile. *I'm in bed.* Sort of.

Do you know how mean that is when I'm stuck on a practice field?

Thrown many interceptions, cowboy?

None. Would you believe it?

Shouldn't you be practicing now? Just in case that changes?

The phone rings and I answer, laughing. All he says is, "Fuck off," before he hangs up. I roll onto my stomach and laugh into the bedspread. Of course he'd say that. He knows I'm one hundred percent right.

When my laughter subsides, I get up and stroll to the window. There's a perfect view of the city skyline, even if the backdrop is currently a bright blue instead of the inky blue this city thrives on.

My phone rings again, and I answer, knowing who it is. "What now?"

"Knock knock," he says at the same time that there are two knocks on the door.

"You—what?" I dart around the bed and toward the door. Pulling it open, I gasp and drop my phone. "What are you doing here? I thought you were at practice!"

"You could at least pretend you're happy to see me," a grinning Corey says, stepping into the room.

"I am. But you're supposed to be practicing."

He laughs and grabs me against him. "We were up at the ass crack of dawn. We got the afternoon off, so here I am."

"How did you know my room number?" I lean back in his tight embrace to look up at him.

"Don't tell my girlfriend, but I charmed that chick at the reception desk," he whispers conspiratorially, looking around shiftily.

"You're an ass." I run my fingers through the hair at the back of his head. "I thought you wouldn't be free until later."

"I wasn't going to be. I was with the guys in that bar across the street when you said you were here. And that was that." He finishes his explanation with a sweet but hot kiss on my lips.

"It didn't sound like you were in a bar when you called."

"I stepped outside, all right, Detective?"

"Don't get cocky, cowboy."

He cups my ass and pulls my hips against his. "I'm very cocky, as you well know." He sucks lightly on my bottom lip. "Would you like a demonstration?"

"We're in New York and you want to have sex instead of

being infuriating tourists?"

"Darlin', I can assure you there's a part of New York you haven't seen yet, and it's between those sheets on your bed. I'd be happy to take the tour with you."

"Deal," I whisper, nipping his bottom lip and walking back to the bed. At the last minute, I turn and whip the top sheet off. "Interesting. I think I've seen the between-the-sheets attraction."

Corey shakes his head, a wildly sexy smile on his face, and pounces toward me. I squeal at how quickly he comes toward me, but instead of jumping over the bed, I fall onto it. He climbs on top of me, pinning my hands above my head and pressing his hips against mine.

"They have different attractions," he murmurs onto my neck. "Creased, fisted, tangled… We have enough time to explore them all."

"We do. I agree." I slip my hands beneath his shirt and run them up his back, enjoying the smooth shapes of his muscles beneath my fingertips. "Once we've been and 'done' New York."

He drops his head, releasing my hands, and groans. "Really? Haven't you done it a million times?"

"Yes," I reply, turning to face him. "But it's my favorite city in the world." I run my fingers through his hair. "Plus, there's the added bonus that us being seen together will quash those rumors that I'm too classy to go out with someone who has naked pictures."

His face darkens a little. "Mmm. You are."

"And you're too hot to go out with someone who lies to everyone about what she does for a living, so we're even."

"Definitely not mmm," he responds, his mouth hovering just above mine. His breath flutters across my lips. "I don't care about them or what they say. I care about you, babe." Corey's hand slowly travels up my side to the back of my head. "I care about you, and if this is your favorite city in the world, then let's go see it all."

"All of it?" I smile.

"We have…" He glances away and presses the home button on my phone so the screen lights up. "We have three hours until dinner. Then until midnight at the latest. Think we can do it?"

"Yes… But why until midnight?"

"Because, at midnight, you're gonna be the Cinderella who doesn't lose her shoe," he whispers into my ear. "I'll give you a slice of your happily ever after if you want it."

My heart skips a beat. Or two. Or ten.

"You mean you're going to fuck me, don't you?"

A slow grin breaks out across his face. "That, too."

Broadway, Rockefeller Center, and Sixth Avenue—all by dinner. I'm impressed. I'm even more impressed by the way we managed to do it fairly unscathed by the media. So they're outside of the restaurant now, trying to get their shot of our apparently 'rocky relationship,' as we knew they would be.

"Where next?" Corey looks up at me. "Times Square?"

I shake my head. "Times Square is better in the dark. All the lights." I sigh happily.

"Oh shit. You're one of them, aren't you?"

"One of what?"

He waves his hand. "Lights and sparkles and fireworks kinda girls."

"Uh, you're aware that I've grown up with a view of Los Angeles and Hollywood, their lights, and their holiday fireworks, right?"

"Yes…"

"And with a superstar for a mom, I'm pretty accustomed to sparkles. As long as they're on someone else." I shrug. "Give me a Murano glass necklace over Tiffany's any day."

Corey tilts his head to the side, his gorgeous, blue eyes intense. He studies me the way he did when we just met—as if he's trying to make sense of what he's hearing.

"You know," he says, looking at me over the top of the glass, "the more I get to know you, the less I understand you."

"I'm a woman. You're not supposed to understand me. It's why you keep coming back. I'm that pretty little algebra puzzle on your test you should know the answer to but can't work out."

His lips pull into a smirk—a smug, cocky, yet happy smirk. "Keep confusing me," he says quietly, leaning forward and grabbing my hand. "I want to keep coming back to you."

"You know, you don't have to be all flowers and roses now that we're in a real relationship. You can still be that cocky guy. I did kinda like him."

"Really? You gave me a ton of shit about him."

"Because it was fun!" I defend. "I miss him. I don't think I'd be here if you kept being this whipped idiot you're being. I mean, come on, Jackson. Grow a pair of balls, okay?"

"You're lucky we're in public with a table between us, babe, or I'd show you what goes with my balls and I'd make sure you never fuckin' forget it."

"There he is." I laugh into my glass. "This guy. He's fun."

"You saying whipped Corey isn't fun?"

"Whipped Corey is sweet. But Cocky Corey is why I'm here. He's the guy who reeled me in."

In all honesty, I can't pinpoint the moment his obnoxious arrogance became something I readily accepted or when his cockiness turned into a personality quirk instead of something that riled me. I can't work out when or how I went from not wanting anything to do with him to needing to be near him—I just know that I did.

I'm totally honest when I say to him that I don't want him to change. I want that arrogant side to come out to play sometimes. It's fun, it's annoyingly endearing, and it makes me laugh because it's true. He is hot. Hell, he's fucking flawlessly gorgeous. He is an amazing football player, as much as I tease him otherwise, and he sure as hell knows his way around my body.

Every girl wants to catch a bad boy and change them. Make them perfect. Coax them into being their dream. It's a challenge between us all: catch him and change him and you've won at life. Here I am, faced with a bad boy, the biggest man-whore with a filthy mouth, and I'm the exception.

So isn't falling for the bad boy the thrill? Isn't it their asshole personality that attracts us? The cocky smirk, the overconfident glint in their eyes, and the unwillingness to listen to the word no? Isn't that what makes them *them*?

Doesn't changing them defy the very reason you fell for the bad boy in the first place?

Not that I've fallen. Not completely, anyway. I could still walk away tomorrow if the powers that be decide that that is what I have to do. It would hurt more than I want to admit, but I could. I'm not so far fallen that I'd be utterly devastated by it.

Although, if he carries on being this intoxicating mixture of sweet and sexy, my heart might just fall those last few inches.

"Let's go." He throws some cash on the dish holding the bill and gets up.

No sooner have I stood up than he wraps his hand around mine and pulls me sharply from the restaurant. Our move doesn't go unnoticed by the paparazzi waiting for us outside, and Corey surprises me by tugging me across the street, where we're still in full view of them, and pulling me into him.

His body is taut, his muscles hard as rock. "You know what my problem was when I acted a total arrogant bastard to you?"

I shake my head.

"I had this insane need to grab you in public and kiss the fuck out of you in front of the cameras. I had an unrelenting desire to make sure every fucker knew you were mine."

I can barely breathe, and what breaths I am taking are short and sharp, but I somehow say, "Do it. Do it now."

Because my heart is pounding and screaming at me to tell the world that *he's mine.*

He crashes his lips down onto mine. Hot and heavy, his hand clasps the back of my neck while the other arm wraps around my back. Then he sweeps his lips across mine in a kiss that reeks purely of possession.

It's not romantic. It's not seductive. It's raw and primal, possession echoing in every clash of our lips.

I feel it everywhere though. It's more than a message to the world. It's a message to me. And I hear it. I hear it loud and fucking clear.

He won't let go. It's as real as real it's gonna get. This is it. There's no turning back.

Any way you can say it, he does—without saying anything at all.

And come on. He's kissing me like I'm his oxygen on the streets of New York while a thousand lights glitter around us. This shit is so real that it floods my veins.

He pulls back, his face still lingering close to mine, and breathes heavily. My body tightens with the words I want to hear, but as a second of silence stretches into a minute, I know they won't come.

I'm crazy because I can't say it back, but that doesn't mean I don't want to hear that he loves me.

I fist his shirt, it not mattering that we're in public, the realization washing over me that he *isn't* in love with me. That maybe he's in the fucked-up emotional limo I am in. That, like we have been from the very beginning, we're on the exact same page in this relationship.

Mom walks into my hotel room with the room service guy and drops onto the bed next to me. I groan and roll over, covering my head with the pillow.

"Go away," I whine, exhaustion wracking my whole body.

Corey left some two hours ago after far too much time creasing, fisting, and tangling these sheets. He also completed the sleep section, which, according to him, topped off the tour of my bed sheets. But still…two. Ugh.

"Rise and shine!" Mom sings, the door closing in the background. "There's coffee in the pot and bacon on the plate."

I sit up, the sheets falling away to reveal the bra I threw on after Corey left. "Bacon?"

"You obviously slept well if you're mentioning the bacon."

"Yes. This bed is comfortable." For sex. I haven't had enough sleep experience yet… "The show is at five, right?"

Mom nods her head. "But there are a few before we also have tickets to. I thought you'd like to come along and spend the day by the catwalk."

I only really want to see mine, but I know Corey is practicing early, and New York is no fun on your own. I was hoping I could wrangle Mom into a trip to Lady Liberty because I know she loves her, but that's obviously totally not in the cards.

"Sure. Why not?" I didn't come last year, after all.

"Corey's busy, isn't he?" Mom smirks, piling some food onto a plate for me.

"Um…"

She laughs. "Honey, you're twenty-two. You don't have to accompany your mommy to everything anymore. I promise. I can take Alex."

"Oh, yes. I can see Alex in the front row of Vera Wang wondering what couture piece he can snag for the next event."

"I'll have you know they approach me for this."

"I know. That's why there's a room full of free clothing in our house."

"Well, yes." She smiles, handing me the plate. "I called Alex this morning. He wanted me to assure you he had great joy finding Cole's Playboy collection from when he was fifteen and subsequently enjoyed teasing him until he drove him out of the house."

"Alex videoed that, right? Right, Mom?" I fight my giggles.

"I told him you'd never approve of him wanting to marry me if he didn't."

I choke on my bacon. "Ex-fucking-cuse me?"

Mom's eyes widen. "Oh, he hasn't proposed!" she says hurriedly. "He just brought it up, and well, we've been dating for a few years. I told him to talk to you."

"I'm not sure asking me is the traditional move."

"Well, Ada already gave him her blessing over biscuits and gravy yesterday morning."

I set my fork down with a sigh. "He fell for the six-sugar

thing, didn't he?"

"Honey, so badly." Mom shakes her head. "I should have warned him. Incidentally, the cookies are now on top of the fridge."

"Smart move."

"Just…out of curiosity… What would you say if Alex were to bring it up with you?"

"Ada's sugar addiction?" I tease. "I don't know. Cole would be pretty annoying to have as a big brother, don't you think? I mean, that Playboy thing…" I shake my head.

"Leah. Please be serious."

I look into my mom's eyes and see hesitance, something I'm not used to seeing. I don't understand it because my father is a giant dickhead, and there's nothing I'd love more than to see her find her happily ever after. She's acted enough—she deserves the real one. And I fucking love Alex.

Still, though… "Tell Alex he'll have to ask me himself."

I can't breathe.

That dress—it's mine. So are the shoes. And the purse. And…and the jumpsuit? That's mine, too. So is the shirt and skirt on the next model. And that pantsuit? Mine. The coat? Mine.

Mine. Mine. Mine. Fucking mine.

My dream. I'm looking at it now. These designs I once scribbled haphazardly onto paper are real. They're not dreams of a sixteen-year-old. They're now my reality, every one perfectly tailored and shaped and enlivened.

My eyes are stinging, but I'm swallowing back any ounce of emotion. I'm trying not to see the pencils scribbling on sheets as the world's most famous people jot down the designs they like. I'm trying not to throw up over the realization that these people like my work.

That these people, who've been to years and years of these shows, like *my* work.

That they don't know that they're sitting almost right next to the designer.

I don't think about the fact that the royal-blue evening gown I'm following with my eyes was originally designed with my mom in mind or that the pale-pink-and-black one following it is my vision for Ryann.

But, as it turns out, I'm thinking about a whole lot of everything, because my mind is whirring at a million miles per hour.

Because that's my dress and my jumpsuit and my evening gown and my skirt and my pants and my purse and my jacket and my coat and my sweater and my dream.

Mom links her pinkie finger with mine in a silent show of solidarity. She knows how hard this is for me. I want to sit here and cry and toast champagne. I want to remember this as the single greatest day ever.

Because, despite the circumstances, I can sit here, front row, and watch what was once in my head walk past as a physical thing.

And there are no words to explain that.

I take a deep breath as the final model disappears backstage and applause fills the room. This is mine. For me. And no one even knows it.

One hour of watching my future clings to me. *Damn.*

I stand up with Mom, our pinkie fingers still linked, ready to break for some food and a drink. She guides me through the bustling people and into the restaurant set up for the show.

"I'm proud of you," she whispers in my ear so quietly that it's barely audible to me. "That was incredible."

I nod because I can't speak. My eyes keep going back to the door that leads to the catwalk—to where my designs just were.

"Grace, darling!" Quinn appears, and obviously, he's left the backstage to his staff. He embraces Mom then turns to me, a proud smile on his face that no one but I can understand, before sweeping me into his arms. "Leah. You fucking star." He kisses my cheek, his words, like Mom's, barely even a whisper. "How do you feel?"

I shake my head because I still can't speak. If I speak, I might cry.

Mom passes me a glass of wine and I drink.

"Surreal," I murmur into it. "Now don't talk to me anymore."

Quinn laughs and asks for a whisky. The amber liquid is passed across the bar to him and he throws it back in one swift mouthful.

"Fuck Fashion Week," he says under his breath. "I'd rather be behind my desk, staring at my prodigy's designs."

Mom gently touches his arm. "You mean in the Bahamas, on a beach, with some gorgeous model, staring at your prodigy's designs."

"Darling, if you're offering..." Quinn eyes her.

"Ew!" I cough, looking between them.

Mom laughs. "He wishes, Leah."

"And for what it's worth, those wishing wells? Bullshit," Quinn adds, leaning in to me.

I laugh as one of mom's friend approaches her. Julia LaFor, editor at the fashion magazine *Riot.* Her articles are always cutting edge, her grasp on the fashion world unparalleled. I have many of her predictions pinned to my boards at home, and surprisingly enough, I haven't met her.

Until now.

"And this is your daughter? Leah?" Julia asks Mom, who nods. Julia turns to me, beaming widely. "Wonderful. You're the star of the show, sweetie!"

I freeze, but somehow, my facial muscles don't move. "I'm sorry. I don't understand."

"Your line? Lea V.? We're all fascinated by you! So young with a collection to rival the golden designers? Fascinating."

"I think...you have me confused with someone else," I say apologetically. "I don't know what you're talking about."

Julia eyes me, a funny glint in her eye. "Really? Word got out just before the show that you're the girl behind them all. We've all been wondering ever since news of the Lea V. line became public knowledge amongst us. Is that incorrect information?"

I look at Mom. Fear paralyzes me. It spreads through my

veins, because no, no, no. This isn't happening. People know? Outside?

"Mom?" I whisper, bile rising up my throat. "Quinn?"

"It was lovely to see you again, Julia," Mom says, kissing her cheek cordially. "But I believe it's best if Leah and I leave now."

Mom wraps her arm around my shoulder and guides me away, Quinn following. As soon as we leave the main room, Mom fielding a whole bunch of people, she turns on Quinn.

"Was this you?"

"If you think I'd jeopardize your daughter's safety for my company, you don't know me."

"He didn't," I whisper, gripping on to Mom. *Oh, God.* "It wasn't him."

I look up at her, and she can surely see the tears filling my eyes, because I can feel them. They threaten to spill over, stinging and taunting.

Only one other person knew.

"Son of a bitch," Quinn growls, guessing correctly. "Get out of here. Get back to your hotel and let us deal with it."

"But—"

He cuts me off, his dark-brown eyes blazing. "Leah, I'm your boss, and I'm telling you to leave and let my team deal with this. Do you understand?" he cuts me off, his dark brown eyes blazing.

I nod, Mom's arms tightening around me.

"And if that sorry bastard comes to see you, then you kick him on his butt. You hear me? I watched the Jaguars do it last season—if they can, you can."

Again, I nod. Because I don't have a choice.

Mom pulls me outside and into a swarm of photographers. Their flashes—they're blinding. Their questions—they're endless. Am I really Lea V.? Have I really kept this secret for six years? Is that why I haven't made my acting debut?

Three security guards approach and circle us. They guide us through the band of insanity outside and toward the cars.

"Leah!"

His voice cuts through me. It prickles across my skin as if I'm a voodoo doll and someone is stabbing me repeatedly with needles, each pin agonizingly painful.

"What?" My voice is stronger than I am inside. I'm crumbling, breaking.

Corey pushes past everyone toward me. "Shit. Babe, you have to know—"

"I know," I reply, gripping the door. "I know everything."

I get into the car and slam the door behind me, turning away so I don't have to look at him.

I don't know what hurts more—that I'll never be the designer I wanted to be or that the guy I trusted with such a big part of me has betrayed that.

chapter TWENTY-EIGHT

Corey

Shit. No, no, no.

She can't think I did this.

I would never fucking hurt her this way. I'd never fucking hurt her any way.

Fuck!

I grab the nearest cab and throw a bunch of bills into his lap to silence his protestations. "The Ivy. And quick."

He pulls away, leaving the money on his lap. It was probably the desperation in my voice. Fuck. I can feel it. I can hear it when I speak, dammit. I mean, fuck it. I've been outside here since the fucking show began because I found out.

I had to tell her that it wasn't me. She has to believe me.

She has to believe she means the world and more to me and I'd never do this.

Fuck, I love this girl. I love her to the fucking end of the universe and back. Hurting her… It's incomprehensible. It physically hurts me. And this…

If I find whoever did this to her, if I find whoever just destroyed her goddamn world, I will hurt that motherfucker so badly that he'll never be able to talk again.

I almost fall out of the car in my desperation to get to her. I need to see her, feel her, hold her. I need to make her pain go away although I don't think she'll let me.

I shove past the media—they can kiss my fucking ass, too. They can kiss every New Yorker's ass for all I care. I'm getting to my girl.

The elevator doesn't move fast enough. No matter how many times I jab my finger into the button, it doesn't seem to move any faster. Just that same, slow bullshit pace it always does.

The doors open on her floor and I run toward her door. I saw the look in her eye, the one that she thought was me. The wrong spark. The wrong fucking belief.

I bang on her door. "Leah! Leah!"

"Fuck yourself!" she screams, her voice hoarse.

"It wasn't me, babe! Fuck, I swear to you! You have to believe me!"

She yanks the door open, and with tears streaming down her cheeks, she stares at me full on. "I don't have to believe a word you say. I never fucking had to, but I did. And I was so fucking stupid!" She slams her hand into her door. "I never wanted to tell you, but you found out anyway, and now this. You know how much this means to me. Why did you do it? Why?"

"I didn't!" I shout. "I didn't! I would never do this to you. I would never do anything that would make you hurt this way."

"Don't lie to me!" Tears keep falling faster and faster, soaking her cheeks. "You are the only person who knows outside of my family. You did, Corey. I know you did. So do us both a favor and turn the fuck around."

I shake my head, pain rippling through me. One by one, the waves hit me, because I've lost her and I didn't do a fucking thing.

"I won't give up on this, Leah. You get that? I won't fucking stop until you believe that I'm not lying. It wasn't me."

She stares at me, every part of her body shaking. Her eyes spit anger and hatred and heartbreak, and each emotion cuts me to my core. It kills a little part of me.

"Leave. Now," she whispers harshly. "Before I call security

and have you removed."

I look her square on although it's killing me. "It. Wasn't. Me."

She pulls her phone from her purse on the side table and dials. Bringing it to her ear, she says, "I need security at room 716. There's someone I need removed."

I stare at her, unable to breathe. I can't believe she really fucking thinks that I did it. I can't believe she thinks I'd betray her that way.

She shuts the door. I hammer on it again and again, because fuck, fucking dammit, she needs to listen to me. She needs to fucking listen and believe because I can't be without her again.

"*Leah!*"

Hands grab my arms and tug me away from the door. I yell once more, but it's pointless. She's made her decision, and now, I have two fucking assholes dressed in black removing me.

Two people who don't care who I am or that my girl has it totally wrong. Two people who haul me into the elevator, down the stairs, through the lobby, and out onto the sidewalk.

Cameras snap and reporters shove microphones in my face. I shove more than one out of my way, but they keep coming, one after another, endlessly.

"Back the fuck up!" Jack roars, shoving one of them out of the way. "Disrespectful motherfuckers."

He grabs my arm and shoves me toward a waiting car. I get in and bury my face in my hands. I don't know. I don't what the fuck I do now without her.

"You're welcome." Jack sits next to me, adjusts the collar of his T-shirt, and slams the door shut.

"Thanks," I mutter, not really giving a fuck if I'd have floored one of those nosy pricks back there.

"What happened?" he asks.

"I knew. She thinks I told everyone." I run my fingers through to the ends of my hair and drop my head so it's between my knees. "Fuck!"

"Did you?"

"No." I sit up quickly, and my head spins, but I look at the closest friend I've had in years. "I'd never fuckin' do that to her, man. Never."

He doesn't say anything. He just looks at me.

"You believe me?"

"Yeah." Jack nods his head. "I've never seen you so fucking cut up about anything, ever. So, yeah. I believe you, bro."

"At least someone does."

She's like a poison spreading through my veins. Her eyes are the worst though. They haunt me, the heartbreak that shone in them and the tears that gave that extra shine I didn't want to see. Even now, I wish I could step forward and wipe them away, kiss the salty wetness from her cheeks. I wish I could hold her until every single inch of that pain disappeared.

I wish I'd stepped forward and done exactly that.

Instead, I stood there when I could have pushed forward. I let myself be taken away from her because the pain of her pain overrode my need to make her understand.

And now, I'm standing in the middle of a fucking football field, trying to make a game happen. It's almost impossible. I can hear her voice teasing me about throwing an interception. I can see her smile as she said it, sassy and sexy at the same time.

"Corey!" Coach bellows into my ear.

I jolt back to the game and call the snap. We're first and goal, and not even I can fuck that up. If I do, I need to hang everything up and fucking quit.

I want to. Right now, I'm hurting so badly that I want to tell Coach to get that prick Anderson out here to take my place.

But I won't because this is my family. The Vipers are my fucking family and I won't let them down because things off the field have turned to shit.

We go through play after play, pickup after interception, after touchdown, and all I can really be thankful for is that I'm not the quarterback being sacked.

And by the time the end of the game is called, all I can really be thankful for is that we have won.

Even with my whole life in shambles, I can still play the game.

Go figure.

I shower and change without speaking to anyone. Jack and Reid try, but I cut them off by turning my back to them. They get the message, and before everyone else can leave, I sling my bag over my shoulder and head toward the door.

I just want to disappear into my hotel room and figure out what the hell I'm gonna do.

There's a figure leaning on my car though, and in my darkness, my heart thumps. Could it be—

"Took your time."

Her Texas accent travels across the parking lot, and I look up at my sister.

"What the fuck are you doing here?"

"I'm being the good daughter and sister and coming to check up on my poor big brother." Lottie straightens, her hands on her lips. "Tell me, Corey. What's it like to finally have your heart broken?"

"Fuck you, Lottie." I slam the back door after throwing my bag in. "Seriously, if you're only here to piss me the fuck off, then turn your ass around and hightail it out of here."

She sighs, tucking her hair behind her ear. "All right, all right. Mom called and asked if I'd come and check on you since it is a weekend and this breakup is all over the news!'" She scoffs. "So here I am, being the good girl, as always."

I open the door of the rental and look at her. "Well, either be nice or fuck off."

"Got a new chick already, Corey?" Zander laughs from across the lot. "You sure attract them!"

"She's my sister, you fuckin' idiot," I snap. "Keep your eyes on your dick and not on her." I turn to Lottie. "Get in the fuckin' car."

"Excuse me?"

"Get. In. The. Fuckin'. Car," I repeat slowly. "These assholes aren't gonna use my sister for their next jack-off material."

Lottie laughs and gets in the passenger's seat. "Protective. Not somethin' I see from you, big brother."

"Guys findin' you attractive. Not somethin' I see, little sister," I shoot back, putting the car into drive and tearing out of the parking lot.

She laughs again, clicking her belt into place. "So he cares. Is it possible there's a heart under there?"

"Hey—you're the one who decided to sit on the sidelines when we grew up. You're the one who avoided me like the motherfuckin' plague. You might piss me off somethin' chronic, but I care about you."

I turn the car toward our hotel. There's a huge line of traffic in front of us, and I remember my mistake from my last trip to the Big Apple.

You never drive in New York.

Lottie doesn't reply. She just sits with her hands in her lap, fidgeting with her fingers. It suits me fine. I don't give a shit if I have to talk to her, especially not now. If Mom wants to know how I am, she can call me for the fourth time today and the seventh time since Leah's identity broke.

It takes us twenty minutes of tense silence until we finally arrive at my hotel. She follows me from the car into the lobby then the elevator.

"Don't you have anything else to do?"

Lottie shrugs. "Mom canceled dinner while she tries to do some damage control. Apparently, you're causin' craziness back in L.A. and she might have to fly back. Hey, Cor, you got room service?"

"No, I'm in an expensive-as-fuck hotel without room service."

She rolls her eyes, typical twenty-year-old, and folds her arms across her chest. When the doors ping open, she follows me out, her eyes burning into the back of my head.

I let us into my room and throw a menu her way. "Have whatever you want."

"Generous," she mutters, looking down at it. "You want anything?"

Sitting on the edge of the bed, I shake my head. Unless Leah counts as 'anything,' I don't want a damn thing.

"Corey," Lottie says softly, and I look at her. She sighs then sits in the chair close to me. "You tried talking to her today?"

I nod and rest my elbows on my knees, leaning forward. "Her phone's off. So is her mom's."

My sister chews the inside of her cheek. "Maybe they were flying home?"

"Probably."

"Why don't you go back to L.A. and go to her house? Talk to her then?"

I wish that were an option. It'll be a fucking media circus outside of her house until God knows when. Besides… "Like she'll let me in."

"I guess." She pauses. "Does it really matter? I mean, I've watched you go through girls quicker than I go through underwear. You'll have another girl on your arm by next weekend."

My eyes narrow. Yeah, it matters. It matters a whole fucking bunch to me. I don't want some other girl on my arm. Hell, I don't even want Leah on it.

I want her in my arms, curled against my body, her fingers fisting my T-shirt as she clings to me.

"Wow," Lottie says softly. "You really care about her, huh?"

I take a deep breath and run my fingers through my hair. Looking at the floor, I say, "I love her, Lottie. And now…" I swallow. "I don't have a clue what to do to make this right."

"Wow," she breathes. "Really? You really do?"

I nod.

"Okay. I think…" She pauses for a moment. "I might be able to help you."

My head snaps up and I meet her light-blue eyes. "Are you serious?"

She tilts her head to one side and shrugs. "I'm gonna need a few days, but yeah. I guess my degree should come in handy at some point in my life."

"Wait… What are you gonna do? Is it legal?"

My sister smiles. "I'll trace the leak to where it originated online. If you really didn't tell, then there'll be a site somewhere with the information. It'll be time-stamped. And yes, it's legal. Kind of."

I sit up straight. "So, you could find the person who did this?"

"Ah, no." She grimaces. "I'm not the NSA, dude. It'll be covered up in so many ways. I won't be able to get past the original source, but that'll be enough. It's probably from the files gathered by the celebrity hacker. Leah's famous by default."

Of course. "Lottie, you're a fuckin' genius."

"I know." She grins. "I'll call you when I've found out." She throws the menu at me. "Now, order me a double vodka and Coke and a bacon cheeseburger."

chapter TWENTY-NINE

Leah

Sometimes it helps to have friends who aren't famous.

Well, Ryann kind of is, but she's still under the radar enough that her apartment makes the perfect hideout from the media circus that keeps pulling its show around me. I took the trash out yesterday and got photographed.

Enjoy putting a picture of me with no makeup, greasy hair, and sweatpants on your front pages, fuckers.

Ryann's place is my place—for now. And tonight, we get the added bonus of Macey for a girls' night in.

And God only knows I need one.

Since I found out that my secret was no longer a secret, my heart has dropped so far that I'm certain it's exited my body completely. If it's still in there, still beating, it's a dull, lifeless throb. Right now, every part of me is giving up.

My worst fears have come to light. All I have is that the most important people in fashion saw the previews of my collection before they knew it was mine. All I can hope for now is some respect from that, not because of who I am.

Everything I worked for has been ripped out from under me, even if my items are already selling out on the QD website. I don't care about that or that the fact that Quinn is probably going to hand me a huge-ass contract to tie me down to him for the next few years. I don't care that everyone is buzzing with the news that Leah Veronica, private and elusive daughter of Grace Veronica, is a big-shot fashion designer.

I don't even care that my friends are amazed or that I had Cole calling me and tearing me a new asshole for keeping it from him.

What I care about is that the dream is over.

And so is the hope that Corey Jackson was something other than the egotistical, selfish asshole I once thought he was.

He proved me right and wrong all in one swoop, and what a way to do it. Expose my biggest secret, the one thing that meant the world to me, right after he spent hours inside me. Nice one, dickhead. He really fucking starred there. Give him a medal, someone.

The worst thing is that, when I think back to the moment I found out, I'm not sure which hurt most. I don't know if the cause of my uncontrollable tears was because I was found out or because he betrayed me.

I don't know which one my heart broke more for. I don't know which one it hurts more right now.

In fact, I'm so numb that I'm not even sure if it hurts anymore.

"I still can't believe you did it for *six* years and nobody found out." Ryann passes me a glass of wine and curls up on the sofa next to me.

"I had to," I say quietly into my glass.

"I get it. Believe me, I do. Like, you have this huge pressure on your shoulders to be as successful as your mom is, right? So, by keeping it secret, it didn't matter if you failed because it would never be connected to you."

"Right. Except now I'll never know because it'll fly by default. It'll fly because my name is attached to it."

"Maybe not." Ryann shrugs. "I'm not saying it's bad. I saw some of your designs in college, and damn, Leah, but the only pressure you have now is keeping it going. It doesn't matter if your work is bad or good. People will buy it if they want it. And hey—if it's shit, the critics will tell you."

"The critics will lie so they don't piss off my mom," I murmur.

"No, they won't. They'll be honest because that's their job. So just go out there, do your thing, and show the world you're not just Leah, Grace Veronica's daughter. You are Leah Veronica and you are a badass and you're going to take over the fashion industry because you can!"

I look at my best friend, a smile growing on my face. Of course Ryann would be the first person to do that. "You're right," I admit. "And hey, at least I can design your Oscars dress now."

She fans herself. "Oh, Lordy, the Oscars. I'm going to die."

"You'll have to go with Cole." I wink.

Ryann freezes then drops her head back, her tongue flopping out one side of her mouth.

"What are you doing?"

"You killed me." She sits up, laughing. "We start filming in two weeks and I can't even be around him. I swear, you're a goddess. How do you keep your ovaries from going boom boom?"

I cover my mouth with my hand. "Um, he's kind of like my brother. I'd be afraid if my ovaries went 'boom boom!'"

She sighs and sips her wine. "I suppose. It's been a while since I had the ovary boom boom, so it's nice to know they're still in there, picking out my future baby daddy."

"I hear you." My smile drops a little. So I never imagined anything with Corey past the right now, but my ovaries definitely did the boom-boom-bop whenever I saw him.

"Shit. That was kind of insensitive. I'm sorry." Ry bites her lip. "Have you spoken to him?"

"No. Since security carted him out of my hotel, he's called a few times, but that's it. I guess he knows I meant what I said. That I'm done." I look into my glass and spin it so the wine swirls.

"You sure you mean it? 'Cause the fight you got going on with your tears tells me something else."

"It doesn't matter." I swipe under my eyes. "He violated my trust in the most brutal way, Ry," I whisper. "He knew what it meant to me to keep it a secret. But he told anyway. There's no way I could ever trust him again. I never should have in the first place."

Ry twists her mouth to the side. "I guess. You'll be okay, you know? He's just a guy. A fit-as-hell guy, okay, but this is Los Angeles. Cocky, arrogant fucktards are all over the place. This love thing is like the lottery. Sometimes you'll meet a guy who gives you a good time, but he's one ball short of the jackpot. Sometimes you don't match any. Then, eventually, if you're lucky enough, you'll nail the Powerball."

"That's a new analogy." I force a smile. "I like this."

"It's true. Look at Macey—she thought Mitch was her Powerball. Really, he was like only matching one or two balls week after week. Turns out, he was a dud ticket, anyway."

"I suppose. And Corey is my 'one ball short of the jackpot,' right? He's nice to look at, can be sweet, and is, you know, killer in the bedroom. It's a shame he's just a giant fuckturd."

"That's the spirit!" Ryann grins. "Just replace his name with Giant Fuckturd and it won't seem so bad. Do it in your phone, too. Just because you can."

She throws it at me, and I stare at her for a moment before setting my glass on the table and bringing up my contacts list. Then I find Corey's name and edit it.

"There." I show her the screen. I now have a lot of missed calls and messages from one Giant Fuckturd.

Oddly, it is better. Mostly because the word 'fuckturd' is fucking fabulous.

"She had the baby," Macey grumbles, shoving the front door open and slamming it behind her. "It's this little fat thing. Looks like a fucking potato on steroids."

I share a startled but concerned glance with Ryann. "Mace, are you all right?"

She nods totally unconvincingly. "Right as fucking rain. Can we please get some tequila and then find me a guy to fuck? *With* a condom, the pill, and the fucking implant. Hell, shove the NuvaRing in there, too."

"You could just call Jack," Ryann snorts, getting up. She grabs a bottle from the kitchen counter and slams it on the coffee table with three shot glasses.

"Hey, you just got a fuck off contract. Why don't you call the realtor for a bigger house?" Macey snaps, grabbing to the shot glass Ry just poured and tossing it back.

"Whoa." I look at her. "We get it, all right? We've been there since Mitch told you he knocked your cousin up. Don't take this out on us. You're not the only one having a shit-ass day."

Macey closes her eyes and takes a deep breath. "You're right. Ry, I'm sorry." She looks between us. "It's just… My aunt sent a bunch of fucking pictures to us this morning. Because, you know, Mitch is such a fabulous catch with his promising law career that's already on hold while he tends to that bitch's swollen ankles and varicose veins. Right."

"And while your cousin is changing shitty diapers and he's feeding a kid at two a.m, you're getting a second degree at college," Ryann reminds her.

"For what though? I can barely pay for the first course," she huffs.

"But when you're this hot-shot lawyer yourself, you'll be able to pay it all off. And he'll still be changing shitty butts." Ryann grins.

"And you don't have swollen ankles or varicose veins," I point out. Hey, if we can focus on her shit instead of mine, it works for me.

"And I'm not going to because I'm too selfish to have a kid. Besides, that would mean commitment and stuff. Mitch beat that shit right out of me with a ten-ton hammer."

"Mace, don't give his cock so much credit."

Her eyes snap to me and she laughs loudly. "Oh, girls. I swear, I don't know why I stayed with him, but it wasn't for his cock. Mr. Jack Rabbit packs more inches *and* girth than he ever did."

"I wonder what Cole's cock is like."

"Oh my God, no!" I hold my hands out to Ryann. "No, no,

no! That's wrong on so many levels!"

"I'm deprived!" she cries, pouring three tequila shots. The doorbell rings and she walks backward toward the door. "I swear, my vagina is so out of action it has cobwebs on its cobwebs. Oh. Er, hi."

"Pizza for Ryann? Or is it cobweb vagina?"

I bury my face in my hands, laughing. Macey isn't as discreet, and she shrieks her giggles, rolling back on the armchair. Ryann stutters something then slams the door.

"Did you pay for that with cash or is he willing to clear your cobwebs?" Macey sniggers, opening one of the boxes.

"Oh my God." Ryann presses her hands to her cheeks. "Why did I not think before I opened the door?"

"Because you're the clumsy one who always makes a bad day good again?" Macey offers, picking up and dropping a pizza slice in half a second. "Hoooo. Hot."

"What she said." I nod toward Macey, grabbing my shot glass. "Ten minutes ago, I was trying not to cry, and now, I'm crying from laughter."

Macey scoffs at me. "Next time you wanna cry over that dickbitch, call me and I'll beat those tears right out of you."

"For real," Ryann adds, her cheeks back to their normal pale pink. "No sad tears. Only happy tears. Especially not over fuckturds. House rules." She grabs some pizza and snatches a bite from the end. With a full mouth, she says, "I need to get my gran to cross-stitch that for me."

"See? You make me laugh." I look from Ryann to Macey. "And you threaten this. This is why it's impossible to be have a broken heart around you guys."

"Psssh! Broken heart my left vagina lip." Macey leans forward. "Your heart is just fine, Leah. Hearts don't break unless the person who hurt you is worth breaking for. And Corey Jackson is definitely not worth your heart breaking."

"I guess so." I smile, but it's fake.

Because she doesn't know him like I do.

And he is worth my heart breaking.

~

"Did your mom tell you my dad wants to marry her?"

I look at Cole, sitting on my bed, playing with my tablet. "She did."

"It's fucking gross. They're old."

"You sound like a petulant six-year-old who doesn't want a new mommy."

He drops the tablet and pouts at me. "Me no want one."

I roll my eyes. "Well, he still hasn't asked my permission. And I'm just saying that, when he does, he should make it convincing."

"Wait. So you're saying you want him to propose to you so he can propose to your mom?"

"That could work." I smile. "Come on. It wouldn't be bad to be my brother, would it?"

"I don't know. Now that Corey's out of the picture, I was kind of considering seducing you. And if our parents got married, it would be kind of awkward, don't you think?"

"Oh, yes. I mean, why wouldn't I give in to your seductive charm?" Again, I roll my eyes. "You're an idiot, Cole."

"It made you smile." He rolls onto his stomach and looks at me. "You've had a face like a wet cat all afternoon and you're pissing me off now."

"I'm sorry my heartbreak is inconvenient to you. Next time, call ahead, asshole."

"I will." He sighs then looks up at me, all traces of joking gone from his face. "Seriously. I hate seeing you upset like this."

"I'm all right, okay? I have a whole bunch of work to do now. I'm a big deal now, you know?"

"Yeah, and I'm mad you didn't tell me. 'Writing my resume' my fucking ass, Leah Veronica!"

I smile apologetically. "I'm sorry. I really couldn't tell anyone. And he… Corey… He found out by accident."

"Your mom told us." He nods slowly, his lips pulled to one side. "What does it mean now though? You gonna keep designing or what?"

"I don't have a choice." I pick some lint from my jeans. "I can't imagine doing anything else, you know? And at the end of the day, I have a job. I don't get to work it the way I want to, and now I'm going to be even more of a media draw than before, but I still get to do it."

"You don't sound that bothered that you were found out."

"No, I am. I'm really upset about it, but I can't change it. I can't reverse Corey's actions. I don't regret keeping it a secret, so I have to do all I can do—design. Quinn has already sent, like, ten million requests from people wanting me to design dresses for award ceremonies and stuff."

"Are you gonna do it?"

"I can't do them all. Besides, the thing I really wanna do is huddle beneath my covers, eat frozen yogurt, and cry for a bit." I shrug. "It's like overnight, my whole world has changed. I'm not sure how I'm supposed to deal with being this person fully in the spotlight. Every move I make is going to be tracked and I don't know how I feel about that."

"It's just a step up from before." He swings his legs around and sits up. "I'm in the same position, remember? Before I did that movie with your mom, I was just Alex Dalton's kid, trying to make a name for myself. I was a guy to watch, sure, but they pretty much left me alone. Now, I can't piss without some dick shoving a camera through my bathroom window."

"I guess. How do you deal with it?"

"You don't. You just hope it'll get better and that they'll eventually leave you alone."

The doorbell rings downstairs and I get up. "True. I'll be right back."

I run down the stairs and through the empty house. With Mom at an audition and Ada having lunch with friends, the house is quiet. Too quiet—and that's exactly why I called Cole.

The bell goes again.

"All right, all right," I grumble, grabbing the handle and pulling the door open. "Corey."

He's right there, in front of me, his hair disheveled and his normally bright, blue-green eyes dull, shadowed by gray. He looks exhausted, completely broken… Much like I feel.

Seeing him jolts me.

"What…what are you doing here?"

"I need to talk to you."

"You've said everything you need to." I push the door shut, but he's stronger and blocks it.

"You haven't let me say a damn thing, Leah."

"I don't want to hear it!" My voice rises. "I don't want apologies or excuses."

"Good, because I don't fuckin' have them. I'm not excusing or apologizing for something that wasn't my fault."

"So you'll lie instead? Awesome. Goodbye, Corey. We're done here."

I shove the door again, but he pushes it hard and it slams into the wall.

"No, we're not fuckin' done, Leah! I told you before that I'm not walking away from you. That counts for now, too." His hands grip the doorframe, his biceps bulging.

I wrap my arms around myself. "It doesn't," I whisper. "We're over, Corey. We never should have started. You know that as well as I do."

He's on me before I can move, his hands framing my face, his lips hot against mine. "Yeah? You think that?"

I nod, my face still held by his.

"You think wrong, darlin'," he whispers huskily. "We're not over. We're not done. We're not history. You got that, babe? No one has ever meant to me what you do, and there isn't a chance in fuckin' hell I'm letting you go without fighting."

"No amount of fighting could ever get me back!" I push his hands away from me and walk backward. "Have *you* got that? Have you, Corey, huh? Have you got that there isn't a single damn thing you could do to make me want you again? We. Are. Over. I will never forgive you for what you did."

"I didn't do it!" he shouts, clenching his jaw. "I feel sick at the thought of hurting you. Fuck!"

"What the hell?" Cole steps up behind me and puts his hand on my back. "Corey, what are you doing here?"

"Trying to make her see clearly!" Corey motions to me.

"As far as I can see, all you're doing is hurting her more, man." Cole glances at me.

I bite the inside of my cheek and look down. I won't cry. Not in front of him. I won't show him just how much I'm dying inside.

Because seeing him is more painful than I thought it'd be.

"Not listening is hurting her. Not being with me is hurtin' her!"

Cole steps in front of me and looks at Corey straight on. "You being here is fucking hurting her. I know her better than you ever could, and my advice to you is to leave right the fuck now and wait until she's ready to talk to you if you're lucky enough for that."

Tension crackles in the air around us, and I reach forward and grab the back of Cole's shirt.

I don't want Corey to go. I don't want him to stay either.

I wish we'd never met each other. That I'd stayed in my room on my birthday like I'd wanted to. That he'd picked some other girl to hit on in the bar.

That I'd never let myself play his game.

Because, in the end, we've both lost.

"Go," Cole says, his voice angry and protective. "That's the best thing you can do right now."

Corey stands there, not moving, and I glance up. My eyes meet his, and his gaze cuts right into my soul. Unwavering but weak, intense but broken, steady but shaken.

And an ounce of doubt slivers into my gut, because you don't hurt someone so deliberately, so publicly, and feel that much pain.

"Leah?" Corey says, his voice rough and like gravel.

"Go," I whisper, looking away from him as soon as I say the word.

I don't want to watch him go. Not again.

There's nothing until the door slams. It echoes through the house and I know he's gone. Again, he's walked away.

Again, I made him.

He's an asshole and he betrayed me, but that doesn't mean I don't care about him. It doesn't mean that I don't love him, because I do. I just didn't know how much until he walked away.

There's falling and there's *falling.* And neither of them really matters. Not a damn bit.

In the end, it doesn't matter how far you fall or how hard and fast you give in to the inevitable rush of it. It'll get you and it'll hurt you. Love is a bastard that knows no boundaries. Pain or pleasure, it doesn't care. Love will push you to the very limit and take everything you have to give, even if you don't have very much at all. Then it'll take some more, until you're left feeling like you need it to live. Like the person you love is the very oxygen you need to breathe. Yeah, love will take you and it will destroy you.

And it doesn't give a shit. It doesn't care if you cry yourself to sleep at night while holding the covers to your chin and flicking through stupid pictures of happier times. It doesn't care about the churning in your stomach at the thought of being without them, and it doesn't care if the very sound of their name stabs you in the chest.

It doesn't care because it doesn't know. All it knows are the frantic beating of your heart when they're around and the way you forget to breathe whenever their bare skin touches yours. Love is pure. It's untainted by stupid words, not bothered by the curses you sling at no one when it hurts, and it's never broken by a mere turn of your back.

All loves cares about it is simply being. It doesn't care about how it happens, when, where, or how fast. Just that it does. Because really, who can live without love?

We all have it. That hilarious, wine, takeout, and deep-secrets love with your girlfriends. The infinite, respect-filled love for the family that have always been there. That first love that's the greatest ever at the time but nothing compared to when you have true love.

That true love. God, that one. The one that sends your body into overdrive. The one everyone craves with every fiber of their being. The one that, when you have it, you should hold on to with everything you have.

The same one you don't know you have. It's there, lingering in the background with every tender touch and each playful kiss, waiting. It's there on the tip of your tongue with every word you say, ready to jump out but never knowing quite when.

And you *never* know. You never know you have it until you don't anymore. You can hold true love in the palm of your hand and wrap your fingers around it in a stealth grip, and you know what? It'll still slip through.

It's invisible yet tangible. Dreamed of yet so very real. Heart pounding yet heartbreaking.

You can turn your back on it without truly realizing what you're doing, because the kind of love that sets your life on fire is the same one that comes crashing in when you least expect it. You realize it when it's too late. At least you do consciously, because subconsciously, you know.

When you meet the person that sets everything you know alight and sends tingles across your skin even when you think you hate them, you know. You know through every argument and sarcastic comment and you know through every goddamn fucking toe-curling kiss.

Because that's love. You know but you don't. When you do, it's too late.

Would I have let him go if I'd have known on Saturday that I loved him with everything I possibly could?

Yes.

Because respect trumps love, and I respect myself more than I love him.

That will never change.

All I've wanted since we met was for him to leave me alone. To get out of my life. Now, all I want is for him to throw Cole out and pin me to a wall and physically make me listen to what it is he has to say.

Because it hurts. It more than hurts. The pain has seared through my whole body from the second I sat in the car. If I wanted to, I swear I could have heard my heart break.

The best love is the one you don't know you have.

It's the one that creeps over you and takes hold of your heart. Your body. Your soul. It's the one you believe in with everything you have and hold on to tighter than you've ever held on to anything.

But it kills you. Fuck, does it kill you.

I feel numb. That's all I can describe it as. There's so much anger and pain and heartbreak coursing through my body that I can't even think of it anymore. I don't want to hold on to it, but I can't let it go either. I can't do anything but sit here, crying into Cole's shoulder, and let it flood me.

The worst kind of love is the one you didn't know you had.

If you don't know you have it, you can't appreciate it. You'll never tell the person who holds your heart in the palms of their hands. You'll never have to tinge every memory with that gorgeous, pink haze that comes with being in love. Because *you don't fucking know.*

And that is absolutely, completely, and utterly the worst kind of love to ever exist.

Everyone should know they're in love, if only so they can tell the person they love. Everyone should know if they make someone's heart beat like crazy, if they set butterflies in their stomach, make their hands tremble with longing. That shit should be common knowledge. *Common fucking knowledge!*

Everyone deserves to know if they're the one person who makes someone's world light up like a thousand city lights illuminating the night.

Tears. On my cheeks.

It's a never-ending flow skimming across my skin with the same speed as I fell in love with Corey.

Fast.

I fell in love with Corey Jackson in the only way I know how. Headfirst, with no regrets or expectations. The very best way to fall in love.

I experienced heartbreak the same way. Headfirst. The very worst way to experience heartbreak.

chapter THIRTY

Corey

Twenty-four hours since I was forced out of her house by some puny-ass fucking actor. If Cole were anyone else and I didn't respect him, I would have had him on his ass and told him to mind his own fucking business.

Instead, I stood there and walked away. I did exactly what I told her I wouldn't.

She told me to.

She also told me once that 'go' means 'stay and fight.'

Either way, I fucked up by going. I just wish I could have stayed and told Cole to get out—told him that he needed to fuck off while I fought for the only girl I've ever loved.

For all I know, Leah's the only girl I will ever love. Right now, I can't see how anyone could compare to her. I don't know how anyone could come close to her smile, her laugh, her touch. I don't know how there could be a single person in this world as fucking perfect for me as she is.

And that's the problem with finding the person you think is 'the one.' No one compares to them. Every girl who walks past me, every chick I see eyeing me up? They're shit on my shoe compared to Leah. She's everything I never knew I wanted, and now that I don't have her, it feels like I have next to nothing.

All I have is football and an empty space where she used to

be.

It's like before I met her—except, this time, I know her beauty. I know the tinkle of her laugh and the sass of her smile. I know the thrill of her fingers across my skin and I know the softness of her body as it presses against mine.

She's everything I never knew I wanted, but everything I've always dreamed of.

But now, it's gone. She's gone. And there's nothing I can do to make her listen to me.

There's a knock at my door, but I ignore it. Fuck everyone else. I don't care.

The door opens and Jack walks in with Reid and Leo.

"Uncle Corey!" Leo yells, running through my house at lightspeed and throwing his seven-year-old body at me. "I caught the ball at practice yesterday and got a touchdown!"

"No way!" I hold up my hand, and he slaps it. "Good job, buddy!"

"Will you come watch my next game? Will you? Will you?"

"I wouldn't miss it. Make sure your dad reminds me, yeah?"

"Done!"

"Hey, bud," Reid says. "Why don't you go out the back and shoot some hoops?"

"All right, Dad." Leo climbs off the sofa and runs through the kitchen to the back yard.

"You look like shit," Reid offers once his son is fully out of earshot.

I rub the side of my head. "Feel it."

"It's quiet here," Jack states.

"No shit. Leah isn't here." It's the truth. She was always the noise in this large, cold house. She was always the person who made this house feel like a home. Whether she was covered in chocolate cheesecake mix, running around the kitchen, or lying on the sofa in her sweatpants, this house has never felt as warm as it did whenever she was here.

Now that she's gone, it's a cold, empty shell with a mere dream of being something.

Now that she's gone, the house is a reflection of me.

"I can't believe you're gutted over pussy," Jack says as they both sit on the sofa opposite me. "There's a fuck-ton of that downtown if you want it."

"It's not about pussy," I reply, meeting his eyes. "It's about her. Fuck, it's her. Always her." I rub my fingers across my scalp roughly.

"Just because you're a cold, hard fucking machine doesn't mean everyone else is." Reid directs that to Jack. I look up and he says to me, "Anythin' we can do?"

"You could pin her arms down and duct tape her mouth so she'll listen to me, but if you value your dicks, it probably ain't the best idea."

Jack chuckles. "Word. She almost had my balls once before."

There's another knock at the door and I lean back on the sofa. Fuck this. What's with all the people in my house?

"Want me to get that?" Jack asks, getting up and walking toward the door without waiting for an answer.

"I guess," I mutter sarcastically.

"Is Corey there?" Cole's voice follows the door opening.

I sit up straight. What the fuck is he doing here?

"Yeah, but who the hell are you?"

"Let him in!" I shout to Jack.

There are no words until the door shuts and Cole appears in my front room. He looks much the same as he did yesterday, and he looks at me seriously.

"Did you do it?"

I shake my head. "No. Never."

He studies me so intensely that I want to squirm. "Come here and tell me it."

"Who the fuck is this guy?" Reid moves to stand, but I wave him off and get up.

"I'm the closest thing Leah's got for a fucking brother, and if Corey's telling the truth, I want to know, all right?" Cole snaps. His eyes find me when Reid doesn't respond. "Did you do it?" he repeats.

I don't say a word. I just meet his stare. If he needs me to tell him, he's a fucking idiot.

"All right. I believe you," he says after a long minute. "And I'm gonna help you make her believe you, too."

"You are?" I frown. "Why?"

"Because she's so fucking hung up on you that it's killing me to see her hurting. And don't tell her I said this, but my dad proposed to Grace last night, and I think I should be some kinda hero in her eyes." He raises his eyebrows. "You get me?"

"I get it. But my sister is already tracing the leak."

"Seriously?"

"She is majoring in computers or some shit. I don't know. She knows more than I do."

"How close is she?"

"Your guess is as good as mine, bro."

Cole nods and shoves his hands in his pockets. "I have a friend who can do the same."

"Pointless."

"Nope." He grins. "Leah will listen to me. If I can show her proof that it wasn't you, she'll believe you and you'll have a shot at getting her back. He'll probably have the leak sourced in twenty-four hours."

"He isn't the guy behind this, is he? My sister has taken almost three days already."

Cole laughs. "No. But he knows what he's doing. Do you want my help or not?"

Leah's face springs to mind. The soft curve of her jaw, the pout of her pink lips, the expression in her eyes, her long, blond hair.

"Yeah. I'll do whatever it takes to get her back."

His phone is by his ear before he's even left the front room. I watch him go without another word exchanged between us.

"Well, fuck me," Jack says, his surprised words ringing out through the silence. "Corey Jackson fell in love."

"Are you sure you're fine?"

I look at Mom. "I'm good, honestly. I'm just…going with

it."

It's not an entire lie. I'm on pins and needles waiting for either Lottie or Cole to call and tell me that they've fixed this mess for me. I'm stuck in a fucked-up sense of limbo where my girl isn't my girl but she is.

Because that fact doesn't change, a fact I have to continuously remind myself of.

Leah is still mine. She can say that she isn't, but she is. As long as she cares and she cries, she's mine. And she does both. I saw it.

Leah Veronica is mine just like she was two weeks ago when I first realized it. She's mine just like she was when I saw her across the bar what seems like a lifetime ago. Mine, mine, mine.

No other way about it.

"Did you know Lottie's flying in today?" Mom hands me a grilled cheese sandwich.

"She is?"

"Yes. Your father is at the airport now to get her."

I blink at her. Lottie's flying in? That better mean she's found the original leak website. If not, I'm gonna kick her tiny little ass.

"Why?" I ask, biting into my sandwich.

"Something about needing to show you something?" Mom frowns. "Why she'd fly across the country to show you something, I don't know, son."

"She's been looking into when the thing where Leah's line got leaked," I explain. "She said she'd call me."

"Your sister has been willingly doing something for you?" Mom exclaims. "Did you drug her?"

"Ha! No. She offered. Maybe we're becoming friends."

Mom sighs. "If only you could have done that when she was in kindergarten."

"Hey. I never let the older boys pick on her. You think I got suspended for punching those guys randomly?"

"Yes."

"Nice. Well, I didn't. They were being dickheads."

"And how about your senior year? Remember when you

punched Ian Nelson?"

"He had his hands all over her!" I protest. "Homecoming or not, no one touched Lottie like that."

Mom holds her hands up. "All right. Well, she's in L.A. now, and she's coming here. For you, I assume."

"I hope so."

Mom nods and turns away. I do, too, but I look out the kitchen window. It faces directly on the driveway, and the last time I wanted to see my sister this badly was when she went out with some asshole in high school who thought third base was acceptable for a first date.

Fortunately—or unfortunately if you were Peter Dart—my sister had more respect, and instead of third base, he got a black eye. I knew then that I didn't have to worry anymore.

I hope that, this time when she comes home, she gives me the same feeling.

Dad's car rolls into the driveway, and my sister's dark hair is visible from the passenger's seat.

Shit. My palms are sweating as I clasp my hands on my lap. I hope to fuck she can give me the only chance I have at getting Leah back. I hope, for once, she's on my side.

I hope that, after years of being a royal asshole, karma won't bite me in the ass any longer.

Lottie walks in with her purse slung over her shoulder and looks around. Her eyes meet mine, and a smile quirks her light-pink lips. "Tell me you love me."

"Don't fuck with me, Lottie."

"Oh, sigh." She actually does sigh. "And here I was, dear brother, thinking we were on teasing terms." She sits next to me, pulls her tablet from her purse, then drops the purse on the floor by her feet.

"Well?"

"It got leaked on some website called '8Open.' I've never heard of it before, but after some research, it seems like it would be a good place to go if you happened to have some gossip on someone famous, or someone popular, at least."

"Like Leah."

"Right. It's a journalist's heaven." Lottie glances at me then goes back to swiping and tapping her screen. "It took me a while to get the website up. It was blocked on the college's Wi-Fi system, so I'm guessing some people know about it. I had to hijack Starbucks's, which was an absolute mess."

"I bet," I mutter, leaning forward.

"This is the site."

She turns the tablet toward me. My eyes flit over the bright green-and-white logo inset on a black webpage, and she clicks on her bookmarks.

"And this is the page where Leah's information was leaked."

The page takes forever to load. The little loading bar ticks a million fucking times before the article finally comes up, along with the front page of what looks like her employment contract. There's no information except stating that Leah has full design control of the line, but all publicity and final designs will be approved by Quinn Deacon of QD designs.

"And e-mails between her and Quinn…" Lottie scrolls down.

Sure as hell, there are a few e-mails with important dates and scanned designs.

"Why were e-mails on her the cloud?"

"She probably saved everything there," Lottie explains, putting the tablet on the table. "It looks like only important e-mails were transferred—maybe so she could access the information no matter where she was without going through an inbox. That's my guess, anyway. I can't tell you more than that, Corey. But this right here is the proof that you didn't tell anyone about her."

"But I could be this"—I look at the username of the poster—"NatGojsh person."

"Ah. No, you couldn't." My sister smiles and swipes a few times. "I traced the username as much as I could. It seemingly originates in the Philippines, but there are lines after. They're just really messy. I could spend ten years going down every line and I'd only have a vague idea of who this person is. And no offense, brother, but the only line you can understand is the line of play."

I smile. "True story. So how do I get this to Leah?"

Lottie grimaces. "I…don't know."

chapter THIRTY-ONE

Leah

My pencil scratches across the page. It's an unconscious movement, one designed to bring comfort and not really anything that makes sense. The irony of this is that, over the last three days, I've gone through approximately two hundred and fifty sheets of paper, and seventy-five of these have been usable designs. To an extent, at least.

Some I might not use for two years, some maybe never. Some I might pull out tomorrow and decide that a change of the neckline will make it a killer piece for my next collection.

The unusable ones are scattered in crumpled balls all over my design room floor. Not that they look out of place, mind you. The whole room is a mess. Fabric scraps litter the floor, too, and there's a range of pins and clasps strewn across my desk. Post-it notes are stuck all over the top of my laptop at angles so random I can see them peeking out at me when I look at the screen. There are a couple of cans of Coke in the trash can, and there might be one behind it because I have a really crappy aim. Might be.

And I have no desire to clean it.

'Cluttered space, clear mind' might be true in some cases, but not in mine. In my life, my space is a reflection of me.

My once-clean, now-messy room is the reflection of how

my life has changed since I met Corey Jackson.

Before him, everything in my life had a place. I knew what happened when. I knew where I had to be, who I had to be with, what I wanted. Down to the minutest detail, I knew.

He destroyed everything I knew.

He came barreling into my life with the force of a hurricane. He battered at my walls incessantly until they fell. He blew into me, beating me down, until I succumbed to his relentless attack and collapsed beneath the force of his determined desire.

And now he's gone and I'm left with the aftermath of his storm. There are a thousand pieces to pick up and unimaginable damage, but somehow, I keep going. Somehow, I can look past the pain and destruction and see how things might be in one, two weeks. Maybe even in a month, when the memories have dulled and the future is brighter than the past.

The only problem is that I can't see a part where he isn't there. And that's my downfall. That's the downfall of every storm—they might not be there, but you'll never forget them.

Corey Jackson grabbed ahold of me and my life and wormed his way in, inch by inch, hour by hour.

I miss him. The thought sizzles through my body, vibrating across my skin, making me hyperaware of the hole inside. That little dickhead-shaped hole where he used to be. It's a dull ache, and the only thing that eases it is when my pencil hits the page and my subconscious takes over.

Only now, my subconscious isn't in control anymore.

I look down at the page and gasp. I didn't draw a dress or pants or even shoes. I've drawn an eye with lashes that curl out at the edges and an eyebrow that quirks at the perfect angle.

From somewhere in my thoughts, I drew Corey's eye.

I snatch the page off the pad and twist it into the tightest ball possible as the doorbell rings. *No, no, no.* Don't say my dumbass mind has summoned him here, too?

"Leah?" Cole yells through the house.

"Upstairs."

There's silence until he hits the stairs. Then the sound of his footsteps fills the air. The hallway floorboards creak under his weight.

"Where are you?"

"Here," I call from my chair and wave my arms above my head. I spin as he turns, and I frown.

There's an envelope in his hands, unsealed but pretty thick. I watch as Cole walks toward me, steps into the room, and looks around.

"Wow," he breathes. "Is this where your magic happens?"

"It's only magic because my name is there." I smile sadly.

"No." He walks to my memo board, where I have random sketches of items. "Trust me. It's the clothes people are going crazy for. I spoke to my mom on the phone this morning and she fucking freaked that you designed some black-and-green lace dress she saw in the QD preview catalog."

My smile brightens, and there's a glint of hope—one that's been absent since I left my show. "Really?"

"Really," he confirms. A moment passes. Then he turns and says, "I have to show you something. But you have to listen to me, all right?"

"Um, okay?" I get up. "Let's go in my room. This place is a, uh…"

"Shithole," Cole answers for me, pushing my bedroom door open.

"Yeah. That."

He drops onto my bed and lays the envelope in front of him. "Come sit down."

"Cole, you're scaring me." I walk toward him with hesitant steps and swallow hard.

"I promise it isn't bad. But you gotta listen to me and not say a word until I'm done, because, shit, Lee."

"What did you do?" I sit down and reach for the envelope.

He snatches it back. "It's what I'm about to do. Baby girl, I'm ten seconds from turning your life upside down and I'm sorry."

He pulls a wad of paper from the envelope before I can reply and puts it front of me. There's a website, 8OPEN, and beneath it is a paragraph connecting me with Lea V. and the front page of my contract. The contract saved to my cloud.

"I…I don't understand." I look up, my voice a mere whisper. "Cole, what is this?"

His shoulders heave with his deep breath. "This is the proof that Corey didn't betray you."

I stare at him, my heart threatening to break again. It's pumping fast, my lungs constricting, and I scramble through the pages. There are e-mails, designs, endless images. All of my work, all connecting me to QD, but the contract is the damning one. That's what connects me to Lea V. One page out of fifty, but that one page is enough.

Cole hands me another sheet of paper. "My friend traced the hacker to the Philippines, then to South Korea, Russia, Malta, and finally, Finland. After that, he surmised that the hacker was leading anyone searching on a wild-goose chase and gave up untangling the lines."

I push that sheet away and stare at the first page, the website screenshot. And all the ones after.

It sinks in slowly.

Like a poison, the truth creeps beneath my skin and invades my bloodstream, flooding my body with its reality, all the while not caring about the shattering of my heart or the ripping of my soul.

My hands shake, and in my eyes, there are tears. They burn and they sting, because it's a slow realization, but it's strong and it's harsh.

After what feels like a million years, I look up at my best friend of a lifetime, my future brother, his face barely visible through the streaming of my tears, and I whisper five words.

"Cole, what did I do?"

I haven't used the punching bag in so long. It doesn't matter that, after ten punches, I hugged it and collapsed to the floor, the weight of the truth too much to bear.

If only I'd listened. If only I'd stopped and thought about

the man I trusted.

If only for one second I'd trusted the man I fell in love with, days and days of heartbreak and misery could have been avoided.

The worst thing is that I don't know if there's any coming back from this. How can he ever forgive me? How can he ever look me in the eye and believe that I'm sorry?

Because I am. And that's what hurts the most right now. My own stupidity and stubbornness has destroyed the one thing I fought so hard about. Yes, I fought to stay away, but in the end, I fought to stay together, too. I wanted Corey, body and soul.

I do want him, body and soul. That never changed despite the fact that I thought he broke my heart. Despite the fact that I thought he betrayed me.

In the end, I betrayed him, and I'm the one who broke our hearts.

My brain excuses it because my world had just been thrown into another solar system's gravitational pull. I was too high on emotion and shock to listen to the logical side of my mind.

And now, I'm standing outside his house, walking back and forth across the entrance to his drive, because I can't decide if I should run away or go and tell him that I'm sorry.

Maybe it won't matter. Maybe it won't make a difference. Maybe he's already moved on.

But maybe I need to do it. I just…

"You just gonna stand at the end of my driveway all day, or you gonna make up your mind if you're comin' in or not?"

A shiver travels down my spine and my heart thumps and my skin buzzes, all at the same time, at the mere sound of his voice. Slowly, I turn. He's shirtless, his hands in the pockets of his jeans making them ride lower than they usually do. I pull my eyes from the bright-blue glimpse of boxer shorts over his waistband and look into his blue-green eyes.

"Probably the former," I reply quietly.

"Let me help. What are you doin' here?"

"Deciding if I should run or ask you to talk," I admit, my eyes still on his. I can't take them away. It's impossible.

"You gonna shout at me? Cuss me out? Tell me to leave?" Pain flits across his face, and I feel sick.

I shake my head without responding verbally because it's too much.

"C'mon, then," Corey says. "Come in and talk to me."

I run my fingers through my hair and pause for just a second. I follow him though. Because I know I have to. I have to tell him that I know it wasn't him and I'm sorry.

He leads me into the front room and I stand awkwardly in the doorway.

"Sit down."

I shake my head again. "I just… I'm sorry," I blurt out. "I know it wasn't you. Cole came over and he showed me where the leak started with the hacker and everything since, and I'm sorry. I never wanted to believe it was you, but I couldn't think of anything, and I was scared and I panicked and I'm sorry."

I cover my mouth with my hand and run toward his front door. I don't care if running makes me weak.

Stand in front of the person you love knowing they might hate you and tell me you can be strong. I dare you.

"Leah!"

I stop halfway down the driveway. I don't know why. Maybe it's the desperation in his voice—the rough, gravelly tone that mirrors the ache inside me. Maybe it's the pounding footsteps running up to me. Maybe it's needing to hear his reply although I'm petrified.

Corey stops in front of me, his hands hovering by my face for what seems like an everlasting moment. Then his fingers curl around my hand and pull it away from my mouth.

I look up, guilt wracking me, my heart aching so painfully that I can't tell if it's beating or not, and I swallow against the tears building in my eyes.

He says nothing. He shakes his head, his lips forming a sad smile, and cups the back of my head. The moment his mouth meets mine is like the cool breeze on a hot summer's day, an eye-closing, toe-curling glimpse of pleasure.

Then it's gone, the touch all too fleeting, and I can't bear to open my eyes. I don't want that to be goodbye.

"Inside," Corey whispers. His arms go around me and he walks me toward his house, his face buried in my hair.

I'm walking backward like a penguin. He's all I have to hold on to, so I do. I wrap my arms around his waist and flatten my hands against his bare, hot skin, committing every sensation to memory.

He's holding on to me tight—so tight that I'm sure he isn't going to let go. I don't want him to let go. I would happily stay here, never speaking another word for the rest of my life as long as Corey's arms are around me.

He spins us by the sofa and drops back, pulling me down with him. I squeak and roll to the side, my grip loosening but his still remaining. He turns with me, his eyes on mine the whole time, a glint I can't decipher sending shivers across my skin. Goose bumps appear in its wake, leaving my arms all pimply and spotty.

"I told you so," Corey whispers, the rough edge still evident.

"You did." I run my fingers along his arm and up to his face. I cup his cheek. "I'm sorry. I'm so, so fucking sorry I didn't believe you."

"I'm not mad. I swear, babe." His hand slides up my back to the back of my head. His fingers splay across my scalp and tangle in my hair. "I never blamed you for not believing me. I just wish I could have been there when you found out. I wish I could have told you. Shit, Leah. Seeing you so heartbroken..." Corey pauses. "Never again. I never ever want to see you fuckin' cry again."

"I should have listened to you." Despite his last words, tears fill my eyes. "I should have trusted you, Corey. I should have believed you'd never do that to me."

"But you didn't." He grabs my hand when I drop it from his face. "That's okay, y'know? When this started, it was a game. You didn't mean shit to me. But now, you do. Shit, you mean everything to me. My whole world just stopped when you walked away from me. I never expected you to trust me. I just had to make it so you could."

"I do," I whisper, linking my fingers through his. "I do trust you, and that's the craziest thing. It was a game for me, too. I thought that, if I gave you what you wanted, you'd give up, but then you didn't, and I realized I couldn't either. I was waiting for you to fuck up, you know? I was waiting to see you on the front page with another girl or for you to dump me with fanfare, but you didn't. You kept going, and every step you took made me come, too. You already made me trust you. You made me believe in you, cowboy."

"I'd never hurt you like that, darlin'. Never. Just understand that, all right? It doesn't make sense to me. You are the most incredible, fascinating, sassy, beautiful person I know." Corey raises our clasped hands to between us and kisses my fingers.

"You went quiet." My voice is still a bare whisper. It's so quiet that I'm surprised he could hear it.

"I didn't know what to do," he admits, holding our hands between us still. "You made me leave. I was…lost. Shit. I was totally fuckin' lost without you, babe. I don't even want to feel that way again."

"You don't have to." I ease my hand from his and touch his cheek again. "If you don't want to, I mean." I bring my face to his, and in a rare show of vulnerability, I whisper, "Please don't ask me to go."

"Never." He pulls me around and onto his lap. With his hands on my back and mine cupping his face, he leans up and says, "I will never ask you to go. Not in a million years. I'd rather get on my knees, say goodbye to every ounce of pride in my body, and beg you to stay than ask you to go."

I close my mouth over his, sealing his words the only way I know how. Sealing a promise with our bodies. The physical act always follows the emotional because that's how we work. Our bodies have to verify our words.

Our chemistry is too consuming to be ignored.

Corey removes my shirt in seconds, the material barely grazing my face as he whips it over my head. "I need to be inside you," he says into my mouth, his words perfectly in time with his kiss. "I need to know you're mine. I need to claim you,

Leah. I need to convince myself that you're back here in my arms and you're mine."

My lips press against his with a ferocity I didn't know I had in me. Yes, yes. Because I need to know I'm his. I need to know he's mine. I need to forget the hell and heartbreak and let Corey work me into oblivion the way only he can.

My bra is gone almost as quickly as his shirt was, my taut nipples rubbing against his hard chest. His hands cup my breasts tenderly yet harshly. His thumbs tease my nipples into harder nubs than they were while his rapidly growing erection pushes against my core between our pants.

But it isn't fast enough. There are too many layers between us, between the parts that really need to be connected. I ghost my fingers quickly down his chest to his pants and undo his button, then mine, so he gets the message.

He shoves at my knees, making me stand, and hooks his thumbs in his waistband. I shove my jeans and panties down my knees and kick them off not so elegantly then leap on him. His hands wind into my hair, not caring, and I lower my hips to his. Shit—his cock is rubbing against my clit. We're so close, so firmly pressed together that I can almost feel the pumping veins that run the length of his shaft.

His hand goes down and he unapologetically plunges two fingers into my pussy. I gasp at the sudden intrusion, but it's what I want, what I need…almost.

I need to be filled by him to the nth degree. I need my body to be so full of him, so consumed, that I can feel nothing but him. Then I know I'm his and he's mine.

Then I know we can battle anything.

Then I know that we are more than just something.

"Please," I whisper. "I need you, Corey. I missed you so fucking much."

He withdraws his fingers and places the end of his cock at my opening. "I missed you, too," he breathes against my skin, his mouth hot, his breath hot, his whole body fucking hot. "Not anymore. Never again."

He slips inside me easily because my body has been waiting

for him. It's been wondering where he was, wondering when he'd come and ease inside me again to kill this ache that's formed.

With every thrust, he eliminates the ache. With every kiss, he eases the sting. With every stroke of his finger across my skin, he takes away the pain that's lingered for days and days and days.

With every touch, he screams. He shouts. He yells from the rooftops that he's mine wholly and completely.

With every bit of him, he sends out a warning that he'll always be mine.

With every bit of me, I send out the warning that I'll only ever be his.

chapter THIRTY-TWO

Corey

She's tucked in my arms. Our legs are tangled, her face is buried in my neck, and her breath skates across my skin with every rise and fall of her chest.

She's exactly where she's supposed to fucking be.

I run my fingers through to the ends of her soft hair, and she tilts her head back to look at me.

"Hi," she whispers like she wasn't moaning my name into my shoulder fifteen minutes ago.

"Hi." My lips tug into a smile.

She blinks up at me, her blue eyes shining and bright. "You're squashing me a little."

I laugh and roll to the side, grabbing the back cushion of the sofa so I don't fall on to the floor. "Is that better, babe?"

Leah nods. "But now, I'm cold."

"I can warm you up again."

"Corey!"

"What?" I get up, holding in my laugh, and retrieve my boxers from the floor. I shove them on and pull Leah to her feet.

She sighs as I run my hands down her body and lift her against me. Her legs wrap around my waist, her arms around my neck, and she rests her head on my shoulder.

"It's better without the underwear," she murmurs, each

stair bouncing her against me.

"I agree, but if I don't have them on, I'm likely to fuck you again." I set her on the edge of my bed and kiss her slowly. "And we still have to talk and shit."

"I don't think I've ever heard you put talking over sex."

I smirk and throw a shirt at her. "That's because I haven't. You forced me in to it once, but that's it." I open the drawer she put her things in when she promised she'd stay with me for a week.

"What are you doing?" She comes up next to me. "You… You kept my stuff?"

"Yep." I pull out a pair of panties and swing them around on my finger.

She purses her lips and snatches them from me. "Why?"

"I didn't do anythin' wrong, did I?" I shrug and lean against the dresser. "It's not like I was never gonna see you again. I figured that, when you found out it was the hacker and not me, you could take your stuff if you weren't interested anymore. I knew it was pretty fuckin' unlikely, but you'd need your panties back either way."

"So arrogant." She rolls her eyes, but the smile playing on her lips contradicts it. "You seem pretty damn sure I was always gonna come back."

"You did, didn't you?" I raise my eyebrows.

Leah puts her hands on her hips. Her eyes rove over my body before she brings them up to meet my gaze. "I came to apologize. I didn't intend to fuck you."

"But you did."

"Obviously." She looks away for a second. "I thought you might…hate me…for not believing you."

I stare at her. *What?* "You thought I'd fucking hate you?"

She nods.

I close the distance between us and cup her face. Our gazes collide, and I shake my head.

"Never. Never could I hate you. I love you, Leah."

Her eyes widen, and she takes a deep breath, those pretty lips parting. "You—you what?"

"I love you," I repeat, quieter this time. "And I should have told you before, when I followed you to the hotel, when I came to your house… I should have just said it. Why are you starin' at me like that?"

She blinks.

"You can say something, you know?"

"I don't know what to say."

"I just told you I'm in love with you and you're just standing there. My ego's really takin' a hit here, darlin'."

She smiles. Then she laughs. She wraps her fingers around my arms and pulls them from her face, and just as I think she's about to step back, she launches herself at me.

"I love you, you pigheaded idiot." Her words are muffled, our lips connected, but I hear them clear enough.

I cup her ass and hold her to me. Her body fits perfectly against mine, and our kiss is a perfect coming together of our emotions.

Her words echo through my mind with every second our lips are connected.

This girl loves me.

My girl fucking loves me.

"*So, what* are you doing about the hacker?" Lottie drops onto the sofa. "Both of you."

Leah shrugs. "Honestly, I don't think there's anything I can do. It sounds like he's crossed so many lines he'll be impossible to find, and I don't know that it's worth suing the cloud provider. I mean, how many people have been exposed and will be doing the same thing?"

"Loads," I tell her. "Neil's been turning away cases because he's got so many for this hacking thing. I'm probably going to pull mine."

"Yeah. That was the vilest thing ever, by the way." Lottie wrinkles her face. "My friends practically orgasmed over your pictures. I vomited, like, ten times."

"Remind me never to meet your friends," I mutter. "Or let

Leah."

Leah laughs. "I haven't seen the pictures, but they were probably more flattering than he deserves."

"Hey!" I grab her leg from my lap and pull her along the sofa. She slides toward me easily. "You sayin' I'm not hot?"

"No. I would never do that."

"Hmm."

Lottie rolls her eyes. "Don't worry. I don't particularly 'like' my friends either. I'm actually looking forward to moving back here after I graduate next summer."

"You're moving back here?"

She shrugs. "New York is nice, but I much prefer the weather here." She grins. "Plus I probably have a better chance of getting a job in L.A. I'm minoring in graphic design, remember?"

"Sis, I can barely remember your fuckin' major."

"Figures. Well, I gotta go. Dad's driving me to the airport." She grabs her purse from the floor by her feet and looks at us with a half smile. "I'm glad you two could figure things out. And, Leah, if he pisses you off too much, just hide the pancake mix. He gets seriously freaking annoying when he can't find it."

"Noted." Leah grins.

"Tell her all my secrets, why don't you?" I grumble, getting up.

"We'll go for drinks next time I'm back and I'll tell her all your sordid stories." Lottie laughs.

"Bitch." I shake my head. "Thank you. For looking for the leak."

"No worries. You're not all bad, brother, and if you're happy, you're not such a prick to me."

I laugh and hug her quickly, something I haven't done for years. "Yeah, well, thanks. Maybe I'll call you next time we play in New York."

"Don't bother. I'll be busy." She opens the front door then leans in to whisper, "I like her. Don't fuck this up."

"You have amazing confidence in me."

"Just warnin' you." She winks and leaves, and I wave to Dad in the car before I shut the door.

I walk back into the kitchen to find Leah rifling through the cabinets. "What are you doin'?"

She glances over her shoulder. "I'm looking for the pancake mix."

"She was lyin'."

"Whatever." She turns back and moves on to a new cabinet. "Are you really going to tell Neil to not file a lawsuit?"

"Probably. It's a lot of hassle that'll probably lead to nothing."

"Exactly why I'm not doing it," she agrees. "Besides, I can't change the fact that the whole world knows Lea V. is my line. I guess my life is about to get ten times crazier."

I come up behind her and wrap my arms around her waist. My lips skim down her neck to her shoulder. "Yep. How horrible it must be to be famous."

She shudders. "Famous. Ugh."

"You being famous is why we met. Are you sayin' you'd change that?"

"Well…"

I spin her and pin her against the kitchen counter. "Answer very, very carefully, darlin'."

A smile creeps onto her face and she slides her hands up my front. "No. I wouldn't change it. I was getting fed up with bad sex."

"Are you saying you're with me for my cock?"

"And your mouth."

"Funny. I happen to be fond of your mouth." So much so that I lower mine to hers and take her bottom lip between my teeth. "And it has a better use than talking."

"So does yours." Leah fists my shirt collar and leans in toward me. Then she tilts her head back and brushes her lips across my jaw. "And I believe that use involves me on my back in your bed with my legs open."

My cock throbs, and I grip her thighs. Lifting her up, I set her ass on the edge of the counter and push up her dress. My fingers hook in the sides of her panties and I tug.

"Mmm," I hum low, nipping her neck. "Who needs a bed?"

EPILOGUE

Leah

If I'd known we'd be this infuriatingly beautiful, I'd have stopped fighting a lot sooner.

Ever since Cole walked in with that envelope full of information and proved to me that Corey was innocent two weeks ago, it's like a switch has flipped between me and Corey. The uncertainty of our relationship before has completely gone, and in its place is a raw honesty.

For the first time since we met, there are no secrets, no games, and no lies. We're the best kind of crazy. He pisses me off as much as he makes me laugh, but he has the best way of making it up to me—usually with his mouth.

"You don't need to do this."

"Too late. I already did it." I glance at him in the mirror and put my mascara into my makeup bag.

"I'd rather you didn't."

"Really? What would you rather do?"

"Hmm, let me think." Corey wraps his arms around me from behind and kisses the side of my neck. "You."

I roll my eyes. "Lottie has flown in for the weekend because of your party. You're not bailing on your own birthday party, cowboy."

"I don't like parties," he grumbles.

I turn and my eyebrows shoot up. "We met in a bar."

"A bar isn't a party."

"You went to my mom's party."

"That was a premiere, not a party."

"You went to the after party."

"Semantics, babe. Semantics." He slides his hands down my body. "Are you wearing underwear right now?"

I laugh and smack his hands away. "Yes, I am. Now come on!"

He sighs and follows me downstairs but doesn't complain anymore. Instead, he stares at me, and I feel his gaze roaming down my back and hovering on my ass.

I stop before I get in the waiting car and tap his cheek. "Smile, you miserable fuck."

"I love you, too," he laughs. "I'd be much happier if you weren't wearing underwear, for the record. That would be the best fucking present ever."

"You're impossible. I need to wear underwear because this dress is so damn short I'll flash everyone if I don't." I expertly climb into the car and tug my dress down my legs.

"I won't complain if you do, for the record." Corey reaches over the back seat and takes my hand in his. His hand is hot and rough, and I smile, linking our fingers.

"Try and behave for one night, cowboy. It's not rocket science."

"You're wearing that sexy-as-fuck dress and you expect me to behave?"

"Yes! Your parents will be here, not to mention your coaches and teammates."

"I don't care. It's my birthday and I'm just sayin' we might disappear into a bathroom for a quick fuck at some point."

I gape at him. "No, we won't!"

"We'll see, darlin'. I happen to be fuckin' charming." He winks. "Who else will be there?"

"Macey, Ryann, and Cole invited some of the girls he used to model with before he started acting full time. They're there to keep Jack happy."

A grin stretches across Corey's face. "Smart move."

"Well, Macey won't go there again. She doesn't do seconds." I frown. "On second thought, she did, so maybe she will do thirds."

"Why not?"

"Her ex is an asshole. We try not to talk about it much because she turns into Medusa." I shrug and get out of the car. "Mom picked the venue, by the way. Not me."

I take Corey's hand and, ignoring the flashes around us, lead him into Rapture. The club has only been open for a few weeks, and it's already one of the most exclusive in L.A. Thankfully, my mom is the queen of Hollywood and they accepted Corey's party before we could blink at them.

I pull him onto the main dance floor with a hesitant smile. Macey, Ryann, and I spent the whole afternoon here decorating. There are banners and streamers and balloons, and the cake is a huge 3D football. Corey looks around in wonder, his eyes flitting between the decorations and the people, and then he stares at me.

"How did you pull this off?" He curls me into his side and brushes his lips over my temple.

I smile and flatten my hand against his chest as I gaze up at him. "I already told you. Mom and the girls helped, and Cole did some inviting."

"But it was your idea."

"Yes."

He drops a deep, lingering kiss to my lips. "You're fuckin' amazing, girl."

"I know." I laugh. "Come on. We're not staying up here all night when the fun is happening downstairs. I want a drink."

Corey walks down with me then pulls me against his front when we're at the bottom. His lips skim my earlobe, and he says, "Don't drink too much. I want you to remember tonight."

"Why's that?"

"Because when we get back, I'm going to give you the best sex of your fucking life to say thank you."

I laugh again, but my muscles clench at the promise in his

words. "Come on, cowboy. Your mom is waving for you."

"Macey looks pissed."

I look at Corey then to where she's standing by the bar. Sure as hell, she looks like she's ready to take her cocktail glass, smash it, then shove the shattered pieces up someone's asshole. I follow her gaze until I see Jack, who's sitting at a table with some other girl but very much looking at Macey.

"Jack should probably disappear if he wants to retain use of his penis," I advise Corey. He laughs but stops as soon as Macey makes her way over to us. "And don't talk to her."

"Why didn't you tell me he'd be here?" she hisses at me.

"I didn't think it was a big deal."

"You know I don't do the whole 'hi, how are you?' thing after fucking a guy."

"Then don't talk to him." I laugh. "Seriously, ignore him, and he'll ignore you."

She grunts and sips her drink. Turns out, she *ignores* me because she's looking at him again.

"Why are you still staring at him?" Corey asks.

I wince.

"Because I fucking want to. He's pretty," she snaps, deliberately turning away from him and finishing her drink. "All right?"

Corey glances at me as if to say, *What the fuck?* and I smirk. I warned him. He will learn to listen to me… Eventually.

"I'm going to get a drink," she mumbles, grabbing her glass and heading back to the bar.

I watch her go, wondering if Jack really did put her in a bad mood or if there's something else riling her.

"I should probably go talk to her," I say to Corey, getting up.

"Hold on." He grabs my hand and pulls me close. "I have something for you."

"What?" I look up at him. "But it's your birthday, silly."

"I know." He drops his head and kisses me. "My present is you accepting what I give you."

"I'm scared."

Corey laughs, wraps one arm around my waist, and digs into his pocket with the other one. Then he brings out something silver and shiny, and I swallow.

"That's a key," I say dumbly when he puts it in front of my face.

He nods. "My key. To my house."

"You're…you're giving me a key to your house?"

"My, you're observant tonight."

"Shut it." I glance at the key then meet his eyes again. "Um, why?"

"Because"—he taps the end of my nose with it—"I want you to have it. I'm not askin' you to move in unless you want to. But you're there most of the time, and now that the season has started, I'm gonna be trainin' late some nights and I want you there when I get back. You can let yourself in."

My lips curve to the side. "So, really, you're doing it so I'm there for your convenience, right?"

He opens his mouth then closes it. "Fuck. Why you always gotta call me out, huh, babe?"

I laugh and step closer, wrapping my hand around his key. "Because it's more fun this way. Yes, I will take your key."

Corey lets go of it, grinning. "Good. Then you can leave half an hour before me and get changed into that white underwear set I put on my bed before we left."

He presses his lips against mine, and I can't help but smile. Presumptuous, arrogant little asshole.

"Okay. Since it's your birthday, I'll cooperate this one time," I say into the kiss.

"Amazin'," he murmurs. "My favorite girl in my favorite color. Happy fuckin' birthday to me."

"Not yet. But it will be."

Look for Macey & Jack's book, *SIDELINED*, coming in March!

Thank you for reading Blindsided! If you enjoyed it, I'd love if you could leave a review, and be sure to sign up to my newsletter to be the first to receive book news, including the release date for Sidelined!

Sign up here: http://eepurl.com/YQvfn

Alternatively, you can join my reader group, **HARTBREAKERS**, and get exclusive sneak peeks of whatever I'm working on!

Join here: http://on.fb.me/1rJk22L

ABOUT THE *author*

By day, New York Times and USA Today bestselling New Adult author Emma Hart dons a cape and calls herself Super Mum to two beautiful little monsters. By night, she drops the cape, pours a glass of whatever she fancies - usually wine - and writes books.

Emma is working on Top Secret projects she will share with her followers and fans at every available opportunity. Naturally, all Top Secret projects involve a dashingly hot guy who likes to forget to wear a shirt, a sprinkling (or several) of hold-onto-your-panties hot scenes, and a whole lotta love.

She likes to be busy - unless busy involves doing the dishes, but that seems to be when all the ideas come to life.

Find her online at:

Facebook: www.facebook.com/emmahartbooks or
www.facebook.com/emma.evelyn
Twitter: www.twitter.com/emmahartauthor
Instagram: www.instagram.com/emmahartauthor
Pinterest: www.pinterest.com/authoremmahart
Website: www.emmahart.org

Made in the USA
Charleston, SC
04 April 2015